P9-CRT-536

SUSAN MALLERY

With more than twenty-five million books sold worldwide, *New York Times* bestselling author Susan Mallery is known for creating characters who feel as real as the folks next door, and for putting them into emotional, often funny situations readers recognize from their own lives. Susan's books have made *Booklist*'s Top 10 Romances list in four out of five consecutive years. *RT Book Reviews* says, "When it comes to heartfelt contemporary romance, Mallery is in a class by herself." With her popular ongoing Fool's Gold series, Susan has reached new heights on the bestseller lists and has won the hearts of countless new fans.

Susan grew up in Southern California, moved so many times that her friends stopped writing her address in pen, and has now settled in Seattle with her husband and the most delightfully spoiled little dog who ever lived. Visit Susan online at www.susanmallery.com.

CHRISTINE RIMMER

came to her profession the long way around. Before settling down to write about the magic of romance, she'd been everything from an actress to a salesclerk to a waitress. Now that she's finally found work that suits her perfectly, she insists she never had a problem keeping a job—she was merely gaining "life experience" for her future as a novelist. She currently writes for Harlequin Special Edition. Christine is grateful not only for the joy she finds in writing, but for what waits when the day's work is through: a man she loves who loves her right back, and the privilege of watching their children grow and change day to day. She lives with her family in Oregon. Visit Christine at www.christinerimmer.com.

New York Times Bestselling Author

SUSAN MALLERY

SHELTER IN A SOLDIER'S ARMS

HARLEQUIN®BESTSELLING AUTHOR COLLECTION

ISBN-13: 978-0-373-01016-5

Shelter in a Soldier's Arms
Copyright © 2015 by Harlequin Books S.A.

The publisher acknowledges the copyright holders of the individual works as follows:

Shelter in a Soldier's Arms
Copyright © 2001 by Susan Macias-Redmond

Donovan's Child
Copyright © 2011 by Christine Rimmer

Recycling programs for this product may not exist in your area.

HARLEQUIN®
www.Harlequin.com

Printed in U.S.A.

CONTENTS

SHELTER IN A SOLDIER'S ARMS

Susan Mallery

To single mothers everywhere.
May your dedication be rewarded with love,
happiness and your heart's desire.

Chapter 1

There was trouble.

Jeffrey Ritter sensed it even before he spotted the flashing light on the security console mounted in his car. At five o'clock in the morning the offices of Ritter/Rankin Security should have been locked down and empty. According to the red flashing light, the building was neither.

Jeff touched several buttons on the console to confirm the information. The front and rear doors were locked, but inner doors were open. Lights were on as well, he noted as he drove into the parking lot and headed for a spot to the left of the double glass doors— glass that was deceptively clear but could in fact withstand severe artillery fire and a small bomb blast.

Trouble, he thought again as he put the car into Park

and turned off the engine. He popped the trunk of his black BMW and stepped out onto the damp pavement. Although it wasn't raining, the air was heavy and wet, as if the Seattle skies were about to do their thing at any moment.

Jeff circled the vehicle and removed his personal firearm, which he checked and slipped into his specially designed holster. Next came the black stunner, designed to immobilize an attacker without permanent injury. He punched buttons on his phone, setting it to standby so that a single touch would alert his partner and the authorities. He didn't usually get the latter involved in his operations, but his office was in downtown Seattle. The local police wouldn't appreciate a predawn shoot-out, and they would absolutely expect an explanation.

He turned his attention to the quiet building. Nothing looked out of place. But in his experience that was common. Danger rarely announced itself with a neon sign.

Jeff walked quickly and quietly, moving around the building to a side entrance without a lock. Only a small keypad allowed access. He tapped in the code and waited for the door to unlock. If someone was waiting in the small alcove, the door wouldn't open. There was a slight *snick* as the locking mechanism released, and he entered the protective space tucked along the main corridor.

He was surrounded on three sides by glass coated to be a two-way mirror. Dropping into a crouch, he surveyed the length of the corridor. Nothing. From the corner of his eye he caught a flicker of movement in the east hallway. It was gone before he could register who or what it was. Damn.

Still crouching, Jeff pushed the concealed button to let himself out into the corridor. He hurried in the direction of the movement, keeping low, running soundlessly. As he rounded the corner, he reached for both the gun and the stunner—only to slam to a halt, as immobilized as if he'd just taken a jolt from his own weapon.

Breath left his lungs. Involuntary impulses forced him to his feet even as he slipped the weapons out of sight. He didn't remember making a sound, yet he must have because the intruder turned and looked at him.

"You hafta be quiet 'cause Mommy's sleeping."

In less than a second he'd scanned the immediate area and absorbed all that he saw. No dangerous intruders, at least not in the traditional sense. Which was unfortunate. Jeff Ritter knew what to do when facing an insurrection, a terrorist hit squad or even a stubborn client. But he had absolutely no experience with children—especially little girls with big blue eyes.

She was small, barely coming to midthigh on him. Dark, shiny curls caught the overhead light. She wore pink kitten-motif pajamas and fluffy, cotton-candy-colored slippers. A stuffed white cat filled her arms.

He blinked, half wondering if she was an illusion. But she remained stubbornly real. As did the woman on the floor beside her.

Jeff took in the cart of cleaning supplies and the woman's casual, worn clothes. Grown-ups he could handle, and he quickly cataloged her flushed face, closed eyes and the trace of sweat on her forehead. Even from several feet away he could sense her fever, brought on by illness. She'd probably sat down to rest and had slipped into semiconsciousness.

"Mommy works hard," the little girl told him. "She's real tired. I woke up a while ago and I was gonna talk to her 'bout why she was sleeping on the floor, but then I thought I'd be real quiet and let her sleep."

Chubby cheeks tilted up as the young child smiled at him, as if expecting praise for her decision. Instead Jeff turned his phone from emergency standby to regular, then flicked on the safety on his gun and switched off the stunner. Then he crouched next to the woman.

"What's your name?"

He was speaking to the adult, but the child answered instead.

"I'm Maggie. Do you work here? It's nice. One of the big rooms is my favorite. It's got really, really big windows and you can see forever, clear up to the sky. Sometimes when I wakes up, I count the stars. I can count to a hundred and sometimes I can count higher. Wanna hear?"

"Not right now."

Jeff ignored the ongoing chatter. Instead he reached for the woman's forehead and at the same time he touched the inside of her wrist to check her pulse. Her heart rate was steady and strong, but she definitely had a fever. He reached to lift an eyelid to examine her pupil reaction when she awakened. Her eyes fluttered open and she stared at him, her expression telling him he was about as welcome as the plague.

A man! Ashley Churchill's first thought was that Damian had come back to haunt her. Her second was that while the cold-looking man in front of her might be second cousin to the devil, he wasn't her ex-husband.

Her head felt as if it weighed three tons, and she

couldn't seem to focus on anything but gray eyes and a face completely devoid of emotion. Then she blinked and brain cells began firing, albeit slowly. She was sitting in a hallway that looked vaguely familiar. Ritter/Rankin Security, she thought hazily. She was working, or at least she was supposed to be.

"I was so tired," she murmured, trying to sound more coherent than she felt. "I sat down to rest. I guess I fell asleep." She blinked again, then wished she hadn't as she recognized the man crouched in front of her. He'd passed her in the hall when she first interviewed for the job. The office manager had identified him as Jeffrey Ritter, partner, professional security expert extraordinaire, ex-soldier.

Her boss.

"Mommy, you're awake!"

The familiar voice normally made her heart leap with gladness, but now Ashley felt only horror. Maggie was up? What time…? She glanced at her watch and groaned when she saw 5:10 a.m. glowing in the light of the hall. She was supposed to have finished her cleaning by two, and she always met the deadline. She remembered something about security systems reactivating after she'd left.

"I'm sorry, Mr. Ritter," she said, forcing herself to scramble to her feet and ignoring the weakness that filled her when she did. "I don't usually sleep on the job. Maggie had the flu last week and I think I caught her bug." In fact, she was sure of it. Not that the stern, unsmiling man standing in front of her would care one way or the other.

He turned his attention from her to her daughter.

Ashley winced, knowing it looked bad. No one had ever explicitly said she couldn't bring her daughter to work, but then no doubt no one had thought they would have to. Four-year-olds didn't belong in the workplace.

"Mommy says preschool is a germ mag-mag-mag-got?" Her rosebud mouth couldn't quite get around the word.

"Magnet," Ashley offered automatically. She smoothed her hands against her jeans and offered her hand to the man who was very likely going to fire her. "Mr. Ritter, I'm Ashley Churchill. Obviously I clean the office. Usually I'm out by two."

"I sleep while Mommy works," Maggie put in helpfully. "Mommy makes me a really nice bed with my favorite kitten sheets. She sings to me and I close my eyes." She lowered her voice and took a step toward the man. "I'm s'posed to go right to sleep but sometimes I peek and look at the stars."

Ashley swallowed against the lump of fear in her throat. "Yes, well, it's not as bad as it seems," she said lamely, knowing it was actually worse. She felt slightly less perky than a fur ball and she was going to lose her job. Talk about a lousy start to her day. At least things could only get better from here.

"Your things are in my office?"

Jeff Ritter spoke for the first time. His voice was low and perfectly modulated. She had no clue what he was thinking, which made her assume the worst.

"Ah, yes."

"Where do the cleaning supplies go?" he asked.

"There's a closet at the end of the hall. I'd nearly finished. I still have to take care of Mr. Rankin's office. Everything else is done."

He took her elbow and led her down the hall. His touch was steel. Not especially rough or firm, but she knew that if she tried to escape he could snap her in half. Like a toothpick.

A charming visual, she thought with a sigh. Her daughter could collect the splintered shards of what used to be her mother and keep them in a little box. She could bring her out at show-and-tell when she went to school and—

Ashley shook her head. She was sicker than she'd thought. Her mind was wandering and she would give almost anything to be in her bed and have this all be a horrible dream. But it wasn't. As they stepped into Jeff's office, the proof of her audacious behavior lay scattered all around.

One of the plush leather sofas had been made up into a bed. There were a half-dozen stuffed animals scattered across the kitten sheets. A juice box and crumbs were testament to a late-night snack, while a baby monitor held the place of honor in the center of the large glass coffee table she'd pushed away from the sofa.

He released her and crossed to the table. When he picked up the monitor, Ashley reached into her pocket and removed the small receiver.

"It's so I can hear her," she said, probably unnecessarily. The man was a security expert. He would have access to listening devices she could only imagine. "I don't bring Maggie to work with me on a whim, Mr. Ritter. I go to college during the day, which is why I work the hours I do. I can't afford to pay someone to spend the night. A sitter would take most of my pay-check and I need that for rent, food and tuition."

She briefly closed her eyes as the room began to spin. He wouldn't care, she thought glumly. He was going to fire her. She would lose both her paycheck and her health insurance. Still, she wouldn't go without a fight.

"She's never been any trouble. It's been nearly a year and no one has ever found out." She winced at how that sounded. "I'm not saying that to excuse my behavior, just to point out that she's not really a problem." *She's not a reason to fire me.* Except she didn't say that.

Maggie moved to her side and took her hand. "Don't worry, Mommy. The nice man likes us."

Oh, yeah, Ashley thought. Maybe served up for breakfast, but not any other way. There was something scary about the man in front of her. Something she couldn't exactly put her finger on. A stillness, maybe? Or maybe it was his eyes—so cold. He studied her like a predator assessing a potential victim.

Jeff Ritter was tall, maybe six-two or -three. His tai-lored suit looked expensive and well cut, but it couldn't conceal the power of his body. He was a honed fighting machine. Maybe a killing one.

He was blond, with eyes the color of slate. In another life he could have been described as handsome, but not in this one. There was too much wariness in his stance, too much danger.

Because of the hours she worked, she didn't have contact with very many people in the office. Once every three weeks she checked in with the office manager. Instructions were left on the bulletin board in the sup-ply closet, her paychecks were mailed to her house. But she'd read articles about the security firm. There had been several write-ups when a computer expert's son had been kidnapped and held for ransom. Jeff had been the one to track down the criminals. He'd brought them back, more dead than alive. The boy had been fine.

A shiver rippled through her. It had nothing to do with fear and everything to do with the fever heating her system. Her stomach lurched and she knew if she'd eaten dinner, she would have just shared it with the world.

Jeff gave her a quick once-over then moved to the sofa. "You're ready to pass out on your feet. You need to be home and in bed."

Before she could protest, he'd gathered the sheets and stuffed them into the tote on the floor by the sofa. Maggie joined in the game, collecting her stuffed animals. While she carefully threw out the empty juice container, Jeff put the baby monitor into the bag.

"Anything else?" he asked.

Just her final paycheck, she thought grimly. But that would be sent to her.

"Nothing. Thank you, Mr. Ritter. You've been very kind."

She didn't know what else to say. Would he respond to begging? Based on the chill in his gray eyes, she didn't think so.

He didn't acknowledge her words. Instead he turned and headed for the front of the building.

"My car's out back," she called after him, then had to lean against the door frame to gather her strength. She needed to sleep. Unfortunately Maggie wasn't going to go down for more than a couple of hours. Maybe that would be enough to get Ashley on her feet enough to get through the day. Or maybe—

"You're too ill to drive," Jeff said flatly. He'd paused at the turn in the corridor. "I'll take you home. Your car will be returned to you later in the day."

She was too weak to argue, which meant he was right about her being in no shape to drive. Slowly she staggered after him. Maggie held her hand.

"Snowball says she wants to sleep with you when we get home," Maggie said sleepily as they walked through the building. "She's magic and she'll make you feel better."

Ashley knew that her daughter wouldn't give up her favorite toy lightly. Touched by the gesture, she smiled at her child. "I think you're the magic one."

Maggie giggled, her curls dancing. "I'm just little, Mommy. There's no place for the magic to go. If I was bigger, there could be some."

Ashley was too tired to point out that Snowball was smaller still. But then, favorite toys were always special in ways that grown-ups didn't understand.

They stepped out into the misting morning to find Jeff holding open the rear door of an impressive black sedan. Ashley didn't have to see the BMW emblem on the hood to know that the car was expensive. Very expensive. If she could make even close to what this car cost, all her troubles would be solved.

She hesitated before sliding across the soft, gray leather. It was cool and smooth and soft. *Whatever you do, don't throw up,* she told herself firmly.

It took only a few seconds to secure her daughter and herself in safety belts. With her arm around Maggie, Ashley leaned back and closed her eyes. Just a few more minutes, she told herself. Fifteen at most. Then she would be home and crawling into her own bed.

"I need your address."

The voice came out of the blackness. Ashley had to rouse herself to speak and even then it was difficult to form words. She started to give him directions, as well, but Jeff informed her he knew the area. She didn't doubt him. He was the kind of man who knew just about everything.

The soft hum of the engine lulled her into that half-awake, half-asleep place. She could have stayed there forever. The early hour caught up with Maggie who snuggled against her and relaxed. Right up until the car came to a stop and she felt more than heard Jeff turn toward her.

"There seems to be a problem."

Ashley forced her eyes open, then wished she hadn't. So much for her day not getting worse.

They were stopped close to her four-story apartment building. Normally there was plenty of room to park right in front of the building, but not this morning. Today, red fire trucks and police cars had pulled into the driveway. Flashing lights twinkled in the light rainfall. Stunned, Ashley stared in disbelief at the river of water flowing down the main steps. Her neighbors were huddled together on the sidewalk.

No, she thought, feeling herself tremble with shock and disbelief. This couldn't be happening. Not today.

She fumbled with Maggie's seat belt, then her own. After opening the rear door, she stepped out, pulling her daughter with her. She was careful to hold Maggie in her arms. The girl's slippers wouldn't provide any protection against the water flowing everywhere.

"Mommy, what happened?" Maggie asked.

"I don't know."

Mrs. Gunther, the retired, blue-haired woman who managed the aging apartment building, spotted her and hurried over.

"Ashley, you're not going to believe it. The main water pipe broke about an hour ago. It's a mess. From what I've learned, it will take a week to repair the damage. They'll escort you inside to get whatever you can carry out, then we have to make other arrangements until the pipe is repaired."

Jeff watched the last trace of color drain from the woman's face. Defeat clouded her eyes, making her tremble. Or maybe it was the fever.

"I don't have anywhere to go," she whispered.

The old lady patted her arm. "I'm in the same situation, dear. Not to worry. They're opening a shelter. We'll be fine there."

Maggie, the moppet with dark curls and a far-too-trusting smile, looked at her mother. "What's a shelter, Mommy? Do they got kittens there? Real ones?"

"I—I don't know."

Ashley shifted her daughter's weight, then stared at the gushing building. "I need to get my textbooks and notes. Clothes for us, some toys."

"They'll escort you in," the old woman said. "I'll watch Maggie while you're there."

Suddenly Ashley seemed to remember him. She turned and blinked. "Oh, Mr. Ritter. Thanks for the ride. I, um, guess I need to get my things out of your trunk."

She moved to the rear of the vehicle and waited until he'd popped open the trunk. When she swung the tote bag onto her shoulder, she had to take a quick step to steady herself.

"Are you going to be all right?"

The question surprised them both. Jeff hadn't planned to ask it. He told himself that her situation wasn't his problem. The woman would be fine in a shelter. His gaze drifted to the little girl all in pink. He was less sure about her doing well under those circumstances.

"We'll be great." Ashley gave him a false smile. "You've been too kind already."

It was his cue to leave. Normally he would have melted into the crowd and been gone before anyone knew he was even there. Instead he lingered.

"You can't take her there," he said, his voice low and urgent. "It's not right."

"She'll be fine," Ashley assured him. "We'll be fine together."

He told himself to step back, to not get involved. He told himself— "I'll pay for a hotel room if you'd like."

Her eyes were an odd hazel color. Neither blue nor green. Not brown. Some swirling combination of all the colors.

"You've been very kind already. Goodbye, Mr. Ritter."

She dismissed him. He accepted her decision, but before she took a step away, he slipped one of his business cards into her jacket pocket. It was an impulsive act, so unlike him. Later he would try to figure out why he'd bothered. Then he did what he was good at. He blended in, moving toward his car. In a matter of seconds, he was gone.

"You plan on joining the conversation anytime soon?"

Jeff looked at his friend and partner, Zane Rankin, and shrugged. "I'm here."

"Physically. But you keep drifting off. Not like you at all."

Jeff returned his attention to the plans on the table without acknowledging the truth of Zane's words. Jeff *was* having trouble concentrating on the work at hand. He knew the cause—he couldn't get the woman and her child out of his head and he didn't know why.

Was it their circumstances? Yet he'd seen hundreds in worse trouble. Compared to a war-torn village with its winter food stores destroyed, Ashley Churchill's plight was insignificant. Was it the child? The girl? Maggie's bright smile, her foolish trust, her pink pajamas and stuffed, white cat were so far from his world as to belong to a distant universe.

Did it matter why they haunted him? Better the living than the dead who were his usual companions.

There were no answers to any of the questions, so he dismissed them and returned his attention to the diagram of a luxury villa overlooking the Mediterranean. The private residence was to host a secret gathering of several international business executives who were responsible for the manufacture of some of the world's most deadly weapons. The threat of industrial espionage, terrorist attack or kidnapping would be high. He and Zane were to provide the security. Step one: learn the weaknesses of the location.

Jeff pointed with his pen. "All this has to go," he said, indicating a lush tropical garden creeping down a hill.

"Agreed. We'll use the latest sensors, hiding them on what's left."

The new high-tech sensors could be programmed to ignore the movement of the security team, yet pick up the wanderings of a field mouse at fifty yards.

"What about—"

The buzz of his intercom interrupted him. Jeff frowned. His assistant, Brenda, knew better than to bother him and Zane while they were involved in tactical planning. She would only do so if there was an emergency.

"Yes," he said, as he tapped a button on his phone.

"Jeff, I know you're busy but you have a call from a downtown shelter. About a Ms. Churchill and her daughter. I didn't know…" His normally take-charge assistant sounded fairly flustered. "Is she a friend of yours? Or should I take a message?"

All of his senses went on alert. "Put the call through," he instructed.

There was a moment of silence, followed by Brenda's voice politely saying, "Mr. Ritter is on the phone now."

"This is Jeff Ritter. How can I help you?"

"Oh, Mr. Ritter. Hi. I'm Julie, a volunteer at the shelter. Ashley and Maggie Churchill are here. The problem is Ashley is very sick. Too sick to stay, but she's refusing to go to a hospital. As she only seems to have the flu, I can't blame her. But we don't have the facilities to take care of her. We found your card in her jacket pocket and I was wondering if you're a friend of the family."

Jeff knew what she was asking. Would he take responsibility? He reminded himself that Ashley Churchill had already refused his offer to pay for a hotel. Then he remembered the defeat in her eyes when she'd seen the ruin that was her home. She was sick, she had a child and nowhere to go.

It wasn't his problem, he reminded himself. He didn't get involved. Not ever. According to his ex-wife he had the compassion of the devil himself and a heart made of stone. Telling the shelter volunteer he wasn't anything to the Churchill females was the only thing that made sense.

"Yes, I'm a friend of the family," he said instead. "I'll be right there to pick them both up. They can stay with me."

Chapter 2

Ashley tried to remember when she last felt this horrible. It wasn't just her unsettled stomach, the pounding in her head or even the weakness that invaded her body. She'd reached the absolute low point of her life. In one morning she'd lost her job and her home, and now she and her daughter were being thrown out of the temporary shelter. In her head she knew that it was wrong of her to stay and expose everyone to the flu. There were several elderly residents, along with mothers with babies. But in her heart she felt incredibly alone. Where were she and Maggie supposed to go? She didn't have the money for a hotel, and even if she did, Ashley knew she was close to physical collapse. If—or rather when—that happened, who was going to watch over her daughter?

Involuntarily her eyelids closed. She desperately wanted to sleep. She wanted this horrible nightmare to end. And just once in her life, she wanted someone else to take charge and make everything better. She wanted to be rescued, just like in those fairy tales she read to her daughter. However, it seemed unlikely a handsome prince would show up to take her away from all her troubles and…

A shadow fell across the cot. Even with her eyes closed Ashley noted the sudden darkening. She forced herself to gather her last bit of strength and look at her visitor. Probably the shelter volunteer, Julie something, who had gently explained she couldn't stay.

But the person looming over her wasn't a too-perky student from the nearby college. Rather he was tall, silent and frighteningly familiar. Not a handsome prince, but the evil wizard—a creature both powerful and deadly.

She knew she was hallucinating, because there was no way her soon-to-be ex-boss was really gathering her up in his arms. She was still lying on the cot, imagining it, she told herself even as powerful male strength surrounded her. The illusion was surprisingly real and in it, he carried her as easily as she carried Maggie.

"You're staying with me until you're better," Jeff Ritter said.

She blinked. The voice sounded genuine and she felt the soft whisper of his breath across her cheek as he spoke. Now that she made herself think about it, she could feel the smooth wool of his suit where her hand rested just below his collar at the back of his neck. She blinked, not sure what was real and what was fever induced.

"Are you carrying me?"

Gray eyes stared into her face. "You're sicker than I thought."

True or not, it wasn't much of an answer.

"We can't—" She pressed her lips together. What couldn't they do? She couldn't remember.

"You'll be safe at my house," he told her.

Safe? Not likely. Suddenly she was being lowered into nothing. She clutched at Jeff, then sighed in relief when he settled her onto a chair.

"Collect her things," he said to someone just out of Ashley's field of vision.

"I'll get her shoes."

The last statement, spoken in her daughter's bright, cheerful voice, brought Ashley back to the land of the living faster than any drug.

"Maggie?"

"She'll be fine."

She shook her head slightly and ignored the subsequent wooziness. With a couple of deep breaths, she managed to clear her head enough to focus on the man crouched in front of her. She hadn't been mistaken—it was Jeff Ritter, all right. Still dressed in his well-tailored suit, still looking distant and the tiniest bit scary.

"Why are you here?" she asked.

"Because you're too sick to stay at the shelter. I'm taking you home until you're on your feet."

She wiggled her sock-clad toes and wondered if he had any idea that she felt as if she was going to be sick forever.

"We can't," she told him. "I mean, we don't even know you."

His steel-gray eyes stared directly into hers. She searched for some flicker of warmth, of humanity, but there was nothing but her tiny reflection in his irises.

"What do you want to know?" he asked. "Should I give you a list of references?"

That would be a start, she thought, but didn't dare speak the words.

Surprisingly Jeff reached out and touched her cheek with his fingers. Just a fleeting moment of contact, during which she felt heat and amazing gentleness.

"Don't be afraid," he said quietly. "I'm not going to hurt you or Maggie. You're sick. You need a place to stay. I'm offering one. End of story. I won't hurt you or pressure you."

"But…"

"You have anywhere else to go?" he asked.

She shook her head. She wished the answer were different, but it wasn't. Her solitary job meant she didn't have any work friends, and she was always rushing into class from dropping Maggie off at school or hurrying out of class to pick up her daughter, so she'd never had time to make friends at the university. Her only acquaintances were her neighbors who were in the same situation she was.

"Mommy, here are your shoes."

She was more awake now and could offer her daughter a hug and her thanks when the happy little girl returned with her athletic shoes.

Before she could bend over and loosen the laces,

Jeff took them from her and began slipping the right shoe on her foot.

The touch of his hand on her ankle was surprisingly intimate. She felt embarrassed and light-headed. The latter sensation could have been from the fever she was fighting, but she didn't think so. Still, it was equally unlikely it was because of what Jeff was doing. He was being kind, nothing more. He was a stranger. A slightly scary stranger. She thought of him as an ice-cold killer, not an attractive man.

"Mommy helps me with my shoes, too," Maggie offered, leaning against Ashley. "With my pink shoes, she has to tie the bow two times instead of just one, 'cause they're so long." Her voice indicated her reverence at the additional work her mother was willing to perform.

"I think I can get by with just one bow," Jeff said, as he finished with the first shoe and started on the second. "Are you ready to go?"

"I need a coat," the girl informed him.

"Do you know where yours is?"

Maggie nodded, then took off in the direction of their cot. Ashley waited until Jeff finished with her shoes and straightened.

The room wasn't spinning so much now and her head felt slightly more clear than when she'd first awakened. Her body still ached and she knew she looked horrible, but as long as her brain continued to function, they would be fine.

"You're acting as if it's all decided," she said.

"Isn't it?" He jerked his head toward the cot where two members of the volunteer staff were already collecting her things. "You need time and a place to recover. I can provide both."

"I want to trust you. As you've already learned, I'm running out of options. But I still have questions. I don't know why you're doing this."

For the first time since he arrived, he wouldn't meet her gaze. He looked over her head, but she doubted he was seeing the bustling activities in the temporary shelter. He'd gone somewhere else, and based on what she knew about it, it wasn't a place she wanted to know about.

Finally he shrugged. "I'm under my good-deed quota for this lifetime."

It wasn't an answer. It wasn't even a good fake answer. She had the sudden thought that maybe he didn't know why he was doing it, either. Which was scary, but not as scary as having nowhere to go. It all came down to whether or not she trusted him. Ashley looked into his face, the strong bone structure, the empty eyes. He had a scar by his mouth and a few gray hairs at his temples. Both her gut and her daughter said he was safe. Was that enough?

"I'm a member of the Better Business Bureau. Does that help?"

The corners of his mouth turned up. The smile transformed him, making him handsome and approachable. It also made her heart beat just a little faster and her breathing increase.

The flu, she told herself. A physical manifestation of her virus. Nothing more.

"Thank you," she said, pushing herself to her feet

and swaying slightly before she gained her balance. "I'm very grateful for your assistance."

"You're welcome."

There was a plus to all this, she thought. If Jeff turned out to be a nice guy in disguise, maybe she could convince him not to fire her from her cleaning job. Then in a few short days, she could return to her regular life and pretend none of this had happened.

The security-soldier business paid better than she'd realized, Ashley thought thirty minutes later when Jeff pulled into the driveway of a two-story glass-and-wood house more than halfway up Queen Anne Hill. The view through clouds and light rain was impressive, with Lake Union down below and the west side of the city visible across the water. She could only imagine how beautiful it would be when the weather was nice.

"Is this yours?" Maggie asked excitedly from the back seat of the luxury car. "It's so big and pretty. Do you have kittens? There's lots of room for them. If you wanted to get one, I'd help you take very good care of it."

"Ever hopeful," Ashley murmured. "Maggie is desperate for a kitten."

"I've noticed."

On their way over from the shelter Maggie had talked about kittens and her school and how nice everyone at the shelter had been. It gave the adults a break from having to make conversation. Ashley, for one, was grateful.

"Where's your 'partment?" Maggie asked as they waited for the garage door to open. "Is it up high? Mommy and me live on the top floor and sometimes it's fun to look out at the city or watch when the storms come. And in 'the summer when it's hot, we open all the windows, 'cause no one can climb in when we're up so high."

Jeff turned off the engine and shifted to face the little girl. "It's a house, Maggie," he told her. "I live here by myself. While you and your mom stay here, I want you to be very comfortable."

Maggie's eyes widened. "It's just you here? Don'tcha get scared being all alone?"

Ashley winced. Until this moment she'd never realized that her daughter hadn't ever lived in a house before. They'd always been in apartments.

"Sometimes it's quiet," Jeff admitted. "But I don't mind that."

He was about to have a couple of days of nonquiet, Ashley thought. Maggie was a sweetheart and very well behaved, but she was a walking noise machine.

He unfastened his seat belt. "Let's get you two inside and settled. I'll bring your bags in later."

Ashley nodded. She could feel the weariness settling over her again. Her consciousness through the drive here had taken the last of her reserves. All she wanted was to sleep for the next four or five weeks.

Jeff climbed out of the car, then opened the rear door to assist Maggie from the vehicle. Ashley trailed after them as they went up the two stairs that led to the main house. Before he opened the door, Jeff punched a long code into a keypad. There was an audible *snick* as the locking mechanism released. She had a brief thought of armed guards waiting on the other side and chuckled at the image of them walking through metal detectors before entering the living quarters of the house.

But whatever security measures existed were concealed because all she saw when she stepped inside was space.

The rooms were huge and sparsely furnished. Jeff showed them the living room, dining room and a study. Only the latter contained any evidence that a person actually lived in the house. The living room had two sofas, a couple of club chairs, along with low tables and a few lamps. But there was nothing personal or decorative. No pictures or photographs on the walls, no magazines, plants or even a pair of shoes marred the solitude. The dining room was the same. A massive table surrounded by chairs. A matching hutch—the glassed-in top of which was empty.

Cream carpet and pale walls added to the sense of space, as did the floor-to-ceiling windows in both the living room and dining room that offered a view of the lake and the shore beyond. The study was at the rear of the house, looking out on extensive gardens. At least here there were papers on the desk and a few books scattered on the leather sofa across from the fireplace.

Ashley looked around without saying anything, then followed Jeff into his huge kitchen. She took in the oversize refrigerator, the six-burner stove and the impressive collection of copper pots hanging above the island.

"You must entertain a lot," she murmured, not able to imagine such a thing. With someone else maybe, but not Jeff Ritter. He didn't appear to be the entertaining type.

"No. It all came with the house." He motioned to the refrigerator. "I eat out, or at the office. There isn't much in the way of food. When I get you settled, I'll take Maggie and go to the grocery store."

She wanted to protest. Surely there was enough for them to get by until she was feeling better. She didn't want to impose. Impulsively she opened the refrigerator, about to make that point. However, the point went unmade.

The interior of the gleaming metal refrigerator was empty. Not just echoing with the stereotypical bachelor fare of beer and condiments. It was as empty as a showroom model. Ashley swallowed, then moved to the pantry. Those shelves were neatly papered and just as bare.

Jeff cleared his throat. "Like I said, I don't eat here much."

"Ever," she corrected. "How can you not have coffee?"

Instead of answering, he indicated that they should follow him toward the staircase at the rear of the house. On the landing it split in two directions. He took the stairs on the right.

"This is the guest wing," he said. "The two bedrooms share a bathroom."

He opened doors, leading the way to well-furnished bedrooms, one larger than the other. The bathroom setup gave them each a vanity and mirror, while they shared the toilet and bath. Maggie hurried to the window seat in the smaller room and knelt on the yellow cushion.

"I like this," she said, holding her stuffed cat close to her chest and smiling. "I can see the water."

"Good."

Ashley hoped her voice sounded pleased. She was

having trouble forming the words as her strength faded. She made her way back into the larger of the two rooms. As it had been downstairs, the furniture was exactly right but there were no homey touches. The walls were blank, as were the surfaces of the dresser and night-stands, except for a clock radio silently illuminating the time.

Ashley found she didn't care about decorating or empty refrigerators. Exhaustion descended with no warning, sucking up the last of her strength, leaving her shaking and breathless.

Jeff seemed to figure out her problem. Without saying anything, he drew back the covers on the bed and urged her to sit on the clean sheet.

"You need sleep," he said, reaching for her shoes and tugging them off. "I'll take care of Maggie. Just rest."

She started to protest. She had to give her daughter instructions to be good, to listen to Jeff and to come running to her if she was afraid. Even as she stretched out on the bed she thought it might be a good idea to stay awake for a while to make sure everything was all right here in the beautiful house on the hill. She ought to—

Jeff watched Ashley fight against exhaustion. Slowly her eyes closed and her breathing slowed.

"We'll be going out for food," he murmured as she drifted off to sleep. "We'll be back soon."

She didn't respond. Maggie bounced into the room, her mouth open to speak. She stopped when she saw her mother asleep, pressing her lips together and then looking at him.

He walked to the door and motioned for her to fol-

low. When they were out in the hall, he stared down
at her, wondering what he was supposed to do now.
Food, he thought. They had to get food. He hesitated,
not sure if he'd ever gone grocery shopping before. As
he'd told Ashley, he ate all his meals at restaurants, or
at work. It's not that he didn't know how to keep food
in the house, he simply didn't bother. Despite the furniture in the rooms and his clothes in his bedroom closet,
this wasn't his home. It was a place to sleep and work
after hours. Nothing more.

"We're going shopping," he announced. "The grocery store."

Maggie hesitated before nodding her agreement. She
looked so small standing there in her pink jeans and
pink-and-white plaid knit sweater. Two tiny clips held
her dark curls off her face. Her Cupid's bow mouth
quivered slightly.

Not knowing what else to do, Jeff crouched in front
of the child. "You know your mom is sick, right?"

"Uh-huh." Her grip on the battered stuffed cat tightened.

"She has the flu. Do you know what that is?"

"It's what I had last week. I was very sick and I got
to watch TV in Mommy's bed and eat Jell-O whenever I wanted."

Was that kid paradise? He didn't know. "But you're
better now, right?"

Another nod.

"So you know your mom is going to be fine in a few
days. I don't want you to worry about her."

Maggie gave him an impish smile. "I know you'll
take care of her."

He hadn't thought about his responsibility in quite those terms, but if it made the kid happy to think that, he wouldn't disagree. "Are you nervous about being with me?"

Delicate, dark eyebrows drew together. "What's nerv-nerv— What's that?"

"Nervous. Upset. Afraid. Anxious." His explanation didn't seem to be helping. He searched his memory for a word a four-year-old could understand. "Scared."

This time, instead of smiling, she laughed. "I'm not scared. You *like* us."

She spoke with a conviction he both envied and admired. If only all of life were that simple, he thought as he rose to his full height.

"Then let's go to the food store."

Maggie trailed after him as they made their way to the car. Jeff hesitated, then decided not to set the alarm in the house. He figured the odds of Ashley opening a door or window were greater than someone breaking in during the short time he would be gone.

He held the back door open for the little girl, then helped her fasten her seat belt. She gazed at him trustingly as he secured her in the car. She sniffed loudly.

"Your car smells nice."

"It's the leather. I've only had the car a few months."

Her eyes widened. "It's new? You have a new car?"

Her tone of reverence made him wonder if Ashley had ever had a new car. Based on her current circumstances, he doubted it. At least not in the recent past. There were so many things in his life that he took for granted.

"I have to call someone I know," he said as he slid

into the driver's seat. "I need to ask her what to buy to make your mom feel better."

"Jell-O," Maggie said firmly.

"Okay, but she'll need other stuff, too." He was thinking in terms of liquids. Or was that for a cold? His first-aid training ran more in the direction of gunshot wounds or emergency amputations.

He backed out of the driveway, then touched a button. A mechanical voice asked, "What name?"

"Brenda," he replied.

Maggie stared at him. "The car is talking!"

He felt himself smile as the sound of a phone ringing came over the built-in speakers. It was nearly five-thirty. Brenda might have gone home.

But his assistant was still at the office. When she answered, he explained that he was taking care of a friend with the flu and needed her advice on what to buy at the grocery store. Also, what would be appropriate to serve a four-year-old for dinner.

With that he glanced at the girl. "Say hi, Maggie."

Still wide-eyed and clutching her stuffed, white cat, Maggie licked her lips. "Hi," she whispered tentatively.

"That was Maggie," he said helpfully.

"Uh, hi, Maggie. Nice to talk to you." His assistant's tone of voice warned him that he would be getting a major third degree when he saw her in the morning.

"Do you even know where the grocery store is?" Brenda asked when she'd recovered from her shock.

"I have a fair idea. I was thinking of soup and juice. Liquids for the flu, right?"

"Uh, yeah, that's right. As for dinner for the little

one, there are lots of options. Rule number one is the less sugar the better. Are you cooking or heating?"

Ten minutes later he had a list along with instructions. Brenda cleared her throat. "Are they going to be staying with you for a few days?"

"Yes. Why?"

"If the mother isn't feeling well, then she won't be up to watching her child. Maggie, do you have a preschool you go to?"

The little girl beamed at being included in the conversation. "Uh-huh. Right by Mommy's school. I stay there until two."

"Ashley is a student at the University of Washington," he clarified.

"Which means she'll be missing class while she's sick."

He heard Brenda writing on a pad of paper. "Can we send someone to sit in for her?" he asked.

"Sure, but I need her schedule of classes first. Some lecture notes are available online. Also, Maggie will need a sitter for the afternoon. I can arrange that. What's your student friend's name?"

"Ashley Churchill. She works for us."

There was a moment of silence. Jeff could practically see Brenda's surprise. She knew everyone who worked for Ritter/Rankin Security.

"The cleaner?"

"Yes."

"How did you meet her?" She coughed. "Sorry. It's not any of my business, of course. I'll get on all of this and call you later tonight."

"Thanks, Brenda. I appreciate the effort."

His assistant laughed. "No problem. You know I'm desperate to break into the spy business. There has to be a market for fifty-something operatives. Finding this information will be good practice."

"I'd be lost without you in the office. I can't afford to let you go into the field."

"So you keep saying. But I think you're just being kind and trying to not hurt my feelings. Oh, well. I'll call you later, Jeff. Bye, Maggie."

"Bye," Maggie piped back.

Jeff disconnected the call, then wondered how Brenda could ever be foolish enough to think of him as kind.

Chapter 3

"They're very good," Maggie said earnestly.

They stood in the cereal aisle of the large grocery store just down the hill from Jeff's house. He'd never been inside in all the time he'd lived in the neighborhood. He doubted Maggie had been here, either, yet she led the way like an expert, wielding her miniature shopping cart around other patrons, calling out names of favorite brands and making decisions with the ease of an executive. Now she held out a box of Pop-Tarts and gave him a winning smile.

"I had them at Sara's house. Her mom fixed them for us. She said only kids could eat something that purple." Her smile broadened. "I said that the purple is the best part."

He looked doubtfully at the picture on the box. It

showed a toaster pastry covered with vivid purple frosting. Just the thought made his stomach tighten. In this case, he'd have to side with Sara's mom.

"You really want those?" he asked, not sure how that was possible.

Maggie nodded vigorously, making her dark curls dance around her head.

"Does your mother buy these for you?"

Big blue eyes suddenly turned away from him. She became intensely interested in the contents of her cart, rearranging the three frozen kid meals he'd bought her. Finally she returned her gaze to him and slowly shook her head.

"No."

Outside of his abilities, he didn't count on very much in the world, but he would have bet his life that Maggie Churchill was incapable of lying—whether because of her age, her character, her upbringing or a combination of the three. He didn't think he'd ever met anyone like her before.

"Would you really eat them if we got them?"

Questions filled her eyes. Questions and hope. She practically vibrated her assent.

"All right." He tossed the package into her tiny cart. "If you're sure."

She gazed at him as if he'd just created a rainbow right there in the grocery store. She threw herself at him, wrapping her arms around his legs and squeezing tight.

"Thank you," she said fervently. "I'll be good. I promise."

He hadn't known she could be anything but.

They continued their shopping, going up and down each aisle. Jeff found that buying bread for sandwiches also meant buying something to go in between the slices of bread. Maggie favored peanut butter and jelly. He thought her mother might appreciate something more along the lines of sliced turkey or beef. Which meant an intense discussion on mustard versus mayonnaise, and an interpretation of whether or not Maggie's shudder at the thought of pickles meant her mother didn't like them, either.

The girl's cart was already full and his was nearly so when they turned the corner and found themselves in the pet food aisle. Maggie touched a can of cat food and sighed.

"Do you have a kitty?" she asked, sounding hopeful. "I didn't see one but maybe she was asleep."

"Sorry. No pets."

"Why? Don'tcha like them?"

"Cats?" He'd never thought about them one way or the other. Dogs could be a problem. Dogs made noise, alerting people to the presence of intruders. More than one mission had nearly been compromised by the unexpected presence of a dog. But cats?

"I travel a lot," he said, then hesitated. Conversing with Maggie was both easy and difficult. He didn't mind spending time in her company, which surprised him, but he wasn't sure what to say. How did people talk to children? He only knew how to talk to adults.

"Pets are a big responsibility," he continued. "It wouldn't be fair to the animal to leave it alone all the time."

She considered his statement, then nodded slowly.

"Mommy and I are home plenty, but she says we can't have a kitten just yet. They can be expensive. Not for her food, but if she got sick or somethin'. Mommy gets sad about money sometimes. She cries in the bathroom." Maggie pressed her lips together. "I don't think I'm supposed to know, but I can hear her, even with the water running. Can you make Mommy not be sad?"

He wasn't sure what to do with the information Maggie shared. Based on the little he knew about Ashley's situation, he wasn't surprised by her financial concerns. But he also wasn't willing to take on responsibility for her emotional state.

"Your mother isn't sad now," he said, sidestepping the issue.

Maggie thought for a moment, then nodded her agreement. "Mommy's happy."

Jeff thought that might be a stretch. Ashley might be relieved to be out of the shelter, but he doubted she was pleased with her present circumstances. His guess was she wouldn't rest easy until she had her life back in order.

While Jeff heated soup in a pan on the stove, Maggie watched her frozen kid's dinner as it warmed in the microwave. The entrée had come with a small toy, which she clutched in her hand as she danced from foot to foot, waiting for the timer to beep.

"I like chicken," she announced. "And macaroni and cheese. I've never had them together before."

It didn't sound like much of a treat to him, but then, he wasn't four. After stirring Ashley's soup, he returned to the task of putting away the rest of the groceries. As the pantry shelves were bare, it didn't take long. He put milk and juice into the refrigerator, along with several cartons of yogurt. Frozen foods went into the freezer.

Grocery shopping and cooking had to be two of the most normal activities, and yet they all felt foreign to him. He didn't eat yogurt from a carton. The last time he'd had the stuff had been during a covert operation in Afghanistan and the goat responsible for the yogurt had watched him warily, as if to make sure he swallowed every spoonful.

He stirred the soup again, then checked on Maggie's dinner.

"Twenty more seconds," she told him, never taking her gaze from the timer.

He dug through kitchen cupboards, pulling out a bowl from a set of dishes he doubted he'd ever used. He also unearthed a wooden tray. After rinsing and drying the bowl, he poured the soup, then, along with a spoon, set it on the tray, next to some toast and a glass of juice. When the microwave beeped, he lifted Maggie's dinner onto the tray, along with cutlery and a drink, and started toward his guest's room.

"I get dessert later, right?" Maggie asked, confirming the reality of her purple Pop-Tart.

"Absolutely. We'll get your mom settled first, though."

"Okay."

He waited while Maggie pushed open the door, then he stepped into Ashley's room. Light spilled out from the bathroom, but the bedroom itself was in twilight. He could make out her still figure on the bed. Her eyes were closed, her breathing even.

He was about to retreat, taking Maggie with him, when the four-year-old flew at her mother and pounced onto the mattress.

"Mommy, Mommy, we brought dinner. There's soup for you and chicken pieces and macaroni and cheese for me. And Mr. Ritter got me Pop-Tarts and they're *purple!*"

Ashley came awake slowly. She opened her eyes and smiled at her daughter, then shifted her gaze so she could take in the room. He both felt and saw the exact moment she noticed him. For a second she looked confused, then she blinked and the questions in her eyes were gone.

Jeff was pleased she didn't appear frightened. He doubted the circumstances were to her liking, but she was in no condition to change them. He'd said and done as much as he could to convince her she was completely safe in his company, but it would take time and experience for her to learn that she could trust him.

"I brought dinner," he said as he flipped on the floor lamp. "Do you think you can eat?"

"I'm going to eat with you," Maggie said, sliding off the bed and walking to the small table by the window. "Is here okay?"

"It's fine, sweetie." Ashley shifted until she was in a sitting position, her back against the headboard. She rubbed her eyes, then looked at the tray. "I'm not hungry, but I haven't had anything since dinner last night, so I should probably try to get something down."

He served Maggie first, carefully putting her entrée in front of her, then setting out a fork, a glass of milk and three napkins. When he carried the tray to Ashley, he noticed that she'd changed her clothes while they'd been gone. She'd traded jeans for sweatpants and her blouse for a loose T-shirt, both in faded navy.

She was pale, with dark circles under her eyes. Sleep had mussed her dark hair. While it wasn't as curly as her daughter's, it was thick and wavy, falling just to her shoulders.

"Maggie promised that you like chicken soup," he said, adjusting the tray so the legs bracketed Ashley's slender thighs.

"What's not to like?" she said, picking up a spoon and taking a sip. "It's great." She paused and looked at him. "You've been more than kind. I really appreciate it. We'll be out of your hair by morning."

"I doubt that," Jeff told her. "You're sick. You're going to need a few days to get your strength back. I want you to feel comfortable enough to do that here."

Her hazel eyes seemed more blue than green or brown. Was it the hour of the day or a reflection of her navy T-shirt? Her arms were thin...too thin. Maggie had a sturdiness about her, but Ashley looked as if a slight breeze could blow her away.

As he continued to stare, he noticed a flush of color climbing her cheeks. At first he thought it was from her fever, but then he had the sudden thought that she might be uncomfortable with his scrutiny. He shifted his attention to her daughter.

"Maggie was a big help at the grocery store," he said. The little girl beamed at him.

"I can only imagine," Ashley said dryly. "She convinced you to buy Pop-Tarts."

"I wasn't a hard sell."

"Mr. Ritter has a magic car," Maggie said between bites of chicken. "A lady spoke to us from the air and everything."

Jeff pulled out the second chair at the small table and sat down. "I called my assistant from the car. I needed some menu ideas."

"She was very nice and said hello to me," Maggie added.

The girl had finished most of her macaroni and cheese, although she wore a good portion of the sauce on her face and hands. Jeff studied the shape of her eyes and her mouth, then glanced at her mother, trying to figure out what traits they shared.

Ashley's features were slightly more delicate. The eye color was different, as well. Did Maggie's blue eyes come from her father?

Ashley tucked a strand of hair behind her ear, using her left hand. Jeff had already noted that she didn't wear a ring, but now he looked to see if there were any telltale marks showing one had recently been removed. He didn't see any tan lines or indentations. A divorce? he wondered. Although having a baby didn't require a woman to marry, Ashley struck him as the marrying kind. He didn't think she would have chosen to have a child on her own. Not without a good reason.

"Is there anyone I should phone?" he asked. "A relative out of state, a friend?"

She paused in the act of drinking her juice and carefully put down the glass. "You mean to let them know where I am?"

"Yes."

A shadow slipped across her eyes and she looked

away from him. He could read her mind as clearly as if she spoke her thoughts. The truthful answer was that she was all alone in the world. If there was no one to care about her, then there was no one to worry if she and her daughter disappeared.

He leaned toward her. "I'm not going to hurt you, Ashley."

She smiled without meeting his gaze. He hated that the fear was back in her eyes. "I know. I wasn't thinking that at all. You've been very good to us."

"Your parents?" he asked, knowing he shouldn't pry.

"Grandma's in heaven with Daddy," Maggie piped up. She'd finished her dinner and was carefully wiping her hands with a napkin.

Ashley a widow? Jeff frowned. She was too young, barely in her mid-twenties. What had happened? A car accident? Murder? Did her husband's death account for her difficult financial circumstances?

Before he could decide if he could ask any or all of those questions, his cell phone rang. He excused himself and stepped into the hall.

"Ritter," he said into the instrument.

"It's Brenda," his assistant said. "I have been my normal efficient self. Are you ready?"

"Just a second." He pulled a notebook and a pen from his suit pocket and started walking toward his study downstairs. "Go ahead."

"I've found a sitter for Maggie tomorrow afternoon. It's one of her teachers from the preschool. So not only is the woman qualified and trustworthy, but Maggie already knows and likes her. Next, I have Ashley's schedule of classes in front of me. She has two tomorrow.

They're advanced classes and don't have Internet lecture notes so I've been in touch with an off-campus service that specializes in taking notes. They will attend both lectures for her and provide me with typed notes by two tomorrow afternoon."

"I'm impressed," he said, sliding behind his desk and settling on his leather chair. "How'd you find her class schedule?"

Brenda chuckled. "I was about to get all high-tech and then I remembered she works here. Her Social Security number is on the job application in her personnel file. After that, it was easy. After all, I've learned from the best."

"Do you mean me or Zane?"

"I refuse to answer that," she said, her voice teasing. "I'll drop by about seven tomorrow morning to help get the little one ready."

"Do you think that's necessary? She seems fairly self-sufficient." After all, she'd talked him into getting just about everything she wanted at the grocery store.

"Do you really want to deal with getting a four-year-old girl ready for school? I'm talking about picking out clothes and doing her hair."

He hadn't thought that part through. "I guess not. Seven sounds fine. I appreciate this, Brenda."

"I know. I just wish you'd let me go into the field. I'd be great."

"Your husband would kill me."

"Probably, but I'd have a fabulous time."

He tried to imagine his fifty-something assistant slinking along the banks of a Russian river, waiting to make a drop.

Brenda sighed. "I know, I know. I don't speak any languages, I'm wildly out of shape, but hey, a girl can dream, right?"

"Absolutely. And comfort yourself with the thought that I'd be lost without you."

"I know." She chuckled. "See you in the morning, boss."

"We'll be here."

He pushed the "end" button and terminated the call, then went back upstairs so he could return to Ashley's room and collect the tray.

He found the larger guest room empty and the sound of running water and laughter coming from the bathroom. Jeff quickly picked up empty dishes and set them on the tray. He was nearly out the door when Ashley appeared.

"I thought I heard you return," she said, leaning against the wall by the bathroom. "Thanks for making dinner. I'm going to give Maggie a bath, then come down with her while she has her dessert. We'll read for a bit and both be in bed by eight."

Weariness darkened her eyes and pulled at the corners of her mouth. She was attractive, in a slender, delicate sort of way.

"You look like you could use a good night's sleep," he said.

She studied him. "I can't decide if I should ask you again why you're bothering, or simply be grateful."

"How about just thinking about getting well?"

She tilted her head slightly. "My daughter thinks you're a very nice man."

"Your daughter is trusting." Too trusting.

"She hasn't had a chance to learn otherwise."

She'd made a statement but he wondered if it was also a warning. As in *Don't teach her differently. Don't give her a reason not to trust.*

Jeff wanted to reassure her that he had no intention of destroying Maggie's illusions about the world. Time would take care of that, and far too quickly for his taste. Oddly, he liked knowing that somewhere a four-year-old little girl laughed with glee because there were Pop-Tarts and kittens.

"Who are you, Jeff Ritter?"

No one you want to know. But he didn't say that aloud because it would frighten her. "A friend."

"I hope so. Good night."

She turned back to the bathroom. He left her bedroom and walked down to the kitchen where he loaded the dirty dishes into the dishwasher then thought about fixing dinner for himself. There were sandwich ingredients and frozen dinners, soup, chili and a couple of apples.

But instead of preparing a meal, he walked into the living room and stared out into the night. The light rain had stopped although clouds still covered the sky. Jeff looked into the darkness, trying to ignore the sense of impending doom. He felt the familiar clenching of his gut and knew that trouble lay ahead. As he wasn't on a mission, he didn't know what form the trouble would take. Obviously it had something to do with the woman. With Ashley.

Even from this distance, he could sense her in the

house. Her soft scent drifted through the air, teasing him, making him wonder how it would feel to be like other men.

His footsteps crunched on the path that led through the center of the village. It was night, yet he could see everything clearly. Probably because of the fire.

The flames were everywhere, licking at the edges of the shabby structures, chasing after the unwary residents, occasionally catching someone off guard and consuming them in a heartbeat.

The fire was alive, fueled by dry timbers and a chemical dreamed up in a lab thousands of miles away. Jeff was familiar with the smell, the heat and the destruction. He hated the fire. It showed no mercy. At times he would swear he heard it laughing as it destroyed.

It was only after he'd gone into the center square of the village that he became aware of the sounds. The *crack* of timbers breaking as they were consumed, the gunshot sound of glass exploding, the screams of the villagers. The soft crying of a lost child.

He knew this village. Every building, every person. He knew that just beyond the rise in the path was the river. He could walk through the fire again and again and never be touched. Because this village was a part of him, a creation of his mind and he was drawn to it night after night. No matter how he fought against the dream, it pulled him in, sucking him toward hell as surely as the fire crept toward the truck at the edge of the square and caught it in its grasp.

A sharp cry caught his attention. He turned and saw

a teenage girl running from a burning building. A support beam creaked and tipped, then fell toward her. Jeff saw it happen in slow motion. He took one step, then another. He reached for the girl, determined to pull her to safety. He put out his hand.

She reached toward him in response. Slowly, achingly slowly, she raised her head until she could see him. Then her mouth opened wider and she screamed as he'd never heard another human being scream before. Sheer, soul-numbing terror.

She jerked away from him and ran toward the river. The support beam tumbled to the ground, narrowly missing her as she fled. Jeff took a step after her. Only then did he notice that all the villagers were racing away from him. They pointed and screamed, acting as if he were a threat worse than the fire.

An aching coldness filled him. Unable to stop himself, he walked toward the river, toward the small pool fed by the flowing water. Fire raged all around him, but he remained untouched by the destruction. People ran past him, screaming, darting out of his way. A mother raced by, a toddler in her arms. The small child cried when he saw Jeff, then ducked his head into the curve of his mother's neck.

They ran and ran until he was alone. Alone and standing by the pool. And even though he didn't want to look, he couldn't help himself. He knelt by the still water and waited for the smoke to clear enough for him to see his reflection.

Then he knew why they ran, why they screamed in terror. He wasn't a man. Instead of his face, he saw the cold metal features of a mechanical creature. A robot.

A metal being not even remotely alive. Fire danced over him, but he couldn't feel it. Nor did it hurt him. He couldn't be burned or damaged in any way. He could only terrify...

Jeff woke in a cold sweat, the way he did every night after the dream. There was no moment of confusion. From the second consciousness returned, he knew exactly where he was and what had happened. He also knew he wouldn't sleep for several hours.

He rose and, in deference to his company, pulled on jeans and a sweatshirt. Then he left his bedroom, prepared to wander through the house like a ghost. Silent, alone, living in the shadows. He tried not to think about the dream, but he was, as usual, unsuccessful. He knew what it meant—that he didn't see himself as human. That he considered himself little more than a machine of destruction. But knowing the truth of the message wasn't enough to make it stop.

As he moved down the hall, he felt a change in the night air. Not a disturbance, just something...different. He could sense the presence of his guests.

Unable to stop himself, he headed in the direction of their rooms. Maggie's door was partially closed. He stood in the hallway and looked in on her.

She slept in the center of the double bed, a small figure guarded by her menagerie of stuffed animals. She was curled up, the blankets tucked around her, sleeping soundly, breathing evenly. A dark curl brushed against her cheek.

He remembered her trust, the sound of her laughter, her delight at the speakerphone in his car. She was a magical child, he thought gruffly, as he noticed one of her fluffy cats had tumbled to the ground. Silently he stepped into her room and put the toy back on the bed. Then, because he couldn't stop himself, he moved through the connecting bathroom and into Ashley's room.

Her sleep was more troubled than her daughter's. She moved under the covers. Her face was slightly flushed, but when he touched her forehead, he didn't feel any heat.

Who was this woman with no family and such dire circumstances? From what he could observe, she was bright and capable. What had happened to bring her to the place where she needed to depend upon his good graces?

Knowing he wasn't going to get any answers, he left her room and walked downstairs. In the living room he walked to the windows and stared out into the night. For the first time since he'd moved into the house, he wasn't alone. How strange. He was always alone. No one came here. Certainly no one had spent the night. When there were women, he visited *them*. He had an animal's need to protect its territory. Yet he had been the one to invite Ashley and her daughter here in the first place. What did that mean?

He asked the question and received no answer. So he moved into his study where he turned on his computer. Ashley Churchill intrigued him. So he would find out what he needed with his special programs and secret information. When all was revealed to him she would cease to be anything but a woman and then he could easily let her go.

Chapter 4

The normally silent morning was filled with changes. Jeff stood in his kitchen, sipping a cup of coffee made in a coffeemaker he hadn't known he owned until he went looking for it a half hour before. Generally he simply got up, showered, dressed and left for the office. He was usually the first one in the building and made coffee when he arrived. He felt strange still being at home when it was almost seven-thirty.

From upstairs came the sound of movement and laughter. Brenda had shown up promptly at seven and was getting Maggie ready for preschool. Jeff glanced at his watch and realized he should check on Ashley before they left. He needed to make sure she would be all right on her own during the day.

He set his coffee mug on the counter then headed for

the stairs. Sleep had taken longer than usual to reclaim him the previous night. He'd been unable to forget he had guests in his house. He couldn't decide if their presence was good, bad or simply different.

He paused outside of Ashley's door and knocked once. A muffled voice invited him to enter. He stepped inside and found Ashley sitting on the edge of her bed. She looked sleepy and flushed. Her hair was mussed and weariness tugged at her mouth, but she held clothes in her arms as if she planned on getting dressed and starting her day.

"How do you feel?" he asked.

"Great. Much better. Thanks."

She was such a lousy liar, he nearly smiled. "Sell it somewhere else. You look dead on your feet and you're not even standing."

She brushed her hair off her face. "I have to get up. Maggie has school and so do I. She needs to get dressed and have breakfast. I have my own classes to attend. Plus, you've already been so kind. I don't want to impose any longer."

Determination stiffened her small frame. She raised her chin slightly, in a gesture of defiance that reminded him of a kitten spitting at a wolf. It looked great and accomplished nothing, except possibly amusing the wolf.

Instead of answering Ashley directly, he called for Brenda to join him.

Brenda bustled into the room. His assistant, a fifty-something blonde of medium height, was dressed in tailored slacks and a silk blouse. She looked efficient and ran his office with the precision and attention to detail of a neurosurgeon at work.

She walked to Ashley and held out her hand. "Hi. I'm Brenda Maitlin. You must be Ashley. Your daughter is such a sweetheart. And you look like death, honey."

Ashley had responded to Brenda's greeting by shaking hands with the woman. As Jeff watched, his assistant took the pile of clothes from Ashley and set them on the dresser. She maneuvered the other woman back under the covers and pulled up the blankets.

"Don't think about anything," Brenda instructed her. "Just sleep and get better."

"But I have to get my daughter dressed and take her to school. Then—"

Brenda cut her off with a quick shake of her head. "You don't have to do a darned thing. Maggie has been fed and dressed. I'm dropping her off at her preschool on my way to the office. Maggie's sitter, one of her teachers from school, is going to look after her after school at her place." She paused as if going through a mental list before continuing. "Oh, and a note taker will go to class for you today, so you don't have to worry about that, either." She turned to Jeff and beamed. "I think that's everything."

Ashley looked stunned. Jeff winked at her. "I know Brenda can be a little overwhelming, but that's why I hired her. Get the best people possible to do the job."

Brenda looked at him. "Then I have just two words to say to you. Field work."

It was an old argument. "I have just one word in response. No. I'd miss you in the office and your husband would kill me."

She glared at him before stomping out of the room.

Jeff returned his attention to Ashley. "She's convinced she would make a great spy. I suspect she's right, but she's late in starting her training and I doubt her family would approve."

Ashley looked confused, as if she was having a difficult time following the conversation. Before she could respond, Maggie burst into the room. The little girl was dressed in purple jeans with a matching purple-and-white sweater. Tiny clips held her hair off of her face. She grinned at Jeff before racing to her mother.

"Mommy, Mommy, Brenda came and cooked me breakfast. We had waffles and I ate a whole one. Then we got me dressed and now I'm going to school in her car. She's got a dog named Muffin and maybe when you feel better we can go visit them."

"A whole waffle. I'm impressed." Ashley raised up on one elbow to study her daughter. "Are you all right?" she asked. "Did you sleep well?"

Maggie laughed. "Mommy, I'm fine." She gave her a quick hug, then dashed out of the room.

Ashley lowered herself back onto the bed. "Thanks for taking care of her. And of me. You're being very nice."

"No one has ever accused me of that before."

"Probably because you didn't give them reason."

Her eyes fluttered closed. Her skin looked soft and smooth. He had an instant vision of touching her cheek, then her mouth. The image was so real, his fingertips burned. Suddenly uncomfortable, he took a step back and tried to figure out what to say.

"I'll be at the office all day," he told her. "Will you be all right by yourself?"

"Sure. I just need to rest a little more."

"The kitchen is well stocked. Take whatever you'd like." He set a business card on the nightstand. "Here's my number, in case you need it."

She nodded slowly, her eyes drifting closed. He knew the exact moment she found sleep. For a second he thought about giving in and touching her cheek...just to see if it was as soft as it looked. But he didn't. Men like him didn't have physical contact with women like her. Men like him remembered they weren't the same as everyone else. And if he tried to forget, the dream was a constant reminder.

Ashley rolled over and glanced at the digital clock on the nightstand: 7:01...a.m. She blinked. As in the morning? She sat up with a hastiness that made her head spin. Morning? That wasn't possible. She last remembered it being seven-thirty in the morning. Had she really slept around the clock?

She threw back the covers and slid to her feet. Aside from a little light-headedness that was probably due to not eating in thirty-six hours, she felt a whole lot better than she had before. But all thoughts of health were pushed aside by the panicky realization she hadn't seen her daughter since the previous morning.

She flew through the shared bathroom and into the adjoining room. It was empty. Empty! Panic tightened her throat. Dear God, what had happened to her daughter? Her eyes began to burn as tears formed. "Maggie," she whispered. "Maggie?"

Just as she was about to scream, she heard a faint sound. She spun in that direction and realized it came from downstairs. There was a low rumble of a male voice followed by childish laughter.

Maggie!

Relief flooded her. Ashley hurried into the hall and made her way to the stairs. Ignoring the shaking in her legs and the dizziness that lingered, she ran down the stairs and raced into the kitchen. With one sweeping glance, she saw her daughter sitting at the table and eating a triangle of toast and jam.

"Maggie!"

Her little girl looked up and smiled with delight. "Mommy, you're up! I wanted to see you last night but Uncle Jeff said you needed to sleep so I was very quiet when I came to say good-night."

As she spoke, Maggie slid off her chair and hurried to her mother. Ashley took in the mismatched shirt and jeans, the smudge of jam on the girl's cheek and the crooked clips in her hair. Her heart filled with love as she gathered her close and held her tightly.

"I love you, baby girl," she murmured, inhaling the familiar scent of her child.

"I love you, too, Mommy," her daughter whispered in response.

Still holding her child, Ashley looked past her to the man sitting at the table. His suit slacks were immaculate, as was his white shirt. His gray eyes seemed to see down to her receding panic. Which was crazy. He couldn't have known that she'd freaked when she'd awakened and Maggie hadn't been in her room. Could he?

"Brenda was delayed by a family crisis," he said. "So we had to get ready without her." He nodded at Maggie. "She picked out her clothes and got herself dressed without any assistance. I did her hair." He smiled self-deprecatingly. "But you probably figured that out."

His smile did something funny to her insides. Or maybe it was just lack of food. Ashley released her daughter and studied her clothes and hair.

"It's perfect," she said.

Maggie beamed. "I've been extra good for Uncle Jeff. I ate all my cereal and I'm going to finish my toast and milk."

Ashley looked at their host. "Uncle Jeff?"

He shrugged. "Mr. Ritter seemed a little formal. I hope you don't mind."

"No. It's fine."

Weird, but fine. She had a hard time imagining Jeff Ritter as an uncle, but he'd obviously done well with Maggie.

He rose to his feet and pulled out a chair. "You must be starving. Let me get you some food."

Ashley was suddenly aware that she'd jumped out of bed without a thought for her appearance. She hadn't showered in two days or brushed her teeth, and her hair probably looked like a rat's nest.

"I, ah, think I'd like to take a shower first," she said, backing out of the room. She glanced at the clock on the wall. "Give me ten minutes."

Because of her recent illness, she wasn't moving as fast as usual, so it was closer to twenty before she walked back downstairs. Her first glance in the mirror hadn't been as horrible as it could have been, but she hadn't been in the position to win any beauty prizes, either. Now she was at least clean, with her hair washed, although still a little damp. Her face was too pale and way too thin. With the onset of the flu, Ashley hadn't been eating regularly for several days. Which meant a loss of weight she couldn't afford. Her jeans were already hanging on her.

She made her way into the kitchen and found Maggie dancing from foot to foot.

"Brenda called," she sang. "She called and she's on her way to take me to school. And—" she paused dramatically before making the most monumental of announcements "—she's bringing one of her dogs with her. The little one. Her name is Muffin and I get to hold her in the car!"

As Maggie spoke, she raced toward Ashley and threw herself at her. Automatically Ashley reached for her daughter, pulling her into her arms. But two days in bed and general weakness from the flu had sucked up all her strength. She staggered slightly and felt herself start to slip.

From the corner of her eye Ashley caught a blur of movement. Suddenly a strong arm encircled her waist, holding her upright. She found herself leaning against Jeff. She had a brief impression of heat and formidable muscles even as he led her to a chair by the table and eased her onto the seat. And then he was back in his chair with a speed that left her wondering if she'd imagined the whole thing.

Except that the left side of her burned from where she'd pressed against him, and she could almost feel his arm around her waist. She shivered slightly. Not from cold, but from… Ashley frowned. She wasn't sure what. Awareness? Because she was suddenly very aware of the man sitting across from her. He didn't seem as much the cold, mysterious stranger this morning.

Maggie shifted on her lap. "Do you think Muffin will like me?"

"How could she not?" Ashley asked. "You're an adorable little girl."

Her daughter beamed with delight. Before she could speak again, there was a loud rap at the front door, followed by the sound of steps on the entryway.

"It's me," a woman called. "Brace yourself, Jeff. I have a dog with me."

Her announcement was unnecessary. A bundle of fur careened around the corner and skittered into the kitchen. The creature was small—maybe seven or eight pounds of multicolored hair and big, brown eyes. At the sight of the animal, Maggie scrambled off Ashley's lap and dropped to her knees. The little dog beelined for the child and sniffed her outstretched fingers, then licked the tips and jumped against Maggie, yipping and licking and wiggling with delight.

"Muffin loves kids," Brenda said as she walked into the kitchen. "But then you probably guessed that." She looked at Ashley. "You seem better."

"I feel better, thanks." Ashley smiled, feeling slightly awkward. While she'd never met Brenda before yesterday, the woman was an employee of Ritter/Rankin Security. What must she think of Jeff bringing a fellow worker into his house and caring for her and her child while she was ill? She felt as if she had to explain the situation, but she didn't know what to say about it.

Brenda handed Jeff a folder. "I'd better get this little one to her preschool," she said. "See you at the office."

He took the folder. "Thanks, Brenda. I appreciate this."

She grinned. "Remember this the next time I request an assignment."

"Yeah, right."

Brenda rolled her eyes, then collected her dog. Maggie scrambled to her feet. "Bye, Mommy. See you when I'm done with school."

They hugged briefly, then Ashley waved as her daughter headed for the front door. "Have a good day," she called after her.

As the front door closed, bread popped out of the toaster. Ashley started to get up but Jeff motioned her back into her seat.

"You're still recovering," he told her. "Until yesterday morning I didn't even know I had a toaster. But that doesn't mean I don't know how to use it."

He rose and put the two pieces of toast onto a plate. Butter and jam already sat on the table. He set the plate in front of her, then poured her a mug of coffee.

"Milk, sugar?"

"Black is fine," she said, slightly confused by his solicitousness.

He set the mug by her left hand, then resumed his seat. "Eat," he said, pointing at the food.

Cautiously she reached for the butter and picked up a piece of toast. This was all too strange. What was she doing in this man's house? Although based on the fact that she'd already spent two nights here, it seemed a little late to be asking questions.

"I spoke with Maggie's teacher yesterday afternoon," Jeff said when she began to eat. "I was told she didn't seem to be suffering any ill effects from being in a strange place."

"Cathy spoke with you?" The preschool had a strict policy of dealing only with parents or legal guardians.

Jeff raised his eyebrows. "Why wouldn't she?"

A simple enough question. Jeff was the kind of man who got what he wanted. That much was obvious from the way he'd brought her and Maggie here, despite her protestations and concerns.

"I'm glad Maggie is doing well," she said in an effort to avoid his question.

"She is. Last night we had spaghetti and salad for dinner. She had a Pop-Tart for dessert."

It might have been her imagination, but Jeff seemed to shudder. She felt herself smile slightly.

"I did not," he continued.

"No real surprise there," she murmured.

A slight upward tilt of the corner of his mouth was his only response. "Then we watched *The Little Mermaid*. Maggie was in bed by eight and asleep by 8:10."

Before she could comment, he passed her the folder Brenda had brought him. "Here are your notes from your classes yesterday. If you're not well enough to attend classes tomorrow, I'll have Brenda arrange for someone to sit in for you. Also—" he took a sip of coffee "—I sent someone over to your apartment building to collect more of your belongings. You'll find them stacked in the living room."

She flipped through the notes—typed and in perfect order—then looked at him. She didn't know what to say. The man had completely organized her life, and made it look simple in the process. She thought of how her daughter had been dressed and fed in plenty of time that morning. He'd prepared dinner the previous night and provided entertainment. By comparison, all the men she'd ever known were incredibly incompetent.

"Maggie's father couldn't even find the clean diapers to change her," she said, "and he sure wouldn't be able to get her ready for school. How do you know how to do all this?"

"I had help from Brenda. She's raised four kids of her own and has a couple of grandchildren. Besides, compared to an antiterrorist campaign, running your life is easy."

"It's anything but that for me," she murmured, thinking it was not possible for their worlds to be more different. "Anything else?"

"Yes. Maggie's class is taking a field trip to the zoo next Friday. The permission slip had to be back yesterday for Maggie to go, so I signed it. Is that all right?"

Ashley sighed. "Of course. I'd meant to take care of that last week. I guess with her being sick and everything else that happened, I just forgot. She would have been heartbroken to miss the trip."

She studied her host. He wasn't just physically strong and a little scary, he was also incredibly competent. She needed that in her life right now, and the urge to let him take over and handle everything nearly overwhelmed her. No one had been around to look out for her since she was twelve.

A nice fantasy, she told herself, but one that had no basis in reality. The truth was she was an employee of Jeff Ritter. For reasons that still weren't clear to her, he'd taken her and her daughter and was making them feel very welcome in his beautiful home. But gracious or not, he was a stranger with a past that made her more than a little nervous.

"You've been really terrific," she said, then took a drink of coffee. "I'm feeling a lot better today. I'm sure that I'll be a hundred percent tomorrow and then we'll be out of your hair." She cleared her throat. "Would it be too much trouble to have someone bring my car here?"

Jeff studied her for a long time. As usual, not a flicker of thought or emotion showed in his steel-gray eyes. He could have been planning sixty-seven ways to kill her with household appliances or deciding on a second cup of coffee. She really hoped it was the latter.

She returned the scrutiny, noting the short, blond hair brushed back from his face and the high cheekbones. He was tall, muscled and extremely good-looking. So why did he live alone in this gorgeous house? Was there a former Mrs. Ritter somewhere? Or was Jeff not the marrying kind? She bit her lower lip. As closemouthed and mysterious as he seemed, she could understand his avoiding a long-term commitment. Was there a series of significant girlfriends? And more importantly, why did she care?

Before she could come up with an answer to the question, he spoke.

"I'm glad you're feeling better, but getting over the flu is no reason to rush off."

His voice was low and well modulated. Controlled, she thought. Everything about him was controlled.

"I think it would be better if we left," she told him.

"Why? Do you really want Maggie living in a shelter until your apartment is fixed?"

Of course she didn't. It wasn't anyone's dream of a housing situation, but she didn't have a choice. "Maggie is resilient. She'll be fine."

"Agreed, but I don't see the need to expose her to that. Why not stay here until your housing problem is resolved? There's plenty of room. You won't be in the way."

"But you don't know us. We're not family. I don't understand why you're—"

His phone went off before she could finish her sentence. Jeff glanced at the screen of the tiny machine, then rose to his feet.

"I have to leave," he told her. "Try to get plenty of rest so you can build up your strength."

Before she could say anything else, he'd grabbed his suit jacket from its place on the spare chair and left the room. Seconds later she heard a door close as he walked into the garage.

"How convenient," she muttered, nearly convinced he'd somehow arranged for his phone to go off at that exact moment. Which was crazy. Even someone like Jeff couldn't do that.

She finished her breakfast, then cleaned the kitchen. After wiping down the counters for the second time, she figured she might as well take a look at the rest of the house before she began studying. Not Jeff's bedroom or anything private, but just to get a lay of the land.

Jeff had made it clear they were welcome to stay until her apartment was fixed. Which could be a few more days. If she got more comfortable in his house, she might be more comfortable with the man. After all, he'd been right about the shelter. It would be far better for Maggie to stay here than to move again.

She wandered through the main floor of the house. There was a large, formal living room with floor-to-ceiling glass windows overlooking the lake. The furniture was expensive, well made and completely impersonal. Her initial impression had been dead-on. There weren't any personal effects anywhere.

The dining room's cherry table could seat twelve, but Ashley had the feeling no one had ever eaten on it. In the family room she found state-of-the-art entertainment equipment, but no books or DVDs.

Ashley paused in the center of the oversize room. The sectional sofa sat opposite the wide-screen television. There weren't any photographs or paintings. Nothing personal. Who was Jeffrey Ritter and why did he live like this? It was as if he had no past—but instead had appeared fully grown. Was he estranged from his family? Were they dead? There weren't even any trophies of war. Maybe he had a secret vault somewhere with all that personal stuff.

The thought should have made her smile, but instead she shuddered as if brushed by a chill. Again the question came to her mind. Who was Jeff?

Ashley shook her head. She decided she didn't want or need an answer. She wasn't looking for a man in her life, and if she was, Jeff wouldn't make the final cut. While he was efficient, thorough and even kind, he wasn't warm and loving. She was only interested in someone who would love her with body, heart and soul. She wasn't even sure Jeff had a soul.

Which meant she should be grateful for his hospitality and should stop analyzing the man. After all, if he let her stay until her apartment was ready, it meant she could take a mini vacation from the trauma that was her life. As her mother used to say, if someone offers you a gift, take it. If you don't like it, you can always exchange it later.

Chapter 5

Ashley spent most of the day studying and sleeping. Around three, the sitter, one of Maggie's preschool teachers, dropped off her daughter.

"Tell me about your day," she said when the sitter had left after refusing payment.

"Cathy read us a whole book and I colored in the number book and we talked about our trip to the zoo next week." Maggie shared the bounty of her experiences over a tuna sandwich.

Ashley listened with half an ear, all the while trying to figure out how to raise the issue of payment with her host. It was one thing to stay in his house, but it was quite another for him to take financial responsibility for Maggie's child care. It's not as if he were the girl's father. In fact, Damian had never once contributed a penny. She rubbed her temples. Thinking about Damian would only make her sad and frustrate her in equal measures, so she wouldn't. And she vowed to talk to Jeff later about him paying for things that he shouldn't.

Maggie swallowed her mouthful of food. "Mommy, are you coming with us to the zoo?" her daughter asked. "Cathy said we need extra grown-ups and I couldn't 'member if you have school."

Blue eyes stared beseechingly. Ashley couldn't help smiling, then touching her daughter's cheek. "I don't have classes, and if Cathy needs help I would be delighted to come along. I love seeing all the animals at the zoo."

"Do they gots kittens?"

"Maybe some really big ones."

"I wish Uncle Jeff had kittens."

"I know you do, sweetie, but he doesn't." She hesitated, not sure how to find out if her daughter was comfortable without scaring her by the question. "Do you miss our apartment?"

"A little."

Maggie drank her milk. The clips Jeff had put in her hair that morning were still crooked. Still, it had been very sweet of him to try.

"I like staying here with Uncle Jeff," Maggie volunteered. "He's very nice." She gave her mother an innocent smile. "Uncle Jeff likes cake. We could make him one."

Ashley couldn't help wondering how much her daughter's generosity had to do with her own affection for the dessert. Although baking something would be a nice gesture, a small thank-you for his kindnesses.

She could even make dinner. Her car had been delivered earlier that afternoon. They could make a quick trip to the store and get everything they'd need.

"You know, munchkin," she said, lifting her daughter down from her chair and tapping the tip of her nose, "that's a very good idea. Let me call Jeff's office and see what time he's going to be home. Then we can make a special cake and a special dinner for him."

She found the business card he'd left her and called his office. When she was put through to Brenda, she asked his assistant what time he would be heading home. Brenda put her on hold while she checked with him. As Ashley listened to the soft music, she had the sudden thought that this was all too weird. Would he think she was cooking for him to capture his interest? The way to a man's heart and all that?

Heat flared on her cheeks. She longed to hang up, but it was too late for that. Brenda already knew it was her on the line. She would have to say that she was offering a thank-you and nothing more.

"He said he'll be home at six-thirty," Brenda announced cheerfully.

"Ah, thanks." Ashley wanted to explain but doubted Jeff's assistant cared one way or the other. She hung up and started her shopping list. She would make sure that Jeff understood everything when he got home.

The chocolate cake turned out perfectly. Maggie insisted on helping with the frosting, which meant there were uneven patches and more sticky chocolate on her arms and face than on the cake itself. Ashley had settled on meat loaf for dinner. It was easy and something most people liked. Plus she had a limited supply of cash that wasn't going to cover anything expensive, such as steaks.

She checked the potatoes and steaming green beans, then glanced at the clock. Jeff was due any second.

"Just enough time to get you cleaned up, young lady," she said, taking the rubber spatula from her daughter's hand and urging her toward the sink.

Just then Ashley heard the door to the garage open. Unexpectedly her heart rate doubled and her throat seemed to close up a little.

His footsteps sounded on the wood floor. She froze in the center of the kitchen, not sure if she should dash for cover or brazenly stand her ground and greet him. The confusion didn't make any sense. Why was she suddenly nervous? Nothing had changed.

Jeff entered the kitchen. He glanced at the pots on the stove, at the cake, then looked at Maggie, covered in chocolate frosting and grinning.

"We made you a surprise," the four-year-old announced.

"I can see that," he told her, and turned his attention to Ashley. "How do you feel?"

She swallowed. It was as if he could see through to her soul, she thought, wondering if she would melt under the intensity of his attention. Heat flared again, but this time it wasn't just on her face. Instead her entire body felt hot. As if she'd just stepped into a sauna.

"Better, thanks," she said, hoping her voice sounded more steady than *she* felt. "I, ah, slept a lot, and studied. The worst of the virus is over." She forced herself to smile, then motioned to the stove. "I made dinner."

"You said you were going to when you called Brenda."

She ducked her head. "Yes, well, I didn't think before I called. I'm sorry. That was really dumb."

"Why?"

She glanced at him from under her lashes. She had a sudden awareness of him as a man. Had his shoulders always been that broad? Why hadn't she noticed before? Was it her illness? Had the flu blunted his effect on her, and if so, how could she get immunized against Jeff Ritter's appeal?

"Ashley?"

She blinked. Oh. He asked her a question. Yeah. Dinner. Why cooking it was dumb. "I didn't want you to feel obligated to come home."

One corner of his mouth quirked up. "I live here."

"I know that. I meant for dinner. You might have plans, or not want to eat with us. The cake was Maggie's idea." She glanced down at her daughter and saw that her four-year-old was following the conversation with undisguised interest.

He smiled at the girl. "It's a beautiful cake. Thank you."

Maggie brightened. "It's really good. Mommy won't let me eat the batter 'cause of eggs, but I licked the frosting and it's perfect."

"Good." He looked back at her. "So what's for dinner?"

"Meat loaf. Mashed potatoes and gravy. Green beans."

"Sounds great. Let me go wash up and I'll join you."

"You will?"

"Unless you don't want me to."

She forced herself to take a deep breath. "No. It would be nice to have you eat with us. Really."

He nodded and left the room. Ashley groaned softly. When had she turned into an idiot? Just this morning she'd had a completely normal conversation with the man. Now she was acting like a freshman with a crush on the football captain. She'd lost her mind, and if she wanted to act like a mature adult, she was going to have to find it again, and fast!

Jeff focused on the report in front of him but he couldn't force any of the words to make sense. He would swear that even from half a house away, he could hear laughter drifting down the stairs and into his study. Earlier he'd heard running water as Ashley prepared her daughter's bath. The nightly routine was as foreign to him as life on another planet, and yet observing it from a distance made him ache inside.

He wanted with a power that nearly drove him to his knees, yet he couldn't for the life of him say *what* he wanted. Connection had never been his strength. Hadn't Nicole told him that dozens of times before she'd left him? Hadn't she hurled the accusation across nearly every argument they'd had? That he'd changed, that he wasn't the man she'd married, that he didn't belong?

And he hadn't belonged with her. In the end, nothing about their life together had been able to touch him. It had been easy when she'd walked away. Or so he'd thought until tonight. Until the laughter of a child and her mother made him wonder what it would have been like if things had been different. If *he'd* been different.

An ache formed inside of him. Deep and dark, it filled him until he couldn't breathe without the emptiness threatening to suck him into a void. He gripped the edge of his desk so tightly, he thought he might snap the sturdy wood...or perhaps a bone in his fingers.

"Uncle Jeff?"

The soft voice made him look up. Maggie stood in the entrance to his study. She wore a pink nightgown under a purple robe. Snowball held the place of honor in her arms. The little girl was freshly scrubbed from her bath, her curls fluffed around her face.

Uncle Jeff. He'd offered that as a substitute for "Mr. Ritter," which had seemed too formal for their present circumstances. Now he questioned the wisdom of claiming a connection where none existed. She would get the wrong idea. Or perhaps it was himself he had to worry about. Perhaps he would be the one to presume affection where there wasn't any. He must never forget who and what he was.

"Are you ready for bed?" he asked, forcing himself to smile at her as if nothing was wrong.

Ashley stepped into the doorway, her hand resting on her daughter's shoulder. "Sorry to disturb you, but she wanted to say good-night."

"Neither of you are interrupting. Sleep well, Maggie."

She bounced free of her mother's restraining hand and raced over to where he sat. Before he knew what she was about, she flung her little arms around his neck and squeezed tight.

She smelled of baby shampoo and honey-scented soap. She was warm and small and so damn trusting. Awkwardly he hugged her back, trying not to press too hard or frighten her in any way. She released him and beamed, then scurried from the room. Ashley lingered.

"Do you mind if we talk for a second?" she said. "After I get her in bed."

"Whenever you'd like."

He tried not to notice how the heat from the bath had flushed her face, nor the way her sweater hugged her feminine curves. He doubted she had all her energy back, but she no longer looked sick.

"Thanks. Give me about fifteen minutes." She turned and left.

Desire filled him. Desire and sexual need. They were both primal and difficult to dismiss. Most of the time he could use work to distract himself from a difficult situation. But not with Ashley. She haunted his thoughts at the office and at his house when he was home. He couldn't forget about her when she walked the halls of the house, leaving proof of her presence in a sound, a scent, a discarded sweater or an open textbook. He had no place to retreat.

However, time and practice had taught him that bodily needs were easily controlled. He'd learned to function without sleep, food or water, while in pain, under stress or physically compromised. Surely he could figure out a way to survive the presence of one woman, regardless of how much she appealed to him. If nothing else, imagining her horror when she figured out the truth about him would be enough to keep his thoughts and actions under control.

* * *

Ashley forced herself to take a deep breath before entering Jeff's study. Her sudden attraction to him hadn't gone away over dinner. The only thing she could figure was that she'd been so sick when she'd first met him that she hadn't noticed the appeal of the man or her own weakness where he was concerned. Now that the virus was under control, she was able to feel the pull. Which made for a great science experiment, but didn't help her current situation: how to get through a conversation with him and not act like an idiot.

Practice, she thought desperately. Maybe this was a case of practice making perfect. That decided, or at least hoped for, she tapped on Jeff's open door and walked into his study.

The room was large, with beautiful bookcases on two walls and a bay window on the third wall, overlooking the garden. His wood desk was big enough to double as an extra bed, and two leather club chairs faced the imposing barrier.

Jeff looked up as she entered. He was still wearing his suit, although he'd taken off the jacket and loosened his tie. A few strands of hair fell across his forehead. They should have softened his appearance, but he was as formidable as always.

"Have a seat," he said, motioning to one of the empty club chairs.

She sank into the dark brown leather seat and tried to relax. She had an agenda and a purpose. She would do well to remember both and not think about how his gray eyes made her think of the sea during a storm or the way his long, strong fingers had looked as he briefly touched her daughter's hair. She wasn't sure if he was a kind man, but he was capable of kind acts. Did that make him any safer for her?

"You've been very good to us," she said, plunging in when it became apparent he wasn't going to speak first, which made sense—she'd been the one to request the meeting. "Putting us up, arranging for Maggie to get to school. It's not that I'm not grateful, it's just that there are some things I need to do myself."

He rose. "Are you taking any medication?"

She blinked at him. "What?"

"Are you taking anything for the flu? I was going to offer you a brandy."

"Oh. No. I'm feeling much better. A brandy would be nice."

It would also give her something to hold so she wouldn't have to worry about her fingers twisting together the way they were now.

He opened the doors of a cabinet built into one of the bookcases and withdrew a bottle of brandy along with two glasses.

"Go on with what you were saying. You need to be responsible for some things yourself. Can you be more specific?"

As he spoke, he poured, then handed her a glass. She took it, careful to keep her fingers from touching his. "Thanks. I was talking about the babysitter. When she dropped off Maggie she wouldn't let me pay her. That's not right."

He poured his own drink, then settled on a corner of the desk. Which meant he was closer to her than he'd been before. Which meant her heart had jumped into her throat, making it impossible to breathe or swallow.

"You have a point," he said.

"I do?"

He nodded.

She forced herself to be calm. Slowly she found herself breathing again. She even managed to take a tiny sip of the brandy. It was hot and wonderful as it burned its way down to her stomach.

"I didn't mean to take over your life," he said. "I'll give you an invoice for the babysitting expenses to date and you can reimburse me."

"I, ah, thank you," she said, surprised he'd seen her side so easily. She also wondered how many times she'd thanked the man since meeting him.

"Anything else?"

As in, did she want to talk about anything else, she supposed. She studied him, thinking that despite the beautiful home and the successful business, he was incredibly alone. Before she and Maggie arrived, there hadn't even been any food in the house. She sensed he lived for work and little else and found herself wondering why.

Of course there could be women, she reminded herself. Maybe it was her own wishful thinking that he spent a lot of time by himself. There could be dozens of girlfriends. But only the kind he didn't invite home, she thought. The house was too silent. There were no echoes of past voices and laughter.

"Ashley?"

"Huh? Oh, sorry. I was lost in thought."

"Want to tell me about what?"

"Not especially." She gave him a false smile, then said the first thing that popped into her mind. "I'm not a widow."

A slight raising of his left eyebrow was his only response.

She closed her eyes and wondered if that had sounded as stupid as she thought. "What I mean is that based on what I said before you probably think I'm a widow, and I'm not. Well, technically Damian is dead, but we divorced first. He died a few months later."

"All right."

She could see he was wondering what possible relevance that information had for him. "It's just that we'd talked about it before. Actually, Maggie mentioned it. She made it sound as if…well…" She cleared her throat and took another sip of her brandy.

"I, ah, should go now," she said, rising to her feet. "You have work and I—"

"You're welcome to stay," he said. "If you're feeling up to a little conversation."

"I—yes, that would be nice." She plopped back onto the seat and smiled. The man made her nervous, but with a little effort on her part, she was sure she could act fairly normal.

"Tell me about school," he said, moving around the desk and settling into his leather executive chair. "Why accounting?"

"It suits me," she said, consciously relaxing in her chair. "I've always enjoyed math and I'm basically an orderly person. I wanted a career that gave me flexibility with my time and didn't tie me down to a big city."

"You want to leave Seattle?"

"No, but I want the option in case that changes."

"Makes sense."

"I started college right out of high school, but with getting married and then getting pregnant, I wasn't able to finish as quickly as I would like."

"But you didn't give up."

He wasn't asking a question. His gray eyes seemed to see past her facade of quiet confidence—if that's what her facade was projecting.

"I'm not the giving-up kind," she admitted, and took another sip of her brandy.

Around them, the night was still. It wasn't raining and there wasn't any wind. In the distance she heard the faint sound of a car, but nothing else. While she and Jeff weren't the only people left in the world, there was an air of solitude in the study. As if they might be cut off from civilization. Oddly, that didn't seem like such a bad thing.

"Who taught you not to quit?" he asked.

She considered the question. "I didn't have a choice. If I'd given up, I wouldn't have survived."

"Why?"

She hesitated, not sure she was ready, or willing, to tell her life story to a virtual stranger. But, despite his emotional distance, Jeff was easy to talk to. Probably because she doubted she could say anything that would shock him. He'd seen and done so much more than she could ever imagine. Her life would be very small in comparison.

"I had a sister who was four years older than me. Margaret…Maggie. I adored her. My dad ran off before I was born, so it was just us three girls. At least that's what my mom used to say." She smiled sadly at the memory. "Mom worked really long hours. She was a waitress. She tried going back to school so she could do something else, but she couldn't make it. She was always so tired. She kept saying that she should have done it when she was young and that we should learn from her mistakes. Don't give up on college no matter what."

"You took her words to heart."

Ashley nodded. "They made a lot of sense."

He continued to study her. Was he taking her measure? Did he find her wanting? Lamplight touched his hair, illuminating the light strands. There wasn't any gold glinting there—just pure blond. A muscle twitched in his cheek.

"You told me you don't have any family," he said. "Where are they now?"

Involuntarily she looked away, lowering her chin and biting her bottom lip. "Gone," she said softly. "Maggie was hit by a drunk driver when she was just sixteen. She and a couple of friends were walking home from the library. It was about nine in the evening and they'd been studying for midterms. All three girls were killed instantly." She hesitated. "It was a difficult time."

The simple sentence didn't begin to explain what she'd gone through. The shock—the incredible pain and disbelief. Her sister, her best friend, was gone.

She clutched the brandy glass in both hands. "Mom was never the same. She sort of disappeared into herself after that. A few months after Maggie died, Social Services put me in a foster home and my mom in a mental institution. One of the times they let her out for a weekend to visit with me, she killed herself."

Jeff didn't say anything. Ashley figured there wasn't all that much to say. She'd had more than her share of tragedy. Most of the time she was able to deal with it, but other times it threatened to drag her down.

"What happened after that?" he asked.

She shrugged. "I grew up in a series of foster homes. Most of them were pretty okay. The people tried to be nice and help me fit in. I had some counseling. I managed to make friends and keep up my grades. Unfortunately I had lousy taste in men. I had a series of loser boyfriends. They weren't mean—they just didn't get anything right."

"Including Damian?"

Ashley tried to remember the last time she'd talked about her past. She usually didn't say anything because there was no way to talk about it without making her life sound like a badly written soap opera. Now she found herself spilling her guts and she couldn't figure out why. She wasn't sure Jeff was even interested.

"Damian tried," she said. "But he wasn't what I wanted him to be. We met during my senior year of high school and I was so sure he was the one. I believed that he would love me unconditionally and forever."

"Is that what you wanted?"

The question startled her. "Of course. Doesn't everyone?"

"No," he said evenly.

Ashley stared in surprise. Who wouldn't want more love in their life? She thought about Jeff. He was a man who spent his life alone. Most likely by choice. But why?

She thought about asking, but she wasn't feeling that brave.

"Damian tried," she continued, picking up the thread of her story. "He cared about me, but he was too young and too much of a dreamer. He would rather scheme than work. He was always going to find the pot of gold at the end of the rainbow. Unfortunately his dreams weren't practical, and when it came time to put food on the table, he took shortcuts. I don't know everything he was involved in, but I suspect it was all illegal. By the time I'd figured that out, we were married and I was pregnant. After Maggie was born, I told Damian he was going to have to change his ways or it would be over. It had been scary enough when it was just me, but with a child to consider—" she shook her head "—I couldn't do it."

She wondered if he would ask for details. She didn't want to talk about the strange men who had come to the house in the middle of the night, or the gun she'd found in her husband's coat pocket.

But Jeff didn't ask about that. Instead he said, "When he wouldn't go straight, you left him?"

"I didn't have a choice. I filed for divorce. Six months after it was final, he was killed in a car accident."

"You've been on your own ever since."

Again, not a question.

She nodded.

He leaned forward and set his drink on the desk. "You're strong, Ashley. You've more than survived all that life has handed you—you've succeeded. Not many people can say that."

His kind words made her squirm. "I didn't have a choice. There was Maggie to think of."

"You named her after your sister."

"I love them both." She cleared her throat. "And things are looking up. In eighteen months I'll have my degree and I'll be able to get a real accounting job, with good pay. Maggie will be entering kindergarten. A couple of years after that, I'll be able to afford a town house for us. We'll be a regular family."

She was counting the days until that time. She was tired of watching every penny and stretching them until they snapped like rubber bands. She wanted to be able to buy her daughter pretty clothes and occasional dinners out. She wanted to go to the movies every couple of months and maybe even afford a trip to Disneyland.

That would come, she reminded herself. The worst of it was behind her. She would—

"I don't want you going back to work at Ritter/Rankin Security," Jeff said.

Her world shattered. In that second, as he spoke those few words, everything changed. Her throat tightened and her hands started to shake.

"Because I brought Maggie to work?" she asked, barely able to breathe, let alone speak. "But Jeff, you have to understand why."

"I do understand. Your schedule is impossible. You don't get any sleep. Your free time is spent studying and taking care of your daughter. You have no savings, no backup. I'm amazed you've stayed as healthy as you have."

So why was he firing her? She needed the money and the benefits the job provided. Where else would she get such perfect hours and medical insurance for her child? Her eyes burned, but she refused to give in to the tears.

She set her glass on the desk and rose to her feet. "You can't fire me," she insisted. "Dammit, Jeff, I do good work. How can you do this—cutting me off without a way to support my child? I'll have to drop out of school. I—"

She couldn't go on. It was so unfair.

"You misunderstand me," he told her. "I'm not trying to make your situation worse. I'm offering you alternative employment. I would like to hire you as my housekeeper. You'll take care of things here—cooking, cleaning, whatever else there is to do. You can live here rent free. In addition, I've spoken with my financial director. There is plenty of contract accounting work. If you're interested, you can do that to supplement your income. The combined amounts should give you about double what you're making now."

As usual, she couldn't read what he was thinking, but she had a good idea. No doubt he was pleased with himself for acting so magnanimous.

"So I'm your charity case for the month?" she asked. "It's an interesting practice, taking people off the street and fixing them. Will you do orphans next?"

"You're overreacting."

"Probably because I'm a woman, right?" She pressed her lips together to hold in the rage. He was playing with her. She didn't understand why, but she recognized the sensation of being manipulated.

"Your offer is generous," she told him. "But I'm not interested. Maggie and I will be fine without you. And we'll be leaving in the morning."

Chapter 6

Ashley hurried to her room. She felt hot and light-headed, as if her flu had returned, but she knew her symptoms weren't that easy to explain. Her eyes burned and her hands balled into fists. She felt angry and embarrassed—but most of all she felt *betrayed*.

How could he have said all that? Offered her all that? It wasn't right. She was a temporary guest in his home and he'd treated her like a—a— She stopped in the center of the upstairs hall and leaned against the wall. She didn't know what he'd treated her like, but it made her feel ugly inside. As if she'd somehow been selling herself. As if… Damn.

Ashley sank onto the floor, pulling her knees up to her chest. Shame flooded her as the truth crashed over her with the subtlety of a Midwestern thunderstorm. She was an idiot. A down-to-the-bones kind of fool.

Jeff Ritter had come out of nowhere and rescued her. There was no other way to describe his taking charge of her life and setting everything right. He'd brought her into his gorgeous home and he'd been kind to her and her daughter. The second the flu bug had departed her system, she'd found out she was incredibly aware of him as a man. She thought he was good-looking and sexually intriguing. That kind of attraction hadn't happened to her in years. In fact she'd been so immune, she'd assumed that part of her was dead.

She'd been startled to feel like a woman again and she'd gone from zero to having-a-crush-on in less than nine seconds. His offers for her to be his housekeeper and do part-time accounting work had blown her fantasy apart in a single breath. She'd been left feeling like an idiot and acting even worse.

It was the stress in her life, she told herself. Too much to do, too little time and money. Years of just getting by had worn her down. At the least little upset, she'd fallen apart. So she'd thought Jeff was the answer to a single mom's prayers and he'd thought she was efficient hired help. Did that matter? He wasn't responsible for her fantasies being destroyed. She shouldn't be having them in the first place.

She leaned her head against the wall and wished she could take back the past fifteen minutes and have them to do over again. This time she would see his offer for what it was—kindness from a stranger, not a rejection from a fantasy lover. Unfortunately time wasn't going to bend just for her.

* * *

Jeff stared at the chair Ashley had used and wondered what the hell had happened. Somehow he'd upset her or insulted her, or both. She was going to leave in the morning and he couldn't stop her. Not that he should want to.

He drained the last of his brandy and hoped the fire burning down to his stomach would ease some of the ache inside. He could almost remember a time when normal conversations had been simple. When he'd been comfortable around people and had taken pleasure in their company. He could remember laughing with Nicole. Touching her, kissing her. He remembered easy words spoken without thinking. Not anymore. Not ever. He weighed each word, wondering if he was getting it right. Because he didn't know how to do that anymore.

He'd been so close, too. Ashley had opened up to him, telling him about her past. He knew enough of the world to be able to read what she *didn't* say as much as what she did. He imagined a frightened girl of twelve, losing both her mother and her sister within a few months of each other. A teenager looking for love with boys who were clueless about what that meant.

Somehow she'd survived, saving both herself and her daughter. She'd even kept her humanity—something he hadn't been able to manage.

He thought about how the light had played on her face, illuminating perfect skin, emphasizing wide hazel eyes. Her smile seemed to come from the heart. She was smart and determined, and thin in a way that made him wonder how many times she'd had money to feed her daughter, but not herself.

Sometime that afternoon he'd come up with a plan to rescue her. He'd worked out the details and then he'd spoken without thinking and he'd insulted her. Because he had a need to fix, to mend. It didn't matter that it wasn't his business or that she wasn't his problem. In an odd and dangerous way, he wanted to be responsible. Which meant that there was something wrong with him. He knew better than to get involved. His soul was too dead to allow for any kind of connection beyond the physical.

Still, he had to make amends. He might not understand the extent of his transgression, but he would do his best to make it right.

He walked through the house to the stairs and climbed to the second floor. He turned toward the guest wing, then paused when he saw Ashley sitting on the floor, leaning against the wall. Faint light from her bedroom spilled into the hallway, illuminating the left side of her face.

Desire rushed through him, making him need with an intensity that sucked the breath from his lungs. She was soft and sweet. Her gentleness called to him. As if he could risk being with someone gentle. As if she wouldn't run in horror if she knew the truth about him, that in the deepest, darkest part of him, he'd ceased to be a man.

She looked up at him and smiled slightly. "I was sitting here trying to talk myself into going back downstairs and apologizing. You've saved me the trip."

Her words didn't make sense. "You have nothing to apologize for."

"What about the fact that I seriously overreacted?

That should count for something. You were just being nice and I took it wrong. At least I assume you were being nice."

Nice? Him? "I was trying to do the right thing. I need a housekeeper and you need to make a change in your work."

She wrinkled her nose. "You do like telling me what to do. Is this a military thing or a male thing?"

"Both."

"Figures." She sighed. "It's not that I don't appreciate the offer, Jeff."

"But you don't trust me."

Her gaze sharpened. "It's not that exactly."

But it was that. He could read it in her eyes. She wanted to believe and she wasn't sure. Could he blame her for that?

I want you.

The words remained unspoken, but they burned inside of him. He wanted and he needed with equal intensity. He wanted to inhale the scent of her body, touch her everywhere. He wanted to feel the silk of her short, dark hair and taste her mouth. He wanted to fill her until they both forgot everything but the heat of the moment.

Instead he drew in a slow breath. "The offer still stands. I hope you'll reconsider."

"I can't."

He wanted to ask why. He wanted to know how she'd figured out the truth about him so quickly. How had she learned that the safest course for her was to run away? He wanted to protest her decision, tell her that she was the closest to caring that he'd come in years. That when he was with her and Maggie, sometimes he forgot he wasn't like everyone else.

What he said instead was "Let me know if you change your mind."

And then he walked away, because if he didn't, he would say something he would regret. He might even tell her the truth.

The next morning Ashley carefully replaced the phone in the cradle when what she wanted to do was throw it across the room and stomp her feet. She hadn't thought it was possible for her life to get any worse, but she'd been wrong. One brief sentence had turned her world upside down. Just one sentence.

"Your apartment building has been condemned."

With that, her home was gone. The city official had been very polite, offering assistance in finding a new place to live. However, there were no plans to help her with the costs of moving, nor was she likely to find such low rent. She was completely and totally screwed.

The timing was incredible. Just last night she'd told Jeff they would be moving out in the morning. Mostly because she'd expected her apartment to be habitable by now. Talk about being completely wrong.

She wanted to go back to bed, pull the covers over her head and wait for the world to go away. Unfortunately that wasn't likely to happen. Instead she had a child to worry about, and classes, not to mention solving her living arrangement issue.

She left her bedroom and moved toward the stairs. Smile, she told herself as she walked down the hall.

Jeff mustn't know she was in such dire straits and she didn't want Maggie worrying, either.

She stepped into the kitchen to find her daughter and Jeff having breakfast together. Neither of them looked up, although she was reasonably confident that Jeff knew she'd arrived. She ignored the man sitting at the table and instead focused on her daughter.

She'd dressed Maggie in her favorite pink corduroy overalls with a matching pink-and-white kitten-print shirt. She'd washed her daughter's face, helped her with her shoes and socks, but she hadn't had time to do her hair. Yet Maggie's curls were drawn back from her face with two tiny, plastic, pink barrettes. They weren't even, or anchored to last the day, but they were in place.

There was no way her daughter had managed to fasten them in her hair, which left only one possibility. Ashley's gaze slid to her host. Jeff was in a suit, as usual. In fact she didn't remember seeing him wear anything else. His white shirt was starched, his tie perfectly in place. He was showered, shaven and ready to start his day.

The breadth of his shoulders spoke of his strength. His firm mouth barely smiled. Yet he'd taken the time to fix a little girl's hair. Something he'd done before. Maggie wasn't afraid of him. If anything, she adored Jeff. She'd trusted him from the first moment they'd met. Was that the intuition of a trusting child, or the hunger of a fatherless girl to interact with a substitute male? Ashley knew generalities about Jeff—that he was a former soldier, a dangerous man who excelled in a potentially deadly occupation. But what did she know about the person inside? What was his story?

"Mommy?" Maggie had looked up and seen her in the doorway. "I'm eating all my cereal."

"Good for you." Ashley raised her chin slightly. "Jeff, may I speak to you for a second?"

He nodded and rose to his feet, then joined her in the hallway. "Is there a problem?" he asked.

She stared into gray eyes. She couldn't read him any better than she had when she'd first arrived. "I talked to someone from the city just now. Did you know my apartment building had been condemned?"

His gaze never wavered. "No, but I'm not surprised. The water damage looked extensive."

"I have to find a new apartment."

He folded his arms over his chest. "Do you have the money?"

"No."

She waited for him to pounce—to again make the offer of a job she was going to have to take. Because in some strange way, she was testing him.

"All right. I'll write you a check to cover the costs. Pay me back when you can. After you graduate from college is fine."

Not the offer she'd expected at all. She sagged against the door frame. "Who are you, Jeff?"

"Why does it matter?"

Because he was making her want to believe in him and she'd learned to never believe in anyone but herself. Besides, he couldn't have made it more clear he wasn't the least bit interested in her skinny self.

A knock at the front door interrupted them. Maggie rushed past, eager to greet Brenda. Ashley turned away from Jeff without answering his question and hurried after her daughter.

Brenda was already inside the house and hugging the little girl. "It's raining this morning," she said. "You're going to need a jacket."

"I know where it is!" Maggie announced, turning around and racing toward the stairs. "I'll get it, Mommy."

"Thank you, sweetie," Ashley called after her, then went to speak with Jeff's assistant.

Brenda smiled at her as she approached. "I know you're feeling better, but I appreciate you letting me take her to school this morning. I just adore her." The older woman sighed. "Grandkids are the best and Maggie is just as sweet as my daughter's little girl."

"You're more than welcome." Ashley glanced over her shoulder to make sure they were still alone, then invited the other woman into the living room. "I need to ask you a question," she said. "It's probably going to sound a little strange and I apologize if it makes you uncomfortable."

Brenda settled on a beige sofa and grinned. "Now I'm wildly intrigued. Go ahead."

Ashley checked again to make sure no one lurked in the hallway, then joined her guest on the couch. "To be blunt, can I trust Jeff? Through an assortment of circumstances, I'm in a difficult situation right now. Jeff has offered me a job as his housekeeper. It would mean living here with my daughter. On the one hand it's a great opportunity. The money is good, the house is terrific. But I don't know him very well and I do have a young child to be concerned about."

"Don't worry about Jeff at all," Brenda said, lightly touching her forearm. "I know he's a little formidable and he doesn't talk about himself, but he's a great guy. I've known him for nearly five years and I would trust him with my life. Better, I would trust him with my grandkids'."

Which was what Ashley needed to know. "Thanks for telling me."

Brenda tilted her head slightly, then tucked a strand of blond hair behind her ear. "At the risk of being presumptuous, I do have one more thing to say."

"Which is?"

"He's not a people person, so don't expect witty banter. And he's very solitary. As far as I know, he hasn't had a serious relationship in the past five years. So don't even think about giving away your heart."

Ashley smiled. "Not a problem. I'm not interested in getting involved."

While she might find the man sexy and appealing on a physical level, emotionally she knew better than to risk her feelings again. If she ever did that again, it was going to be with someone who could love her more than anyone else in the world.

"Then you should be just fine."

Maggie burst into the living room. She had her jacket dragging from one arm and her backpack trailing from the other. "I'm ready," she announced.

Ashley laughed. "Not exactly, young lady. Come here."

In less than five minutes, Maggie was ready to leave for school. Ashley kissed her goodbye and promised to pick her up promptly at two. Brenda gave her a quick wave and a thumbs-up, then they left. Ashley was alone with Jeff. It was decision time.

She found him in his office, packing his briefcase. Had he worked into the night? she wondered. She hadn't been able to sleep much, mostly because she'd been thinking about his offer and how badly she'd acted. What had kept him up through the long dark hours?

She knocked on the open door, then stepped inside. "Do you have a minute?"

"Of course."

He motioned for her to take one of the seats in front of his desk. She did, choosing the one she hadn't sat in the night before. He relaxed into his chair.

She licked her lips. "I want to ask if your offer is still open."

"For the loan?"

"No. The job."

He raised his eyebrows and nodded instead of speaking.

Good. At least she hadn't blown it so much that he'd changed his mind.

"I'm interested," she told him. "But I need to know why you're bothering. You could get someone in here a couple of times a week to do the cooking and cleaning. Why a full-time live-in housekeeper and why me?"

He didn't answer right away. Instead he seemed to consider the question. Which made her squirm in her seat. Was she being inappropriate with her questions? Would he get angry? Did she want to work for him if his temper had such a short fuse?

"I know you well enough to trust you in my house," he said at last. "Besides, I like your daughter."

Her nerves were frayed. One snapped. "Then have a couple of kids of your own."

Thoughtful gray eyes turned toward her. "I can't."

She'd been expecting half a dozen answers, but not that one. "I don't understand."

"I have a low sperm count. It makes conception highly unlikely."

She blinked. Her mind seemed to sway slightly as a couple hundred questions formed in her mind. How had he known? That wasn't the sort of information one learned in a routine examination. He had to have been tested for fertility. Which meant what? That he'd been trying to get someone pregnant at one time? So at one time…

"You were married?"

A slight smile tugged at the corners of his mouth. "I know that's hard to believe."

"No, it's not that."

Although it was. She couldn't imagine Jeff on bended knee, proposing. And married? As in living with a woman? Being casual in jeans, maybe, or walking around unshaven, wearing a robe? It boggled the mind.

"I was married for several years. We tried to have children. When she didn't get pregnant, we were both tested. The fault was mine."

Was that why he wasn't married anymore? Was that— She realized that it was none of her business. "I'm sorry," she murmured. "I didn't mean to pry."

"I understand your concern. While I like Maggie, I don't think of her as a substitute daughter."

He picked up a pen and studied it. On anyone else,

Ashley would swear the action was a stall for time. Finally he set the pen down.

"I don't make a habit of being a nice guy, which is why I'm doing this so badly," he said. "You work for me. I have no intention of firing you. If you want a loan for relocating to another apartment and your old job back, you're welcome to both. If you'd like to try being my housekeeper on a trial basis, that's fine, too. I don't want anything from you or your daughter." He paused. Something dark passed across his face. "If you're looking for an explanation for my actions, think of them as atonement."

"For what?"

He shrugged. "I'm damn good at what I do. I was better as a soldier. That comes with a price."

She didn't want to ask any more because she didn't want to know what he'd done. She remembered the article that mentioned his time in special ops. There were hints about covert assignments. Assassinations. Secret battles.

He was dangerous. She knew that in her head, but she couldn't feel it in her heart. As if she was exempt from the ruthlessness. Was that possible?

"I have a small child," she said. "Considering your line of work, I'm assuming you have guns in the house. Will she be safe?"

Instead of answering in words, he rose to his feet. At the far end of the room, he touched a book on a shelf and the entire bookcase swung open. Ashley rose and followed him. He pointed to the large safe built into the wall.

"There's no key or combination lock. It requires a

retinal scan. The mechanism has its own power source so it won't be disabled by an electrical blackout. Everything dangerous is kept in there."

She thought about asking what all might be in inventory, but figured she was better off not knowing.

"Maggie is perfectly safe," he said. "I wouldn't let her stay here otherwise."

Ashley shivered. She wanted reassurance that she would be safe, too.

"I'd like the housekeeper job," she said, shoving her hands into her jeans pockets and taking a step back. "Just for a couple months, until I get my feet under me."

"Fair enough." He closed the bookcase. "Are you interested in the accounting work, as well?"

In for a penny, as they say. "Yes."

"Good."

He stared at her. Something flickered against his irises. For a second she would have sworn she saw fire—the kind that burned bright from passion's desire. If he had been any other man, she would have thought he was interested. But not Jeff. Certainly not in her.

Chapter 7

It took Ashley less than forty-eight hours to invade his world. Jeff had always had a biweekly cleaning service that took care of the house and washed his sheets and towels, but now he had a *housekeeper*.

Ashley took her work seriously. Pieces of furniture that had simply been dusted were now polished. Surfaces gleamed and the scent of lemon filled the air. He found vases of flowers on tables and light filtering in through sparkling windows. His sheets and towels were softer, his cupboards stocked with food and meals had become multi-course and nutritional. When he gave her accounting work, she did it quickly and accurately, returning it to him the following day.

Jeff hadn't realized how careful she'd been to keep to herself while she was simply a guest in his house. Now her presence was everywhere. Her perfume lingered in the hallway. A couple of Maggie's toys found their way to the family room. Schoolbooks stacked up on an end table. It was as if a family lived here.

A family. The concept was unfamiliar. He knew intellectually that there had been a time when he'd belonged to a family. He'd been born to parents who lived in suburbs, just like regular people. Jeff knew he'd been a part of that world once—playing sports in high school, hanging out with his friends. But those memories weren't real to him. It was as if he'd seen a movie about someone's past. A past that happened to be his own. He couldn't relate to those images and he didn't know how to act now that he was no longer alone.

He glanced at his watch. It was late, nearly midnight. Maggie was long asleep, but Ashley was still up, studying in the kitchen. The need to go to her compelled him to rise to his feet, even though he knew he shouldn't bother her. He walked toward the light, knowing he had no right to want to be with her, even when all he expected was simple conversation.

She haunted him. Much like the ghosts of his past, she was a constant presence in his mind. Yet unlike the memories of the dead, she made him feel better for occupying his thoughts. She made him anticipate— something he hadn't done in years. She made him need, which reminded him he was alive. But was that good or bad?

He reached the kitchen and stood in the doorway. The overhead light glinted off her dark hair. She wore jeans and a sweater. Her feet were bare and she'd tucked one up under her on the straight-backed chair. Several books lay open across the table. She glanced at one, then returned her attention to the accounting paper in front of her.

One curl caressed her cheek. Looking at it made him press his fingers into his palm. He wanted to touch the curl...and the cheek. He wanted to feel the silk of her skin and the warmth of her body. He wanted...

"Are you just going to stand there, or are you going to join me?" She spoke without looking up.

Jeff frowned. He knew he hadn't made any noise. "How did you know I was here?"

She glanced at him and smiled. "It's a mom thing. Internal radar. The same mechanism tells me when Maggie is doing something she shouldn't." She pushed her foot against the chair next to her, moving the seat toward him in invitation. "I'm due to take a break." She pointed at the closest open textbook. "It's cost accounting, so you're doing me a favor by taking me away from it for a while. There are fresh cookies. Want one?"

He followed the direction of her finger and saw a heaping plate of cookies on the counter. "You're always trying to feed me."

She smiled. "That's because you don't eat very much. I'm a compulsive feeder."

"Another mom thing?"

"Probably. I want to take care of the world."

He moved toward the table, but didn't take the seat next to her. Instead he settled across from her—as much to see her as to make sure he wasn't close enough to touch. Something about the late hour made him question his ability to do the right thing. The need inside seemed to grow with each tick of the kitchen clock.

"Not all mothers are compelled to take care of everyone," he said. "It's about being a giver more than being maternal."

"Maybe." She rose to her feet and walked over to the cookie plate. After moving a couple of her books, she set it in the center of the table, then headed to the refrigerator. "What about your mother? What was she like?"

"A homemaker," he said as Ashley poured them each a glass of milk. "She liked to sew and bake. My dad worked for Ford. On the assembly line."

She put a full glass in front of him and resumed her seat. "Let me guess. You played football and were something of a flirt."

"I'll admit to the football."

Ashley had been kidding when she'd asked the question. She couldn't imagine Jeff as a young man. She'd never seen him out of a suit. Even now, despite the late hour, he wore a white shirt and slacks. He'd discarded his tie and rolled up his sleeves, but he hadn't bothered changing into something more casual. Did the man own jeans?

Not that it mattered. She was glad she had the cookies and milk to give her something other than Jeff to look at and touch. Otherwise she wasn't sure she could control herself around him. She'd never once in her life wanted to be sick, but right now she couldn't help wishing for a bit of the flu bug to return because it seemed to be the only thing that kept her immune to Jeff's masculine charms.

She hated the way she noticed the strength in his hands and wrists and the shivery sensation in her belly as she studied the stubble darkening his jaw. His voice sent ripples of need dancing along her spine and the darkness of the night made her think of bed and tangled sheets. She tried to convince herself it was a lack of male companionship that made her overreact to her new boss, but she was afraid it wasn't that simple. Something chemical happened when she was around the man and she didn't know how to make it stop.

Conversation, she told herself as her breathing increased slightly. Talk about something normal and maybe he won't notice the sexual tension in the air.

"What sent you into the army?" she asked.

"I didn't want to go to college. I liked sports, but I wasn't a big fan of school. I wanted to see the world."

"Did you?"

He picked up a cookie. "I saw a lot of places I didn't want to see."

"Is that where you met your wife?"

He bit into the cookie and chewed. "No. She and I had dated in high school. We married right before I enlisted."

It sounded so normal. A guy marrying his high school sweetheart. Ashley looked at Jeff and frowned. She couldn't imagine a moment of it. "You two were pretty young," she said.

"Agreed. Too young. I'd signed up for four years. From day one I knew I'd found where I belonged. I was sent into special operations almost right away. Nicole and I had thought we would be together after boot camp, but that didn't happen. They didn't allow dependents in the places I went, so we were apart more than we were together. That was hard on both of us."

"Marriage is difficult under the best of circumstances," she pointed out, trying not to notice the intimacy of the night. The overhead light illuminated the table, but the rest of the kitchen was in shadows. Outside, the darkness was silent. There weren't even any cars driving by.

"Things changed," he said. "I had assignments that were…" He hesitated as if searching for the right word. "Challenging. I couldn't talk about most of what I did, and what I could talk about she didn't want to hear. After a while we stopped talking."

Ashley knew he'd seen things she couldn't even imagine. There were horrors in the world that no sane person would want to know about. But what of the people who had no choice but to live through those experiences?

"You changed," Ashley said, making a statement rather than asking a question.

His gaze sharpened. "That's what Nicole said."

"Wasn't she telling the truth? How could those circumstances not change you?"

"You're right." He stared into the distance, as if exploring his past. "In the end she decided it was easier to leave than to make the marriage work."

"Do you regret that?"

"No."

She wondered if he was telling the truth. "Accepting that a relationship isn't going to work is really tough," she said, then nibbled on a cookie. "I had to make that decision when I was married to Damian. When it was just the two of us, his irresponsibility didn't seem like such a big deal, but after Maggie was born, it mattered more."

She sipped her milk. "Some of the reason I resisted the truth was that I didn't want to admit that I'd made a wrong decision. I'd been so sure he was the one. But within the first couple of months, I knew he wasn't. Still, I tried to fix him. I tried to make him see that working hard at a good job was better than all his dreams about getting rich quick. I wanted the marriage to work."

"Wanting isn't always enough."

She sighed. "I learned that one in spades. Finally I saw that the only person I could save was myself. Damian was getting involved in some scary stuff. I couldn't risk that. I had a daughter to take care of. So I left and hoped he would save himself."

She stared at the table, then began pushing around the cookie crumbs. "It's like with my mom. After my sister was killed, Mom just lost it. Physically she was in the room, but her mind was somewhere else. I begged her to stay with me, to get better, but I couldn't fix her or save her."

Her throat tightened. She didn't usually allow herself to think about her past—certainly not the time when she lost both her sister and her mother, albeit in different ways.

"You're strong," Jeff told her. "A lot of people would have cracked under the pressure, but you survived. That's admirable. You kept your head and your sense of humor."

His praise made her flush. "Yeah, well, sometimes that's all I did have. At least until Maggie. Now she keeps me focused on what's important. As long as we're together we'll be fine."

"Your daughter is very lucky. I respect you, Ashley. I know this has been a difficult time for you. I won't do anything to betray your trust in me."

She looked up and met his steady gaze. Suddenly the room was filled with crackling electricity. She felt mesmerized and incapable of thinking for herself.

Jeff stood. Involuntarily she found herself doing the same. Her chest was tight. Her fingers began to tremble. As he moved around the table, she knew with a certainty that she couldn't explain that he was going to kiss her. Right there in the kitchen. Her heart thundered, her breath came in gasps. Anticipation filled her as her breasts seemed to swell and that secret place between her legs grew damp.

Now, she thought desperately as he got closer. The world around them faded. There was only the night and the man.

They stood less than a foot apart. She kept herself from reaching for him because she desperately wanted him to touch her first. She knew how it would be between them. An explosion. There would be nothing subtle or gentle, but she found she didn't mind that.

"Good night, Ashley," he murmured, and then he was gone.

Her lips parted and she gasped a protest, but it was too late. As quickly as it had blossomed to life, the moment died, leaving her feeling cold and incredibly alone.

Had she been wrong? Hadn't he planned to kiss her? She would have sworn he'd been thinking about it as much as she had. Yet he'd resisted.

She wanted to run after him. She wanted to follow him and beg him to take her, to say that they didn't need promises or commitments. She would accept just the moment and expect nothing more. Instead she sank onto her chair and closed her eyes.

She was a single mother—she couldn't afford to live for moments. She had to be responsible. Whatever insanity caused her to think such thoughts about Jeff had to be ignored. Did she really plan to have sex with her boss? Talk about stupid. She was staying in the man's house.

She sucked in a deep breath and forced herself to resume her studying. She had a lot of work to get through before she could go to bed, and the alarm would go off very early. But instead of numbers and text, she saw Jeff's gray eyes. She remembered the fire she'd seen burning there and wondered how she'd ever thought his eyes were cold.

Ashley hovered outside of Jeff's at-home office. She didn't like to think of herself as a person who hovered, but no other word fit. Except maybe *lurked* and she liked that choice even less.

It's not that she'd been avoiding him in the past couple of days. Okay, maybe she hadn't exactly been around as much, but that was mostly because the kiss-that-had-never-happened had left her feeling embarrassed and stupid. She'd been thinking warm, fuzzy thoughts about Jeff and he'd been thinking less than nothing about her.

So in an effort to keep herself from making a complete idiot of herself, not to mention losing a great job, she'd stayed out of his way. Until now, when she was hovering and trying to gather the courage to step into his office and just ask him.

Finally she simply sucked in a breath and stepped into the study. It was early—only a few minutes after seven in the morning—but Jeff was already showered and dressed for the office. He was putting several folders into his briefcase, which made her wonder how late he'd been working the previous night and did the man actually sleep?

He looked up at her and gave her a slight smile. "Good morning. What can I do for you?"

She thought of about a dozen things, most of which had nothing to do with her reason for being in his office and everything to do with the large bed in his room and the soft feel of bare skin on sheets.

She had to clear her throat to speak. "It's...um—" Her voice failed. What was she doing here? There was no way Jeff would even consider doing this.

"Ashley?"

She sighed. Idiot or not, she was going to have to ask. "I spoke to Cathy, at Maggie's school. Today is their field trip to the zoo and they're short a couple of parents. I'm already going, but Cathy asked if I knew anyone else who would be interested in accompanying the kids and I thought maybe..." She pressed her lips together and stared at the carpet. "You like Maggie and, well, it was a stupid idea."

"Are you inviting me along?"

She nodded then forced herself to meet his gaze. What was he thinking? Please God, don't let him be able to see her uncontrollable and growing attraction. That would be too humiliating to bear.

"Cathy likes to have one adult for every couple of

kids, so if you went, we'd be responsible for four. One of them would be Maggie, of course."

"You'd stay with me?" he asked. "I wouldn't have to be alone with the children?"

She couldn't help grinning. "Jeff, they don't bite."

"Sometimes they do." He closed his briefcase. "I'd be happy to come along. Give me ten minutes to call the office and leave Brenda a message, then change my clothes."

"Sure. Great."

She backed out of the office before he could sense the elation that swept through her. He was joining her. They would spend the entire day together. Okay, they would have four rug rats with them and this was more about Maggie than her, but still. A shiver of pleasure rippled through her.

Ten minutes later Jeff walked down the stairs. Ashley was busy helping Maggie into her coat, which meant she was kneeling on the floor. A good thing because she probably would have fallen over if she'd been standing.

He'd changed his clothes. Nothing unusual in that. People did it all the time. But she'd never seen Jeff in anything but a suit, and in jeans and a sweater he was gorgeous. Broad shoulders pulled at the woolen fabric. His chest narrowed to his waist, where his jeans emphasized his slim hips. Soft, faded denim clung to thighs as solid and well shaped as a Greek god's.

Maggie squealed when she saw him. "Mommy said you're comin' with us to the zoo. I wanna see *all* the animals. And baby kitties. And elephants, 'cause next to the kitties, I like them the best. Because of their ears."

Jeff squatted next to her daughter, which put him way too close to herself. "Not the trunks?"

Maggie wrinkled her nose. "Trunks are silly. But they have neat ears."

Jeff grinned. Ashley's heart froze for a second, before attempting a land speed record in thumps per second. Jeff occasionally joked and he smiled fairly regularly, but he didn't grin much. There were almost dimples in his cheeks and great crinkles by his eyes. If he did that grin thing too much, he could generate enough heat to melt the polar ice caps.

Sensible, she reminded herself as she finished helping Maggie with her coat and rose. She had to be sensible. She wasn't looking for a relationship with a man. She preferred her life to be simple. When she was finally ready to get involved again, she wanted someone who could love her best. She had a feeling that Jeff wasn't in a position to open his heart to anyone. So why go looking for trouble?

"Here you are."

She turned and saw Jeff holding up her coat for her. As she slipped into it, she accidentally brushed her cheek against his hand. Fire burned from the point of contact. She sighed. It seemed like she wasn't going to have to look for trouble. It was finding her all on its own.

Four-year-olds found everything about the zoo endlessly fascinating. Jeff watched in amazement as his charges raced toward the giraffe exhibit. The kids were as excited by the drinking fountains and benches as they were by the animals.

"What are you thinking?" Ashley asked. "Having second thoughts?"

"Never."

"I'm glad, because you're great with the kids."

He risked glancing at her, taking in the perfect smoothness of her skin and the laughter lurking in her hazel eyes. She was endlessly pretty, he thought, and more than appealing. He was finding it more and more difficult to spend time with her and not give in to his need. He'd come close a couple of times, compelled by a desire that grew so quickly, it was difficult to contain.

When he'd first brought Ashley home, she wanted to know who he was and what he was doing in her world. Now he wanted to ask her the same question. Who was this woman who had made a place for herself in his cold and empty life?

"Jeff, Jeff, pick me up so I can see 'em!"

The instruction came from a blond little boy named Tommy. For reasons that weren't clear to Jeff, the boy had latched on to him from the second they'd been introduced.

Jeff bent awkwardly and lifted the boy in his arms. "There you go."

The slight weight shifted as the kid squirmed to get a better look at the giraffes strolling through their compound.

"Are the elephants next, Mommy?" a familiar voice asked.

"Yes, Maggie. In just a few minutes. Aren't the giraffes pretty, with their long necks?"

Maggie glanced at him as if to say her mother simply wasn't getting it. Cats and elephants were the only animals that interested Maggie.

"Can I touch 'em?" Tommy asked.

Jeff shrugged. "Do you want to keep all your fingers?"

Tommy's blue eyes widened. His hands curled into fists. "They eat fingers?"

"No, but they bite. Animals in the zoo aren't pets. We have to treat them with respect because they're wild creatures."

The boy regarded him solemnly. Tommy had a stain on the front of his flannel shirt and a cowlick that sent a lock of hair up toward the heavens.

"Are you Maggie's daddy?"

The question caught Jeff off guard. He lowered the boy to the ground. "No."

Two of the kids pushed to get closer to the fence, keeping visitors away from the animals. In the process, one of the kids, a girl in pigtails, landed on her butt. Before she more than opened her mouth to scream, one of the mothers pulled her to her feet and distracted her by pointing out the baby giraffe.

Jeff looked at the group of children and parents. They moved and interacted with a grace and rhythm he couldn't understand or copy. He was very much the outsider, but he couldn't decide if he wanted to be anything else.

"Elephants next," Cathy, the preschool teacher, called. "Let's go this way."

The children yelped with excitement and hurried after her.

"Not exactly special ops in the jungle, huh?" Ashley

said as she stepped next to him. "So, is this more or less challenging than your last security job?"

"It's different."

"Mommy, Uncle Jeff, elephants," Maggie called as she raced past them.

"Don't run, young lady," Ashley instructed. Her daughter slowed marginally.

The late-morning air was cool. There hadn't been any rain in a couple of days and most of the clouds had blown away to the east. Jeff inhaled the scent of the trees and plants around them and tried to ignore the sweet scent that was Ashley alone.

She made him ache with wanting. She made him want to kiss her and touch her, even though he knew he could never do either. Being with her would destroy them both, because she would eventually figure out who and what he was. Then where would they be? Life was easier when he remembered his limitations.

"Why are elephants gray?" one of the boys asked. "Why do they have trunks? Why are they so big? Do they eat people?"

Ashley laughed. "I'll bet we can read all about the elephants when we get there."

The boy wasn't impressed. "Don't you know?"

She turned to Jeff. "What about it, big guy? Want to take the elephant questions?"

"I had to answer questions in the bug house, and that was a lot harder."

"I don't believe you."

They walked toward the re-creation of a tropical forest for the elephants. Other children from a different school were already chattering about the big mammals.

Jeff paused to count heads, making sure the entire group was still together. He could—

A sharp cry cut through the morning. Jeff turned and was moving toward the sound before he even understood what he heard. Tommy had fallen and sat cradling his small hand against his chest. As Jeff approached, he saw the child had skinned his palm. Fat tears spilled from his blue eyes.

One of the mothers got there first. She reached for the boy, but Tommy pushed her away. Instead, still crying, he stumbled to his feet and swayed toward Jeff.

"I have disinfectant and stick-on bandages with me," someone said.

Jeff stared as the boy approached. His small body shook with the force of his sobs. Not knowing what else to do, Jeff picked up the child and held him against his chest. Tommy buried his face in Jeff's neck. His tears were hot. The boy hiccupped.

"Let me see," Ashley said softly, gently tugging on the boy's arm so she could free his hand.

Tommy shrieked in protest.

"Come on, big guy," Jeff said, feeling awkward as everyone stared at them. "Let's look over the damage. I'm gonna bet we can fix you right up."

The boy raised his head and sniffed, then held out his hand.

Jeff looked over the wound. It was superficial and barely bleeding. There was a bit of dirt in the scrape, along with a couple of small pebbles.

"It needs washing, disinfectant and a bandage," Ashley pronounced. "Want me to take care of him?"

Jeff wanted nothing more, but at her words Tommy shrieked and wrapped his arms around Jeff's neck.

"I'll do it," he said and took the supplies from one of the mothers. He found a sign pointing toward the restrooms and headed in that direction.

"We'll wait here for you," Ashley called after him.

"I hate elephants," Tommy murmured. "They're bad."

"But the elephants didn't make you fall. Sometimes we fall all on our own and it's not anyone's fault."

The boy continued to cling to him. Still feeling like an idiot, and as if he was doing everything wrong, Jeff gently touched the boy's shoulder. The child was so small and fragile. He could span the kid's back with his hand. Confusion filled him. What the hell was he doing here? He didn't know how to take care of a child.

But there wasn't anyone else around and Tommy was depending on him. Jeff figured it couldn't be any worse than taking out a bullet or setting a bone in the field. Except emergency care for his team had never made him feel strange inside. As if something was cracking. But what he didn't know was if the ice around his heart was letting go or if his wall of protection was being breached. Or were they the same? And how long would it take to find out if the change was going to destroy him?

Chapter 8

"But what about the camels that lost their humps?" Maggie asked that night, her eyes wide. "Aren't they sad?"

"Some camels only have one hump. They haven't lost anything. They're just different."

Ashley bit back a smile. After ten minutes of grilling by her daughter, Jeff was still the picture of patience. He put down his fork and leaned toward her daughter.

"Remember the elephants you liked so much? There are two kinds of those, African and Asian elephants. It's the same with camels. Some have one hump and some have two."

They were sitting around the kitchen table at dinner. Ashley tried to ignore how good Jeff looked and the way the meal made her able to think of them as a family. They weren't a family. They barely knew each other. The fact that Jeff had insisted they all eat together was just him being nice.

She frowned. "Nice" didn't exactly describe his actions. Now that she thought about it, why *did* he want to eat with them? Not that she was complaining. Mealtimes were always interesting when he was around.

"Why are camels different?" her daughter asked.

Jeff hesitated, as if forming an answer. Ashley decided he might need a little help. Four-year-olds were nothing if not persistent.

"It's like dogs," she told Maggie. "There are many different kinds of dogs. Some are big, some are small. But they're all still dogs. There are two different kinds of camels."

"Do the camels with one hump feel sad because they're different?"

Jeff leaned toward her. "Maybe the two-humped camels are the different ones."

Maggie's eyes unexpectedly filled with tears. "I don't want the camels to be sad."

Ashley hadn't seen that one coming. But before she could reach for her daughter and offer comfort, Jeff shocked her down to her toes by gently pulling the little girl onto his lap. He held her securely, as if he'd done it a thousand times before.

"Are you sad because you have brown hair?"

Maggie tilted her head so she could stare into his face. "No," she said slowly. "Mommy says I have pretty hair."

"Mommy's right. So you're not sad about how you

look because you look perfect for you. Camels are the same. They know they're exactly what they should be."

The tears disappeared as quickly as they'd arrived. "So camels are happy?"

"Nearly all the time."

Maggie beamed, then scrambled back to her seat where she picked up her spoon and went to work on her carrots. But Jeff didn't resume his own meal. Instead he continued to stare at the little girl.

"Maggie, you must promise me something. You must promise me to always be special and never change."

Maggie paused, her spoon half raised to her mouth. She grinned. "I'm gonna be a big girl soon."

"I know."

Something tightened in Ashley's chest. For the first time since she'd met Jeff Ritter, she knew what he was thinking. He was staring in wonder at her child and wishing life could always be exceptional for her. He wanted to protect her from all the bruises and scrapes she would encounter, both physical and emotional. Somehow little Maggie had found her way past Jeff's protective wall.

How was she supposed to resist a man who adored her daughter? To use her daughter's language, she would be very sad to leave this man. He'd only been a part of their lives for a short time, but he'd made an impact. When she returned to her already-in-progress life, nothing was going to be the same.

"What are you thinking?" Jeff asked, switching his attention to her.

"That Brenda was right. You're an honorable man."

He stiffened. "I'm no one's idea of a hero. Don't make me one."

She knew that there were ghosts in his past, but they didn't matter to her. He was honorable in the ways that counted. He would never leave a woman or a child in a bind. He was dependable. He wouldn't run off with the rent money, or borrow from a loan shark and disappear, leaving his wife to face the consequences. He was nothing like Damian.

Before she could explain what she meant, Jeff rose from the table. She glanced at his still half-full plate.

"Aren't you hungry?" she asked. "It's been a long time since lunch."

"I have work."

He left the kitchen without saying anything else. Maggie stared after him.

"Is Uncle Jeff mad?"

"No, honey, he's just busy."

And conflicted. Ashley sensed the battle within him. She knew that they were the reason, but she didn't know why. Part of her wanted to go after him and talk, but a part of her wanted to run in the opposite direction. Jeff might be logistically dependable, but he was still risky in other ways. She was determined to only get involved with a man who could love her unconditionally. Jeff wasn't in a place to love anyone. Not until he'd dealt with his past. Attraction was acceptable—which was good because she couldn't control hers. But anything else was foolhardy. And she'd already been a fool for a man more than once in her life. She wasn't about to do it again.

* * *

"Kirkman is worried about a kidnapping attempt," Zane said the following week when he and Jeff met to discuss their upcoming job in the Mediterranean.

Jeff studied the diagrams spread out on the large conference table. "Kidnapping's the least of it," he replied. "At least then there's the chance he'll be held for ransom. They'd want to keep him alive. If I were him, I'd be more concerned about an outright hit."

Zane grinned. "You want to tell him that?"

"Not especially." Jeff leaned back in his chair and glanced at his partner. "But I will when I meet with him next week."

"Rather you than me. I suspect he's something of a screamer."

"Screamer" was the indelicate term used to identify clients who couldn't handle the reality of their situation. They didn't want to hear about the actual or potential danger, and they frequently resisted making changes in their lifestyle to keep themselves and their family safe. Yet they were the first to start screaming the second something went wrong, most often when it was their own fault.

"I don't doubt it." But screamer or not, Kirkman had to be dealt with.

Zane tossed his pen onto the table and looked at his partner. "So, tell me about the woman in your life."

"There is no woman."

"That's not what the rumors say. And I happen to know that you have a female living in your house with you."

"She works for me. She's my new housekeeper."

Zane raised his dark eyebrows. "And?"

"And nothing. Her name is Ashley. She used to work here in the office and now she works at my house. It's a business arrangement, nothing more."

Even if he wanted it to be more, he wasn't going to act on the wanting. Because it would be dangerous for them both. He couldn't be what Ashley needed him to be, while she…

He returned his attention to the diagrams in front of him, even though he wasn't seeing anything remotely resembling the floor plan of the main villa. Instead he saw hazel eyes bright with laughter and inhaled a sweet scent he would remember for the rest of his life.

Ashley could be very important to him, he acknowledged. But he wasn't going to let that happen.

"What about her daughter?" Zane asked. "Kids can be tough to ignore."

Jeff smiled. "What would you know about children?"

"I know enough to avoid them," his partner joked. "And so have you, until recently. So what's going on, Jeff? If you keep this up, people are going to start thinking you're actually human."

It was an old joke—one that Jeff didn't find especially humorous. He also wasn't willing to answer any questions about Maggie. Not when the little girl was rapidly becoming important to him. Something had happened during the field trip to the zoo. Being with the children, taking care of Tommy when he'd skinned his hand, had cracked some part of his protection. Now Maggie slipped inside until he found himself thinking about her throughout the day, worrying about her.

Would the teachers at the preschool remember to make sure she wore her jacket outside when she played? Did she finish her lunch? Had anyone treated her unfairly?

He still remembered when he'd actually taken her onto his lap to comfort her. His reaction had been pure instinct—and filled with more feelings than he cared to admit.

Both the Churchill females were making a mess of his life.

He pointed to the papers on the table. "We need the security plans finalized by the end of the week."

"No problem."

Zane leaned forward, resting his elbows on the table. Like Jeff, he wore a suit and tie to the office. Unlike Jeff, he tended to relax during the day, rolling up his sleeves and loosening his collar. He tapped the pages in front of them.

"I can do this myself," his partner said quietly. "It's time to let me take charge. You know, leave it to the younger guys."

"Why?" Jeff knew he wasn't getting old or soft. What was Zane's point?

"I can do this," Zane insisted.

"That was never a question."

"Wasn't it? Then why do you take all the dangerous assignments for yourself? You leave me babysitting the wives, while you stake out the trouble spots."

Jeff studied his partner. The man was only three or four years younger, but sometimes the age difference felt like decades. Zane had a lot of the same experiences, but he was a sharpshooter and a tactician. He'd spent most of his military years planning the operations or taking out the enemy from a distant location. Zane had had his share of kills, but less experience with the horror.

"I don't have family," Jeff said. "The guy who has nothing to lose volunteers for the most dangerous job. It's an old habit. One I've had trouble breaking."

Zane's dark eyes never wavered. "Like I have a family to go home to?"

Jeff shrugged. Zane didn't have anyone in the world, either. "So we're even."

Zane frowned. "I thought—" He hesitated. "Hasn't that changed? I mean with the woman and the kid."

"Nothing's different."

Jeff's voice and words were firm. It was true, he told himself. Absolutely true. Having Ashley and Maggie in his life didn't change anything. He ignored the whispering voice deep inside that reminded him he was lying. Nothing had changed, he insisted to himself. He couldn't afford to let circumstances be different. He had to remember what had happened with Nicole—and the dream. Always the dream.

"I'd like the chance," Zane told him. "You owe me that."

Jeff looked at him. "Free license to kill yourself?"

"Isn't that what this job is about? Putting it all on the line for the client?"

Jeff knew that was true, but what he couldn't explain was why it made sense for him to do it over and over again, but when Zane wanted the same, Jeff couldn't help thinking it was a waste.

* * *

"I was at the bookstore at lunch," Jeff said, standing in the entrance of the kitchen and shifting his weight from foot to foot.

Ashley stopped stirring the pot of spaghetti sauce. Her boss actually looked nervous. He wouldn't meet her gaze and there was a distinct hint of color tingeing his cheeks. The mighty hunter embarrassed about something? She moved toward him, both intrigued and charmed.

"I had long suspected you could read," she told him. "But thanks for the confirmation."

His mouth twisted. "That's not the point. I have a trip coming up in a few weeks. I wanted a book for the flight home."

She started to ask about the flight there, then realized he would probably spend that preparing for whatever assignment he might be involved with.

"Okay," she said. "Well, I hope you enjoy your book and thanks for sharing the information with me."

"You're mocking me."

She couldn't help smiling. "Maybe just a little. Why are you telling me this?"

"Because there was a display of kids' books and I bought one for Maggie."

He moved his left arm. As he did so she realized that he'd had his left hand tucked behind his back. He held up a pink-and-white gift bag overflowing with glittering pink-gold tissue paper. Obviously he'd not only bought the book, but he'd had it wrapped, as well.

"Is it okay?" he asked.

She knew he wasn't asking about the presentation,

but instead about the gift itself. Which left her with her own questions. Did he want to know if it was okay to give Maggie a book, or okay for him to give her daughter a present at all? Maybe he didn't know which he was asking, either.

Her chest tightened slightly as she remembered what had happened the previous week when Maggie had been upset about camels and Jeff had comforted her. He'd reacted impulsively. She'd seen the shock in his expression when he'd realized what he'd done, but by then it was too late to stop. Maggie was settled on his lap, leaning against him. Trusting and small, she was impossible to resist. Ashley knew—she'd been unable to keep from loving her from the moment she'd first held her.

But she was *supposed* to love her child. She'd wanted to have a baby and had been excited when her daughter had been born. But what about Jeff? Did he want children? He'd told her he couldn't have them. He'd also said that Maggie wasn't a substitute for his own child, but she was growing less confident of that. Did the little girl fill a hole in his heart Jeff didn't even know was there?

Ashley wasn't sure how she felt about her boss connecting with her child. She liked knowing he had a soft spot, but was she creating a problem for all of them?

He stepped forward and set the book on the table. "You could tell her it was from you if that makes you more comfortable," he offered.

She shook her head. "You give it to her," she said, even as she wondered why Maggie's father couldn't have been half as open to her presence in his life. Damian had never had any interest in his child. He'd seen her as one more drain on his resources.

Jeff picked up the bag and headed for the family room. Faint sounds of an afternoon cartoon drifted through the house. Ashley followed him, wanting to see what happened yet knowing she was putting herself in danger by doing so.

"Uncle Jeff!" Maggie bounced to her feet when she saw him enter the room. She pushed the mute button on the television and grinned. "Whatcha got?"

"A present."

Big blue eyes widened. "For me?"

"Maybe."

Maggie grinned. "It's for me. What is it?"

"Why don't you find out for yourself?"

He held out the gift bag. The little girl practically vibrated with excitement. She took the offering and reverently placed it on the coffee table. Carefully she pulled out the tissue paper, then reached inside for the book.

Only, it wasn't just a book. An oddly shaped box held a storybook and a stuffed pink kitten. Maggie's mouth worked, but she couldn't make any sound. Obviously Jeff had figured out that anything feline was her favorite.

"Please read to me," she said, thrusting the box at him.

He freed both the book and the cat, handing the latter to her, then settled on the sofa. Maggie plopped down next to him, her body leaning against his, her expression joyful and trusting. She cradled her new stuffed cat in her arms.

Jeff opened the book. "'Once there was a pink kitten named Pooky Girl, which was a rather silly name.'"

Maggie tugged on his suit sleeve. "This is the bestest present ever," she said.

"I'm glad you like it."

Ashley turned away. It wasn't that she didn't want to hear about the adventures of Pooky Girl, it was that she didn't want either Jeff or Maggie to notice the tears in her eyes.

Why did he have to be so darn *nice?* He was making her like him more than she should. He was making her think of him as warm and caring. That, combined with how hot he looked in jeans or in a suit, not to mention the tango her hormones performed every time he was within spitting distance, was enough to make her crazy. And dangerously vulnerable.

Jeff couldn't be a part of her life. He was too different. He was scary, although even as she said the words, she didn't believe them. Not anymore. But while she might have changed her opinion about him, one thing had stayed exactly the same. He was dangerous to her plans for the future. She wanted love and she had a bad feeling that Jeff's heart had died a long time ago.

It was well after midnight when Ashley awakened. She couldn't say what had startled her from sleep. The house was silent, and when she got up to check on her daughter, Maggie was sleeping peacefully in her bed and holding her new stuffed cat in her arms.

Ashley told herself it had been nothing and that she should just go back to bed, but something compelled her to pick up her robe and head for the stairs.

"Oh, right. Like I'm going to check all the windows

and doors," she muttered softly to herself as she walked onto the main floor.

Jeff's house was a fortress. She didn't understand his complex security system, and she knew that everything was safe. Even so she had to see for herself.

She checked the kitchen and Jeff's study, then headed to the front of the house. As she crossed by the living room, she saw a shadow by the window. Her mind froze, but her heart recognized. The nanosecond of fear faded.

Jeff.

He was looking out into the darkness, studying the night, or perhaps staring into a past that she couldn't begin to imagine.

He wore jeans and nothing else. His back was broad, his skin smooth. Muscles rippled and bunched as he shifted slightly. She felt her mouth water, something that had never occurred while she'd been looking at a man. Chocolate, sure. There was nothing like the smell of the confection to get her salivary glands all excited, but she hadn't noticed the same man-generated effect until this moment.

She had the strongest impulse to cross the room and touch him. To stroke his bare skin, to press her mouth to his shoulder and taste him. A shiver rippled through her. It was just hormones, she told herself. She was in the middle of her cycle, so biologically she was predisposed to want sex. Mother Nature at work. But her desire didn't *mean* anything—not in the real sense of the word. It was interesting information she wasn't about to act on.

"I'm sorry I woke you."

Jeff's voice cut through the night, startling her. She

hadn't realized he knew she was there. "No. You didn't. I just…" She couldn't explain how she'd come to be awake. "Sometimes I'm compelled to cruise through the house, making sure things are the way they should be. What's your excuse for being awake at this indecent hour?"

She'd made the comment lightly, but when he didn't instantly answer, she realized she might have crossed over some invisible line in their relationship.

"Sorry," she said quickly. "I was making conversation, not prying. You don't have to answer that."

"I don't mind." His voice was low and hoarse—as if speaking were difficult for him. "I have a recurring dream. It wakes me up and it's a while before I can get back to sleep."

She suspected his dreams weren't anything like hers in which she found out she had a final exam in a class she'd never attended or was supposed to pick up her daughter but suddenly couldn't remember the address of the preschool.

"Want to talk about it? Sometimes that helps."

She made the offer without thinking, then thought about retracting it. After all, did she really want to know the deep dark secrets trapped in Jeff's subconscious?

He shoved his hands into his jeans pockets. He still stood with his back to her. "I—" He cleared his throat. "There's a village. It's on fire. As I walk through it, I realize the people there are more frightened of me than of the destruction of the flames."

Ashley listened to the stark words as he told her what happened. She took a step toward him, visualizing the running children, hearing their cries of pain and fear.

Her breath caught when he told her what he saw in the reflection of the shallow pool.

Not human? Is that what he really thought?

"No, Jeff," she said, moving closer still. "I'll admit that you're a little intimidating, and until I got to know you I thought you were a little scary, but I never saw you as other than a man. And Maggie's adored you from the beginning."

"She's very special."

"So are you," she told him. "You're not the easiest guy to get to know, but you have many wonderful qualities."

He glanced at her over his shoulder. "My ex-wife, Nicole, wouldn't agree."

"Then she's wrong."

He still faced the window. The room was too dark for her to see his reflection clearly, but she could see the shadow. He shook his head.

"Nicole saw the truth," he said slowly. "She knew what I was. She said she was glad we never had children together. She told me that the reason I couldn't have a baby wasn't because of my low sperm count but because I wasn't human anymore. I'd become a soldier and in the process, I'd forgotten how to be just a man."

"No," Ashley breathed, as she instinctively reached out and rested her fingers on his bare shoulder. "No, that's not true at all. You're just as human as the rest of us. Just as—"

Without warning, he spun to face her and grabbed her hand. His touch was strong and firm, but not bruising.

"Don't touch me," he growled. "Don't start something you can't finish."

For a second she thought she'd violated some fighter code. That touching him made him think he was being threatened and put her in danger. But then she noticed that he hadn't released her fingers and was instead rubbing them with his own. There was something sensual about the caress. Something that made her bones start to melt.

"Jeff?"

He stared at her and she wondered how she could have ever thought of his eyes as cold. They weren't cold at all. Instead fire raged in them. Fire and need and a hunger that made her lick her lips in anticipation.

She might not have a whole lot of experience with men, but she recognized the powerful desire ripping through him. He was a barely controlled, sexually ready male.

She should have turned and run for the hills. Or at the very least, her own bedroom. Wasn't there a lock on the door? Wouldn't she be safe there?

Except she found she didn't want to be safe. Not when the alternative was being held in Jeff's arms. She felt her own body flaring to life. Needs long denied awoke and stretched, making her ache.

Slowly, very slowly so he could know what she was about to do, she reached toward him with her free hand and placed her fingers on his chest. She felt warm skin, cool, crinkly hair and a faint tremor.

He swore and clutched her shoulders. "Ashley."

The way he said her name made her want to purr. There was desperation in his voice, and a hunger that cried out from the soul. She raised herself on her toes and pressed her lips to his.

"I have every intention of finishing this," she murmured against his mouth. "So what are you waiting for?"

Chapter 9

Ashley should have known that she would be in no way prepared for his kiss. Jeff's strong arms came around her and he pulled her against him. She'd barely absorbed the feel of his rock-hard body, so unyielding against her own, when his lips claimed hers in a moment of possessive need that robbed her of all will.

He didn't explore or ask or hesitate. Instead he pressed his mouth against hers as if his life depended on them kissing at that exact moment. His aggression should have frightened her, she thought hazily, except she felt that she needed him just as much. There wasn't any air in her lungs and he was her only source of life.

She parted for him instantly, not needing to be seduced, but instead wanting to be taken. She wanted to experience possession at Jeff's hands.

He was a man. She'd been with men before—she had the child to prove it. But no other man had kissed her in quite the same way. Maybe it was a soldier's attention to detail; maybe it was just good luck on her part. Because instead of accepting her silent invitation to invade her mouth, he continued to kiss her lips. He was aggressive and demanding, yet his barely suppressed violence left her feeling feminine and tender. He slowly explored her lips, making her shiver with anticipation.

Mouth on mouth, hands on body. Their breath became one. Finally, when he'd discovered her to his satisfaction, he finally stroked her bottom lip with his tongue. The damp heat made her knees tremble. She clutched at his shoulders, needing to anchor herself in a suddenly spinning universe.

Finally, when she was sure she couldn't take it anymore, he slipped into her mouth.

She gasped. If she'd had the breath or strength, she would have screamed. At the first stroke of his tongue against hers, fire ripped through her body. Her breasts swelled, and between her legs a sensation of heaviness and desire made her squirm.

He tasted completely masculine and perfectly of himself. He stroked her, teased her, discovered her. He was completely in control and she found that made her relax. There was no reason to worry about being awkward. Jeff wouldn't let her misstep. Lack of fear allowed anticipation to build. She raised herself on tiptoe so she could fit herself more fully to him, absorbing his strength. His large hands began to stroke up and down her back.

She arched into his touch. She wore a cotton nightgown and a flannel robe. Underneath both garments was a cotton pair of panties. Suddenly the layers were heavy and unnecessary. She wanted to feel his fingers against her bare skin. She wanted the same attention to detail that he gave to their kiss brought to her breasts and other parts of her body.

He cupped her face and held her slightly away from him. His gray eyes burned bright with need. His fingers trembled slightly, and she was aware of the hard ridge of his desire pressing against her belly.

"Ashley, I—" His voice was low and hoarse, as if it was difficult for him to speak. "I need you to be sure."

She managed a shaky smile. "I'm very sure," she whispered. "I know it's crazy for about a thousand reasons, but I want you."

She blushed as she spoke, not used to being so bold. But she didn't call the words back. She did want Jeff more than she'd ever wanted anyone. Even the man she'd been married to.

He ran his fingers through her mussed hair, then dropped a quick kiss to her mouth. "I don't have any protection with me." He shrugged. "I don't sleep around much, I've had a recent blood test and I'm not exactly a pregnancy risk."

She couldn't help smiling. How like Jeff to reassure her that she was safe with him.

She leaned forward and pressed her mouth against his bare chest. He tasted faintly of salt. "Did you think I would want to stop?"

He didn't answer with words. Instead he pressed his mouth to hers and hauled her up against him. They kissed deeply and she felt herself disappearing into the experience. Perhaps later she would think that she was crazy for giving in. Perhaps after they'd crossed the line that would change everything, she would have regrets, but not now. Not this night. She sensed that as much as Jeff wanted her, he needed her even more. And it was that need that made him impossible to deny. Well, that and her own aching body that longed for the release *his* body promised.

He moved his head slightly so that he could kiss her cheek, then her jaw. Damp kisses tickled her skin and made her gasp. He moved lower, down her neck to the collar of her robe. Once there, he exchanged lips for hands and continued his journey. She sucked in a breath as his hands found and cupped her breasts. Before she could beg him to never, ever stop, he slipped to her waist and her hips. His thumbs brushed the jutting bones there.

Ashley had a moment of feeling self-conscious. She knew that she was too skinny by at least ten or fifteen pounds. At one time she'd been a tad more lush, but a limited food budget, not to mention the need to provide for her child, had changed that. Still, Jeff didn't seem to be complaining.

Instead he dropped to his knees. Once there he pushed at her robe and nightgown, shoving them up to her waist, then moving her hands so that she would hold the fabric. He tugged on her panties, pulling them down. Without thinking, she stepped out of them.

Ashley felt heat climbing her face. He couldn't possibly be going to— It was too soon and he was… Well, he just couldn't.

But he could and he did. Before she'd figured out a

way to act casual about the whole thing, he pressed his mouth to her belly. The kiss touched her down to her soul and made her gasp his name.

He tenderly nibbled along the sensitive skin there, pausing only to tease her belly button. Her legs began to tremble. She had to brace herself to keep upright. He moved lower and lower still until he reached the most secret part of her. Once there, he gently parted the protective folds of her feminine place and licked her.

Ashley bit her lip to keep from screaming. Inside her head, a thousand voices echoed with a single cry of pleasure. It was as if he knew her better than she knew herself, she thought hazily, barely able to remain upright as he kissed her over and over.

He urged her to shift so she could part her legs. She tried to do as he requested, but it was too difficult to maintain her balance. Suddenly she stumbled and was falling, only to be caught in his strong embrace.

Jeff smiled at her as he lowered her to the carpet in the living room. He settled her on her rear, then carefully drew her robe off her shoulders and pulled her nightgown over her head. She was naked and found that she didn't much mind. It felt right with him. Maybe a sensible woman would have been nervous or even scared, but all she could think was that she wanted him to pick up exactly where he'd left off.

Unfortunately he didn't read her mind. However, what he did instead turned out to be just as wonderful. He bent over her breast and drew one tight nipple into his mouth. The other received attention from his fingers. He licked, he nibbled, he teased until she was writhing on the floor and desperate for more.

After he'd switched so that her other breast had equal attention, he shifted so that he knelt between her legs and kissed his way down her stomach. Her breath caught as she stiffened in anticipation. Finally he bent low to give her the most intimate kiss of all. The one that made her cry out his name as she drew back her knees and dug her heels into the carpet.

His hands cupped her hips. His breath was hot, his tongue insistent. She couldn't stand what he was doing to her. Not for another second.

"Don't stop," she gasped. "Please."

She felt more than heard a low, throaty sound of laughter as he continued his ministrations. Then suddenly the world tilted and flew out of control. Before she could prepare herself, a powerful wave of release crashed through her. She was caught up and carried away, drowning in the most amazing sensations she'd ever experienced.

Once again Jeff caught her in his strong arms. Caught her and held her as she slowly, very slowly, returned to normal.

When she finally surfaced enough to open her eyes, she found herself staring into his face. He smiled down at her. She felt her own lips curve in response.

"Mission accomplished," she murmured. "They teach you that at boot camp?"

"No. In special forces. I took the advanced course."

Her own smile turned into a grin. "Jeff, you could teach the course."

He touched her face, then smoothed back her hair. "I wanted it to be good for you," he told her. "I'm glad you were pleased."

"*Pleased* doesn't begin to describe it."

He was so gentle, she thought. Despite the fire still raging inside of him. She felt the insistent pressure of his arousal. He was as hungry as she had been just a few moments before. Yet he'd taken the time to satisfy her very thoroughly. This from a man who dreamed he wasn't human and kept mostly to himself?

She wanted to ask what it meant that they were doing this. But even more, she wanted to feel his bare skin against hers as he entered her.

She stroked his back, then slid her hands around to his chest. "I think it's time for the second act," she said and brought his mouth to hers.

As they kissed, he moved his fingers against her breasts, then slipped them lower. She was still slick and swollen and it didn't take much to get her blood boiling all through her. In a matter of minutes she was writhing against him, as hungry as she'd been before.

He shifted so that he could pull off his jeans, then returned to kneel between her legs. The only light in the room came from outside—a diffused illumination from the streetlights' glow in the damp night. His face was in shadows and she couldn't see his eyes. Yet she wasn't afraid. Not even when she felt his arousal pressing against her.

She slipped a hand between them to guide him inside. With one smooth thrust, he filled her completely. She gasped as her muscles relaxed to admit him, then immediately tightened around his width.

He braced himself on his hands and stared into her eyes. She kept her gaze on him. Even as he entered her again and again, even as her own body began to react to the tension filling her, she refused to look away.

Jeff knew he wasn't going to be able to last much longer. His lack of control wasn't about not having been with a woman in a long time, although that was true enough. Instead his legendary self-control was being destroyed by a wide-eyed gaze and the feel of slick walls contracting in pleasure.

He felt the first release ripple through Ashley's slender body. She clutched his arms and arched back her head, all the while gasping for breath and pleading with him to follow. He told himself to hold back. That his waiting would make it better for her. But suddenly he didn't have a choice. He couldn't wait, couldn't do anything but fill her again and again, shifting back on his haunches as he grabbed her hips and pulled her closer.

And then he was at the point of no return. He thrust into her deeply, making them both cry out. He surrendered to the release, losing himself in a perfect moment of paradise.

Jeff rolled over and pulled Ashley into his arms. The night was still except for the sound of their breathing. She cuddled against him, her head on his shoulder, her breath tickling his chest.

"When was the last time you did it on your living room floor?" she asked.

"Never."

He thought about telling her more. That he'd never invited a woman to his house. He'd never made love here before.

Made love.

The words stopped him, but he couldn't deny them. Ashley was more than just sex.

"What about you?" he asked.

She propped herself up on her elbow and grinned down at him. "I've never made love on your living room floor before, either."

Her humor made him wrap his arms around her and pull her against him. He liked the feel of her naked body pressing into his.

"How do you feel?" he asked as he stroked her from shoulders to rear.

"Good. Better than good." She sighed. "You were pretty amazing. All that ability to focus on the task at hand. I should have guessed how well it would translate. Now if only my rug burn will fade by morning."

"Rug burn?"

He started to sit up to look at her back, but she laughed and pushed him back onto the carpet.

"I'm kidding. My back is completely unscathed."

"Good."

She turned onto her side. He slid his hands over her hip and felt the prominent bone. "You're too thin," he told her.

She glared. "I take back all those nice things I just said. It's incredibly tacky to criticize a woman's body at any time, but never more so than after you'd just done the wild thing and while she's still naked."

She was being playful, but he didn't smile. "I'm not being critical, I'm stating a fact. You haven't been eating enough. Why do I know that it's more about money than looking good in clothes?"

She sat up and turned so she was facing away from

him. "Don't, Jeff. I don't want to talk about that. Please don't spoil the mood."

Her request answered his question. He hated that money had been so tight for her that there were times when she didn't get enough to eat. He wanted to fix her life. He needed to make it better. Except he was the wrong person for the job. Nicole had been right when she'd pointed out that he didn't know how to be like other men. At least he'd given Ashley a good job. As long as she worked for him, she would be safe.

"You're supposed to say something reassuring," she muttered.

"I'm sorry." He touched her bare skin. "I don't want to spoil the mood. Please come back here and let me hold you."

She turned toward him. The lamplight filtered through the partially open drapes, illuminating her body. Her breasts were surprisingly full for her slight frame. The nipples were tight. As she moved, her breasts swayed slightly. She was an erotic image brought to life by the night.

Unable to stop himself, he leaned over and took her right nipple in his mouth. She grasped his head and moaned. Suddenly he was touching her everywhere, needing her, desperate for her. He told himself that it was too soon.

"I don't want to hurt you," he murmured.

"Don't worry about it."

She pressed herself against him as they kissed.

He was hard in a heartbeat. Hard and hungry, as if they hadn't made love less than an hour before. He cupped her breasts and teased her nipples. She ran her fingers through his hair and down his back. He put his hands on her hips and urged her to straddle him. She did so; then in one easy, sexy movement she settled on top of him and let him find his way home.

Ashley couldn't believe they were making love again. She was generally a once-every-three-or-four-days kind of girl. But with Jeff she couldn't seem to get enough. The second he began to fill her, she felt herself contracting around him. The first release made her arch her head back in an attempt to catch her breath. The second made her frantic to have him fill her more and more and more.

She raised and lowered herself with a pace she thought might be too fast until she realized that his hands guided her hips, keeping her in place and her rhythm steady for both of them. Every few seconds another contraction filled her. She hadn't known it could be like this.

Suddenly tension spiraled through her. Tension and need. It consumed her until she had no choice but to shudder with the glory of it all. Just as she reached her pinnacle, she felt Jeff stiffen and cry out. Together they clung to each other as their bodies reveled in the moment of being one.

Ashley slept like one of the innocent, Jeff thought later when they were both in his large bed. Her even breathing spoke of her rest. He couldn't find the same solace; he didn't dare.

When was the last time he'd made love? Not had sex, but actually made love with a woman? He couldn't recall. Not since Nicole. And with her it had been before things had started to go so desperately wrong. Sex was a bodily function. He understood and respected his body's need for release. But this was different.

He closed his eyes but didn't allow himself to sleep because the dream lurked in the world of the unconscious and he didn't want to have it twice in one night. Not with Ashley sleeping so peacefully beside him. She might think that she understood him, but she had no idea of his real self.

So instead of sleeping he held her close, ignoring the very male part of him that wanted her again. He told himself that the wanting was allowed for this night but no longer, because wanting was dangerous. Wanting made a man weak and careless. Either could get him killed.

In the morning he would walk away without looking back. He would never allow himself to do this again or even to think of it. That would be best for both of them. But until morning there was the night. He closed his eyes and breathed in the sweet scent of her skin.

The next morning Ashley was fighting both a mild case of rug burn and a major case of the guilts. She tried to act as normal as possible as she fixed her daughter's lunch, even though Jeff was also sitting at the table, looking as if nothing had happened the previous night. Fortunately Maggie didn't sense the tension between the adults and chattered away as if this was an ordinary morning.

Ashley had awakened to the sound of Jeff in the shower and had used the moment of privacy to escape to her own room. When they'd met up in the kitchen, she'd managed to greet him and pour him coffee without melting into a puddle of desire, or worse, clueing in her daughter that something was different.

As she spread peanut butter on bread, Ashley tried to reconcile the well-dressed conservative man sitting at the table with the one who had licked her entire body the night before. Or the one who had awakened her just before dawn so they could make love yet again. She couldn't wait for round two.

Just hold on one minute, she told herself as she reached for the jar of jelly. There wasn't going to be a round two. Last night had been amazing. It had been special and perfect and it had to be a one-time event. Jeff wasn't the kind of man a woman like her settled down with, and she didn't want a casual, sexual relationship. For her, the act of physical intimacy had always been closely tied to love. She didn't love Jeff; she didn't want to love Jeff. To make sure that didn't change, she was going to have to stay out of his bed.

She would tell him as soon as they were alone.

That decided, she finished her daughter's sandwich and put it in the small, plastic, cat-covered lunch box.

"It's gonna be Easter soon," Maggie was saying.

Jeff smiled at the little girl over his coffee mug. "What happens then?"

Maggie looked shocked that he didn't know. "Mommy and me go to church where they have lots and lots of pretty flowers and we listen to the min— min—" She glanced at her mother for help.

"The minister," Ashley said.

Maggie beamed. "And when we come home we find what the Easter bunny left for me. Last year he was very nice and left me lots of chocolate." She leaned toward Jeff and lowered her voice. "I'm hopin' he's nice to me this year."

Maggie turned to her mother. "Mommy, can I take my new book to school to show my teacher?"

Ashley nodded.

Maggie jumped from her seat and raced toward the stairs. Which, unfortunately, left Ashley alone with Jeff. He turned his attention to her.

"How are you feeling?"

Was it her imagination or did his tone sound different this morning? She barely stopped from slapping herself in the forehead. Of course it was different. *They* were different. Their intimacy the previous night had changed everything.

"I, ah, I'm fine," she said, barely able to meet his gaze.

She could feel the heat flaring on her cheeks. What was he thinking? Was he, too, remembering what it had been like when they'd been together? Should she tell him now that it had been wonderful but really couldn't happen again?

"Jeff, I—"

"I found it! I found it!" Maggie's singsong voice filled the kitchen as the little girl flew into the room, her new book clutched to her chest.

She dashed over to Jeff and flung herself into his arms. "Thank you for my book. And the kitty. They're my bestest presents ever."

Ashley watched her daughter's small arms go trustingly around Jeff's neck. She saw the large man she now knew to be tender and considerate, hug her back. Suddenly she was aware of the sound of her own heartbeat and the way the room seemed to tilt slightly.

She'd been worried about getting involved with a man who wasn't right for her. She'd been concerned about having her heart engaged in futile longing for a man who could never love her back. But she'd never once thought anyone else was at risk.

Now, as she observed the tall, dangerous man and the trusting little girl, she knew that Maggie was the one who had already given her heart away. Maggie had bonded with Jeff, viewing him as the father she never had. Maggie would have dreams and expectations, and there was nothing Ashley could do to warn her about holding back.

An ache filled Ashley's chest. She wanted to protect her daughter, but she didn't know how. Should they leave? Should they—

Jeff whispered something in Maggie's ear and her daughter laughed. Ashley knew it was too late to keep Maggie from connecting with Jeff. And taking her away now, before they had to go, seemed cruel. Perhaps it would be best to let the child enjoy Jeff while they were in his house. Later they would both have to deal with the impossible task of getting over Jeff Ritter.

Chapter 10

Jeff left his office with the Kirkman file under his arm. He knew he could have asked Brenda to do the research on the small town just neighboring the Mediterranean estate, but he needed something with which to distract himself. Something that would take his mind off Ashley.

They hadn't spoken that morning. Maggie provided a perfect buffer and he hadn't seen the point of trying to get Ashley alone for a few minutes of conversation. It was ironic. He who had faced numerous terrorists, enemy soldiers and certain-death assignments without flinching was nervous about talking with a woman. He grimaced. Nervous didn't begin to describe how he felt. He was flat-out terrified.

He didn't know why she'd agreed to make love with him last night. He'd told her about the dream; he'd bared something close to the truth about who and what he was. And yet she hadn't run away. Maybe she hadn't figured out what it all meant. Maybe that would come later.

He didn't want to think about that. He didn't want to see her features tighten in disgust or fear. He didn't want her backing away from him when he entered a room.

And yet, despite all that could still go wrong, he wasn't sorry. How could he be? Last night had been perfect.

He stepped into the research room and settled at one of the computers. Even as he typed on the keyboard, he thought about what it had been like to be with her. How she'd looked and felt and tasted. How she'd sounded. The way that she'd clung to him, losing herself in the moment.

No, he couldn't be sorry about that. Even if it meant that he could never sleep again.

He frowned slightly. The dreams lurked in the back of his mind, an ever-present enemy. He knew that they would extract their revenge for his temporary assumption that he could be like everyone else.

"Where's Brenda?"

The question came from behind him. Jeff turned and saw his partner lounging in the doorway to the research room. Zane raised a questioning eyebrow and continued, "Did she call in sick?"

"No. She's around."

Zane sauntered over to the chair next to Jeff's and took a seat. "So why are you in here?"

Jeff shrugged. "I had the time."

Zane didn't look convinced. "Are you all right? You

haven't been yourself for the past few days and today it's worse."

"What are you talking about? What's worse?"

"I'm not sure." Zane studied him. "It's the woman, isn't it? The one staying at your house."

Jeff didn't think he'd been acting any differently, but obviously he'd been wrong. Zane was observant and he didn't make mistakes.

"Nothing's changed," he bluffed, knowing it was a lie. Having Ashley and Maggie come live with him was just the first of many changes.

"Don't get me wrong," Zane told him. "I think you having a woman around is a good thing. I'm all in favor of that. You need some normalcy."

Jeff didn't agree, but he wasn't about to argue. Ashley was dangerous to him because she distracted him. In his line of work, a distraction could cause a mistake. Just one misstep, one unnoticed detail, would mean the difference between living and dying.

Zane jerked his head toward the open door. "You ready for the meeting?"

Jeff glanced at his watch, then nodded. They had four new recruits going through orientation. A quiet, competent woman in her early thirties, and three ex-military men.

"What do you think?" he asked his partner as he closed his folder and followed Zane out of the research office.

"They're all right. The youngest of the three, Sanders, is a little gung ho for my liking. He still thinks the protection business is glamorous."

Jeff grimaced. "Just what we need. Someone stupid. How'd he get this far?"

"Great credentials and impeccable recommendations. They're genuine," Zane continued as he paused just outside the conference room. "I checked them myself."

Then they hadn't been faked, Jeff thought. Zane didn't make those kind of mistakes, either.

Jeff stepped into the conference room with Zane on his heels. Jack Delaney, former Secret Service agent and arms expert, nodded as his bosses walked to the front of the room. The four recruits sat at a conference table facing the podium. Jeff looked them over, noticing the even gazes that met his own. The woman sat a little apart from the rest. She had long red hair and a body that would make traffic stand still. He briefly wondered what had brought someone that good-looking to this line of work, then dismissed the question. Her appearance didn't matter if she was the best.

He glanced at the three men. The youngest was easy to pick out. He wore a grin the size of Texas.

"These are the men who sign your paychecks," Jack said easily. "Jeff Ritter and Zane Rankin." He nodded and stepped away from the podium.

Jeff took his place. He looked at each of the recruits, trying to size them up. Only two people would be hired and that decision wouldn't be made for at least a month. He and Zane were particular about whom they worked with. After all, the team members risked their lives together. To trust that much, everyone had to depend on each other.

"There is no room for mistakes," he said by way of

introduction. "Nor do we bring our egos, our tempers or our prejudices to any assignment. Every job puts it all on the line. Before we invite you to join our company, we will attempt to find out your weaknesses, your faults and what makes your skin crawl. Because the kind of clients who employ us expect the best."

He paused to make sure he had their attention. "A British banker had handled some delicate foreign transactions a couple of years back. He noticed that there were some irregularities and traced them to the source. Along the way, he discovered his bank was being used to launder billions in drug money. The men responsible for the deposits were not pleased to be exposed. In an effort to keep the man quiet, they kidnapped his only child. The man's wife had died in childbirth. He had no other relatives."

Jeff leaned forward, resting his elbows on the podium. "A half-dozen kidnappers holding one small boy. There was no margin for error. As it turns out, we got lucky. A clean shot from a hundred yards. How many of you would be comfortable in those circumstances? No second chance, no room for errors."

He didn't wait for anyone to answer. "In case you're wondering why you didn't read about this in the paper, it's because that's how we prefer to work. While there is occasional press coverage, it's the exception rather than the rule. If you're in this for glamour, fame or a chance to get laid, tell me now."

This time he did pause. The woman grinned. "Gee, boss, and I was so in it for the sex."

Her comment made everyone chuckle, easing the tension in the room.

"Kidding aside," Jeff said when the room was quiet again. "Each of you has to question if you have what it takes. The best operatives are loners. No connections, no ties. It's harder to be afraid when you have nothing to lose. Good luck."

With that he turned and walked out of the room. Zane would speak next, but Jeff had heard the speech a couple dozen times. Besides, he was too distracted by his own thoughts to pay attention.

He'd told the recruits the truth. It took having nothing to lose to stop being afraid. He'd lived by that code for years; it gave him his edge. But what if that had all changed? He hadn't been able to stop thinking about Ashley. She haunted him like a sensual ghost determined to win his soul. He couldn't afford the distraction. He couldn't afford to get involved.

If he felt pleasure, what would be next? Weakness? Hesitation? Would he worry about her to the point where he would hesitate a split second?

That wasn't an option. There was only one solution to the problem. He could never be intimate with her again.

Ashley knew she was grinning like a sheep but she couldn't help herself. There was something wonderful about the way her thighs hurt from what she'd been doing the previous night. Okay, yes, she knew that she and Jeff could never have a normal relationship. And yes, having an affair with one's boss, however brief, was never clever. But there was something to be said for a romantic, and slightly sexual, glow.

She felt as if she wasn't actually touching the ground when she walked. Everything seemed more brightly colored and nothing could upset her good mood. The downside was she'd had a darned difficult time concentrating in class. She'd found herself doodling Jeff's name instead of paying attention to the lecture.

She had it bad.

Ashley walked to the refrigerator to pull out the chicken she wanted to roast for dinner. As much as she wanted to be with Jeff again, she knew that it could never work between them. There was no future here. She wanted to make a safe haven for herself and her daughter. She had no clue as to what Jeff wanted, but she suspected it was something very different. He wasn't the kind of man who would love her more than anything. He would never promise to love her unconditionally, the way she would want to love him.

She froze in the act of removing the chicken from the shelf. Not that she was saying she loved Jeff. She didn't. She liked him a lot and she thought he was hot, which was very different from love. Jeff was not the man for her—he had a past that was too different from her own. They obviously couldn't make love again, even if he wanted to. She would have to tell him as soon as he got home.

Jeff couldn't remember another more cowardly act in his life. However potentially difficult or painful, he'd never taken the easy way out until tonight. Instead of coming home at his usual time and facing Ashley, he'd had Brenda phone to say he had to work late.

It was after eleven when he pulled into the garage and turned off the engine. The situation had been worse than he'd realized. Not only didn't he want to face her, he hadn't been able to stop thinking about her while he'd been at the office. Despite his long hours, he hadn't gotten anything accomplished.

He climbed out of the car and headed for the house. As he'd driven up, he'd noticed faint light from behind the drapes, so he wasn't surprised to see that Ashley had left on a few lamps. As he crossed toward the kitchen, he tried to remember if he'd ever not come home in the dark.

He found a piece of paper waiting for him on the kitchen table. "Uncle Jeff" spelled out in very uneven, very large block crayon letters was followed by an arrow pointing to a plate with a slice of chocolate cake. The dessert looked too tidy to have been made by Maggie, but the welcoming note was pure little girl.

His chest tightened. He couldn't recall anyone ever doing something like this for him. Maggie had actually thought about him while he'd been gone. Had Ashley, as well?

His house was no longer empty and impersonal. He told himself it didn't matter, but it did. He told himself he shouldn't like it—but he did.

Swearing under his breath, he ignored the dessert and headed for the stairs. He had to get himself under control. Distractions weren't allowed. He promised himself the situation would get better with time. It had to.

She was waiting in his bed. Jeff stepped into the room and flipped the switch. Ashley lay curled up on top of the covers, one arm bent and supporting her head. She wore a lace nightgown that covered everything and concealed nothing. He forgot to breathe.

"Hi," she said, slowly pushing herself into a sitting

position. "I wasn't sure what time you'd be home and I didn't want to miss you."

He couldn't speak. He could barely set down his briefcase. His throat was tight, his groin was on fire. He didn't care. He wanted to spend the rest of his life looking at her slender curves and remembering what it had been like to make love with her.

"It's about Easter," she said. She sounded calm. She *looked* calm.

He blinked. He couldn't have heard her correctly. "Easter?"

"You know, that holiday we have in the spring? Maggie's been talking about it, as you may remember. The thing is, I always hide Easter eggs for her. I would like to know if it's all right for me to do that in your yard this year." She wrinkled her nose. "Unless it rains. That would be a drag."

He couldn't understand what she was saying. Didn't she know she was practically naked and making him crazy, lying there on his mattress? Yet she acted as if everything were perfectly fine.

"Use the yard," he managed to say. "For the eggs."

"Good. Also, when I talked to Brenda today, she invited us to brunch at her house. I hope you don't mind that I said yes. So I figured we'd do the Easter egg hunt, then go to church, then over to Brenda's. Of course if you object to church, you could meet us there."

He was losing his mind. "Brenda invited the three of us?"

Some of her calmness faded. He sensed her tension. Suddenly Ashley wouldn't look at him. "Yes, well, I thought that was odd. Then I figured she'd run it past you and you'd agreed."

Brenda hadn't said a word.

Ashley slid to the edge of the bed, then stood. She was barefoot and nearly naked.

"The thing is, I'd told myself I was going to be practical," she said, moving closer to him. Her hazel eyes glinted with humor. "Having an affair with my boss is not only crazy, it's potentially dangerous. I have goals, you have goals and they're not the same, right?"

He suddenly wanted to hear all about her goals. Instead he nodded.

"So it would be dumb to get involved."

As she spoke, she put her hands on his shoulders and pushed off his jacket. The thick fabric slid down his arms and slipped to the ground.

She pressed her fingers against his chest. "But you're so darned cute when you're all stoic and soldierlike. I'm not sure I can resist that. There's also the way you're patient with Maggie and incredible in bed. All that attention focused on what I want. Call me spineless. One minute I was getting ready to crawl between my own sheets and the next I was here. Want me to go away?"

Instead of answering with words, he cupped her face in his hands and kissed her. She responded the instant his mouth brushed hers, leaning into him and groaning softly. Desire filled him, making his blood heat and his arousal flex against her belly. He wanted her. He'd been fooling himself by thinking he could share the same house and ignore her.

He swept his tongue against her lower lip. She parted for him, but he waited before entering, brushing back and forth until she trembled. Only then did he slip inside and taste her sweetness.

She clung to him. Bodies pressed, heat flared, need grew. He felt the rapid pounding of her heartbeat and knew that his own beat just as fast. Desperate for more, he broke the kiss so he could nibble his way along her jaw and down her throat. She groaned and arched her head back.

"Jeff," she gasped. "You don't have to do the Easter thing if you don't want to. I mean I won't change my mind about wanting to make love with you."

He couldn't help chuckling as he tugged on her lace nightgown. "I'll do the Easter thing," he said softly, pulling down her short sleeves and baring her to the waist. "Right now I'll promise to do anything you want."

Chapter 11

Jeff awakened shortly before dawn. He jerked out of a sound sleep only to find himself right where he was supposed to be—in his bedroom. It was nearly a full second before he was able to register two important facts: he hadn't had the dream and he wasn't alone.

He didn't know which startled him more. After he and Ashley had made love the previous evening, they'd slipped under the covers. He'd held her close, fully expecting to spend another night staring at the ceiling, not daring to close his eyes and experience the nightmare. Instead he'd drifted off without being haunted by the specters of his past.

He turned toward the feminine warmth pressing against him, only to find Ashley watching him. She smiled slowly.

"Good morning."

Her voice was velvet, her body silk. He found himself instantly aroused by her presence and the acceptance he saw in her eyes.

"How'd you sleep?" he asked, turning toward her and touching her cheek.

"Really well." She hesitated. "At the risk of starting your day with the words every man hates to hear...we have to talk."

Her hair was a mess. Dark curls teased at her face and shot out in every direction like an uneven halo. Her skin was slightly flushed and the scent of their lovemaking clung to the sheets. Her need to have a conversation didn't disturb what he considered a perfect moment.

He knew what she was going to say. A casual relationship with him wasn't her style. This wasn't sensible; they had to end it. He told himself that he didn't mind. The past two nights had been more than he'd expected. They would be enough.

"Talk away," he said easily, propping his head on one hand.

"Oh, sure. Make me be the one." She flopped onto her back, then turned her head toward him. "Jeff, what are we doing?"

He wanted to say they had been sleeping and now they were having a discussion, but he knew that wasn't exactly what she meant. "What would you like us to be doing?"

"If anyone else gave me that answer, I would instantly accuse the man of hedging, but I suspect you're asking because you genuinely want to know. Am I right?"

He nodded. She wanted to talk about *them*. About their potentially mutual goals and desires. He didn't have either—at least none that included a normal relationship with a very nice woman.

She pressed her lips together. "I'm going to take a wild guess here and say that I think you're out of your element with me. Am I right?"

He nodded again. Now it was his turn to settle onto his back.

"Jeff, is there anyone special in your life?"

He knew what she was asking. "No. I wouldn't be here with you if there was."

"That's what I thought but I had to be sure." She slid her hand toward him under the covers and lightly touched his arm. "Has there been anyone special recently?"

He thought about the question. Recently there had been no one. "No. There hasn't been anyone in my life since Nicole."

And in an odd way, Nicole hadn't been in his life at all. The young man she'd married had disappeared in a matter of months. By their second anniversary, it was as if that Jeffrey Ritter had never existed.

He saw now that he shouldn't have married her. Or having married her, he shouldn't have gone into Special Forces. He'd changed so much so quickly. Their marriage had never had a chance. As for other women since then, they had existed but not the way Ashley meant. They had been nameless, faceless companions of the night. Strangers who welcomed him for an hour or a day. One woman had hung on for nearly two weeks.

"I haven't been with anyone since Damian," Ashley confessed. She shifted, curling against him. "There were a few guys before I met him, but I was pretty young then. It didn't really count."

"You're still pretty young."

"Jeff!"

He looked at her as she raised herself up on one elbow. "I'm twenty-five. That's hardly a baby."

"I'm thirty-three."

"So what? That makes you an old man?"

He was older than she could know. He'd seen so much that no one should ever see.

She sighed and settled back against him. He could feel her bare breast pressing against his arm. "You make me crazy," she murmured. "You're not that old."

"If you say so."

"I do. Besides, that wasn't the point. Damian was the first man I'd ever been with, which makes you the second."

Her words stunned him. He heard them and turned them over in his brain without having a clue as to what to do with them.

"Ashley?"

"Yeah, yeah, I get it. More than you wanted to know."

"Why did you tell me?"

"Because…" She pressed her lips to his bare arm. "Because I want you to know that I think what we have is very special. I think *you're* special."

She thought they had something. A relationship? Was that possible? He wanted to tell her that he didn't know how, that he wasn't safe. That *this* wasn't safe. Not for either of them.

"I didn't want this," she continued. "Getting involved, I mean. Based on how you live your life, I'm guessing you didn't want it, either. Which means we should probably assume it's just hormones and that whatever it is will pass."

He risked looking at her and nearly lost himself in her beautiful eyes. "What didn't you want?"

She smiled. "The complication. The attraction. I spent yesterday being completely schizophrenic— bouncing between grinning like an idiot and promising myself I would end this immediately."

So she'd been feeling the same things he had. "If you planned on telling me it was over last night, the lace nightgown was a mixed message."

"I know." Her smile faded. "Jeff, neither of us wants this. The timing is bad, it's confusing. There are probably a hundred reasons to pretend it never happened, but that's not what I want."

"What do you want?"

She settled her head on his shoulder and closed her eyes. "To play it by ear. To enjoy my time with you without getting too personally involved or getting hurt."

Until it's time for me to leave.

She didn't say those last words, but he heard the message and knew she was correct. They could pretend for now. Pretend that they were allowed to be lovers and act like other people. But they both knew the truth. Eventually she would walk away from him because he could never give her what she needed and deserved. And he would let her go because to keep her in his world meant being distracted. One mistake on an assignment could easily be the end of him and the client.

"I need to keep my own room," she said. "So Maggie doesn't get confused. I don't want her to know about this. I thought I'd plan on heading back there before she wakes up."

She was talking about spending her nights with him. Of them being together in the same bed for hours at a time. Not just making love, but holding and touching and sleeping together. Longing filled him. A need to inhale the scent of her and be with her until the memories were so strong that he could never forget.

"So what do you think?" she asked. She opened her eyes and looked at him. "You haven't said what you want."

He knew this was all pretend, but it was more than he had ever had, so it was enough. "I want to make you happy," he said. "I want to do whatever you would like."

She grinned. "Really?"

He turned her onto her back and slid one thigh between hers. "Absolutely anything."

"How wonderful," she murmured. "I'll give you a list of requests tonight."

"Why don't we start right now?"

"Mommy, I found one!" Maggie squealed with delight, then held up a brightly colored yellow plastic egg. "Uncle Jeff, look!"

"How many is that?" he asked.

Maggie glanced into her basket. "Four," she said with a reverence generally used by chronic shoppers at a twice-yearly sale.

Ashley smiled at her daughter and fought against an unexplained urge to cry. Her eyes began to burn and her throat tightened. She blinked rapidly until her wayward feelings were under control.

Her weakened emotional state was easy to explain, she thought as she sat next to Jeff on the rear step of his house. Ever since she was twelve years old, she'd been fighting to keep her world together. First she'd had to deal with her sister's death and the subsequent loss of her mother. Then she'd struggled to keep afloat in the foster home system. She'd managed to graduate from high school and start college, only to find herself in love with a charming loser who had no business being a husband let alone a father. Then she'd been a single mother, barely able to keep her world together.

For the past thirteen years, life had been one challenge after another. For the first time since the trouble all started, Ashley had a chance to relax and just breathe. Thanks to her job as Jeff's housekeeper and the part-time accounting work she did, she actually had a savings account. She was current in her studies, every day her graduation from college was that much closer, Maggie was happy and healthy and they had a very impressive roof over their heads.

All because of Jeff.

Ashley glanced at him out of the corner of her eye. He'd dressed for church in a beautiful navy suit, but she happened to know that shortly after six that morning, he'd been outside in jeans and a sweatshirt, hiding Easter eggs. He'd concealed them just enough that Maggie wouldn't think the Easter bunny had gone soft on her, yet she was finding every single one of the plastic eggs.

Last night Jeff had helped Ashley prepare the eggs, filling the hollow plastic with chocolates, stickers and gaudy Day-Glo rings. He was growing on her; he was growing on them both.

Ashley recognized the danger signs. It wasn't just that Jeff made love to her every night with an attention to detail that left her breathless. Somehow the three of them had created rituals. Jeff and Maggie went grocery shopping twice a week. Fridays were movie-and-popcorn nights, complete with a Disney flick and plenty of cuddling on the sofa. Jeff had watched Maggie two evenings before Ashley's last set of midterms.

He always asked about both their days, listening intently as if the information were essential to world peace. Or maybe it was just essential to his own well-being. He talked about work, explaining he had a business trip to the Mediterranean late the following month, and kept her updated on the performance of the new recruits.

"Six!" Maggie hollered as she held up another plastic egg.

Jeff stood. "Well done, young lady. Most impressive. As I believe the quota for each child is six eggs per Easter bunny visit, you've found them all."

"Really?" Maggie's blue eyes glowed with pride. "Mommy, I found them all!"

"You are a very clever little girl," Ashley said, holding out her arms to her daughter.

Maggie ran to her for a hug, then turned to Jeff and held up her free arm. The tall, dangerous man bent low and scooped the child into his arms. Ashley's heart tightened in her chest. Both she and her daughter had it bad. Jeff no longer scared them, if he'd ever scared

Maggie. He was kind and gentle and he paid attention. How was she supposed to resist him?

Jeff headed for the back door. Ashley rose and followed. He was so good with her daughter. How tragic that he couldn't have children of his own. He would be the best kind of father. Nicole had been wrong to tell him he wasn't human. Jeff Ritter was very much a man—as flawed and frail as the next. But he was also decent.

She stepped into the kitchen where Maggie and Jeff had already opened several of the plastic eggs to discover the goodies inside. Her daughter laughed with excitement over a bright orange ring in the shape of a daisy. She looked up at her mother and grinned.

"This is the bestest Easter ever. Can we go to church now, and then to Brenda's where I can see Muffin again?"

Ashley nodded and held out her hand. "Let's put on our Easter dresses and get all pretty for Uncle Jeff."

Maggie clasped her hands together in front of her chest. "We have hats," she said happily.

Jeff raised his eyebrows. Ashley smiled. "I know it's silly, but it's a tradition. New Easter hats."

"I can't wait to see them."

His gaze met hers. Ashley's heart squeezed a little tighter. In that moment she knew that she'd fallen for Jeff. Fallen hard and fast with no hope of walking away without being crushed.

"Why is everyone staring?" Ashley asked in a low voice as they walked through Brenda's house in Bellevue.

Jeff had also noticed the interested looks they were receiving. He put his hand on the small of Ashley's back. "It's because you're so lovely."

She glanced up at him and laughed. "Yeah, right."

He took in her dark, wavy hair, the hazel eyes that seemed to see down to his soul, the way her mouth turned up slightly at the corners. She wore a cream-colored dress with long sleeves. The heavy fabric outlined her curves, falling gracefully to her calves. Atop her head sat a small scrap of lace and fabric that could only be called a hat under the loosest of interpretations. She looked beautiful and elegant and he couldn't believe they were here together.

"Maybe it's you," she murmured. "After all, you're not so bad looking yourself."

"I'm sure that's it."

She chuckled and took a glass of orange juice from a tray circulated by a tuxedo-clad waiter.

Brenda's house was spacious. Her husband had joined Microsoft in the days when the computer firm was in its heyday. Their wealth was reflected in the elegant furniture and attractive artwork. But while Ashley admired the decorator touches, Jeff counted exits and planned escape routes. He knew there was no point, but old habits died hard.

"So tell me about this brunch," Ashley said. "She goes all out."

"It's a yearly tradition." He glanced around the crowded living room. "Most of the employees from the security company are here, along with a lot of people from her husband's work. The rest are friends and family."

"Do you come often?"

"No."

He didn't bother to tell her that this was the first time he'd attended. That combined with him showing up with a gorgeous woman and her daughter explained all the attention they attracted, but he wasn't about to tell Ashley that, either. From what he could figure out, she thought of him as relatively normal. He didn't want to do anything to change her opinion before circumstances did it for him.

"Well, well, fancy seeing you here."

Jeff held in a groan. Fate hadn't taken long to burst his bubble, he thought as he turned to greet his partner.

Zane Rankin stood with a young woman clinging to his arm. She was in her early twenties, with long blond hair and a chest so large, it threatened her ability to stay upright. Her scrap of a dress barely covered her from breasts to thighs.

Jeff turned and shook hands with his partner, then introduced Ashley. Zane's date, Amee—"No *y* just a double *e*"—giggled.

"Zane says you're really dangerous, like him. That you could kill someone with your bare hands."

Jeff shot Zane a death look that was depressingly ineffective. "This isn't the sort of place I can demonstrate that," he said coldly.

"Oh." The young woman glanced around at the crowd. "I guess not. It's Easter. I guess we have to be nice to each other today, you know?" She cuddled against Zane. "Maybe you can tell me about it later."

Zane leaned close her to ear. "Honey, I'll give you a personal tour of the vulnerable areas."

Amee giggled again. She disentangled her arm and touched Ashley's hand. "I have to go to the little girls' room. Want to come?"

Ashley shot Jeff a helpless look before following the other woman out of the living room. Jeff glared at his partner.

"Just once I'd like to see you with a woman whose IQ was slightly larger than her chest."

Zane grinned. "My normal response to that would be to say that I'd like to see you with a woman. But you're with one. I'm surprised, Jeff. And impressed. What you lack in quantity, you make up for in quality."

"Thank you."

Maggie raced toward him, a moplike ball of fur tagging along. "Uncle Jeff, Brenda said I can brush Muffin and we're going to watch a movie together."

She raised her arms as she approached and he automatically swept her up against his chest. Muffin raised herself up on her back feet, her front paws scrambling against his legs as if she, too, wanted to be picked up.

Zane raised his dark eyebrows. "Uncle Jeff, why don't you introduce me to this lovely young woman?"

Jeff would rather have left the brunch. Too many people were watching him, talking about the shock of seeing him with a child. He knew they were right, that he had no business being with an innocent like Maggie. But for reasons that weren't clear to him, the little girl wasn't afraid. He hoped he didn't do anything to change that.

"This is Maggie," he said. "Ashley's daughter. Maggie, this is Zane Rankin. I work with him."

Maggie's blue eyes widened. "Uncle Jeff is very important. He keeps bad men away. Do you do that, too?"

"Sure," Zane said easily. "But Uncle Jeff is the best."

Maggie snuggled close to him. "I know." She pressed her tiny rosebud mouth against his cheek, then motioned for him to put her down. "Muffin really wants to see the movie," she explained, gave him a quick wave, then disappeared into the crowd.

As soon as they were alone, Zane's gaze turned speculative. "I hadn't realized you and the kid were so close."

Jeff shrugged. "She's pretty easy to like."

What he didn't say was that Maggie terrified him. He didn't want to do anything to hurt her and the knowledge that he could was just one more thing that kept him up nights.

Zane looked as if he wanted to say something else, but then he stepped back. "The ladies have returned."

Jeff turned and saw Ashley and Amee approaching. Zane was watching them, as well, but Jeff noticed his friend was paying as much attention to Ashley as to his own date.

Something hot flared to life inside of his chest. It took him a moment to recognize the bitter heat of jealousy. No way, he told himself. Jealous of Zane? Ashley hadn't looked twice at the man. Besides, Zane would never try anything. Ashley wasn't his type. But despite the logic, the feeling remained, making him uncomfortably aware of being out of his element.

He wasn't prepared to be a part of society's mainstream, he reminded himself. The cries of the dead were never quiet and he would do well to remember that.

"Amee was telling me the most interesting things about your business," Ashley said as she stepped close to him. "Did you and Zane really single-handedly save the British royal family from certain death?"

Jeff shot Zane a questioning look. His partner grinned. "Okay, so I might have exaggerated the story a little."

Ashley moved close to Jeff. "How much? I want to hear the part where you threw yourself on the queen to save her from a flying bullet."

Amee beamed. "Aren't they just the bravest men? Zane has over a dozen scars. You should see them."

"Maybe another time," Ashley murmured.

Jeff looked into her eyes and saw the humor lurking there. "There was no incident involving the royal family," he said softly into her ear. "They have their own security."

"I figured as much, but Amee was so proud."

They watched as the blonde bombshell ran her manicured fingers up Zane's arm. "Zane's offered to show me what he does," the young woman said, "but I'd be too frightened."

"You mean, take you on an assignment?" Ashley asked, sounding doubtful.

"No. They have an executive training course in a couple of weeks." Amee sighed. "But it's just too scary for me."

Zane winked at Ashley. "Maybe you'd like to go. It's just for a weekend. You could check out what it is Jeff does with his day."

Jeff hesitated. His first instinct was to change the subject. No way did he want Ashley to see what he did in his world. She would be terrified. Which meant it probably wasn't a bad idea. Her being scared would be the safest way to end the relationship before he did something stupid and hurt her. Her current view of him wasn't based in reality. The weekend away would change that.

"I'm intrigued," Ashley admitted. "What happens during the training weekend?"

Zane shrugged. "It's no big deal. A dozen or so executives join us in the mountains. We have a special resort we use. It's rustic, but not unpleasantly so. We teach them some basics about staying safe, how to recognize a terrorist threat, that sort of thing."

"Why do I think it's slightly more complicated than that?" Ashley asked.

"You'd be perfectly safe," Jeff assured her. "If you're interested, I'm sure Brenda would be willing to babysit."

She stared at him. "Do you want me go?"

No, he didn't. But he also knew it was important that she saw a piece of his reality. Being around her was changing him, and not for the better. He was getting weaker, softer. If she saw the truth, she would back off.

"I think you'd find it interesting," he said. "There's nothing dangerous for the participants. It's not survival training."

"Are there bugs?"

He grinned. "Just little ones. You could take them."

"Okay. Sounds like fun. If Brenda doesn't mind watching Maggie, I'll go."

"Great." Zane gave her a thumbs-up. "I'll arrange everything."

Just then Brenda announced that brunch was being served in the main dining room. Jeff put his hand on the small of Ashley's back and ushered her toward the doorway. Amee said something about shoes and the subject was changed. But he couldn't stop thinking about the weekend retreat, two short weeks away. Nothing would be the same at the end of those forty-eight hours. He wasn't sure if his friend had done him a favor or just sent him a one-way ticket to hell.

Chapter 12

The site of the executive security camp was a lodge on the east side of the Cascade Mountains. As always, the weather was better than on the Seattle side. Ashley stepped into sunshine as she exited Jeff's BMW.

"Now here's something I haven't seen in a while," she joked as she raised her face to the warm rays.

The past few weeks had been typical for spring in Seattle. Plenty of cool days and lots of rain. The weather people kept hinting at sunshine but then changing the forecast.

Her feet crunched on the gravel parking lot as she moved to the rear of Jeff's car and waited for him to open the trunk. She glanced at the cars around them. "Lexus, Jaguars, Mercedes and…" she counted "three limos. So, Jeff, tell me about these clients of yours."

He pulled her shabby suitcase from the cavernous truck. His own bag was soft, black leather. It was so smooth to the touch, she wouldn't mind a coat in the same material.

"Executives," he said. "I told you that."

"Yeah, but I was thinking about my local bank branch manager. These people are way different."

He grinned. "I think one of our participants might own your bank. That counts."

"Oh, sure. We can have a detailed conversation about the way the ATMs seem to always go out at five o'clock on Fridays."

She looked at the lodge, noticing for the first time that it seemed much more elegant than rustic. She returned her attention to Jeff and realized he was dressed in one of his tailored suits. Why did she suddenly have a bad feeling that she was completely out of her element?

"Jeff, maybe I don't belong here."

He set his bag on the ground, then draped an arm around her. "Don't be nervous. You have as much right to be here as anyone else. They're all going to feel just as awkward because they're all out of place. This is combat, not the boardroom. My staff and I make sure everyone attending is clear on who are the experts."

She leaned into him, inhaling the familiar scent of his body. "Like that's making me feel better." She felt his mouth brush against the top of her head. Which did ease some of her tension. "So why are you in a suit?" she asked. "You told me to dress casual."

He had, in fact, insisted on jeans, sweatshirts and boots or athletic shoes. The sky might be a whole lot clearer on this side of the mountain, but the air temperature wasn't much warmer.

"I have to impress the clients during the introductory session. If I dress like them, they'll relax."

"So later you'll show up in your soldier's clothes?"

"I promise."

She glanced up at him and grinned. "Can I swoon?"

"Do you want to?"

"With every breath I take."

"Liar," he murmured, then kissed her briefly before releasing her and grabbing her suitcase as well as his own.

She followed him into the lodge.

The main room was huge, both wide and tall, soaring up three stories. On the far wall was a fireplace large enough to host a committee meeting. There was plenty of wood and trophy heads mounted on the wall. The reception desk stretched for about fifty feet. It was midafternoon on a Friday and the place should have been crowded. Instead she saw only one other guest. Jeff had told her they rented the entire place even though their client list was kept at less than twenty-five. She couldn't imagine what the executives were spending on the three-day course. Although if the information kept them alive, how could they put a price on the weekend?

This was Jeff's world and she was about to get an inside view of it. She couldn't decide if that was good or bad. Maybe—

Jeff stopped just short of the reception desk and turned to her. "What did you want to do about a room?" he asked.

Ashley blinked. "A room? I'd prefer to have one.

Sleeping in the car has never been my idea of a good time."

"Did you want one of your own?"

It took her a second to figure out what he was asking. A room of her own, as in did she want them to share a room?

"We're not at home," he continued, avoiding her gaze, which was so unlike Jeff. "I thought you might prefer to have the privacy."

He was nervous, she thought suddenly. And embarrassed, if his shuffling feet were anything to go by. She wouldn't have thought Jeff capable of either emotion.

"Will I be in the way if I stay with you?"

His gray gaze settled on her face. His look was so intense, it was almost like being touched by him.

"I'd prefer us to be together," he said, "but it's your call."

She raised herself on tiptoes. "Do you think they have a room with a mirror on the ceiling?"

He grinned. "I'll ask."

He moved to the reception desk. As he registered them, Ashley felt a fluttering sensation in the center of her chest. A warm, mushy kind of fluttering that occurred more and more when she was with Jeff. She knew what it meant and it scared her to death. She did *not* want to be falling for this man. Especially when she didn't know what he was feeling about her. She wanted to think that this mattered to him, that it was more than just casual, but she couldn't be sure.

"Ready?" he asked.

"What?"

She glanced around and saw that their bags had

been whisked away. He handed her a room key, then put his hand on the small of her back to urge her forward. They walked down a long corridor that led to the conference rooms. Double doors stood open. A young woman smiled and handed Jeff a clipboard and Ashley a name tag. Only her first name had been printed in block letters.

"Let's go," he said, and motioned for her to step into the conference room. Ashley prayed for courage, then did as he requested.

The room was about forty by forty, with several conference tables set up, facing front. About two dozen people stood talking in small groups. There were only two other women and they were both older than Ashley by at least a decade.

All the name tags had first names only, with no indication of who was whom or where anyone was from. She noticed several of Jeff's staff standing around the perimeter of the room. Zane was up in front, talking with one of the hotel staff. When he saw Jeff, he shook hands with the staff member and moved toward his partner. Ashley took a seat at the end of one of the tables. No one might be identified by location and occupation, but she could tell that everyone here was wealthy, powerful and probably tipped more than she made in a year. Why on earth had she let herself be talked into this?

"Welcome," Jeff said as he moved to the front of the room. "Ritter/Rankin Security is pleased to have you here for our executive security weekend retreat. I'm Jeff Ritter and this is my partner, Zane Rankin."

Everyone took a seat. A short, round man sat next

to Ashley. He appeared to be close to sixty and had the most gorgeous diamond pinky ring she'd ever seen. His suit looked softer than her flannel pj's and she would swear she'd seen his face in the international financial section of the Seattle paper. Please God, don't let him want to exchange business cards, she thought humorously.

"One of our staff members is moving among you, passing out a schedule for the weekend," Jeff continued.

Ashley took the offered notebook and opened it.

"We're here to teach you about being safe," Jeff went on. "In one afternoon and two days, you're not going to become experts. That's not our goal. What we want to teach you is preparedness and awareness. You need to know what kind of security you're going to need so you can hire the best available.

"The first lecture is on security preparation. We'll touch on various dangers, what is likely and what is unlikely to happen to you when you travel. We'll talk about threats to your family. We will also discuss the duties and responsibilities of a security detail.

"Later this afternoon we'll have our first session on weapons. This will occur at the firing range away from the lodge. You'll be handling everything from a handgun to a submachine gun.

"Saturday morning we'll focus on terrorist threats. Who, where, how and when. This will include information on both bombs and booby traps. Saturday afternoon is evasive driving.

"On Sunday everyone will participate in three different mock terrorist situations. The goal is to make you aware and cautious. If that means putting the fear of God into each and every one of you, all the better. Nobody dies on my watch. Any questions?"

Ashley had to consciously keep from letting her mouth drop open. She thought about all the time she'd spent with him and how they laughed and talked and made love late into the night. She was having trouble reconciling that man with the man in front of her. She'd wanted a chance to find out about Jeff's world. Now that she was here, it was a little late to be having second thoughts.

"When in doubt, trust no one," Zane said later that afternoon as he paced the length of the conference room. He pointed to a man in the front row. "John, tell me a bit about your business."

The man, a forty-something British executive, adjusted the front of his khaki-colored shirt and cleared his throat. "The company is a multinational software conglomerate. We have—"

"Any kids?" Zane asked, interrupting.

"Yes, three. Two boys and a girl."

"Any of them away at school?"

"One son is at Eton."

"You must be proud."

"I am. Margaret and I—"

"Margaret's your wife?"

"Yes. She and I have been most fortunate in that our children are..."

John's voice trailed off when he realized one of the security staff was typing into a laptop. Seconds later the printer shot out several pieces of paper.

"What is going on here?" he demanded, rising to his feet.

Zane took the pages and handed them to him. Then he turned his attention to the group. "John just gave the lives of his wife and children to a terrorist group determined to make its mark. In the time it took him to share some general information about his occupation, the type of company he worked for, the name of his wife and the number of his children, we were able to pull together a relatively complete file on him. The data bank already exists. Incomplete profiles are stored and as more details are learned, the profiles grow. One slip—a son in Eton, the name of a spouse—can bring it all together."

John flipped through the pages and swore softly. "I didn't know."

"Most people don't. You got off lightly this time. We've screened everyone. No lurking terrorists. Next time you might not be so lucky." He pointed to John's name tag. "That's why first names only." Zane turned to Ashley. "Tell us about yourself."

She couldn't help smiling. "I don't think I know you well enough to share any details. But thanks for asking."

"Exactly right," Zane said, winking at her. "Better to be considered rude than be found dead. Remember, if you don't know the person, don't take the risk. It's not worth it." He glanced at his watch and nodded at Jeff. "Let's switch subjects. If you'll turn to the next section in your notebooks."

"Security," Jeff said by way of introduction. "Having too much staff is just as useless as having too little. Don't get caught up in the game of looking good with an entourage."

He continued talking, but Ashley wasn't paying attention to his words. She was too mesmerized by how he looked. She took in the fatigues, the baseball-style military cap, the gun strapped to his waist. He was a stranger—a very exciting, very dangerous-looking stranger. He was—

Both sets of side doors burst open and nearly a dozen armed, masked men poured into the room. Someone screamed. Ashley thought it might have been her, but her throat was too dry. Her heart leaped into her throat, making it impossible to breathe.

Before she knew what was happening, the men were grabbing people and forcing them toward the rear of the room. Everything happened so quickly. There was a gunshot and a cry. Instinctively she turned to catch sight of Jeff. At first she couldn't see where he was but then she noticed him by the front wall. He was checking his watch.

She felt someone grab her arm and roughly thrust her toward the rear of the room. Seconds later a voice yelled, "Clear!"

Jeff looked up. "Thirty-two seconds. That's how long it took my men to collect you into an easily manageable group. Give them another twenty-five seconds and you'd all be dead."

The man who had been "shot" scrambled to his feet. He was one of the security staff. He patted his chest and grinned. "Blanks on a bulletproof vest. I didn't feel a thing."

"Now that I have your attention," Jeff said, "let's talk about buying the best. Don't be cheap. Get the best people and give them the most dependable equipment available. Newer isn't always better. Figuring out what they should have isn't your job—you have experts for that. But don't skimp. Yes, a clip that holds more bullets costs more. So what? Isn't your life worth that?"

He put down his clipboard. "Let's take a fifteen-minute break so that your heart rates can get back to normal."

Ashley pressed her hand to her chest and wondered if that would ever happen. At least her heart had returned to her chest. She moved over to the table set up with sodas and water. She opened a can of a diet drink and sipped. A few of the other participants chatted to each other while most pulled out their cell phones and made calls.

Zane walked over to where she stood and he grinned. "Great, huh? Did you ever feel so alive?"

"Yes," she said. "I felt very alive before I thought I was going to die. That was not my idea of a good time."

Zane laughed as he moved away, but she didn't think it was funny. She turned her attention to Jeff who was busy answering questions. For the first time she was starting to understand who and what he was. A warrior.

She remembered he'd told her Nicole had said he wasn't human. Ashley disagreed. He was very human. He was just better trained and more willing to die than most people. He was also very special. How many men like him would be willing to take the time to braid a little girl's hair or read her a story? How many would bother with things like Easter egg hunts or remember to compliment her on a new hat?

Yes, he was a warrior and she loved him.

Ashley closed her eyes against the sudden burning

behind her lids. She didn't want to start crying here, but emotion overwhelmed her. She loved Jeff. It was a thousand kinds of stupid and yet she hadn't been able to stop herself.

To make matters worse, along with the love came fear. She knew what she wanted in her life—someone who would love her completely, more than he'd ever loved anyone else ever. She desperately needed to be first in his life.

Was that Jeff? Did he care about her that way? She wanted to believe it was possible, but she wasn't sure. Could the warrior open himself that much? His life was so different from hers. She couldn't go where he went. Would he be willing to stay on her side of the line?

She felt a hand on her shoulder, turned and saw Jeff standing next to her.

"Are you all right?" he asked, concern deepening his voice.

She forced herself to smile. "Zane seemed to feel it was all a joke, designed to make us feel alive. I told him I was plenty alive enough before. If anything, the attack scared about three years of life out of me."

"That's the adrenaline. It's a powerful chemical, but it will fade."

She touched her chest. "So I'll be able to breathe without gasping?"

"Just give it a minute." He brushed his fingers against her cheek. "How are you holding up? Any regrets?"

"About four dozen, but I'm still enjoying myself. It's really different from my ordinary life."

"Are you surprised?"

"By the differences? No." She shrugged. "I knew

what you did, but I never understood the details. There are way too many ways to kill people."

"My job is to make sure that doesn't happen."

"Agreed, but is it what you do or who you are?"

She knew what she wanted him to say. Unfortunately she also knew what he was going to say.

"It's who I am," he told her. "That can't change."

"I know," she said with a lightness she didn't feel. "But a girl can dream."

He dropped his hand to his side. His gaze grew more intense. "What do you dream about, Ashley? What do you want?"

She wanted him to be different. To be an ordinary man who worked in a bank or a factory. She didn't want someone who saved the world because causes were often so much more important than people. She wanted him to be the kind of man who would love her back.

She was as foolish as a child crying for the moon.

"Pizza," she said at last. "The all-meat kind with sausage and pepperoni. What do think? Is there a take-out pizza place around here?"

At first she didn't think he was going to let her change the subject. But she suspected Jeff didn't want to discuss their differences any more than she did.

"I happen to know a great little place in town. We'll have it delivered."

"Sounds perfect." She turned away, then glanced at him over her shoulder. "And while we're waiting, we can take a bath…together."

"I've never been much for speeding," Ashley said uneasily the next afternoon. She eyed the souped-up dark town car parked in front of her, then glanced at the oval course laid out in a field about ten miles from the lodge.

The sealed concrete road went straight for about a quarter mile before curving through a series of turns. It disappeared behind a screen of trees, but she knew that on the far side of the track someone was spraying the surface with a slick mixture designed to make the tires slip. Assuming she survived that, the next section of the course would include an ambush, complete with gunshots and explosions. Being a passenger had been harrowing enough. Now it was her turn to drive.

She understood the point of the exercise. The people who took this course for real were powerful enough to be kidnapping targets. Should that happen on the road, they had to be prepared. This afternoon wouldn't substitute for a professional driving course, but it was an introduction. Ashley tried to find humor in the situation by wondering if the training would help her get a better parking place at the grocery store.

Zane patted her back. "You don't get special concession just because you're female."

She glared at him. "Did I ask for any?"

He shrugged. "You look kinda whiny."

She planted her hands on her hips. "Do you think annoying me is going to make me drive better?"

"It'll keep you from being nervous."

Jeff strolled over and glanced down at the list on his clipboard. "Ashley, you're up next as the driver. Are you ready?"

"Only if I get to kill Zane when I get back."

Jeff chuckled. "Is he getting on your nerves?"

"Like nails on a chalkboard."

"Were you scared?"

She looked at the big car and then at the course. "Maybe."

"So it worked."

She sighed. "I hate it when you two act all superior just because you're professional soldiers."

Jeff opened the driver's door and reached inside for the safety helmet. "Relax, concentrate and drive fast."

"Can I do just two out of three?" she asked.

"No. All three are required."

Grumbling under her breath, she fastened on the helmet, then slid behind the wheel of the town car. Two men, bankers from New York, got into the rear. Zane rode shotgun. Jeff stood at the side of the track with a clipboard in one hand and a stopwatch in the other.

"Whenever you're ready," he called.

Ashley nodded. She took a deep breath to try to ease the tension in her body. It didn't work. She wiped her damp palms on her jeans and tried to tell herself that this was just pretend. Nothing bad was going to happen. Except she knew that it could. One of the participants had overturned the other town car an hour before. No one had been hurt but the car had been totaled.

She glanced at her passengers. "Helmets on, gentlemen," she said.

When everyone was safely buckled in, she started the car and drove onto the track.

The purpose of the exercise was to feel what it was like to have to drive evasively. They'd all seen a video on the subject and watched a demonstration. Now they were being given a chance to practice it for themselves.

Based on the way the cars had fishtailed all over the road, Ashley knew she was in for a challenge.

"You're driving like a girl," Zane said blandly as she eased into the first curve.

She didn't bother looking at him. "This kind of strategy may work on your recruits," she said, "but as I am a girl, it doesn't do a thing for me."

As she left the first curve, she accelerated. The exercise was timed, but she would lose points for skidding off the road.

There were three *S* curves in succession, then a long straight section. At the end of it, the concrete glistened from the slick substance she would have to pass over. Gritting her teeth, Ashley floored the car, then eased up as they approached the oily mixture. She barely touched the steering wheel, so as not to change the direction of the car.

The vehicle moved straight for the first twenty feet, then began to slide off the road. Ashley had watched the other drivers try to fight with the car. Instead she guided it to the side of the road. Once they settled onto the dirt shoulder, she pressed on the accelerator. The tires had traction and she was able to steer around the last of the slick trap.

Only when she was back on the road did she risk glancing at Zane. He didn't react at all. "Not bad," he murmured.

Ashley allowed herself a grin. She knew she'd done a whole lot better than not bad. She was about to tell him so when gunfire exploded all around the car.

"Get down," she yelled.

A smaller vehicle pulled out next to her and moved close, trying to crowd her off the road.

She ignored the gunfire and the other car, instead concentrating on the track in front of her. She gunned the engine, shooting forward. There was an explosion off to her right, but Ashley ignored it. Another car came up on her right. She swung her car toward it, bashing it once, then sped off toward the finish line.

It was only when she'd stopped the car that she realized her heart was racing. She'd done it! She'd completed the course.

"What's my time?" she asked Zane.

"Three seconds behind Henry's."

"Three seconds?" She jumped out of the car and practically danced to where Jeff was standing with a clipboard of his own. "I'm right behind Henry. In second place."

"I know," he said without looking at her.

She slapped the back of her hand against his upper arm. "Come on." She leaned close. "Admit it. You think I'm pretty hot stuff."

He looked up. She saw the pride and affection in his eyes. "I'm more impressed than you know."

Chapter 13

A sharp cry cut through the night. Ashley's first thought was that this was yet another trick of Jeff's staff at the executive retreat. But when she opened her eyes, she recognized Jeff's bedroom in his large house on Queen Anne Hill. This wasn't a drill.

She blinked in the darkness and tried to figure out what she'd heard. Was Maggie having a bad dream? Her daughter didn't usually—

The cry came again, but not from down the hall. Instead, the sharp outburst of pain came from the man lying next to her. Ashley turned toward Jeff. As she did so, she glanced at the clock and saw that it was nearly two in the morning. Often she returned to her own bed to sleep, but tonight something had compelled her to stay with Jeff. Now, as she watched him fight with the covers and speak harsh, unintelligible phrases, she was glad she was there for him.

She reached out to touch his arm, then remembered the weekend they'd just spent together. He was very much a warrior. While she'd had clues about his skills before, now she had firsthand knowledge. She wanted to wake him up without finding herself in some kind of death grip. She knew he wouldn't deliberately hurt her, but she had no idea of the content of his dream. In the second or two it took him to return to reality, he could do a lot of damage.

So instead of touching him, she turned on the light sitting on the nightstand and softly spoke his name.

He came awake instantly. His eyes opened and he made a quick, visual search of the room. When his gaze settled on her, he stiffened.

"I was dreaming."

She nodded. "You cried out. Are you all right?"

It was only as she spoke the words that she realized he was both sweaty and ashen. The sound of his harsh breathing seemed to fill the room.

"Jeff? What's wrong?"

"Nothing. I'm fine."

He was anything but. She nibbled on her lower lip, not sure what to do with him. She couldn't force him to talk nor could she physically make him relax. Not knowing what else to do, she left the light on, but slid back under the covers and snuggled close to him. She lay with her head on her pillow but her arm across his chest. She pressed her legs against his and waited.

Slowly he began to relax. His breathing evened out and his heated body cooled. While she'd slipped on a nightgown after they'd finished making love, Jeff was still naked. She ran her fingers through the hair on his chest, pausing when she felt a long, slender scar running the length of his rib cage.

"What is this from?"

"A knife fight."

"Where'd you get it?"

"Afghanistan."

She sighed. "Jeff, was it like the dream you told me about before? The one where the village is burning and the people are running from you?"

"Yes."

He wasn't being overly chatty. "There's more to it, though, isn't there? You've had the dream before when I was with you and I don't remember you crying out."

He half turned away.

She raised herself up on one elbow and touched his cheek. "Jeff? You can tell me. I'm not afraid of you. If this is a privacy issue, that's one thing, but if it's about protecting me, I'll have to slap you."

Her last comment made him turn back to her. He smiled slightly. "Zane told me you were offended by all his 'girl' comments. I have to remember to inform him you don't take a lot of guff from anyone."

"That's right. I've had natural childbirth. I know about suffering. I don't think you can say anything to shock me. So if you want to talk, I'm happy to listen."

His smile faded and he closed his eyes. "It was a different dream," he said quietly. "A visitation from the souls of the dead."

At first she didn't understand what he was saying. And then she knew. The souls of the dead were from people he had killed. She settled back on the bed, resting her head on his shoulder.

"You were a soldier. You did what you were told."

"Does that make it right?"

"I don't know. I do know that it doesn't make you a monster. Despite your ex-wife's claims to the contrary, you're not inhuman."

He swallowed. "Maggie was there. In my dream. She was screaming for me to save her and I couldn't. Every time I got close enough to reach her, she saw me and ran away."

Ashley shuddered. She didn't want to hear any more. She didn't want to know what Jeff had suffered in the process of defending his country and doing his job. She wished there were a way to heal him.

"There's a psychological reason that Maggie has suddenly appeared in your dreams," she said. "You care about her and you want to keep her safe. I have a friend who has a recurring dream about losing a baby. Her kids are long grown and gone, but that doesn't ease the worrying."

"Knowing that doesn't make it any less real in the dream."

"I know." She pressed a kiss to his shoulder. "Jeff, I'm really willing to listen if you think it will help."

He didn't answer. She continued to hold him close. Eventually his eyes fluttered shut and she thought he might have gone back to sleep. She hoped so. He needed his rest. But after a time, he started speaking.

"I can't tell you anything more," he said. "I would never do that. If you knew the truth, you'd never be able to close your eyes again."

At first she didn't believe him, but then he turned to face her and she saw the truth of his words in his expression. She remembered all he'd talked about over the recent weekend. The lessons, the casually told stories. The professional attitude of a man who knows his subject. Suddenly she was cold. A shiver passed through her. She didn't want to know the horrors of his past.

Without meaning to, she recalled a lecture from the weekend. It had been about bombs and booby traps, and the damage they could do on the human body. Jeff's knowledge didn't come from a book; it came from experience. From watching people die. There had been so much horror and Jeff had been caught in the middle of it.

"I so want to make it better," she breathed, and touched his cheek. "Jeff, I don't know how."

He took her hand and pressed his mouth to her palm. In that moment, every last doubt she'd ever had faded as if it had never been. She was more sure than ever that she loved him. She'd probably loved him from the first. It didn't matter how he felt about her, if he loved her or not. He owned her, heart and soul.

"Why are you crying?" he asked, his voice a whisper.

She sniffed. "I didn't realize I was."

He brushed tears from her face. "Why?"

How could she explain? "Hearing about your past makes me sad. I want to fix it and I can't."

He collected more tears on his fingers then rubbed them against his thumb, as if testing if they were real.

"No one cries for me."

She wasn't sure if he was telling her that no one was supposed to cry for him, or if no one ever had.

"I can't help it," she said. "I feel your pain."

He frowned. "But I'm not like everyone else."

"I know."

"So you're disappointed in me?"

She couldn't help smiling. "No. I'm honored to know you. I'm honored to be a part of your life."

He shook his head. "I still don't understand the tears."

"I'm crying because I care."

Nearly a week later her words still didn't make sense. Jeff tapped his pen against the pad of paper in front of him. He had retreated to his study after dinner, supposedly to work. Instead all he could think about was Ashley and the strange conversation they'd had the previous Sunday night.

She'd cried because of him. He didn't understand that, nor did her saying she was crying because she cared make sense. As far as he could tell, nothing between them had changed. She was still sharing his bed, still trusting him with her daughter. He wanted to believe that everything was all right between them, but he wasn't sure. He had a sense of impending doom. He knew he was waiting for her to get angry and come after him.

Hadn't she gotten it? She'd spent the weekend with him, seeing him for what he was. If the lectures and demonstrations hadn't scared her away, his nightmares should have. Hell, he'd dreamed that Maggie was in danger, yet too afraid of him to allow him to rescue her. Didn't Ashley understand? Didn't she know that meant that when it really counted he was going to let her down?

He didn't want to. He would rather cut out his own heart than hurt either Ashley or Maggie, but he wasn't going to have a choice. He couldn't help himself. He wasn't like other men. He was—

The door to his study flew open. Ashley stepped inside and planted her hands on her hips. She glared at him.

Despite her obvious temper, he drank in the sight of her. She was beautiful, with her flashing eyes and flushed skin. Her sweater hugged her slender torso and her worn jeans outlined narrow hips. He couldn't help smiling when he saw the fluffy cow socks on her feet.

"Oh, sure, go ahead and laugh," she announced. "But you, mister, are in so much trouble."

His humor faded as if it had never been. This was it. She knew the truth and she was leaving him.

He didn't speak. What was he supposed to say? He'd always known it was going to end like this.

She walked toward the desk. "You're avoiding me. You've been avoiding me all week, and don't even think about telling me you're busy with work. What's going on?"

"I *do* have work," he insisted. "I have the Kirkman case. It needs my attention."

Ashley didn't even blink. "Sell it somewhere else. What's wrong? I've been thinking about the sequence of events in recent days. As near as I can figure it, you started acting weird last Monday. Which means it was after that dream you had. The one we talked about

What's the problem, Jeff? Did we connect? Are you concerned because I'm getting too close?"

She was, but not in the way she meant. He was waiting for her to figure out the truth about him and then run.

She sighed. "What is it? Are you mad at me?"

"No. Of course not."

"Oooh, he speaks." She glared. "Okay, you're not mad. What about having Maggie and me here. Are you changing your mind about that?"

Her question stunned him. He half rose to his feet before settling back in his leather chair. "I don't want you to move out. I enjoy having you here."

She took another step closer to the desk. "Finally we're getting somewhere. Okay, so you're not mad and you want us here. Are you happy?"

He wasn't even sure what she meant, let alone figuring out the emotion itself.

"I can see from your face that you're not," she said with a sigh, and settled into the chair opposite his desk. "Okay. Not mad, not happy, yet you still want me here. Care to explain all this?"

She was trying. He could tell that he'd confused her and he needed to make things more clear. The problem was he didn't know how.

"It's about the dream," he told her, staring at the desk, not wanting to see her expression. "I don't like that I have it. I don't like what it says."

"You mean you're uncomfortable about your past?"

"No." He sucked in a breath. "You saw my weak spot."

When she didn't say anything, he looked at her. She

stared at him blankly. He nearly groaned. How much more was he supposed to explain? Why didn't she get it? Weakness was danger. Weakness was to be despised. He wanted to be with her and he was terrified of her getting too close. He was a soldier and he needed a soldier's detachment. When he was around her, he couldn't stay detached. Not anymore.

For the first time in his life he was afraid. Of what was inside of him. Of losing someone important.

She leaned toward him and rested her arms on his desk. "Was the weakness that you shared it with me or was it what you talked about?"

"What we discussed."

She stared at him. "Okay. We talked about the dream and your inability to rescue Maggie. Is it that you failed?"

He shifted in his seat. Was she torturing him on purpose? "Yes."

"Are you afraid I'll use your perceived weakness against you or think less of you?"

He sprang to his feet. "Dammit, what else would it be?" he demanded.

She rose and glared at him. "Don't you yell at me. I'm not the idiot in this room. You are." She circled around the desk and pushed in front of him.

"I'm not the enemy," she said as she poked a finger into his chest. "Stop treating me like I am. Stop hiding out because you act like a human being. It's more than allowed. It's the sort of behavior I would encourage."

She placed her hands on his arms and tried to shake him. "Don't you get it? I care about you." She paused as if she wanted to say more, then continued. "I won't hurt you. I won't think less of you. In fact, I admire you very much. Maybe in soldier-speak you've violated some manly code. Maybe in that world, showing your softer side is dangerous. But when it comes to a personal relationship between a man and a woman, being vulnerable is generally a good thing. I want you to trust me the way I trust you."

"You trust me?"

She threw up her hands. "Is that *all* you got out of what I said?"

"No."

He'd heard every word; he just wasn't sure he believed it.

"Jeff, here's the news flash, so pay attention. I care about you *more* because of your confession. Knowing about your pain and the darkness in your soul makes me feel closer to you. It doesn't make me want to run away. So if that was your goal, you failed."

His throat was dry and it was difficult to speak. "What about the weekend? Did that change anything?"

"Zane got on my nerves a little, but aside from that, no, nothing is different." She paused and looked up at him. "I take that back. I think I have a clearer understanding of what it is that you do. I respect your abilities more. But that's it."

He felt as if someone had lifted the weight of the world off his shoulders. She wasn't mad, she wasn't running away.

"I'm glad," he said simply.

She smiled. "Prove it."

At first he wasn't sure what she meant. Then he saw the passion flaring in her eyes. She wanted him. She wanted to make love and have him touch her everywhere.

He didn't know how that was possible, but he wasn't about to ask questions or turn her down. Instead he wrapped his arms around her and picked her up until he could set her on the edge of the desk. Then he dropped his mouth to hers and kissed her.

By now he was familiar with the taste of her mouth. He slipped between her lips, savoring the soft sweetness waiting there. They touched and circled, performing a dance that was uniquely their own. Need filled him—a growing heat and desire that made his blood throb and that most male part of him flex against her belly.

She was perfect for him, he thought hazily as he broke the kiss and pressed his mouth to her jaw, then her neck. Everything about her was exactly right. The texture of her skin, the scent of her body, the way her hands rubbed against his chest, igniting fires before fumbling with his shirt buttons.

He grasped the hem of her sweater and tugged upward. She leaned back enough to allow him to pull the garment over her head and toss it to the floor. Her bra was next. He quickly unfastened the slender hook and slid the scrap of lace down her arms.

Her nipples were already tight buds, thrusting toward him in the faint coolness of the room. He cupped her breasts, absorbing their weight, their temperature and their silky smoothness. Need hummed hotter inside of him. He longed to rip the rest of her clothes from her body and thrust himself inside of her. But he held back. Giving Ashley pleasure first made his own release better. Not only was she slick and ready for him, he'd learned that once she climaxed, she would release again and again when he entered her. Those rapid contractions were the best part of making love with her.

He lowered his head and took her right nipple in his mouth. As he swirled his tongue around the beaded flesh, he settled his hands on her waist and began unfastening her jeans. Her fingers tangled themselves in his hair. She arched into his licking caresses, breathing heavily and murmuring his name.

With one quick tug, he shoved off her jeans and panties. She wore only socks scrunched around her ankles. The sight of her in them and nothing else was oddly erotic, so he left the socks in place. He shrugged out of his shirt and placed it on the desk behind her.

"Lie down," he instructed. "It's time I went to work."

She laughed even as she stretched out on the desk. He settled into his chair and pulled it close to her. She'd parted her legs and now he moved between them. He could already feel the heat of her arousal. She would be damp and ready for him. He knew exactly how sweet she would taste, how she would moan at the first stroke of his tongue, how her muscles would tense and her legs would draw back as she approached her climax.

Just thinking about how it would be made his own arousal tense painfully. Pressure throbbed at the base of his groin, but he ignored the sensation. There would be time for him later. Now he wanted to concentrate on Ashley.

He rested his hands on her belly and slid them up her body as he moved closer. As his fingers tickled her ribs, he nibbled his way up her thighs. First one side, then the other. Licking, kissing, biting gently. She gasped and giggled and breathed his name. Her hands settled on top of his, urging him higher until his palms settled on her breasts.

She shifted so that she could rest her feet on the arms of his chair, opening herself for him. He accepted the silent invitation and slowly licked her most feminine place. She gasped in pleasure. Her thighs parted more. He explored all of her, the place he would enter later, the sweet mysteries of her desire, before kissing that one spot designed to make her moan.

He found it easily, and knew exactly what to do. As his fingers toyed with her tight nipples, his tongue circled her center, moving over and around, teasing, rubbing, kissing, licking. He moved fast, then slow. He made her moan and then he made her beg. Only when her legs were trembling and her body slick with sweat did he give in to her demands and move in the steady rhythm designed to make her fall into ecstasy.

It took less than ten seconds. He licked her over and over, guiding her to her release. Then she shuddered in his intimate embrace. Her body quivered as her insides spasmed.

He held back as long as he could, waiting until she had finally stilled. Only then did he stand and reach for his belt. He fumbled with the zipper before finally unfastening it. As he shoved down his pants, he pushed the chair out of the way and urged her to wrap her legs around his waist. Bracing his hands on the desk, he stared into her beautiful face and plunged into her.

One deep, slow thrust that had them both gasping. She clamped her muscles around him and smiled. Her eyes were still glazed with the lingering aftershocks of her release. As he moved in and out of her, he watched her expression tighten. At the same time he felt her body convulse around his. She moaned. He swallowed hard and struggled for self-control.

She didn't make it easy. He knew that as long as he moved in and out of her, she would climax, rippling against him, drawing him in deeper, forcing him over the edge. He pulsed his hips, then swore, knowing it wasn't supposed to be this good and never wanting it to stop.

Wait, he told himself. Hold back. But he couldn't. Using her legs, she pulled him closer, sending him in deeper, then gave herself up to the release. As she breathed his name, he felt himself losing control. He grasped her hips and pumped hard and fast. The sound of his blood rushing through his body filled his ears. He couldn't think, couldn't breathe, couldn't do anything but feel the intense release as he spilled himself into her.

When he'd recovered, he bent over her and kissed her mouth.

"Amazing as always," she said with a sigh. "You are a man of many talents."

He touched her cheeks, her nose, then her lower lip. "I aim to please."

"You reduce me to a puddle. That's more than pleasing." Her hazel eyes darkened. "No more hiding away, okay?"

He couldn't deny her anything. Even when it made sense to do so. "I promise."

Jeff typed in his notes on the report the team had prepared. They were getting close to finishing up the security plan for Kirkman and his associates. The meeting was in several days.

His phone rang and he took the call, but when he was finished, he found it difficult to return to his report. He wasn't concentrating very well these days. Ashley was always on his mind.

It had been nearly a week since she'd accused him of hiding out. A week during which their relationship continued to complicate his life. He knew that he should give her up but he couldn't seem to find the words to tell her goodbye. While being disconnected was the safest course of action, he found himself resisting returning to his solitary world. He enjoyed the warmth and the laughter Ashley and Maggie brought to his life. He enjoyed the passion Ashley brought to his bed. He liked knowing she was home, waiting for him, thinking about him. He trusted her.

While he'd trusted men with his life on a mission, he'd never trusted a woman before. Not with his heart and soul. He could almost imagine himself doing that with Ashley.

There were times when he wondered what was going to happen. How would he survive her walking away? He thought that—

The door to his office flew open and Ashley raced into the room. While he took in the fury in her eyes, a part of his brain acknowledged that she burst into his life on a regular basis. She was fearless, which he admired. Hers was real courage—she was brave even when she had something to lose.

She slammed the door behind her. "What the hell were you thinking?"

Her rage was a tangible life force in the room with him. Jeff turned away from his computer so that he could face her. Even as he wondered what she was talking about, he realized she'd never visited him at work before.

"Ashley, what seems to be the problem?"

Her eyes flashed with fire. "Don't give me that. Don't pretend you don't know. What was it, Jeff? A game? Did you think it was funny? How dare you play with my life! Were you even thinking? Didn't you care that I had goals and a plan? Damn you."

He didn't know what was wrong. He rose and walked around the desk so that he was standing in front of her. Had she finally figured out that his dreams weren't strange images from his subconscious, but were, in fact, the truth? Had she realized he wasn't like other men?

Tears filled her eyes. She angrily brushed them away. "Say something."

"I still don't know what's wrong."

Her mouth thinned. "How like a man. What am I supposed to tell Maggie? Did you even give her one thought in all of this?"

At the mention of her daughter's name, his heart froze. "Is something wrong with Maggie? Is she hurt?"

"She's fine. This has nothing to do with Maggie." She shoved him away from her. "You and your big sob story. To think I bought into it. I'm such an idiot. You lied to me. How could you?"

"Ashley?"

She glared at him. "I'm pregnant."

Chapter 14

Ashley continued to talk but Jeff wasn't listening. He couldn't believe what she's said.

Pregnant?

He tried to figure out what, if anything, he was feeling, but he couldn't tell. It was as if his entire brain had shut down. Pregnant. He turned the word over and over in his mind wondering how it could be possible.

"And don't for a moment think that you're going to say something stupid like 'Who's the father?'" she said, still glaring at him. "You know exactly where I've been spending my nights. This baby is yours."

A baby. That was more real than hearing her say she was pregnant. Had they really produced a child together? A living being growing inside of her that would become an infant and grow into a child.

He hadn't thought he was human enough to father a child. He remembered what the doctor had talked about when there had been problems with Nicole. That he, Jeff, had a low sperm count. Something about less than optimal numbers. That it was unlikely he could father a child in the traditional manner, although there had been other alternatives if they'd been interested. By then, Nicole wasn't interested. She'd said that the reason he couldn't father a child wasn't about his sperm count but the fact that he was no longer human.

She'd been wrong.

Jeff had never thought to question the doctor further. Until Ashley had entered his life, he'd used condoms for health reasons. Although with her that had never seemed necessary. He knew he was healthy, so he hadn't worried about passing anything on to her. But he'd never considered that he might be able to get her pregnant.

"Are you even listening to me?" she demanded.

Something bright and alive flashed inside of him. It was hot and pure and it took him several seconds to recognize the feeling.

Joy. Pure, wonderful joy.

He grabbed her at the waist and swung her around the room. She shrieked and hung on to his shoulders.

"Jeff! Put me down. I'm not happy about this."

He knew, but he couldn't help smiling at her. "We're having a baby."

"I believe I was the one who informed *you* of that. Stop grinning like a sheep. This isn't good news."

He tried to sober. "I know. I'm sorry. I wasn't playing with you, Ashley. I didn't know I could get you pregnant. Based on what the doctor had told me before, I never thought it would be an issue. I really do have a low sperm count. If you would like the name and phone number of the doctor, I'll give it to you. I wasn't being irresponsible on purpose."

She pulled away from him and moved over to the leather sofa by the back wall. Once there, she sank onto a cushion and dropped her head into her hands.

"I know," she said softly. "I never thought you planned this. I mean I know I sort of implied it by what I said, but that was more shock and temper than anything else." She raised her head and looked at him. "You might not have many sperm but the ones you have seem frisky enough."

She drew in a shaky breath, then swore and started to cry. "I can't believe this is happening to me. I thought I finally had my life all together. I had so many plans for Maggie and myself and now I'm going to have a b-baby."

The last word broke on a sob. Jeff knelt beside her. As he had before when she'd cried, he touched her tears, marveling in her ability to feel so much. To let herself live in the world rather than outside of it.

"I know you're confused and upset," he said soothingly. He was neither. The path was obvious to him. He'd created this problem in her life and he was going to fix it. "You don't have to be. Your plans will be different now, but that's not necessarily a bad thing. I'll be providing for you, Maggie and the baby. You can finish your degree or not. It's your choice."

She blinked and several more tears ran down her cheeks. "That's crazy, Jeff. We're not your responsibility. Well, maybe the baby is, but not the rest of it."

"I want the responsibility. I want to take care of you. I want you to marry me."

Married? *Married!* Ashley stared at Jeff, unable to form any more words in her brain. Married?

"You want to marry me?" she asked, not able to believe what he'd said.

"Yes. As soon as possible."

She shook her head. When she'd first suspected the truth, she'd dismissed the possibility of being pregnant. Never one for a regular period, the length of time since her last one hadn't been much of a concern. But as the days had turned into weeks, she'd begun to wonder. Then yesterday when she'd stopped at the drugstore to buy vitamins for Maggie, she'd found herself in the family-planning aisle, studying the different pregnancy kits. Even as she'd told herself it wasn't possible, she'd bought one. Two hours ago, she'd had her hunch confirmed.

She'd been so angry, first at Jeff for what she'd thought were his lies, but mostly at herself. She knew better. She was smart and responsible. So why had she gotten so careless with something as important as birth control? She'd always wanted more kids, but not like this.

"You don't have to do this," she told him. "While I'd appreciate some help until I get my degree, marriage isn't necessary."

She wished he wouldn't talk about it anymore. She didn't want to be married to someone who didn't care about her. She didn't want to be an obligation.

He cupped her face in his large, strong hand. Despite not knowing how she was going to put her life back together, she couldn't help rubbing her cheek against his palm. If she had to have an unexpected pregnancy, she would prefer Jeff to be the father. At least she knew she was getting a very strong, intelligent gene pool.

"I want to marry you," he said, gazing into her eyes. "Not because it's the right thing to do, but because I don't want to let you go. I'm not willing to lose you, Maggie or the baby."

Happiness crashed over her like a wave. She flung her arms around him and pulled him close.

"You care!" she said, starting to cry all over again, but this time they were tears of happiness. "Oh, Jeff, I'd hoped you did, but I wasn't sure. You never said anything. You could be distant. I was afraid you were just in it for the sex."

She sniffed and straightened, then kissed him on the mouth, on his nose, on his cheeks, before hugging him again.

"I love you," she whispered fiercely. "I have for a long time. At least it's been coming on for a while. I knew for sure that weekend we went away. My very own warrior."

"Ashley."

He was the one to pull back this time. He wiped away her tears.

"You don't have to say this. I want to marry you."

"No. It's not because of the baby." She grasped his hands in hers. "Please don't think it's because of that or gratitude. I really mean it. I love you so much. You're everything I've ever wanted. I can't believe I got so lucky to find someone like you. Someone so good and strong. You're different from any man I've ever known."

She sniffed, then smiled. "I know the whole emotional thing is really hard for you, so I'm doubly honored that you would trust me with your heart. I swear, I'll never give you a reason to regret this. I'll love you forever."

He leaned forward and kissed her. "You make me very happy," he told her.

"And I'm even a pretty decent evasive driver," she teased, then kissed him back.

All her dreams were finally coming true, she thought as he pulled her close and hugged her. Jeff loved her more than anyone in the world. In his arms she could feel safe, loved and at home.

"Mommy, you have a secret," Maggie complained that night at dinner. "I can tell."

Jeff wasn't surprised the little girl had figured out something was different with her mother. Ashley practically glowed. Her smile was radiant, her step extra bouncy, her conversation excited.

"A secret?" Ashley said, her voice teasing. "You think so?" She turned to smile at him, a smile full of adoration. "What do *you* think, Jeff? Is there a secret?"

He knew she was playing a game and wanted him to be a part of it. But he couldn't be as lighthearted about the situation. He was confused and felt guilty. Which didn't make sense because he'd been telling the truth when he'd said he would marry her. He *wanted* to marry her. However, she thought he loved her.

Love. Jeff didn't know what the word meant. Not anymore. Perhaps there had been a time when he'd been a part of a family, just like everyone else. Those long-ago memories didn't have any place in his current reality. So when she said she loved him, he wasn't sure if he understood what that meant.

He believed in Ashley's capacity to love. He'd seen it firsthand with Maggie. Ashley was patient and caring. She'd seen him at his worst and she was still here. Wanting to be with him. Claiming to love him.

"Mommy, tell me!" Maggie pursed her lips together in a scowl. "I want to know!"

Ashley pulled her daughter onto her lap and hugged her. "Okay. It's a really good secret. I think you're going to be very happy."

Maggie's blue eyes widened. "Are we getting a kitten?"

"No. It's better than that."

Now that Ashley had Maggie's attention, she hesitated. Jeff knew her well enough to know that she was searching for the right words. She wanted to explain the situation simply and in a way that left the four-year-old feeling safe.

He was glad he wasn't the one who had to figure the best way to say it. Words had never been his strong suit. Actions had always been easier.

As Ashley started talking about how nice it had been to live in "Uncle Jeff's" house, he studied them. The overhead kitchen light illuminated their faces, making the similarities between them easy to spot. How much would their child look like Ashley? Or would the child look like him?

The questions startled him, reminding him again of the fact that he and Ashley were going to have a baby together. He dropped his gaze to her flat stomach. A baby grew in there. He was still stunned that he'd been able to get her pregnant. Now that she and Maggie were going to be a permanent part of his world, he was determined to take care of them.

"Well," Ashley was saying, "what if we never had to leave Uncle Jeff's house? What if we lived here for always?"

Maggie looked at him, her rosebud mouth parting. "We can stay? Promise?"

His throat tightened. The sensation was unfamiliar. "I'd like that."

Ashley tucked a curl behind her daughter's ear. "Maggie, I love you very much. I will always love you."

"I know, Mommy. I love you, too."

"I also love Jeff. And he loves us. I'm going to marry him."

Jeff waited, his throat tight, his heart seemingly still. He and Ashley had discussed waiting to tell Maggie about the baby. She would need time to get used to her new family before having to adjust to having a younger sibling.

Maggie looked at him. "Will you be my daddy when you and Mommy get married?"

Odd feelings crashed through him. He couldn't identify any of them so he didn't know what they meant. However, they made it tough to talk. He had to swallow a couple of times before he could get out the words.

"Would you like that?"

She threw herself at him. "When we went to church on Easter I asked God to send me a new daddy, and he did!"

Her small arms wrapped tightly around his neck. Her weight settled on his body. He hugged her back. With a fierceness that surprised him, he vowed to himself he would always keep this precious child safe. If that wasn't love, it was the best he could do.

"So you're okay with this?" Ashley asked. "You're happy that I'm marrying Jeff?"

"Daddy," Maggie said, planting a sticky kiss on his cheek. "You're marrying Daddy."

Tears filled Ashley's eyes. She wrapped her arms around them both. For the first time in many years, Jeff felt as if he was a part of something important and special. Daddy. The word felt both odd and right.

He shifted so he could reach his suit jacket, hanging behind him on the chair back. In the right outside pocket was a small box. He'd stopped to pick it up on his way home. Now he grabbed the box and held it out to Ashley.

Both females stared at the square of dark blue velvet.

"What is it?" Ashley asked.

"What do you think?"

She shrugged, then lightly touched the top of the box. "Maybe an engagement ring?"

"Got it in one."

He was suddenly nervous. Should he have waited and asked her if it was all right to buy her a ring? Should he have taken her shopping with him? He'd actually just stopped to look when he'd seen the elegant design and had known right away that it was perfect for her.

"Open it," he told her.

She took the box and did as he requested. Both Ashley and Maggie gasped as she drew out an emerald-cut diamond on a platinum band. Smaller baguette-cut diamonds were set into the band. Light caught the larger gem and made it glow.

"It's gorgeous," Ashley breathed.

"Do you really like it?"

She looked stunned for another second or two, then threw her arms around his neck and hugged him close. "Jeff, it's so beautiful and way too expensive. You didn't have to do this for me."

"I wanted to."

"Thank you. You've made me very happy."

Her scent, the feel of her body, the pressure of her mouth on his were all familiar. They filled him with a confidence that he'd never felt before. In that moment he knew he could take on the world and win.

"Oh, Jeff."

Ashley snuggled against him in his bed. She curled herself around him, resting her head on his shoulder and gazing up at her engagement ring.

"I still think you spent way too much money."

"I don't, and it's my money. At least until we get married."

She turned and looked at him. "No. It will always be *your* money. I want you to keep everything you made before the marriage separate. That way it's not community property."

He frowned. "Why would you want that?"

"Because I'm not marrying you for your money. I love you. But if I start asking for things or taking what's yours, you'll start to question me, and I don't want that. Everything has happened so fast. Your last experience with marriage wasn't exactly positive. I want this to be different. I want it to be forever. So I need you to trust me."

He smoothed her hair off her face. "I trust you with my life," he said. Didn't she know that trusting or not trusting wasn't the problem?

"Good. Then keep everything you have now in your own name and it will never be an issue between us. Besides, in a couple of years I'm going to be the one making the big bucks, and then you'll be worried about *me* thinking *you're* in it for the money."

She grinned and he couldn't help smiling in return. What twist of fate had brought this beautiful, giving woman into his life? How had he gotten so lucky as to have won her heart and that of her daughter?

"Speaking of my career, or the training thereof, I have finals in a couple of weeks." She rested her hand on his chest and her chin on her hand. "I have to really buckle down and study, so I was thinking we could get married after that. Or did you want to wait longer?"

"I will marry you whenever you say," he told her. "After finals works for me. What do you want to do?"

She wrinkled her nose. "Something small is fine with me. Maybe just a couple of friends with a justice of the peace and then we all go out to dinner?"

"What about a honeymoon?"

She arched her eyebrows. "What did you have in mind?"

"A couple of nights somewhere by ourselves. Maybe San Francisco. Then a week or so with Maggie."

She sighed contently. "This is why I want to marry you. You're such a great man, Jeff. Thoughtful and caring. It means a lot to me that you're willing to bring Maggie."

"I wouldn't want to leave her behind."

"I agree." She hesitated, then ran her free hand through the hair on his chest. "Do you think we did the right thing, not telling her about the baby? I mean, there's plenty of time. I won't really be showing until I'm well into my fourth month."

"The wedding is enough for her right now."

"Okay. That's what I thought, too." She looked at him. "What about your family? Do you want to tell them about us? You've never said very much about them. Are you seriously estranged?"

His family? He hadn't thought about them over the past few years. "No one got angry and stalked out," he said, "if that's what you're asking. My visits made my folks uncomfortable so I stopped going."

"Why?"

"For the same reason Nicole divorced me. I was different."

"I bet they'd like to see you now," she told him. "It's been a long time and I'm sure they miss you. Maybe you could give them a second chance."

He shrugged. He didn't have an opinion one way or the other.

"You're their son," she persisted. "You matter. They love you."

"Do they?" he asked, because he wasn't sure. "What does that mean? What do you feel when you say you love me? How can you be sure?"

She laughed and rolled onto her back. "I'm sure because it's written in the stars. Because I hear the sound of the ocean when we're together, not to mention a choir of angels."

"No. Seriously. What do you feel? How do you know?"

She sat up, leaned against the headboard and pulled the covers up over her bare breasts. Her humor faded and her eyes darkened. "You're not joking? You really want to know what I feel when I say I love you?"

He nodded.

"Jeff?" She paused and licked her lips. "Why are you asking me that?"

Her voice sounded very small. He could see her pulse beating in her throat. As she watched him her heart rate increased and her skin paled.

He knew then that he'd made a huge mistake pursuing that line of questioning. He wished he could call back the words and talk about something else.

"You don't love me," Ashley breathed. Her hands tightened around the covers she held in front of herself. "Dear God, why didn't I see it before? You don't love me. You want to marry me because of the baby."

"No," he said quickly, even though it was true. "I care about you and Maggie very much. You're both important to me. More important than anyone has been in a long time. Maybe ever. I want to keep you both close and take care of you. I want to be there for you, your daughter and our child. I want to learn to be a good husband and father."

Tears filled her hazel eyes. "But you don't love us."

Deep inside of him something began to ache. He knew that if he told her the truth, he risked losing her. But he couldn't lie.

"I don't know how. I don't know what love is. I feel something," he said, touching his chest. "I want you.

I miss you when we're apart. I want the best for you, Maggie and the baby. Is that love?"

Ashley felt the tears on her cheek. She told herself to say something, to scream, to run, but she was immobilized by disbelief and shock. All her life she'd wanted only one thing—to be loved by someone who would love her more than anything else in the world. Foolishly she'd given her heart to Jeff even knowing that he wasn't likely to care about her that way. When he'd proposed, she'd allowed herself to believe that he was more than she'd imagined.

She thought she'd finally found everything she'd ever wanted in the world, but she'd been wrong. It was all just an illusion.

"I can't," she murmured, not sure what she was saying she couldn't do. Stay? Marry him? Keep breathing?

Feeling returned to her limbs—a tingling pain as if they'd been asleep for a long time. She forced herself to climb out of bed and reach for her robe. Her body ached and it was difficult for her to walk.

"Ashley, where are you going?"

"To my room. I have to think." She had to figure out how everything had gone so terribly wrong.

Jeff lay in the darkness, listening to the silence in the house. Ashley had left him several hours before. While he knew what had gone wrong, he didn't know how to fix the situation. Was he supposed to go after her? Should he try to explain? Except what was there to say?

She wanted a piece of his heart. He'd figured out that much. He would have offered all of it, had it been his to give. But that tender organ had long since died, leaving him only a hollow shell of a man. There had been no other way to survive the horrors of what he'd seen and experienced. He'd ruthlessly cut out any delicate feelings because they were dangerous. He'd had to become a machine to survive. Now he was in a situation that required him to be a tender man and he no longer remembered how.

He rose and walked to the window. The night sky was surprisingly clear. He studied the stars as if the answers could be found there. Cold seeped in through the glass. He shivered.

Suddenly the coldness came from within. It was thick and dark and froze him to the center of his being.

She would leave him now.

Jeff leaned his forehead against the cool glass and held in the cry of anguish. No, he thought. She couldn't go. If she left, he would not survive. He could not. Without her he would turn into the robot of his nightmares. Without her he wouldn't have a chance.

Hurrying, he left his room and found his way to hers. The light was off, but she wasn't asleep. He could hear the soft sound of her weeping. Without saying anything, he climbed into her bed and pulled her close. She came to him willingly, holding him tight, pressing her cheek against his chest.

"Stay," she whispered.

"I will. Just don't leave me."

He breathed in the scent of her, the heat of her, needing her to chase away the chill. But the ice lingered, fueled by her tears and his knowledge that nothing had been resolved.

Chapter 15

Three days later Ashley was just as hurt and confused as she'd been when she first realized that Jeff didn't love her. What was she supposed to do? Stay with him? Marry him anyway, knowing that he didn't love her? They were going to have a child together, which meant something to her. She thought it meant something to him. And Maggie adored him.

She pushed aside her accounting theory textbook and rose to her feet. With all the emotional conflict in her life, she was having a difficult time studying. Maybe a break would help.

She went in search of Jeff and Maggie. He'd offered to take care of her daughter for the evening, giving Ashley time to study. She'd appreciated the offer and had accepted. Not only so she could hit the books, but because she found it difficult to be with Jeff these days. She kept trying to figure out what he was thinking and feeling.

As far as she was concerned, the formula was simple. If he didn't love her, she wasn't staying. They could work out some kind of arrangement for their child later, but she wouldn't be married to a man who didn't love her. So why was she still here? What was she waiting for? Was it inertia, or something more? Was she stalling for time because she was hoping for a miracle, or did she really believe that Jeff's feelings were deeper than he realized?

Ironically, while her life before Jeff had been more difficult financially, in other ways it had been a whole lot easier. Her choices had been simple. Now she found herself deciding one minute to stay because she couldn't imagine life without Jeff, then the next minute, telling herself they would leave in the morning.

She walked into the family room. Jeff and Maggie sat on the floor, her daughter on his lap, his back pressed against the sofa. They were watching a cartoon movie based on the Tarzan legend.

Maggie was draped across Jeff, her head leaning trustingly against his chest. One of his big hands rested on her belly and she absently tugged on his fingers. On the floor lay a half-dozen dolls in various stages of dress, surrounded by scattered clothes. Obviously they'd been playing one of Maggie's favorite games of pretend: Fashion Show.

Ashley couldn't help smiling as she imagined Jeff fumbling with the miniature fastenings of the small but intricate clothing. Yet she knew without having been in the room that he'd been patient with Maggie, following her lead and making her feel special. She knew that he would have little interest in the Tarzan movie, yet he would watch it as if it was a matter of world peace. That next week he would willingly watch it again.

She leaned against the door frame and folded her arms over her chest. She wanted answers. Ashley shook her head. No. She wanted a sure thing. She wanted to know that Jeff was the one. As if there were only one perfect person. She didn't want to make a mistake; she didn't want another loser in her life.

She wanted him to promise that he would love her forever. And when he couldn't say the words, she wanted to leave him. But what about his actions? What about the fact that when it had really counted, he'd show up for both her and Maggie? What about every kind thing he'd done? What about how he'd taken her into his world, afraid it would drive her away, yet needing her to see the truth of what he did? What about him wanting to marry her because he'd made a baby with her?

He was, she realized, the most honorable man she'd ever known. How could she have doubted him?

Jeff might not know how to tell her how he felt but he *showed* her every day. And isn't that what mattered? Wasn't it all about actions rather than any slick words? He might not know the state of his heart, but with every kindness, every moment of caring and patience, he demonstrated what he felt.

"Ashley?"

She looked up and saw that he'd seen her. She read the questions in his eyes. Things hadn't been right since they'd had that late-night talk. She glanced at her daughter and knew this wasn't the time.

"I just wanted to say hi," she told him. "And that I love you."

Hope flared in his eyes. "Still? Even..." His voice trailed off.

"Still," she assured him and felt contentment. He was the one she wanted, for always.

After Maggie was in bed that night, she went searching for him. He was in his study, going over some papers. As she approached, he set down his pen.

"We have to talk," he said.

"I know." She circled around the desk and slipped onto his lap. Then she wrapped her arms around his neck and kissed him. "I've decided that we're going to be all right. You need some time to come to grips with all that's happened between us. It's been fast and a real change. I understand that. You've spent the past, what, fifteen years living like some Rambo guy. Family life is going to be an adjustment. I trust you. Completely."

"I'm glad," he said, setting her on her feet and standing next to her. "Because we have to go over a few things before I leave."

"Leave?"

"My trip to the Mediterranean. The Kirkman case."

"Oh. Yeah. You told me." In all the emotional trauma, she'd forgotten. She followed him over to the leather sofa and settled next to him. She pointed to the folder waiting on the coffee table. "State secrets?"

"No."

"A security plan?"

"Not exactly."

She tilted her head. "Okay. You're not being wildly chatty. Why don't you take over the conversation."

"I want to talk about my will." He opened the folder and drew out a thick document. "I saw my lawyer yesterday to get a new will. I've left everything to you, except for two separate life insurance policies I had set up for Maggie and the baby. You're the trustee for both policies. It should be enough to cover raising them, along with college."

She stared at the document, but couldn't make it come into focus. A will? "I don't understand."

"If things don't go well, I want you to be taken care of. The business is set up with an automatic sale of my half to Zane, if something happens to me, and the same if he dies. You'll receive the proceeds from the sale, along with the house. I have a 401k, investments, checking and savings accounts. Brenda will get in touch with my financial adviser if anything happens, and Jerry can walk you through it all."

"No." She pushed the folder away. "I don't want to talk about this. Not now. I told you. I'm not interested in your money."

His gray gaze was steady. "I understand that, Ashley, and I believe you. However, if I don't come back, I want you taken care of."

If I don't come back.

She slid into the corner of the sofa. "Don't come back? What are you talking about?"

He sighed. "Probably nothing. This isn't an extremely high-risk operation."

Operation? "Are we talking about your business trip?"

"It's a security detail. These men are very highly placed. There have been both death and kidnapping threats. We've prepared for the worst and I'm sure everything will be fine. But if something happens, I want you to have financial security."

She sprang to her feet. "No. I don't want financial security. I want you to come back."

"I'm sure I will."

She pointed to the folder. "You're *not* sure. That's why we're having this conversation. Jeff, are you telling me that you could die on this trip?"

He shifted uncomfortably on the sofa. "It's unlikely."

"How unlikely?"

"Less than a thirty percent chance."

Her mouth dropped open. Thirty percent? There was a thirty percent chance he could die? While he was gone?

"No," she said firmly. "No. You can't go. You cannot die. Not until we're both old. I don't want you to die." She'd just found him. She refused to lose him.

"Ashley, be reasonable. This is what I do."

"You're crazy, then. How can you walk out on Maggie and me? And what about the baby?" She paced to his desk, then spun to face him. "You can't. You just can't. Dammit, Jeff, you're not some solitary soldier giving his all for God and country. This is just some assignment. You can't leave like this. It's wrong. You have a responsibility to us. We need you to come home to us."

"This is what I do."

"No, it isn't. You run a security company. You have a staff. You have other people to do this kind of thing."

"So I should send someone else out there to die?"

She felt as if he'd hit her in the stomach. She clutched her midsection and bent at the waist.

He was going to die. That's what he was trying to tell her. The claim of it only being a thirty percent chance had been a lie designed to calm her fears.

"Ashley—"

"No!" she shouted, straightening and glaring at him. "All my life the people I've cared about and loved haven't loved me back. Not enough to stay. Not enough to keep from dying. I thought you were different. I thought you really cared, but because of your background you couldn't get in touch with your feelings. But now I know that I was wrong. You can't express your feelings because you don't have them. I thought you would change and realize you love us, but you won't. You don't love us. You're going to leave me and die, just like everyone else. You don't think I'm worth living for."

He rose. "You're wrong. You are worth living for. I have every intention of coming back to you."

"That's not good enough. I don't want you to go."

"I have to go. It's my job." He hesitated. "You knew what I was before, Ashley. Nothing has changed."

"Yes, it has." Before, she hadn't realized the truth. "Loving someone means wanting to stick around."

As soon as she said the words, she braced herself for him to say he didn't love her at all, so what did staying matter. But he didn't. Instead his expression turned sad.

"I would have thought loving someone meant accepting every part of that person," he said. "You knew who and what I was when you first met me, so I don't understand why it's suddenly a problem. It's ironic. Nicole could accept what I did, but not what I'd become. You understand who I am, yet you won't accept what I do. I guess we both expected more of each other."

Ashley felt as if he'd slapped her. She'd been so sure she was the one in the right and that he was wrong. But his words caught her off guard. Too stunned to speak, she could only watch as he walked out of the room.

Jeff waited the entire night, but she never came to him. He'd tried to go to her, but her door had remained closed and she hadn't answered his light knock.

The next morning he packed his suitcase and made his way downstairs. He'd left the folder on the coffee table in his study. If something happened to him, he wanted Ashley to be able to find it.

She was in the kitchen with Maggie. The dark circles under her eyes told him that she, too, had had a restless night. As they stared at each other, he wished he could find the words to make it right between them. He wished there was a way to explain why he had to do this job—why he had to do every job. That stepping into the line of fire was the only way to atone.

Maggie saw him and scrambled out of her seat. "Daddy, Daddy, Mommy says you have to go away and I don't want you to go."

She flung herself at him. With an ease he wouldn't have believed possible just a couple of months ago, he set down his suitcase, bent low and picked her up, swinging her into his arms. She clung to him.

"Don't go," she said, her big blue eyes filled with tears.

"I have to. This is about work. But I'll be home in about a week."

"A week is a very long time."

"I know. I'll miss you."

As he spoke he looked over her head toward Ashley, but the woman who had so changed him wouldn't meet his gaze. She sat at the table, carefully stirring her coffee.

Maggie rested her head on his shoulder and sighed. She was so small, he thought uneasily. How could she possibly survive? He found himself wanting to stay, to make sure that she was going to be all right. But he couldn't. He had a job to do.

"I'll bring you something," he told her as he set her on the floor.

She brightened immediately. "A kitten?"

"No. Mommy and I have to talk about that first. But something nice."

"Something for Mommy, too?"

He looked at Ashley. She was still staring intently at her coffee. "Yes, something for Mommy."

Jeff hesitated. He wanted to say something that would make things better between them. He wanted to heal the breach, but he didn't know how. In the end all he did was pick up his suitcase.

"I need to get to work. I'll guess I'll see you in a week."

"Will you call?" Ashley asked without looking up.

Phone her? He'd never considered the possibility. But he could. Staying in touch would be easy.

"Sure." He calculated the time difference. "Say the early evening, after dinner?"

She nodded. "That would be nice. Thank you."

He wanted to go to her and pull her to her feet and into his arms. He wanted to beg her to tell him that she wouldn't give up on him, that it wasn't over between them. He wanted to know how he was supposed to make her happy when everything about their relationship confused him.

Instead he said nothing. He turned on his heel and walked out of the kitchen. Maggie called after him.

"Mommy and I love you."

He could only hope it was still true.

Six hours later he pored over the diagrams of the villa one last time. The private jet would take off from Boeing Field at four. The team was already assembled, the equipment checked.

"I can't believe you're doing this," Zane said as he walked into Jeff's office.

"What are you talking about?" he asked his partner.

Zane stalked over to the table and stabbed at the papers. "I can't believe you're really going to do this."

"The job? It's my responsibility."

"No. It's *our* responsibility. I'm a partner in this, remember. I can do this job." Zane glared at him. "It was bad enough when you wanted all the glory for yourself, but now you have a family to think about."

Glory? "Is that what you think?" Jeff asked. "That taking the most dangerous assignments is about glory? I never wanted my name in the papers. None of that mattered."

Zane's dark eyes were bleak when he spoke. "If it's about the dead, don't you think I have some ghosts of my own? Just because I was a sharpshooter doesn't mean I wasn't involved. Killing from a distance is still killing, Jeff. When I had to plan operations, the numbers of the dead weren't faceless. I studied the recon photos afterward to see how my plan had been carried out. I could see what I'd done in every shade of color."

Jeff stared at his partner. "I hadn't realized," he said.

Zane shrugged. "Before, it wasn't important for you to know, but things are different. You have Ashley and Maggie now."

And the baby, but Zane didn't know about that yet. A family. That's what his partner was saying. Jeff had responsibilities for more than the job. At one time he would have agreed, but not now. Ashley might claim to love him, but he doubted it was true. She loved parts of him. The parts she could admire. But the true blackness of his soul was beyond her. He thought she understood who and what he was, but he'd been wrong. She was already pulling away.

What he couldn't admit to Zane, what he could barely think to himself, was how much it hurt. He'd allowed himself to believe. When she'd heard about his nightmares and hadn't turned away, he'd experienced his first spark of hope. Later, instead of being frightened off by the executive retreat, she'd had fun. He'd told her more details about his past and still she'd stayed, eventually claiming to love him. And he'd believed her because he'd been desperate to keep her in his life.

But in the end, she couldn't handle what he did. She wanted him to change, to take a job that wouldn't put him in danger. She wasn't willing to love all of him.

"I don't think Ashley and Maggie are going to be

sticking around much longer," Jeff said, gathering up the diagrams. "Ashley doesn't approve of these kind of missions."

"Can you blame her? Who wants to see someone she loves facing down a bullet?"

"It's what I do."

"That's complete bull and you know it. You choose how you participate in the assignment. You hire the best and train them to be better, then instead of letting them get on with their job, you meddle." Zane took a step closer to him. "You know what I think, Jeff? I think you're afraid. You care about Ashley and her daughter and that scares you. You've never had to care before. Suddenly, after all these years, you have something to lose. What if your edge is gone? What if at the last minute you don't want to take the bullet? But instead of celebrating the fact that you have a chance at a normal life, you walk away."

Zane glared at him in disgust. "You're an idiot. Don't you get it? Chances like this don't come along very often."

"You don't have anyone in *your* life," Jeff said, trying to ignore the truth of his friend's words.

"You're right. Because the one person I was supposed to be with died. There's not a single day that goes by without me thinking about her, wishing things could be different. I lost my chance. What's your excuse?"

Jeff wasn't sure what to say. "I'm sorry," he mumbled. "I didn't know."

"Yeah, well, now you do. So quit being a jerk who would rather take a bullet in the back than admit he might have fallen in love."

* * *

Ashley couldn't get Jeff's words out of her head. She kept telling herself that he was wrong, that she hadn't betrayed him. She was the injured party. But no matter how many times she told herself that, she couldn't quite make herself believe it.

She paced the length of the kitchen, ignoring her open accounting books. While she knew she should be studying, she couldn't stop thinking about Jeff. Thinking and watching the clock. His plane would take off in less than two hours. After that she wouldn't see him for a week…or maybe not ever again.

"I can't go through this," she said, squeezing her eyes shut. "I can't sit around waiting for him to die. All I wanted was someone to love me back. To want to live for me and love me more than anyone. An unconditional love."

She opened her eyes and stared unseeingly out the window. Jeff was never going to love her that way.

She wanted to scream her frustration. She wanted to throw something. She knew in her heart she wasn't as angry about his work as she was about the loss of her dream. She'd thought they would have a chance, but she'd been wrong. Damn the man for not loving her on her timetable and in the way she'd always imagined. Didn't he know he was messing with her lifelong dream? Ever since her sister had died, she'd ached to feel safe again. But with Jeff running off to throw himself in front of a bullet, she could never feel that way.

She could never—

Ashley froze in the center of the kitchen. She blinked

once, then again. She wanted Jeff to love her on her timetable. She wanted him to love her unconditionally. *She* wanted.

But what about Jeff? Didn't he deserve the same wants and desires? Wasn't he entitled to a love that encompassed all of him, not just the parts she really liked? Who was she to dictate his life? As he'd pointed out the previous night, she'd known what he was when she'd met him. So why was she so angry about it now? Was it possible that she wanted to be loved unconditionally without doing the same in return?

As if showing a movie, her brain flashed pictures of her time with Jeff. From the first moment they'd met, he'd been giving, gentle and kind. He didn't know how to be a husband or a father, yet he was willing to take on both jobs. The second she'd told him about the baby, he'd wanted to marry her. In the past couple of months, he'd started to change, opening up more, feeling more. Perhaps he didn't know what was in his heart; perhaps he could never say the words. But she knew. He was a man deeply committed. He was a man in love.

How could she have been so incredibly stupid? Was she really going to let him walk out of her life, possibly get killed, thinking she was mad at him? He was everything she'd ever wanted. Why on earth was she willing to let him go?

She glanced at the clock and panicked. There wasn't much time.

"Maggie?" she yelled, running toward the family room. "We have to go out right now. I want us to say goodbye to Jeff."

* * *

Jeff crossed to the waiting area. The jet was due to take off in about ten minutes. His team was in place. They'd finished their last equipment check and were getting ready to board when he heard a high-pitched voice.

"Daddy! We want to say goodbye."

Stunned, Jeff turned slowly and saw Maggie and Ashley waving from the entrance to the building. The little girl broke away from her mother and ran toward him. She held out her arms and threw herself at him.

"Mommy drove really fast," Maggie confided before giving him a wet kiss on his cheek. "We didn't want to miss you."

He looked at Ashley for confirmation. She shrugged sheepishly. "I wasn't reckless and I didn't go over the speed limit—much."

A smile tugged at the corners of her mouth. She wore jeans and a sweater and she was the most beautiful woman he'd ever seen.

"You're not mad at me anymore?" he asked, not sure what could have changed her mind.

She moved close and joined her daughter in wrapping her arms around him. "I'm sorry, Jeff. I shouldn't have said all those things." She looked up at him and grinned. "Just because you're an idiot doesn't mean I'm going to stop loving you."

Her words were like a soothing balm on the open wounds of his heart.

"Besides," she said. "You have to come back and marry me. Maggie wants you to be her dad. I want you to be my husband and we have that other consideration."

He knew she was referring to the baby. He put Maggie on the ground and took Ashley's hands in his. "But this is what I am. I'm not going to change. I'm a soldier, Ashley. Parts of me will never see the light of day."

"I know. While that doesn't make me happy, I accept and love all of you. Just don't you dare die out there. I'll be so angry, I'll hunt you down in the afterworld."

"Are you sure?"

She nodded. "I understand why you have to question me, Jeff. I'm sorry for how I acted. You're the best man I've ever known. It's okay that you can't speak from your heart yet. I even get that you may never be able to say the words. But your actions have a voice of their own and they tell me how you feel."

She hesitated, then shrugged. "All my life I've wanted someone to love me more than anything. I finally figured out I'd better be worth that kind of devotion. Which means I don't have the right to change your life. As you pointed out to me last night, I knew exactly who and what you were when I fell in love with you."

She rose on her toes and kissed him on the mouth. "We'll miss you while you're gone and we'll be waiting for you to return. I love you."

Jeff released her hands. Ashley watched him embrace her daughter, then he hugged her one last time. She tried not to cling to him, but it was hard. She wanted to beg him to stay. She wanted to plead her case one last time, telling him that they needed him alive. But she didn't. He had a job to do and she needed to respect that.

So she put on a brave face as he walked away and kept the tears at bay until he walked out of the hangar and toward the jet waiting on the runway. She saw

Zane climbing the stairs. Jeff was right behind him. It was only then that she allowed herself to give in to the sadness filling her.

"Mommy, why are you crying?" Maggie asked.

"I'm going to miss Jeff very much."

Tears spilled out of her daughter's eyes. "Me, too. I'm going to pray for him every night."

Ashley would do the same. Pray and wait and love him because he was the best part of her.

She picked up Maggie and held her close. Together they made their way to the car.

"We're a mess," Ashley said, trying to stem the flow of tears. "Look at us."

She managed a feeble smile. Maggie attempted one, as well, but it wasn't very successful. Ashley fumbled with her keys. She set her daughter on the ground so she could push the metal into the lock. Moisture blurred her vision. Behind them, the whine of the jet engine increased. He was leaving and she had to let him go.

She shoved the key into the lock, but it wouldn't fit. Then a warm, strong hand settled on top of hers, steadying her, guiding her, and the key slid home.

Ashley turned and saw Jeff standing behind her.

"How…? What…? Oh, thank you."

She flung herself into his arms, clinging as if she would never let go.

"Zane said I was an idiot for leaving you and Maggie," he murmured against her hair. "I finally figured out he was right. Besides, he always did hate sharing the glory."

She didn't know what to say. Happiness flooded her, filling her so much, she thought she might start to glow.

"You're really here? You're not leaving?"

He bent and picked up Maggie. "No more dangerous assignments," he promised. "I can't be fearless anymore. After all, I have something wonderful in my life now. Three somethings I don't want to lose."

"I can count to three," Maggie informed them. "Daddy, if you're not going away, can I have a kitten?"

"Absolutely."

Ashley laughed, then kissed Jeff. He held them both close.

"I get it," he said softly, staring into her eyes. "I finally understand what I've been fighting for so long. I know what's in my heart. It's why I couldn't leave. I love you, Ashley. And Maggie and—" he glanced at her stomach "—you know."

"Really?"

"More than anything in the world. For always. With you I can finally find my way home."

Epilogue

The summer sun was warm and bright in the sky. Jeff looked up from the book he was reading as Maggie and her best friend, Julie, ran across the backyard. They were followed by two golden retrievers, sisters from the same litter. Laughter filled the air, making him smile.

He turned his attention to the shade in the corner where Ashley lay on a blanket, an eighteen-month-old blond boy snuggled at her side. As he watched the woman he loved and his firstborn son, he felt a familiar sensation of happiness and contentment. He could never have imagined his life turning out like this.

David Jeffrey Ritter had arrived exactly on schedule, claiming the attention of the entire family. Last May, Ashley had graduated with honors. She'd taken a job with a local accounting firm whose female partners gave generous maternity leaves and provided on-site day care.

It was too soon for her to be showing, but Ashley was pregnant again. This time they were hoping for a girl. If she turned out to be half as wonderful as Maggie, Jeff knew he would be the luckiest man around.

"What are you thinking?" Ashley asked in a sleepy voice.

Jeff glanced at his watch. "That my parents will be here soon."

"I should probably get up and start lunch."

"I'll do that. After all, they're my parents."

Ashley closed her eyes and smiled. "No. They said they're mine, too. Remember? At Christmas."

At his wife's urgings, Jeff had contacted his folks and found that they were more than willing to be a part of their son's life. With Ashley's help, he was slowly learning to connect with people. The dream of the village and fire came less often now and when it woke him, instead of pacing in the solitary darkness, he held on to his wife whose tender embrace promised to never let him go.

Snowball, their very real white Persian cat, rubbed against his legs and purred. He reached down and patted her. Everyone and everything he loved in the world would soon be in this house. Life was good, he thought happily. Life was very good.

* * * * *

DONOVAN'S CHILD

Christine Rimmer

To all of you wonderful readers
at Harlequin.com who encouraged me
to write this book. Thank you.

Chapter 1

"Impress me," Donovan McRae commanded from behind a matched pair of enormous computer screens.

The screens sat on a desktop that consisted of a giant slab of ash-colored wood. The slab of wood was mounted on a base hewn from what appeared to be volcanic rock. The desk, the screens and the man were way down at the far end of a long, slant-roofed, skylit space, a space that served as Donovan's studio and drafting room in his sprawling, half-subterranean retreat in the West Texas high desert.

Impress me?

Abilene Bravo could not believe he'd just said that.

After all, she'd been imagining this moment for over a year now. At first with anticipation, then with apprehension and finally, as the months dragged by, with growing fury. She'd waited so long for this day—and the first words out of the "great man's" mouth were *Impress me?*

Hadn't she already done that? Wasn't that how she'd won this prize fellowship in the first place?

And would it have killed him to emerge from behind that fortress of screens, to rise from that volcano of a desk, to gesture her nearer, maybe even to go so far as to offer a handshake?

Or, hey. Just, you know, to say hello?

Abilene gritted her teeth and tamped her anger down. She reminded herself that she was not letting her big mouth—or her temper—get the better of her.

She did have something to show him, a preliminary design she'd been tinkering with, tweaking to perfection, for months as she waited for this all-important collaboration to begin. Donovan's assistant had led her to a workstation, complete with old-school drafting table and a desk, on which sat a computer loaded up with the necessary computer-assisted design software.

"Well?" Donovan barked at her, when she didn't respond fast enough. "Do you have something to show me or not?"

Abilene saw red, and again ordered her heart to stop racing, her blood not to boil. She said, in a voice that somehow stayed level, "I do, yes," as she shoved her memory stick into an empty port.

A few clicks of the mouse and her full-color introductory drawing materialized in front of her. On his two screens, Donovan would be seeing it, too.

"My rendering of the front elevation," she said.

"Self-evident," he grumbled.

By then, her hand was shaking as she operated the mouse. But beyond that slight tremor, she kept herself well under control as she began to show him the various views—the expanded renderings of classrooms, the central cluster of rooms for administration, the negative spaces that made up the hallways, the welcome area, the main entrance and vestibule.

She intended to cover it all, every square inch of the facility, which she had lovingly, painstakingly worked out—the playgrounds, the pool area, even the parking lot and some general landscaping suggestions. From there, she would go into her rough estimate on the cost of the project.

But she didn't get far. Ninety seconds into her presentation, he started in on her.

"Depressing," he declared darkly from behind his wall of monitors. "Institutional in the worst sense of the word. It's a center for underprivileged children, not a prison."

It was too much—all the months of waiting, the wondering and worrying if the fellowship was even going to happen. Then, out of nowhere, at last—the call.

That was yesterday, Sunday, the second of January. "This is Ben Yates, Donovan McRae's personal assistant. Donovan asked me to tell you that he's ready to begin tomorrow. And to let you know that instructions will be sent via email...."

She'd had a thousand questions. Ben had answered none of them. He'd given her a choice. She could be flown to El Paso and he would pick her up there. Or she could drive her own vehicle.

She'd opted to drive, figuring it was better to have

her own car in a situation like this. In order to arrive before dark, she'd been on the road before the sun came up that morning.

The drive was endless. An eight-hour trek across the wide-open, windblown desert to this godforsaken corner of Texas.

And now she was here, what? She'd met the great man at last. And she found him flat-out rude. As well as dismissive of her work.

He demanded, "What were you thinking to bring me lackluster crap like this?"

Okay, worse than dismissive.

The man was nothing short of brutal. He'd seen a fraction of what she'd brought. And yet he had no compunction about cutting her ideas to shreds.

Abilene had had enough. And she said exactly that. "Enough." She closed her files and ejected her memory stick.

"Excuse me?" came the deep voice from behind the screens. He sounded vaguely amused.

She shot to her feet. Upright, at least she could see the top half of his head—the thick, dark gold hair, the unwavering gray-blue eyes. "I waited a very long time for this. But maybe you've forgotten that."

"I've forgotten nothing," was the low reply.

"We were to have started at the beginning of last year," she reminded him.

"I know when we were scheduled to start."

"Good. So have you maybe noticed that it's now January of the *next* year? Twelve months I've been waiting, my life put virtually on hold."

"There is no need to tell me what I already know. My

memory is not the least impaired, nor is my awareness of the passage of time."

"Well, *something* is impaired. I do believe you are the rudest person I've ever met."

"You're angry." He made a low sound, a satisfied kind of sound.

"And that makes you *happy?*"

"Happy? No. But it does reassure me."

He found it *reassuring* that she was totally pissed off at him? "I just don't get it. There's such a thing as common courtesy. You could at least have allowed me to finish my presentation before you started ripping my work apart."

"I saw enough."

"You saw hardly anything."

"Still. It was more than enough."

By then, she just didn't care what happened—whether she stayed, or whether she threw her suitcases back into her car and headed home to San Antonio. She spoke with measured calm. "I would really like to know what you were doing all year, that you couldn't even be bothered to follow through on the fellowship you set up yourself. There are kids out there who desperately need a center like this one is supposed to be."

"I know that." His voice was flat now. "You wouldn't be here now if I didn't."

"So then, what's up with you? I just don't get it."

Unspeaking, he held her gaze for a solid count of five. And then, bizarrely, without moving anything but his arms, he seemed to roll backward. His torso turned, his arms working.

He rolled out from behind the massive desk—in a wheelchair.

Chapter 2

A wheelchair.

Nobody had mentioned that he was using a wheel-chair.

Yes, she'd heard that he'd had some kind of accident climbing some snow-covered mountain peak in some distant land. But that was nearly a year ago. She'd had no clue the accident was bad enough for him to still need a wheelchair now.

"Oh, God. I had no idea," she heard herself whisper.

He kept on rolling, approaching her down the end-less length of the room. Beneath the long sleeves of the knit shirt he wore, she could see the powerful muscles of his arms bunching and releasing as he worked the wheels of the chair. He didn't stop until he was directly in front of her.

And then, for several excruciating seconds, he stared up at her as she stared right back at him.

Golden, she thought. He was as golden up close and personal as in the pictures she'd seen of him. As golden as from a distance, on a stage, when she'd been a starry-eyed undergraduate at Rice University and he'd come to Houston to deliver an absolutely brilliant lecture on form, style and function.

Golden hair, golden skin. He was a beautiful man, broad-shouldered and fit-looking. A lion of a man.

Too bad about the cold, dead gray-blue eyes.

He broke the uncomfortable silence with a shrug. "At least you're no doormat."

She thought of the apology she probably owed him. She really should have considered that there might be more going on with him than sheer egotism and contempt for others.

Then again, just because he now used a wheelchair didn't mean he had a right to be a total ass. A lot of people faced difficult challenges in their lives and still managed to treat others with a minimum of courtesy and respect.

She returned his shrug. "I have a big mouth. It's true. And my temper rarely gets the better of me. But when it does, watch out."

"Good."

It wasn't exactly the response she'd expected. "It's good that I never learned when to shut up?"

"You've got guts. I like that. You can be pushed just so far and then you stand up and fight. You're going to need a little fighting spirit if you want to have a prayer of saving this project from disaster."

She didn't know whether to be flattered—or scared to death. "You make it sound as though I would be doing this all on my own."

"Because you *will* be doing this all on your own."

Surely she hadn't heard him right. Caught by surprise, she fell back a step, until she came up against the hard edge of the drafting table. "But…" Her sentence trailed off, hardly begun.

It was called a fellowship for a reason. Without his name and reputation, the project would never have gotten the go-ahead in the first place. The San Antonio Help the Children Foundation was all for giving a bright, young hometown architect a chance. But it was Donovan McRae they were counting on to deliver. He knew that every bit as well as she did.

The ghost of a smile tugged at the corners of his perfectly symmetrical mouth. "Abilene. You're speechless. How refreshing."

She found her voice. "You're Donovan McRae. I'm not. Without you, this won't fly and you know it."

"We need to carry through."

"You noticed. Finally."

A slow, regal dip of that leonine head. "I've put this off for way too long. And as you've already pointed out, there's a need for this center. An urgent need. So I'll…supervise. At least in the design phase. I'll put my stamp of approval on it when I'm satisfied with what you've done. But don't kid yourself. If it gets built, the design will be yours, not mine. And you will be following through in construction."

Abilene believed in herself—in her talent, her knowledge, and her work ethic. Yes, she'd hoped this fellowship would give her a leg up on snaring a great job with a good firm. That maybe she'd be one of the fortunate few who could skip the years of grunt work that went into becoming a top architect. But to be in charge of a project of this magnitude, at this point in her career?

It killed her to admit it, but she did anyway. "I don't know if I'm ready for that."

"You're going to have to be. Let me make this very clear. I haven't worked in a year. I doubt if I'll ever work again."

Never work again?

That would be a crime. She might not care much for his personality. But he was, hands down, the finest architect of his generation. They spoke of him in the same breath as Frank O. Gehry and Robert Venturi. Some even dared to compare him favorably to Frank Lloyd Wright. He blended the Modern with the Classical, Bauhaus with the Prairie style, all with seeming effortlessness.

And he was still young. Not yet forty. Many believed an architect couldn't possibly hit creative stride until at least the age of fifty. There was just too much to learn and master. Donovan McRae's best work *should* be ahead of him.

"Never work again…" She repeated the impossible words that kept scrolling through her mind.

"That's right." He looked…satisfied. In a bleak and strangely determined sort of way.

"But why?" she asked, knowing she was pushing it, but wanting to understand what, exactly, had happened to him to make him turn his back on the kind of career that most would kill for. "I mean, there's nothing wrong with your *brain,* is there?"

An actual chuckle escaped him. "You *do* have a big mouth."

She refused to back off. "Seriously. Have you suffered some kind of brain damage?"

"No."

"Then why would you stop working? I just don't get it."

Something flashed in those steel-blue eyes of his. She sensed that he actually might give her an answer.

But then he only shook his head. "Enough. I'll take that memory stick." He held out his hand.

She kept her lips pressed together over a sarcastic remark and laid the stick in his open palm.

He closed his fingers around it. "Ben will show you to your rooms. Get comfortable—but not *too* comfortable." He backed and turned and wheeled away from her, disappearing through a door beyond the looming edifice that served as his desk.

"Abilene?" said a quiet voice behind her. She turned to face Ben Yates, who was slim and tall and self-contained, with black hair and eyes to match. "This way."

She grabbed her bag off the back of her chair and followed him.

The house was a marvel—like all of Donovan McRae's designs. Built into the side of a rocky cliff, it had seemed to Abilene, as she approached it earlier, to materialize out of the desert: a cave, a fortress, a palace made of rock—and a house—all at the same time.

It was built around a central courtyard. The back

half nestled into the cliff face. It had large glass doors and floor-to-ceiling windows all along the courtyard walls, giving access to the outside and great views of the pool and the harsh, beautiful landscaping. The facade side had windows and glass doors leading to the courtyard, as well. It also offered wide vistas of the wild, open desert.

Abilene's rooms were on the cliff side.

Ben ushered her in ahead of him. "Here we are."

The door was extra wide. The one to the bedroom was wide, as well. She ran her hand down the rough-hewn door frame.

Ben said, "Donovan had all the rooms made wheelchair-accessible, so it would be possible for him to get around anywhere in the house."

She set her leather tote on a long table by the door and made a circuit. First of the sitting room, then of the bedroom. She looked into the walk-in closet where her own clothes were already hanging, and also the bathroom with its open shower and giant sunken tub.

The walls of the place seemed hewn of the rock face itself. And the furniture was rustic, made from twisted hunks of hardwood, starkly beautiful, like the desert landscape outside. French doors led out to the pool, and to the paths that wound through the courtyard.

Donovan's assistant waited for her near the door. "The pool is yours to use as long as you're here. There's also a large gym downstairs. Check with me if you want to work out there and I'll give you a schedule. Donovan uses the gym several hours a day and prefers to do so alone. The desk, computer and drafting table you used today in the studio are yours whenever you need them.

Anytime you're hungry, the kitchen is to your left as you exit your rooms. Just keep going until you reach it. Or you can ring. Press the red button on the phone. The housekeeper will answer and see that you get anything you need."

"I know I'll be very comfortable. Thank you."

"I had your suitcases unpacked for you."

She gave him a wry smile. "You assumed I would stay?"

"I did, yes."

"I have to tell you, it was touch and go back there in the studio. Your boss can be rude."

Apparently, Ben felt no obligation to leap to Donovan's defense. He spoke in his usual calm, unruffled tone. "Don't let him run you off."

"I won't. It's a promise."

"That's the spirit." Did he almost smile? She couldn't be sure. "Drinks at seven, just you and Donovan."

"That sounds really fun." She said it deadpan.

Ben took her meaning. "Only if you feel up to it. If you'd prefer, I can have something sent here, to your rooms."

"I definitely feel up to it."

"Excellent. If you follow either the courtyard breezeway or the interior hall in either direction, you'll eventually reach the front living room off the main entrance. Or you can simply cross the courtyard. It's chilly out, but not too bad."

"I'm sure I can find my way."

"Good, then. If you need anything—"

"I know. Press the red button on the house phone."

"I'll see you at dinner." He turned to go.

"Ben?"

He paused in the doorway, his back to her.

"I had no idea Donovan was in a wheelchair."

A silence. And then, reluctantly, he turned to her again. "Yes. Well, he's very protective of his privacy lately."

"A little communication goes a long way."

"You should be discussing this with him."

"Probably. What happened to him?"

Ben frowned. She was sure he would blow her off— or tell her again to ask Donovan. But then he surprised her and gave it up. "You may have heard about the ice-climbing accident."

"Just that there was one."

"He fell several hundred feet. Both legs sustained multiple fractures. His right tibia was driven up through the knee joint into the thigh."

She forced herself not to wince. "So…it's not his spine? I mean, he's not paralyzed?"

"No, he's not paralyzed."

"Will he walk again?"

"It's likely. But with…difficulty—and I've said more than enough. Seven. Drinks in the front living area."

And he was gone.

Abilene got out of her tired traveling clothes and jumped in the shower. In twenty minutes, she was freshened up and ready to go again. She considered exploring the house a little but decided to ask Donovan to show her around personally later. It might be a way to break the ice between them.

If such a thing was possible. The man was as guarded

as they came. She had her work cut out for her, to try to get to know him a little.

Stretching out across the big bed, she stared up at the ceiling fixture, which consisted of tangled bits of petrified wood interwoven with golden globe-shaped lights that seemed strung on barbed wire. With a sigh, she let her eyes drift shut. Maybe what she really needed about now was a nice little nap....

The faint sound of her cell ringing snapped her awake. She went to the sitting room to get it. The display read Mom.

She answered. "I'm here. Safe. Don't worry."

"Just what I needed to know. Your father sends his love."

"Love to him, too. Did Zoe and Dax get away all right?" Saturday, which had been New Year's Day, Abilene's baby sister had married her boss and the father of her coming baby. The newlyweds were to have left for their honeymoon on Maui that morning.

"They're on their way," her mother said. "Dax says to say hi to Donovan." Zoe's groom and Donovan were longtime acquaintances. "And your sister says to tell your new mentor that he'd better treat you right."

"I'll give him the message—both of them," Abilene promised.

"Have you...spoken with him yet?" Aleta Bravo asked the question carefully. She knew how upset Abilene had been with the whole situation.

"We spoke, yes. We...had words, I guess you could say. He was rude and dismissive. I was forced to tell him off."

"Should I be concerned?"

"Not as of now. I'll keep you posted."

"You can always simply come home, you know. It won't be that difficult to find a place for yourself. You're a Bravo. And you graduated at the top of your class."

"Mom. There are plenty of architects. But an architect who's worked closely with Donovan McRae, now that's something else altogether. A fellowship like this—one-on-one with the best there is—it just doesn't happen very often."

She considered adding that Donovan had been facing some serious challenges lately and possibly deserved a little slack for his thoughtless behavior. That he used a wheelchair now.

But no. Ben had made it painfully clear that McRae didn't want the world butting into his private business. She would respect his wishes. At least until she understood better what was going on with him.

Aleta said, "You're determined to stay, then?"

"Yes, I am."

"Well, then I suppose I won't be changing your mind…."

"No. You won't." And then, from her mother's end of the line, faintly, she heard the deep rumble of her father's voice.

Aleta laughed. "Your father says to give him hell."

"I will. Count on it."

After she said goodbye to her mom, she checked in with Javier Cabrera.

Javier was an experienced builder—and the first person she'd called when she got the summons yesterday from Ben. He owned his own company, Cabrera Construction, and had been kind enough to hire Abilene to work as a draftsperson on a few of his projects over the endless months she'd been waiting to get started on the fellowship. He'd even allowed her to consult with him at his building sites, giving her the chance to gain more hands-on experience in construction. He had become not only her friend, but something of a mentor as well.

His connections to her family were long-standing and complicated. Once the Bravos and the Cabreras had been mortal enemies. But now, in the past few years, the two families seemed to have more in common than points of conflict.

"Abby," Javier said warmly when he answered the phone. "I was wondering about you."

"I'll have you know I have made it safely to Donovan McRae's amazing rock house in the middle of nowhere."

"Did he tell you how sorry he was for all the time he made you wait and wait?"

"Not exactly."

"You get in your car and you come back to SA. I have work for you. Plenty of work."

She smiled at the driftwood and barbed-wire creation overhead. "You're good to me."

"I know talent. You will go far."

"You always make me feel better about everything."

"We all need encouragement." He sounded a little sad. But then, Javier *was* sad. He was still deeply in love with his estranged wife, Luz.

Abilene confided that Donovan had said her design was crap.

Javier jumped to her defense, as she had known that he would. "Don't listen to him. Your design is excellent."

"My design is...workmanlike. It needs to be better than that."

"You're too hard on yourself."

"I have to be hard on myself. I want to be the best someday."

"Stand tall," he said. "And call me any time you need to talk to someone who understands."

"You know I will."

They chatted for a bit longer. When she hung up, it was ten minutes of seven. She combed her hair and freshened her lip gloss and walked across the courtyard to the front of the house.

Donovan was waiting for her.

He sat by the burled wood bar, watching, as she approached the French doors from the courtyard.

She wore a slim black skirt, a button-down shirt with a few buttons left undone and a long strand of jade-colored beads around her neck. Round-toed high heels showed off her shapely legs, and her thick chestnut hair fell loose on her slim shoulders.

She pushed open one of the doors and stepped inside as if she owned the place. There was something about her that had him thinking of old movies, the ones made way back in the Great Depression. Movies in which the women were lean and tall and always ready with a snappy comeback.

From that first moment in the afternoon, when Ben ushered her into the studio, he had felt...annoyed. With her. With the project. With the world in general. He wasn't sure exactly why she annoyed him. Maybe it was all the energy that came off her, the sense of purpose and possibility that seemed to swirl around her like a sudden, bracing gust of winter wind.

Donovan didn't want bracing. What he wanted was silence. Peace. To be left alone.

But he had chosen her, sight unseen, by the promise in the work she'd submitted, before it all went to hell. And he would, finally, follow through on his obligation to the Foundation people. And to her.

They were doing this thing.

She spotted him across the room. Paused. But only for a fraction of a second. Then she kept coming, her stride long and confident.

He poured himself a drink and set down the decanter of scotch. "What can I get you?"

"Whatever you're having." She nodded at the decanter. "That's fine."

"Scotch? Don't women your age prefer sweet drinks?" Yeah. All right. It was a dig.

She refused to be goaded. "Seriously. Scotch is fine."

So he dropped ice cubes into a crystal glass, poured the drink and gave it to her, placing it in her long-fingered, slender hands. They were fine hands, the skin supple, the nails unpolished and clipped short. Useful hands.

She sipped. "It's good. Thanks."

He nodded, gestured in the direction of a couple of chairs and a sofa. "Have a seat." She turned and sauntered to the sofa, dropping to the cushions with artless ease.

He put his drink between his ruined legs and wheeled himself over there, rolling into the empty space between the chairs. "Your rooms?"

"They're perfect, thanks. Is it just you and Ben here?"

"I have a cook and a housekeeper—a married couple, Anton and Olga. And a part-time groundskeeper to look after the courtyard and the perimeter of the house." He watched her cross her pretty legs, admired the perfection of her knees. At least she was a pleasure to look at. "Did you rest?"

"I had a shower. Then my mother called. She told me to tell you that Dax sends his regards and my sister says you'd better be nice to me."

"Your sister and Dax...?"

"They were married on Saturday. And left on their honeymoon this morning."

"I hope they'll be very happy," he said without inflection. "And then what did you do?"

"Does that really matter to you?"

"It's called conversation, Abilene."

Her expression was mutinous, but she did answer his question. "After I talked to my mother, I called a... friend."

He took note of her hesitation before the word *friend*. "A lover, you mean?"

She laughed, a low, husky sound that irked him to no end. A laugh that said he didn't intimidate her, not with his purposeful rudeness, nor with his too-personal questions. "No, not a lover. Javier is a builder. A really good one. I've been working for him over the past year, on and off. He also happens to be my half sister Elena's father. And the adoptive father of my sister-in-law, Mercedes."

He sipped his scotch. "All right. I'm thoroughly confused."

"I kind of guessed that by the way your eyes glazed over."

"Maybe just a few more details…"

She swirled her glass. Ice clinked on crystal. "My father and Javier's wife, Luz, had a secret affair years ago."

"An adulterous affair, that's what you're telling me."

"Yes. That's what I'm telling you. Luz was married to Javier. My dad to my mom. The affair didn't last long."

"Did your father love your mother?"

"He did—and he does. And I believe that Luz loved—and loves—Javier. But both of their marriages were troubled at the time."

"Troubled, how?"

She gave him a look. One that said he'd better back off. "I was a toddler when all this happened. I don't know all the details, all the deep inner motivations."

"Maybe you should ask your father."

"Maybe you should stop goading me."

"But I kind of like goading you."

"Clearly. Where was I? Wait. I remember. Javier—and everyone else except Luz—believed that Elena, my half sister, was his. But then, a few years back, the truth came out. It was…a difficult time."

"I would imagine."

"However, things are better now. Slowly, we've all picked up the pieces and moved on." She uncrossed her legs, put her elbows on her knees and leaned toward him. With the glass of scotch between her two fine hands, she studied him some more through those arresting golden-green eyes of hers. "So what did *you* do while I was busy talking on the phone?"

"Mostly, I was downstairs in the torture chamber with one of my physical therapists."

"You mean the gym? You were working out?"

"Torture really is a better word for it. Necessary torture, but torture nonetheless." And he had no desire to talk about himself. "What made you become an architect?"

She sank back against the sofa cushions. "Didn't I explain all that in my fellowship submission?"

As if he remembered some essay she had written to go with her original concept for the children's center. As if he'd even read her essay. Essays were of no interest to him. It was the work that mattered. "Explain it again. Briefly, if you don't mind."

She turned her head to the side, slid him a narrow look. He thought she would argue and he was ready for that—looking forward to it, really. But she didn't. "Four of my seven brothers work for the family company, BravoCorp. I wanted to be in the family business, too. BravoCorp used to be big into property development."

"And so you set out to become the family architect."

She gave him one slow, regal nod. "But since then, BravoCorp has moved more into renewable energy. And various other investments. There's not much of a need for an architect at the moment." She set her drink on the side table by the arm of the sofa. "What about your family?"

He put on a fake expression of shock. "Haven't you read my books?"

She *almost* rolled her eyes. "What? That was a requirement?"

"Absolutely."

"Well, then all right. I confess. I *have* read your books. All four of them, as matter of fact. Will there be a quiz?"

"Don't tempt me. And if you've read my books, then you know more than anyone could ever want to know about my family."

"I'd like to hear it from you—briefly, if you don't mind." Those haunting eyes turned more gold than green as she gave his own words back to him.

He bent to the side and set his drink on the floor, then straightened in the chair and braced his elbows on the swing-away armrests. "I hate all this getting-to-know-you crap."

"Really? You seemed to be enjoying yourself a minute or two ago. But then, that was when you were asking the questions."

"You are an annoying woman." There. It was out.

She said nothing for several seconds. When she did speak, her voice was gentle. "You're not going to scare me off, Donovan. If you want me to go, you'll have to send me away—which means you'll also have to admit, once and for all, that you're backing out of the fellowship."

"But I'm not backing out of the fellowship."

"All right, then. Tell me about your family."

He was tempted to refuse. If she'd read his books as she claimed, she knew it all anyway. But he had the distinct impression that if he refused, she would only badger him until he gave it up.

So he told her. "My father was never in the picture."

From where he sat, without shifting his gaze from her face, he could see out the wide front windows. He spotted the headlights of a car approaching down the winding driveway. When the car pulled to a stop under the glow of the bright facade lights, he recognized the vehicle.

A red Cadillac.

He ignored the car and continued telling Abilene what she no doubt already knew. "My mother was a very determined woman. I was her only child and she set out to make me fearless. She was a force to be reckoned with. Adventurous. Always curious. And clever. It was her idea that I should write my autobiography when I wasn't even old enough to have one. She said I needed to cultivate myself as a legend and an authority. And the rest would follow. She died when I was in my early twenties. A freak skydiving accident."

Abilene had her elbow braced on the chair arm, her strong chin framed in the L of her thumb and forefinger. "A legend and an authority. I like that."

"It's a direct quote from my second book. If you really had read that book, you would remember it."

"This may come as a shock, but I don't remember everything I read."

"How limiting for you."

She gave him a slow smile, one that told him he was not going to break her. "Did you ever find your father?"

"To find him implies that I looked for him."

"So that would be a no?"

An atonal series of chimes sounded: the doorbell.

Abilene sent a glance over her shoulder and shifted as if to rise.

"Don't get up," Donovan said.

"But—"

"Olga will take care of it."

Abilene sank back to the couch cushions as his housekeeper appeared in the wide-open arched doorway that led to the foyer. Olga cast him a questioning look. He gave a tight shake of his head.

Olga shut the thick archway doors before answering the bell. Seconds later, there were voices: Olga's and that of another woman. The heavy foyer doors blocked out the actual words.

He heard the front door shut.

And then Olga opened the doors to the living area again. "Dinner is ready," she announced, her square face, framed by wiry graying hair, serene and untroubled.

"Thanks, Olga. We'll be right in." Out in the driveway, the Cadillac started moving, backing and turning and then speeding off the way it had come. Abilene had turned to watch it go. He asked her, "Hungry?"

She faced him again. "Who was that?"

"Does it really matter? And more to the point, is it any of your business?"

Abilene stood and smoothed her skinny little skirt down over those shapely knees. "I can see this is going to be one long, dirty battle, every step of the way."

"Maybe you should give up, pack your bags, go back to San Antonio and your so-helpful builder friend, who also happens to be the father of your half sister, as well as of your sister-in-law. To the loving arms of your large, powerful, wealthy family. To your father, who loves your mother even though he betrayed her."

Her eyes went to jade, mysterious. Deep. "I'm going nowhere, Donovan."

"Wait. Learn. The evening is young yet. You can still change your mind."

"It's obvious that you don't know me very well."

Chapter 3

Dinner, Abilene found, was more of the same.

A verbal torture chamber. But at least it was brief.
She saw to that.

Ben joined them in the dining room, which was the
next room over from the enormous living area and had
more large windows with beautifully framed views of
the desert and distant, barren peaks.

There were several tables of varying sizes, as in a
lodging house, or a bed-and-breakfast. They ate at one
of the smaller ones, by the French doors to the courtyard, just the three of them. Olga brought the food and
a bottle of very nice cabernet and left them alone.

Abilene asked, "Why all the tables? Are you thinking of renting out rooms?"

Donovan raised one glided eyebrow. "And this is of
interest to you, why?"

Ben answered for him. "Once, Donovan thought he might offer a number of fellowships...."

Abilene smiled at Ben. At least he was civil. "Students, then?"

"Once, meaning long ago," Donovan offered distantly. "Never happened. Never going to happen. And I decided against changing the tables for one large one. Too depressing, just Ben and me, alone at a table made for twenty." He gave Ben a cool glance. "Ben is an engineer," he said. "A civil engineer."

Ben didn't sigh. But he looked as though he wanted to. "I had some idea I needed a change. I don't know what I was thinking. I was a very good engineer."

"I saved him from that," Donovan explained in a grating, self-congratulatory tone. "In the end, an architect knows something about everything. An engineer knows everything about one thing. It's not good for a man, to be too wrapped up in the details."

Ben swallowed a bite of prime rib and turned to Abilene. "But then, my job here is to deal with the details. So I guess I'm still an engineer."

She sipped her wine. Slowly.

Donovan glared at her. "All right. What are you thinking?"

She set down her glass. "I'm thinking you need to get out more. How long have you been hiding out here in the desert?"

A low, derisive laugh escaped him. "Hiding out?"

She refused to let him off the hook. "Months, at least. Right? Out here a hundred miles from nowhere, with your cook and your housekeeper and your engineer."

"Are you going to lose your temper again?" he asked

in that so-superior way that made her want to jump up and stab him with her fork.

"No. I'm not."

"Should I be relieved?"

She glanced to the side and saw that the corners of Ben's mouth were twitching. He was enjoying this.

Abilene wasn't. Not in the least. She was tired and she was starting to wonder if maybe she *should* do exactly what she'd told everyone she wouldn't: give up and head back to SA. "I'm just saying, maybe we could go out to dinner one of these nights."

"Go out where?" Donovan demanded.

"I don't know. El Paso?"

He dismissed her suggestion with a wave of his hand. "It's a long way to El Paso."

"It's a long way to anywhere from here."

"And that's just how I like it."

"I did go through a small town maybe twenty miles east of here today."

"Chula Mesa," said Donovan in a tone that said the little town didn't thrill him in the least.

Abilene kept trying. "That's it. Chula Mesa. And just outside of town, I saw a roadhouse, Luisa's Cantina? We could go there. Have a beer. Shoot some pool."

"I'm not going to Luisa's."

"You've been there before, then?"

"What does it matter? I'm not going there now. And as for Chula Mesa, there is nothing in that dusty little burg that interests me in the least."

"Maybe you could just pretend to be interested."

"Why would I do that?"

"Sometimes you have to pretend a little, Donovan.

You might surprise yourself and find that you actually do enjoy what you're pretending to enjoy."

"When it comes to Chula Mesa, I'm not willing to pretend. Wait. I'll go further. I'm not willing to pretend anywhere. About anything."

She really did want to do violence to him. To grab his big shoulders and shake him, at least. To tell him to grow up. Snap out of it. Stop acting like a very bright, very spoiled child. She took a bite of prime rib, one of potato. Dipped an artichoke leaf in buttery sauce and carefully bit off the tender end.

Donovan chuckled. "Fed up with me already, huh? I predict you're out of here by morning."

Ben surprised her by coming to her defense. "Leave her alone, Donovan. Let her eat her dinner in peace."

Donovan's manly jaw twitched. Twice. And then he grunted and picked up his fork.

They ate the rest of the meal in bleak silence.

When Abilene was finished, she dabbed at her lips with her snowy napkin, slid it in at the edge of her plate and stood. She spoke directly to Ben. "Would you tell the cook the food was excellent, please? I've had a long day. Good night."

"I'll tell him," Ben replied pleasantly. "Sleep well."

"My studio," Donovan muttered. "Nine o'clock sharp. We have a lot of work to do."

She let a nod serve as her answer, and she left by the door to the interior hallway.

In her rooms, she changed into sweats and then sat on the bed and did email for a while. The house had wireless internet.

Really, it was kind of a miracle. Way out here, miles

from nowhere, her cell worked fine and so did email and her web connection. She would have been impressed if she wasn't so tired and disheartened.

What she needed was sleep, but she felt restless, too. Unhappy and unsatisfied. All these months of waiting. For this.

She knew if she got into bed, she would only lie there fuming, imagining any number of brutal ways to do physical harm to Donovan McRae.

Eventually, she turned on the bedroom TV and flipped through the channels, settling on The History Channel, where she watched a rerun of *Pawn Stars* and then an episode of *Life After People,* which succeeded in making her feel even more depressed.

Nothing like witnessing the great buildings of the world rot and fall into rubble after a so-enchanting evening with Donovan McRae. It could make a woman wonder if there was any point in going on.

At a few minutes after ten, there was a tap on her sitting room door.

It was Ben, holding two plates of something sinfully chocolate. "You left before dessert. No one makes flourless chocolate cake like Anton."

She took one of the plates and a fork and stepped aside. "Okay. Since there's chocolate involved, you can come in." She poked at the dollop of creamy white stuff beside the sinfully dark cake. "Crème fraîche?"

"Try it."

She did. "Wonderful. Your boss may deserve slow torture and an agonizing death, but I have no complaints about the food."

They sat on the couch and ate without speaking until both of their plates were clean.

"Feel better?" He set his plate on the coffee table.

She put hers beside it. "I do. Much. Thank you."

Ben stared off toward the doors to the darkened courtyard. "I started working for him two years ago, before the accident on the mountain. At the time, I really liked him. He used to be charming. He honestly did."

"I know," she answered gently. "I heard him speak once. He was so funny. Funny and inspiring. He made it all seem so simple. We were an auditorium full of students, raw beginners. Yet we came away feeling we were brilliant and accomplished, that we could do anything, that we understood what makes a building work, what makes it both fully functional and full of…meaning, too. Then, after he spoke, there was a party for the upperclassmen and professors, with Donovan the guest of honor. I was a freshman, not invited. But I heard how he amazed them all, how fascinating he was, how full of life, how…interested in everything and everyone. We all wanted to be just like him when we grew up."

"I keep waiting," Ben said, "for the day I wake up and he's changed back into the man he used to be. But it's been a while now. And the change is nowhere on the horizon."

She asked the central question. "So. What happened to him? Was it the accident on the mountain?"

Ben only smiled. "That, I really can't tell you. You'll have to find out from him."

She scoffed. "I don't think I'll hold my breath."

"He likes you."

That made her laugh. "Oh, come on."

"Seriously. He does. I know him well enough by now to read him a little, at least. He finds you fascinating. And attractive—both of which you are."

Was Ben flirting with her? She slid him a look. He was still staring off into the middle distance. So maybe not. "Well, if you're right, I would hate to see how he treats someone he *doesn't* like."

"He ignores them. He ignores almost everyone now. Just pretends they aren't even there. Sends me or Olga to deal with them."

She gathered her knees up to the side. "This evening, before dinner, someone arrived and was sent away, someone in a red Cadillac. I didn't see who, but I heard a woman's voice talking to Olga at the door…."

Ben shrugged. "People come by, now and then. When they get fed up with him not returning their calls. When they can't take the waiting, the wondering if he's all right, the stewing over what could be going on with him."

"People like…?"

"Old friends. Mountain climbers he used to know, used to partner with. Beginning architects he once encouraged."

"Old girlfriends, too?"

"Yes." Ben sent her a patient glance. "Old girlfriends, too."

She predicted, "Eventually, they'll all give up on him. He'll get what he seems to be after. To be completely alone."

Ben's dark eyes gleamed. "With his cook and his housekeeper and his engineer."

She told him gently, "I didn't mean that as a criticism of you."

He smiled. A warm smile. "I know you didn't."

"I just don't get what's up with him."

"Well, don't worry. You're not the only one."

"How will he live, if he doesn't work? This house alone must cost a fortune to run."

"His books still make money."

"But an architect needs clients. We're not like painters or writers. We can't go into a room and lock the door and turn out a masterpiece and *then* try to sell it...."

"I know," Ben said softly. He admitted, "Eventually, there could be a problem. But not for a few years yet, anyway...." There was a silence. Ben was gazing off toward the courtyard again.

Finally, she said, "You seemed pretty stuffy at first."

He chuckled. "Like the butler in one of those movies with Emma Thompson, right?"

"Pretty much. But now I realize you're not like someone's snobby butler, not in the least. You're okay, Ben."

He did look at her then. His dark eyes were so sad. "I was afraid, after the way he behaved at dinner, that he'd succeeded in chasing you off. I hope he hasn't. He needs a little interaction, with someone other than Anton, or Olga. Or me."

"A fresh victim, you mean."

"No. I mean someone smart and tough and aggressively optimistic."

"Aggressively optimistic? That's a little scary."

"I meant it in the best possible way."

"Oh, right."

"I meant someone able to keep up with him—I could use someone like that around here, too, when you come right down to it. Someone like you…"

"I wouldn't say I'm exactly keeping up with him."

"Well, I would."

She drooped back against the couch cushions. "Okay, I'm still here. But it's going to take a lot of chocolate, you know."

"I'll make sure that Anton keeps it coming." He got up. "And I'll let you get your rest."

She waited until he reached the door before she said, "Good night."

"'Night, Abilene." And he was gone.

"It's not a *horrible* arrangement of the space," Donovan announced when she entered the studio the next day. He was already at his desk, staring at his computer screens.

She saw that her design for the center was up on the computer at the desk she'd used the day before—which meant he was probably looking at the same thing on his two ginormous screens.

Just to be sure, she marched down the length of the room and sidled around to join him behind his desk.

Yep. It was her design. Up on display like a sacrificial offering at a summoning of demons. Ready to be ripped to shreds by the high priest of darkness.

He shot her an aggravated glance. "What? You do have a desk of your own, you know."

She sidled in closer, and then leaned in to whisper

in his ear. "But yours is so much bigger, so much…
more impressive."

He made a snarly sound. "Did I mention you annoy
me?"

"Yes, you did. Don't repeat yourself. It makes you
seem unimaginative." He smelled good. Clean. With
a faint hint of some really nice aftershave. How could
someone who smelled so good be such an ass?

It was a question for the ages.

"You're crowding me," he growled.

"Oh, I'm so sorry…." She straightened again, and
stepped back from him, but only a fraction.

"No, you're not—and I don't like people lurking behind me, either."

"Fair enough." She slid around so she was beside him
again, put her hand on his sacrificial slab of a desk and
leaned in as close as before. "I slept well, surprisingly.
And I'm feeling much better this morning, thank you."

He turned his head slowly. Reluctantly. And met her
eyes. "I didn't ask how you slept."

"But you should have asked."

"Yeah. Well, don't expect a lot of polite noises from
me."

She heaved a fake sigh. "I only wish."

"If you absolutely have to lurk at my elbow, pay
attention." He turned back to the monitors, began click-
ing through the views. "Have you noticed?"

This close, she could see the hair follicles of his just-
shaved beard. His skin was as golden and flawless from
beside him as from several feet away. He must get outside now and then, to have such great color in his face.

And his neck. And his strong, lean hands. "Noticed what?"

"It lacks a true *parti*." The *parti,* pronounced *par-TEE*, as in *We are going to par-tee,* was the central idea or concept for a building. In the process of creating a building design, the *parti* often changed many times.

She jumped to her own defense. "It does not lack a *parti*."

He sent her a look. "You never mentioned the *parti*."

"You didn't ask."

"Well, all right then. What *is* the *parti?*" He let out a dry chuckle. "Nestled rectangles?"

Okay, his guess was way too close. She'd actually been thinking of the *parti* as *learning rectangles*. Which somehow seemed ham-handed and far too elementary, now he'd taken his scalpel of a tongue to it.

"What's wrong with rectangles?" She sounded defensive and she knew it. "They're classrooms. Activity rooms. A rectangle is a perfectly acceptable shape for a classroom."

"Children deserve a learning space as open and receptive as their young minds."

"Oh, wait. The great man speaks. I should write that down."

"Yes, you should. You should carry a notebook around with you, and a pen, be ready to jot down every pearl of wisdom that drops from my lips." He spoke with more irony than egotism.

And she almost laughed. "You know, you are amusing now and then—in your own totally self-absorbed way."

"Thank you. I agree. And you need to start with

some soft sketches. You need to get off the computer and go back to the beginning, start working with charcoal, pastels and crayons."

"Starting over. Wonderful."

"To truly gain control of a design," he intoned, "one must first accept—even embrace—the feeling that everything is out of control."

"I'm so looking forward to that."

"And we have to be quick about it. I told the Foundation we'd be ready to bring in the whole team in six weeks." He meant the builder, the other architects and the engineers.

"Did you just say that *we'd* be ready?"

"I decided it would be unwise to go into how I won't be involved past the planning stages."

"Good thinking. Since you know exactly how that would go over—it wouldn't. It won't. They're counting on *you*."

"And they will learn to count on you."

"So you totally misled them."

He looked down his manly blade of a nose at her. "Better that they see the design and the scale model and love it first, meet you at your most self-assured and persuasive. You can give them a full-out oral presentation, really wow them. Make them see that you're not only confident, you're completely capable of handling the construction on your own."

"Confident, capable, self-assured and persuasive. Well. At least I like the sound of all that."

He granted her a wry glance. "You have a lot of work to do. Don't become *overly* confident."

"With you around? Never going to happen."

Loftily, he informed her, "March one is the target date for breaking ground."

She put up a hand, forefinger extended. "If I might just make one small point."

"As if I could stop you."

"I can't help but notice that suddenly, you're all about not wasting time. What's that old saying? *'Poor planning on your part does not constitute an emergency on mine.'*"

"The tight timeline has nothing to do with my planning, poor or otherwise."

"Planned or not, you're the one who kept us from going ahead months ago."

"Since you seem to be so fond of clichés, here's one for you. Can we stop beating the same dead horse? Yes, I put the project on hold. Now I'm ready to get down to work."

"And the timeline is impossibly tight."

"That may be so."

"How generous of you to admit it."

"But in the end, Abilene, there is only one question."

"Enlighten me."

"Do you want to make a success of this or not?"

Okay. He had it right for once. That *was* the question. "Yes, Donovan. I do."

"Then go back to your work area, get out your pastels, your charcoal, your fat markers. And stop fooling around."

Chapter 4

From that moment on, for Abilene, work trumped everything else. From nine—sometimes eight—in the morning, until after seven at night. Donovan supervised. He guided and challenged her. But he fully expected her to carry most of the load.

It would be her project in the truest sense. Which made it the chance of a lifetime for her, professionally. And also absolutely terrifying.

She drove herself tirelessly and mostly managed to keep her fear that she might fail at bay.

Donovan was not always there in the studio with her. He would set her a task or a problem to solve and then disappear, only to return hours later to check on her progress, to prod her onward.

Often during the day, when he wasn't with her, he

took his personal elevator down to his underground gym to work with one of his physical therapists. Now and then, she would see them, Donovan's trainers. And the massage therapists, too. They were healthy, muscular types, both men and women. They came and went by the kitchen door. Anton, the cook, who was big and barrel-chested with a booming laugh and long gray hair clubbed back in a ponytail, would sometimes feed them after they finished putting Donovan through his paces.

Donovan seemed dedicated to that, at least, to taking care of his body, to making it stronger—though he continued to do nothing to heal his damaged spirit.

Or, apparently, his broken relationships. As had happened the first night, people Abilene never saw showed up at the front door to ask to speak with him. Olga or Ben always answered the doorbell when it rang. And they always sent whoever it was away.

More and more as the days went by, Abilene found herself wondering about that. About the people who cared for Donovan, the people he kept turning his back on. She would wonder—and then she would catch herself.

Really, it wasn't her concern if he refused to see former friends. She didn't even *like* him. Why should she keep wondering what had happened to him? Why couldn't she stop puzzling over what could have made him turn his back on other people, on a fabulous career?

There was the climbing accident, of course. That seemed the most likely answer to the question of what had killed his will to work, to fully engage in his own life. It seemed to her that *something* must have happened, something that had changed him so completely from the outgoing, inspiring man she'd admired from a distance back in college into someone entirely different.

She found she was constantly reminding herself that she was there to work, not to wonder what in the world had happened to Donovan McRae. She told herself to focus on the positive. If she could pull this off, create a design that would wow the Foundation people *and* hold her own overseeing construction, her career would be made.

And there were *some* benefits to being stuck in the desert with Donovan—Olga, for one.

The housekeeper was helpful and pleasant and ran the big house with seeming effortlessness. And beyond Olga, there was Anton's cooking; every meal was delicious and nourishing. And the conversation at dinner, while not always pleasant, did challenge her. Donovan might not be a very nice man, but he was certainly interesting. Ben provided a little balance, with his dry wit, his warm laughter.

Abilene really did like Ben. As the days passed, the two of them became friends. Every night, he came to her rooms for an hour or two before bedtime. Often, he brought dessert. They would eat the sweet treat, and he would commiserate with her over Donovan's most recent cruelties.

And beyond the great food, the comfortable house, the very efficient Olga and Abilene's friendship with Ben, there was music. Anton played the piano, and beautifully. Sometimes after dinner, in the music room at the east end of the house, he would play for them. Everything from Chopin to Gershwin, from Ray Charles to Norah Jones.

One night, about two weeks into her stay in Donovan's house, Anton played a long set of Elton John songs—songs that had been popular when Abilene's parents were young. Anton sang them, beautifully, in a smoky baritone, and Olga, who had a good contralto voice, sang harmony. Abilene felt the tears welling when they sang "Candle in the Wind."

She turned away, hoping Donovan wouldn't notice and torment her about it.

But it was never a good bet, to hope that Donovan wouldn't notice.

When the last notes died away, he went for the throat. "Abilene. Are you *crying?*"

She blinked the dampness away, drew her shoulders back and turned to him. "Of course not."

"Liar." He held her gaze. His was blue and cool and distant as the desert sky on a winter afternoon. "Your eyes are wet."

She sniffed. "Allergies."

He refused to look away. She felt herself held, pinned, beneath his uncompromising stare. She also found herself thinking how good-looking he was. How compelling. And how totally infuriating. "It's winter in the desert," he said. "Nobody has allergies now. You're crying. You protect yourself by pretending to be cool and sophisticated. But in your heart, you're a complete sentimentalist, a big bowl of emotional mush."

It occurred to her right then that he was right. And she wasn't the least ashamed of it. "Okay, Donovan. I plead guilty. I *am* sentimental. And really, what is so wrong with that?"

"Sentimentality is cheap."

Ben, sitting beside her, shifted tightly in his chair. "Cut it out, Donovan."

"Ben." She reached over and clasped his arm. "It's okay."

He searched her face. "You're sure?"

"I am positive." She turned her gaze on Donovan. "A lot of things are cheap. Laughter. Honest tears. Good times with good friends. A mother's love. A baby can have that love by the mere fact of its existence. Of its very vulnerability, its need for affection and care. Cheap is not always a bad thing—and I'll bet that when you were a child, you used to pull the wings off of butter-flies." She regretted the dig as soon as it was out. It wasn't true and she knew it. Whatever had shriveled his spirit had happened much more recently than his childhood.

He totally surprised her by responding mildly. "I was a very nice little boy, actually. Sweet-natured. Gentle. Curious."

The question was there, the one that kept eating at her. She framed it in words. "So then, what is it, ex-actly, that's turned you into such a bitter, angry man?"

He didn't answer. But he did look away, at last.

And for the rest of the evening, he was quiet. The few times he did speak, he was surprisingly subdued about it, almost benign.

Ben brought her red velvet cake that night. "I figured you deserved it, after that dustup in the music room."

"It wasn't so bad, really. I shouldn't have said that about him torturing butterflies."

"It got him to back off, didn't it?"

"Yeah. But…"

"What?"

"I don't know. Sometimes, in the past few days especially, I don't feel angry with him at all. I only feel sorry for him."

Ben put on a frown. "So then you don't want this cake…."

She grabbed for it, laughing. "Don't you dare take that away."

He handed over one of the plates and she gestured him inside. They sat on the couch as they always did when he brought dessert.

She took a couple of slow, savoring bites. "I don't know how Anton does it. Red velvet cake always looks so good, you know? But as a rule, it's a disappointment."

He nodded. "I know. It's usually dry. And too sweet."

"But not Anton's red velvet cake." She treated her mouth to another slow bite. "Umm. Perfect. Moist. And the cream cheese frosting is to die for. So good…"

Ben laughed. "You should see your face."

"Can you tell I'm in heaven? Good company *and* a really well-made red velvet cake. What more is there to life?"

"You're happy. I like that."

She gave him a bright smile, ate yet another dreamy bite of the wonderful cake. "You know, we really should go into that little town, Chula Mesa, one of these nights."

He swallowed, lowered his fork. His dark eyes shone. "We?"

"Yeah. You. Me. Donovan."

"Donovan." Ben spoke flatly now. "Of course, Donovan."

"No, really. I think it would be good for him, for all three of us, to get out of this house for a while. We could invite Anton and Olga, too. Make it a group outing."

Ben wasn't exactly jumping up and down with excitement at the prospect of a night out with his boss. "Have you brought this up to him?"

"Just that first night." She made a show of rolling her eyes. "You remember how well that went."

"What can I say? You can't make him do what he doesn't want to do."

"Ben, he needs to get out. He's…hiding here. He's made this house into his fortress—you know that he has. It's not good for him."

Ben lowered his half-finished plate to his lap. "Listen to you. You're getting way too invested in him."

"What's wrong with that? You said it yourself, that first night. You said he needed someone like me around."

"I didn't mean that you should make him into a… project."

"But I'm not."

"Abilene. You're his protégé. Not his therapist."

"Which is a very good question. Does he *have* a therapist—a counselor I mean, someone to talk to? If he spent half as much time trying to figure out what's going on inside him as he does in the gym downstairs, he'd be a much happier person. Not to mention, more fun to be around."

"No. He doesn't have a counselor."

"Well, he should. And he should get out. We should

work together on this, you and me, make it a point to get him to—"

"Abilene. Stop." Ben set his plate down, hard.

She blinked. "What?"

"*I'll* go with you, okay?" He spoke with intensity. With passion, almost. "Into Chula Mesa, to Luisa's. We can have a few drinks. A few laughs, just the two of us."

Just the two of us.

Suddenly, the rich cake was too much. She set it down, half-finished, next to Ben's. "Ben, I…"

He sat very still. And then he smiled. It was not a particularly pleasant smile. "Not interested, huh?"

"Ben…"

His lip still curled. But now, not in any way resembling a smile. "Just answer the question."

There was no good way to say it. "No. I'm not. Not in *that* way."

He let out a slow breath, and then smoothed his hair back with both hands. "Well, at least you didn't say how much you *like* me. How much you want to be *friends*."

"But, I do. On both counts. You know I do." She wanted to touch him. To soothe him. But that would be beyond inappropriate, given the circumstances. "But my liking you and wanting to be your friend…neither of those is the issue right now, is it?"

"No, they're not. The issue is that I want more. And you don't." Now he looked openly angry. "It's Donovan, right?"

She gaped. "Donovan? Not on your life."

He grunted, nodded his head. "Yeah. It's Donovan."

"Ben. Come on. I don't even *like* him."

"Yeah. You do. You like him a lot." He stood. "I think that you and I need to redefine the boundaries."

She hated that. But he was right. "Yes. I agree. I think we do."

"If you want to know about Donovan, you should ask him yourself. If you want to go to Chula Mesa with him, tell him so. If you think he needs a shrink, say so. Say it to him. Leave me out of it. Please."

He left her, shutting the door a little too loudly behind him.

"What did you do to Ben?" Donovan demanded when she walked into the studio the next morning bright and early.

As if she was answering that one. "Why do you ask?"

"Oh, come on. I know he's got a thing for you."

She took a careful breath. Let it out slowly. "If you knew that, you might have mentioned it to me before now."

"I thought it was none of my business."

"Oh, right. Because you're so considerate of other people and all." She was standing in front of her drafting table.

He rolled out from behind his twin computer screens and came at her, fast, stopping cleanly a foot from her shoes. "He left a half hour ago."

Her throat clutched. She gulped. "What do you mean, left?"

"He packed his suitcases and he left. He said he needed to get out of this house, away from here. Far away."

"For...how long?"

Donovan blew out a breath. "Abilene. He quit."

She felt awful. Yes, Ben had been upset last night. But she'd never imagined he would just pack up and move out, just walk away from a job he'd had for two years now. "But where will he go?"

Donovan stared up at her. His sky-colored eyes, as always, saw far too clearly. "If you cared that much, you wouldn't have turned him down when he made his play, now would you?"

She eased backward, around the drafting table, and sank into the swivel chair behind it, not even caring that Donovan would see the move for what it was: a retreat. "How would you know if he made a play for me?"

He let out a low sound—dismissive? Disbelieving? She couldn't tell which. "I guessed. And since you're not denying it, I'm thinking I guessed right."

She threw up both hands. "What do you want me to say?"

"How about the truth?"

"Fine. All right. He did ask me out. I said no." She glared at him, daring him to say one more word about it.

He said nothing. He only sat there, his strong hands gripping the wheels of his chair, watching her face.

She dropped her hands, flat, to the drafting table, making a hard slapping sound. "Where will he *go,* Donovan?" Tears of frustration—and yes, guilt, too—tried to rise. She gulped them down, hard.

He rolled a fraction closer and spoke with surprising gentleness. "Stop worrying. He owns a house in Fort Worth, near his family. And he's an excellent engineer. I gave him a glowing letter of recommendation. He'll easily find another job. Plus, it wasn't just you. I think he was getting a little tired of things around here. A little tired of the isolation, of dealing with me. He was ready to move on. And he definitely has options as to what to do next. So please, take my word on it, Ben is going to be fine."

She stared at him, vaguely stunned. He had just been *kind* to her, hadn't he? He'd made a real effort to soothe her worries about Ben.

Had he ever once been kind to her before?

Not that she recalled. And Donovan McRae being kind...that was something she would definitely have remembered.

She pressed her hands to her flushed cheeks, murmured softly, "It's...kind of you, to say that."

"Not kind," he answered gruffly. "It's only the simple truth."

A weak laugh escaped her. "You just can't stand it, can you? To have someone call you kind?"

"Because I'm not kind. I'm a hardheaded SOB with absolutely no consideration for anyone but myself. We both know that."

She closed her eyes, pressed her fingertips against her shut eyelids and wished she could quit thinking about the things Ben had said last night—about how she had a thing for Donovan. About how, if she had questions for Donovan, she should gut up and ask them of the man himself.

Well, she absolutely did *not* have a thing for Donovan. Not in the way Ben had meant. She was only...intrigued by him. She was curious about him.

And yes, she wanted to help him get past whatever

was eating at him, whatever had made him turn his back on his own life.

Was that so wrong?

He was watching her. Way too closely. "All right." He pulled a very clever sort of wheelie maneuver, leaning back in the chair, so the wheels lifted a fraction, turning while the wheels were lifted, and then rolling the chair backward until he was sitting beside her at the drafting table. "What terrifying thoughts are racing through that mind of yours?" He almost sounded...friendly.

So she told him. "I think you need someone to talk to."

"About what?"

"About...all the stuff that's bothering you. I think you need to see a trained professional."

He craned away from her in the chair. "A psychiatrist. You think I need a shrink."

"I do. Yes."

"No."

"Just like that?" She raised a hand and snapped her fingers. "No?"

"That's right. Just like that."

"Donovan, you're a very intelligent man. You have to know that there's no shame in seeking help."

"I didn't say there was shame in it. I only said no. And since I am perfectly sane and a danger to no one, I have that right. I'm allowed to say no."

"It's not about being sane. I know you're sane."

"That's a relief." He pretended to wipe sweat off his brow.

"I just thought that if you could talk it out with a professional, if you could—"

"I'll say it once more, since you have a bad habit of not listening when I say things the first time. No."

She could see she was getting nowhere on the shrink front. So she moved on to the next issue. "Then how about this? Will you go into Chula Mesa with me some evening?"

He actually groaned. "Didn't I make it clear two weeks ago that I was not going to Chula Mesa—with you, or otherwise?"

"You could rethink that. You could change your mind. People do that, you know, change their minds?"

"Abilene. Have you ever been in Chula Mesa?"

"Well, besides driving through it, no, I haven't."

"I've been in Chula Mesa. I've seen it all, been there. Done that. I don't need to go there again."

"Just…think about it. Please."

"I fail to understand what a visit to Chula Mesa could possibly accomplish."

"We'll get out of the house, see other people, broaden our horizons a little."

"If I wanted a broader horizon, I wouldn't look for it in Chula Mesa."

She was becoming irritated with him again. "You really should stop saying mean things about Chula Mesa."

"I will be only too happy to. As soon as you stop trying to drag me there."

"I'll leave it alone for now, okay? I'll bring it up again later."

"Why is it I don't find that comforting in the least?"

She still had a thousand unanswered questions for him. "One more thing…"

"With you, it's never just one more thing."

"Tell me about what happened, on that mountain, when you broke both your legs."

He slumped back in the wheelchair. "It's barely nine in the morning and already, you've exhausted me."

"Please. Tell me. I do want to know."

"You should have asked Ben, before you broke his heart."

She wanted to slap him. But then, that was nothing new. She schooled her voice to an even tone and reminded him, "A moment ago, you said he left more because of you than of me. Now you say I broke his heart."

"Figure of speech."

"Hah. Right—and since you brought it up, I'll have you know that I *did* ask Ben, that very first day. He told me that you fell several hundred feet down the side of a mountain, that both of your legs were badly damaged in the fall, each sustaining multiple fractures. He also said there *was* a possibility you might someday walk again."

"I can already walk." He smiled in a very self-satisfied way. "Your mouth is hanging open."

She snapped it shut. "But if you can walk…?"

"The chair is much more efficient," he explained. "And you have to understand that when I say I can walk, I mean with crutches. And also with considerable pain. Slowly, I'm improving. Very slowly."

"Well. That's good, right? That's excellent. What mountain was it, where?"

"What difference does the mountain itself make?"

"I would just like to know."

"We do eventually need to work today." He spoke in an infinitely weary tone.

"What do you mean, 'we'? Last I checked, all the work was on me. What mountain?"

He shook his golden head. "I can see it will take more energy to keep backing you off than to simply answer your unnecessary question."

"What mountain?"

"It's called Dhaulagiri." He pronounced it *doll-a-gear-ee*. "Dhaulagiri One. It's in Nepal, in the Himalayas. The seventh highest peak in the world. It's known as one of the world's deadliest mountains. Of all who try to reach the summit, forty percent don't come back. At least, not alive."

"So of course, you had to try and climb it."

"Is that a criticism?"

"No. Just an observation. So what happened—I mean, after you fell?"

"My climbing partner managed to lower himself down to me. And then, with him dragging me and me hauling myself along with my hands as best I could, we ascended again, to a more stable spot. He dug the ice cave. I wasn't much help with that. He dragged me in there. After that, he had to leave me to get help. That's a big no-no, in the climbing community. You never leave your partner. But we both agreed it was the only way, that since both of my legs were out of commission, there was no possibility I could make it down with only him to help me. So he made the descent without me. I was fortunate in that the weather held and a successful helicopter rescue was accomplished—but only after I spent three days alone on the mountain."

"In terrible pain," she added, because he didn't. "And is that it, then, those three horrific days? Are they why you say you won't work again, why you've retreated from the world?"

He studied her face for several very uncomfortable seconds, before he demanded, "What does it matter to you? What difference can it possibly make in your life, in the work that I'm perfectly willing to help you with, in the things I'm willing to teach you about the job I know you love?"

"Donovan, I want to understand."

He watched her some more. A searching kind of look. And then he said, "No."

She didn't get it. "No, you won't tell me?"

"No, it wasn't the three days in the ice cave—not essentially."

"So you're saying that *was* part of it, right?"

"No, that's not what I said."

"But if you—"

He put up a hand. "Listen. Are you listening?"

She pressed her lips together, nodded.

"If I'm a different man than I was a year ago..." He spoke slowly, as if to a not-very-bright child. "...it's not about my injuries. It's not about how I got them or how much they hurt. And it's not about the endless series of surgeries that came after my rescue, not about adapting to life on wheels. Society may ascribe all kinds of negative values to my situation, may view what happened to me when I fell down the mountain as a tragedy, blow it up all out of proportion to the reality, which is that I survived and I'm learning to live in my body as it is now."

She couldn't let that stand. "But Donovan, you're not learning to live, not in the truest sense. You're still... angry and isolated. You have Olga turn people away at the front door, people who care about you, people who have to be suffering, wondering what's going on with you."

He grunted. "Since you don't even know who those people are, how would you know that they're suffering?"

"You turn them away without even seeing them. That's just plain cruel. And on top of all the rest, you never intend to work again. *That* is a crime."

"Don't exaggerate."

"I'm not exaggerating. It *is* a crime, as far as I'm concerned. It's not right. Work is important. Work is… what we do."

"We?" He tried really hard to put on an air of superiority.

She wasn't letting him get away with that. "Yes, we. People. All people. We work. We all need that. Purposeful activity. Especially someone like you, who is the absolute best at what he does."

"You're going too far." His voice was low, a rumble of warning. "Way too far. You have no idea what I need. What I *have* to do."

"Well, all right. Then tell me. Explain it to me."

"Let it go, Abilene."

"But I want—"

He cut her off. "What *you* want. Yes. All, right. Let me hear it. You tell me what you want."

"I want to understand."

He leaned in closer to her. His eyes were the dark gray of thunderheads. "Why?"

"Well, I…" She was just too…aware of him. Of the

scent of him that was turbulent, somehow. Fresh and dangerous, like the air before a big storm.

He prodded her. "Answer me."

"Because I..." She couldn't go on. All at once, she realized she wasn't sure. Not of what she really wanted. And certainly not of what was actually going on here.

"Leave it alone," he said low. And then he wheeled away from her, swinging the chair effortlessly around the jut of her drafting table and out into the room. Halfway to his own desk, he spun on her again. "Will you just leave it now?"

She stared across the distance between them. And for no reason she could fathom, she felt her face flood with heat. And she felt guilty, suddenly. Guiltier even than when he told her that Ben had gone. She felt thoroughly reprehensible now, as if she'd been sneaking around somewhere she had no right go to, peering into private places, touching secret things.

"All right," she said, the words ragged-sounding, barely a whisper. "I'll leave it alone. For now."

"Leave it alone once and for all. Please." He waited for her to say that she would.

But she didn't answer him. She gave him no agreement, no promise that she would cease trying to learn about him, to understand him.

She couldn't make that kind of promise.

She couldn't tell that kind of lie.

Chapter 5

Donovan needed distance.

The painful conversation in the studio the morning that Ben quit was too much. He never should have let that happen between him and Abilene, and he set about making sure that nothing like it would happen again.

During work hours, he took care to set himself apart from her, to be only what he actually was to her: a teacher, the one who had set himself the task of helping her accomplish her goal. She was in his house for one reason—to get the design for the children's center ready to be presented to the Help the Children Foundation.

He was not her friend, he reminded himself repeatedly. They were not equals. She had a task to accomplish with his guidance. And that was all.

She did him the courtesy of letting him claim the distance he needed. He was on guard constantly, waiting for her to step over the line again, to badger him under the guise of trying to "understand" him.

But she didn't. She worked and she worked hard.

In the evening, all that week, by tacit agreement, they skipped the usual cocktails in the sitting area. They saw each other in the dining room, for dinner. They spoke of the progress that had been made on the design.

After they'd eaten, they said good-night.

He placed an ad in the local weekly paper, the *Chula Mesa Messenger,* for a new assistant. No, he didn't hold out much hope that he'd get an acceptable applicant that way. But he gave it a try.

The ad appeared when the paper came out on Thursday. Friday morning, four days after Ben's departure, he had three replies. He held the interviews that day.

One of the applicants seemed worth giving a trial. Her name was Helen Abernathy, and she was a retired secretary from Austin. Helen agreed to start that following Monday. She preferred not to live in, to return nightly to her own house and her retired husband, Virgil.

Helen's living at home was no problem for Donovan. He didn't really need a live-in assistant anymore, anyway. He'd become reasonably adept at taking care of himself by then. He could get into the shower by himself, dress himself, even drive himself in the specially modified van he'd bought, should he ever want to go anywhere. He only needed someone to handle correspondence, to pay the bills and field phone calls.

Since Helen would be going home at six, that would leave only him and Abilene at dinner. And when she re turned to San Antonio, which would be in three weeks now, if all went as planned, he would eat alone.

That was fine with him. Perfect. It was the choice he had made.

Saturday, Abilene knocked off work at about four.

Donovan knew she would use the pool, which he kept heated in the winter. Lately, she'd been swimming every day after she finished working.

Donovan knew this because he'd happened to be in his rooms around five on the afternoon of the day Ben quit. He glanced out the French doors of his sitting room—and saw her by the pool.

He watched her swim that day.

And each day since.

She wore a plain blue tank suit, a suit that showed off the clean, sleek lines of her body. She had slim hips and nice breasts, breasts that were beautifully rounded, high and full—but not too full. The breasts of a woman who had yet to bear a child.

He admired her pretty body in the same way that he admired her spirit and her quick mind. Objectively. From the safe cocoon of his own isolation. He felt no desire when he watched her. It wasn't sexual. It was simple appreciation of the beauty of her healthy, young female form.

When she emerged from her rooms, she would toss her towel on a bench and dive right in. She would swim the length of the pool, turn underwater, and swim back to where she had started, turn again, and head back the other way.

Back and forth, over and over. She swam tirelessly.

After twenty minutes or so, she would emerge, breathing hard. She would towel off quickly, and disappear into her rooms again.

That Saturday afternoon, when she climbed from the pool, as she was reaching for the towel she'd left thrown across a stone bench, she paused. She turned her head until it seemed to him she was looking directly at him, where he sat in his chair just inside the French doors.

She simply stood there, water sliding off her slim flanks, her hair slicked close to her head. She stood there and she stared right at him through those eyes that seemed fully golden right then, not so much as tinged with the faintest hint of green.

He knew she couldn't see him, that the light was wrong—and so what if she did see him? It wasn't any big deal, that he had seen her swimming.

Still, he rolled his chair backward until he was out of her line of sight.

Dinner was at seven-thirty, as usual. He went to the dining room with apprehension tightening his chest, sure she was going to give him a hard time about spying on her while she swam.

But when she joined him, she seemed the same as always—or at least, the same as she had been since they'd both said too much on the morning Ben left. She was quiet. Polite. Professional. They spoke of the project. They agreed that it was going well.

Olga was just clearing off to bring the dessert when the doorbell rang. The housekeeper straightened from gathering up the dirty dishes.

Abilene leaped to her feet. "It's okay, Olga. I'll get

the door." She spoke to the housekeeper—but she was looking straight at him. Daring him. Challenging him.

Olga hovered in place at the edge of the table, not sure what to do next.

So be it, he thought. "All right, Abilene. Go ahead. Get the door."

It was almost worth having to deal with whoever waited outside, to see the look of surprise on her face, the frank disbelief that he was finally going to let someone else in the house.

Olga calmly went back to clearing off.

And Abilene disappeared through the archway into the living area and the front hall beyond.

Abilene opened the door.

On the other side stood a pretty woman with thick black hair that fell in shining curls to below her shoulders. Small and shapely, the woman wore snug skinny jeans, a tight sweater and very high heels. She might have been thirty, or forty. Hard to tell. Behind her, in the dusty turnaround in front of the house, a red Cadillac waited—no doubt the same Cadillac Abilene had seen the night she first came to Donovan's house.

"Hello. I'm Luisa. Luisa Trias."

"Abilene Bravo." She shook the woman's offered hand. "I'm working with Donovan for a few weeks. Come on in…"

Luisa eased her fingers free of Abilene's hold and moved back a step. "Is Donovan here?"

"He is, yes. In the dining room. We're about to have dessert. Join us, why don't you?"

"Oh, I don't want to butt in. I only want to know that

he's all right. I've driven out here twice before. Both times, I was told that he wasn't at home...."

Abilene hesitated. Really, how much did she have a right to say? Maybe jumping up and insisting that she would answer the doorbell hadn't been such a brilliant move, after all.

But then Donovan spoke from behind her. "Luisa. How are you?" Abilene glanced over to see him sitting in the archway to the living area.

The pretty black-haired woman gasped. Clearly, she'd had no idea that he was using a wheelchair now. But Abilene had to hand it to her. She recovered quickly.

The woman scowled at him. "I've been calling. You never call back. And I've been out here, to try to see you. Your housekeeper keeps sending me away."

"I'm sorry, Luisa. Truly." He actually sounded remorseful. "I haven't been feeling like seeing anyone lately."

"Lately? It's been months since you came back." The huge dark eyes grew just a little misty. "A friend is a friend. You should know that. How is it that you've become such a bastard, Donovan? A big, selfish bastard, who cares so little for those who care for him?"

He had the grace to look ashamed. "It's a long story. Too long."

She touched the gold crucifix at her throat. "Are you all right?"

"I am. I'm fine. I promise you." He spoke gently, with what sounded to Abilene like real concern for Luisa's feelings. "Come in. Have some crème brûlée with us."

Luisa looked at him sideways. "I shouldn't forgive you...."

His smile was rueful. "Please. Come in."

"Are you sure? I needed to know that you're all right, but we can speak later if you—"

He put up a hand. "I repeat, crème brûlée. *Anton's* crème brûlée."

Finally, Luisa allowed herself to be convinced. She joined them in the dining room, where Olga served the dessert and coffee.

Luisa ate with relish. "Ah. Anton. That man can cook. Someday, when I open a real restaurant, I might have to steal him away from you."

"Luisa owns the local roadhouse, Luisa's Cantina," Donovan explained. He glanced fondly at the dark-haired woman. "It's a couple of miles outside of Chula Mesa."

Abilene sipped her coffee. "You mean the roadhouse I keep trying to get you to go to?"

He turned his gaze to her, his expression cool now. "That would be the one."

Luisa laughed, a husky, sexy sound. "Yes. It's a good idea, Abilene. Why don't you both come? And soon."

"We'll see," said Donovan. "One of these days…"

Abilene set down her coffee cup. It clinked against the saucer. "*I'll* be there next Friday night. Count on it—whether I can talk Donovan into coming with me, or not."

Luisa grinned. "Good. I'll look forward to seeing you." She sent Donovan a look from under her thick, black lashes. "You, too. I mean it. You've been acting like a stranger for so long now. It's time you stopped that."

"Luisa. I get the message. You can quit lecturing me."

"Come with Abilene, Friday night."

He looked away. "I'll think about it."

Luisa clucked her tongue. "I've been tending bar for almost two decades. I know what it means when a man says he'll think about something. It means that he's already done whatever thinking he is willing to do—and the answer is no."

He set down his spoon. "Enough about Friday night."

Even as he gruffly ordered Luisa to back off, there was real affection in his tone, in his expression. And Luisa seemed so fond of him, too.

Abilene knew she ought to make her excuses and go, give them a little privacy. No doubt the two of them wanted some time together, had things to say to each other that they wouldn't feel comfortable saying with someone else in the room.

Yet for reasons she refused to examine, she felt a certain reluctance to go, to leave him alone with a good-looking woman, a woman who'd most likely once been his lover.

Who might still be. Or plan to be.

Or...

Well, whatever the situation between the two of them was, exactly, Luisa and Donovan probably wanted some time to themselves.

She made herself rise. "I'm sure you two have a lot to catch up on, and I'll just—"

Luisa cut her off with another husky laugh. "Sit down, chica. It's not that way." She sent Donovan a teasing look. "Tell her. Make her see."

He made a gruff sound, something midway between a grunt and a chuckle. "Luisa's right. It's not that way. Though I did give it my best shot, back in the day."

Luisa made a face at him. "We met nine years ago, when he came out here to build this house. He came in my bar often then. And he was a big flirt. But I explained to him that I'm no longer a wild, foolish girl. I don't need a man to sweep me off my feet and then break my heart. But I can always use a true friend. And so we became friends—or so I thought." The corners of Luisa's full mouth drew down. "Until you stopped taking my phone calls."

He looked back at her levelly. "We're still friends, Luisa. You know we are."

She seemed to weigh the truth in his words. Finally, she nodded. "Okay, then. Prove it. Come with Abilene to my cantina next Friday night."

He tried his most forbidding expression. Luisa seemed completely unaffected by it. And then he demanded, "Will you stop pushing me? I said I would think about it."

"Less thinking, more doing," Luisa advised. She turned to Abilene. "Where are you from?"

"San Antonio."

"A beautiful city. Chula Mesa is not very exciting. It's like many small towns. Not a lot to do, but we have a nice little diner. I like to have my breakfast there on Sundays, after eight o'clock mass. Maybe you would meet me, tomorrow morning at a little after nine? We can get to know each other."

"She doesn't have time for that," Donovan grumbled. "We're on an important project, with a very tight timeline. She works seven days a week."

Abilene ignored him and spoke to Luisa. "I would love that, Luisa. I'll be there."

"Well, then." Luisa's pretty smile bloomed wide. "I'll look forward to seeing you."

They chatted some more, about casual things. And then Luisa got up to leave. Donovan and Abilene followed her to the door.

The minute she was gone, Donovan turned on Abilene. "I'll give you her number. You can call her and tell her you can't make it tomorrow, after all."

Abilene lounged back against the arch that led into the living area. "Why in the world would I want to do that?"

"Because you need to be working. There's no time to waste driving out to the Chula Mesa Diner."

"I can work into the evening some night, if I have to. I'm going, Donovan."

He gave her a long, smoldering look. "What for?"

"I like Luisa. And I can use a little break. I'll be back by eleven, at the latest."

He started to speak again—and then he didn't. Instead, he neatly whirled the chair around and rolled away from her.

Abilene had no trouble finding the diner. It was on Main Street, between Chula Mesa Hardware and Chula Mesa Sunshine Drugs.

She got there before Luisa. She chose a booth with a clear view of the door and ordered coffee for both of them.

Luisa arrived a few minutes later, wearing a snug-fitting V-neck navy blue knit dress and navy blue heels as high as the ones she'd worn the night before. She spotted Abilene immediately and her face lit up with her gorgeous, open smile. "Hey!"

"Hey."

Luisa hurried to join her in the booth. "So you came," she said, leaning across the table, pitching her voice to just above a whisper. "I wasn't sure you would make it."

Abilene frowned. "But I said I would be here."

"You did. But I thought that Donovan would try to change your mind about meeting me alone."

"He did try. But as you can see, my mind is my own."

"Yes, I do see." Luisa said the words approvingly. "But Donovan can be very persuasive, as I'm sure you know."

"Persuasive?" Abilene laughed at that. "No. That's not a word I would use to describe him. He's gruff and exacting. Demanding. Overbearing. Sometimes cruel, though not so much lately. But persuasive? Uh-uh. Not in the least."

"He *used* to be persuasive."

"Yeah? Well, he used to be a lot of things."

Luisa leaned even closer. She reached out, touched the back of Abilene's hand. "He's changed a lot."

"Yeah."

"He must guess that we'll talk about him. He'll hate that."

"Too bad."

The waitress came over. Luisa introduced them. "Margie, this is Abilene...."

When Margie had taken their orders and left them alone, Luisa sipped her coffee and leaned close again. "I do have a few questions. And I'm thinking it will be easier to get the answers from you than from Donovan."

"Ask. Please."

"I heard he had an accident during one of his climbing trips...."

Abilene quickly filled Luisa in on all she knew, from the fall on Dhaulagiri One, to the days alone in the ice cave, to the chain of surgeries. She spoke of his dedication to his physical rehabilitation. And she included what Donovan had told her the morning Ben left—that he *could* walk, though with difficulty, using crutches.

"He seems so sad," said Luisa. At Abilene's nod, she asked, "So what is this project you're working on with him?"

Abilene told her about the children's center, explained that she was the architect who'd won the fellowship he'd offered.

Margie came with the food. She gave them more coffee and left them alone again.

Luisa said, "I remember, a couple of years ago, he mentioned a plan he had to build a center in San Antonio for children in need. He was passionate about that."

"Well, it's finally happening. We're pulling the design together now. In a few weeks, we'll..." She corrected herself. "*I'll* be going back to SA, to supervise construction."

"He won't go with you? But why not?"

"He says he'll never work again."

"But that's impossible. He loves his work."

"I know. But he says that's all over now."

"He used to travel often, all around the world, building fine hotels, houses for rich people, museums, skyscrapers...."

Abilene set down her slice of toast after only nibbling the crust. "It seems so wrong, I know. He's locked himself up in his house. He won't come out and he won't let anyone in."

"But he let you in."

"I think he finally felt he had to. For the sake of the children who need the center we're building."

"And you've helped him," Luisa said.

"I don't know if I'd go that far."

"Abilene, you let *me* in. And he allowed it."

"Yeah. That's true. He did. Finally."

"You're changing his mind," said Luisa, as if it were such a simple, obvious thing. "You're making him see that life goes on—and life is good. That there's hope and there's meaning. That he can't hide in his house forever, nursing his injuries, feeling sorry for himself. That there's more of life ahead for him, much more. Years and years."

Abilene blew out a breath. "You make it all sound so…possible."

"But of course, it's possible. You're showing him that it is."

"I've been trying, believe me. I don't know *why* I'm trying, exactly. But I am." She fiddled with her napkin, smoothing it on her lap, though it really didn't require smoothing. "I can't…seem to stop myself."

Luisa said simply, "You care for him. There's no shame in that."

She glanced up, met the other woman's waiting eyes. "But I…"

Luisa's smile was soft and knowing. "Yes?"

"Well, I only mean…" She felt suddenly breathless, awkward and tongue-tied. "It's not that we're…intimate. We're not."

Luisa ate a careful bite of her breakfast. "But you do care for him, don't you?"

Abilene sat up straighter. Why should that be so difficult to admit? "Yes, all right. I do. I care for him." A low, confused sound escaped her. "But the way he behaves a lot of the time, I have no idea why."

Luisa laughed. "I know what you mean. Caring for him has to be a very tough job, given the way he is now. But someone's got to do it, got to reach out for him, got to…stick with him, no matter how hard he seems to be pushing everyone away."

"Yeah." Abilene laughed, too, though it came out sounding forced. "I guess I should look at it that way."

"And he is stronger than he knows."

"Oh, Luisa. You think so?"

"I know so. He will come back, to himself, to the world."

"I hope you're right."

"Trust me. I know him. Yes, he suffered a terrible accident. So?" She waved a hand, an airy gesture. "What is all that? What are months of operations and painful rehabilitation? Nothing. Less than nothing, next to losing a child…"

Abilene didn't know what to say. "Luisa, I'm so sorry. I had no idea you'd lost a child."

Luisa pressed her hand against the small gold crucifix at her throat. "Oh, no. Not me."

"But you said—"

"I meant of *his* child. Donovan's child. Elias."

Chapter 6

Abilene could not draw breath.

She felt, suddenly, the same as she had back in the third grade, when the class bully, Billy Trumball, had punched her in the stomach for coming to the defense of a smaller boy. That punch had really knocked the wind out of her. It was an awful, scary feeling, to fear her breath would never come, to gape for air like a landed fish.

She pressed her hand to her stomach, hard. And all at once the air rushed in again. She managed to whisper, "I didn't know...."

Luisa seemed shocked. "He never told you?"

Abilene shook her head. "I know I said we weren't intimate. But even that's an exaggeration. We are so much less than intimate. We're not friends, not even

close. I find that I want to understand him, you know?
But he's not an easy man to understand. And Ben—
Donovan's assistant?"

"Oh, yes. I remember Ben."

"Actually, he quit last Monday, which is another story
altogether. But what I'm getting at is that Ben and I,
well, I thought we got along. We talked some, about
Donovan. About what had happened to make him retreat from the world. I guess I thought I knew more
than I did."

"Ben never told you…?"

"Not a word. And Donovan never so much as hinted
at such a thing." She leaned across the table, pitched her
voice to a whisper. "I just can't believe I never knew.
Donovan's a famous man—I mean, to another architect,
like me, he's pretty much a living legend. You'd think
I would have heard from someone, at some point, that
there was a child. And then there's Dax…."

"Dax? I don't know him."

"Dax Girard, my new brother-in-law. He and my
baby sister got married a few weeks ago. Dax *knows*
Donovan. Not really well, I don't think. But still. Dax
never said anything about a lost child."

"Maybe it never came up," Luisa suggested gently.
"Elias has been gone for a while now."

"How long?"

"About five years."

"But Luisa, there are no pictures of a child in the
house—none that I've seen, anyway."

"No pictures…" Twin lines formed between Luisa's
dark brows. "But there were pictures a year ago. One
on the piano, of Elias at the beach in California, hold-

ing a starfish, smiling his wide, happy smile. One over the fireplace, a large portrait from when he was two or three, in the front room..." Her frown deepened. "I didn't look, last night, when we went through there on the way to the dining room. I didn't notice if Elias's picture was still above the fireplace. And I didn't go into the music room."

"No pictures," Abilene repeated. "Not in the public rooms of the house, anyway. How old was the child—Elias—when he died?"

"Six, I think."

"So you're saying Donovan was married, then?"

Luisa was shaking her head. "Abilene..."

"I just, well, I had no idea he'd been married."

"Please, Abilene."

She sat back in her chair. "What's the matter?"

"I can't say any more."

"But I was hoping, if you could just explain to me—"

"I can't. It's not right." Luisa reached across the table, caught Abilene's hand and held on. Her dark eyes were tender, her expression firm. "I've said too much already. You know I have. The rest is Donovan's to tell."

Donovan went to the studio at a little after ten.

Abilene was still in Chula Mesa with Luisa, wasting the valuable morning hours when she should have been working. He wondered what the two of them were talking about—and then he told himself to stop wondering.

It didn't matter, he tried to convince himself. Whatever they found to chatter about, it had nothing to do with him.

He reviewed, for the second time, the work Abilene

had done the day before. He made notes on her progress, notes on what she ought to get accomplished that day. And also notes on what she should be tackling in the next week. She was doing well, was actually a little ahead of where he'd hoped she might be at this time.

The truth was that she continued to thoroughly impress him, with how quickly she learned, with her dedication to the work. In fact, she could probably afford a Sunday morning at the Chula Mesa Diner with Luisa.

Not that he would ever admit that to her face.

She came in at ten forty-five. He felt a rising apprehension at the sight of her, in narrow gray slacks, a coral-colored checked shirt and a jacket nipped in at the waist. Her hair was windblown, her cheeks a healthy pink. He wanted to ask her if she'd had a nice time with Luisa.

But that would have been too friendly. He tried to be careful, not to get friendly with her.

Plus, he really didn't want to know about her breakfast with Luisa. He had a strong intuition that his name had probably come up. Maybe more than once. And he just didn't want to hear what those two might have said about him.

"Ready to work?" He rolled toward her.

She nodded, but didn't say anything as she slipped in behind the drafting table.

He circled the table and glided in beside her. That close, he could smell the light, tempting perfume she wore. She reached up, smoothed her hair. He found himself staring at the silky flesh of her neck, at the pure line of her jaw.

She slid him a look, frowned. "What is it?"

He cleared his throat. "I have notes, a lot of them."

"Well, all right then." Her voice sounded...what? Careful? Breathless? He wasn't sure. She added, "Let's get started."

He had dual urges—both insane. To ask her if everything was all right. To run the back of his finger down the satin skin of her neck, and to feel for the first time with conscious intent, the texture of her flesh.

Seriously. Was he losing his mind?

They went to work.

An hour later, he left her to continue on her own. He checked on her at three, then changed into sweats and went down to the gym where he worked out on his own, a long session with the free weights and then another, equally long, of simple walking, back and forth, with the aid of the parallel bars, sweating bullets with each step.

His legs really were getting stronger. Recently, he'd found he was capable of standing long enough to make use of a urinal, even without a nearby wall or a bar to brace himself with. It was a milestone of which he was inordinately proud.

At five, he returned to the main floor. He dropped in on her again before he went to clean up, because it was getting late and he was afraid she'd have left the studio if he took the time to shower first.

She was still there. "Just getting ready to wrap things up for the day," she told him. That green-golden gaze ran over him. "Good workout?"

"Yes, it was." He felt sweaty and grungy, and he probably smelled like a hard-ridden horse. But he should have thought of that before he came wheeling in here without a shower. "Let's see how you're doing...."

She showed him what she'd come up with in the past hour and a half. They briefly discussed what was going well. And what wasn't quite coming together.

They agreed that they had a good handle on the arrangement of space now. But they'd also decided the design had to speak of fun, of possibility. Probably of flight. That, they had begun to think, was the eventual *parti:* early flight.

Somehow, they needed to get the theme of flight into the facade and the main entry, so that when parents and children and teachers came to the center every day they felt a sense of uplift, that anything could happen in this special place, that they, the children who grew and learned there, could do anything they set their young minds to accomplishing.

This was the central idea for the structure. And that meant they needed to get a serious grip on it soon, since the rest of the complex would be likely to change, once they found the true heart of the project.

"Soon," he said, affirming what they both knew needed to happen. "I know you're going to find it soon."

She was straightening her workspace by then. "Well, probably not tonight. Right now, I think I could use a long, hard swim."

He had a sudden, stunning vision of her, emerging from the courtyard pool, all wet and gleaming, the water sliding off her body in glittering streams.

"Uh. Yeah," he said stupidly. "A swim. Good idea. Clear your head."

She regarded him. It was a strange, piercing sort of look. He almost wondered if she could see inside his mind, if she knew that he had watched her, in her blue tank suit, out in the courtyard, when she thought she was alone.

Well, if she did suspect him of spying on her, she could stop worrying. He would never do such a thing again.

"See you at dinner," she said, still eyeing him in that odd way—or at least, so it seemed to him.

"Yes," he answered distractedly. "See you at dinner."

And she left him.

He made himself stay behind in the studio, which was one of the few main floor areas without a view of the courtyard—and the pool. He went to his desk and he pushed his computer monitors out of the way, and he spent an hour sketching, plugging away at the facade problem.

At six-thirty, no closer to any kind of solution than he had been when he started, he went back to his own rooms to shower before dinner.

The lights in the courtyard were on by then. And before he turned on any lights in his sitting room, he went to the glass doors and gazed out.

The pool was deserted—which he had known it would be.

And he felt disappointed, that she wasn't still out there, after all—a feeling he knew to be completely reprehensible.

He whirled and rolled through his bedroom, and the wide-open double doors to the bathroom, where he tore off his sweats and used the railings he'd had installed months ago, to get into the open shower and onto the bathing stool waiting there.

Twenty minutes later, he was clean and dressed and on his way to the dining room.

Abilene was already there, in a simple long-sleeve black dress, standing at the doors that looked out on the courtyard. She turned when he entered.

In her eyes, he thought he saw questions. His guard went up.

But then she smiled. And all she said was, "There you are." Now she seemed almost happy to see him.

And he was glad, absurdly glad. That she hadn't asked any questions. That she had smiled.

They went to the small table that Olga had set for them. He wished he could stand up, step close to her, pull back her chair. Such a simple gesture, but not something he could do. Not yet, anyway.

And possibly, not ever.

She sat. He wheeled around the table and took the waiting place across from her. Olga had lit the candles, and already served the soup. And the wine was there, opened.

He poured. For Abilene. And then for him. He raised his glass. She touched hers to it. They sipped. Shared a nod.

Ate the soup.

Olga appeared with the salads. She took their empty bowls away, refilled their wineglasses. And vanished again.

They ate the salad, sipped more wine.

The whole dinner was like that. He didn't talk. Neither did Abilene.

But he felt…together with her, somehow. In collusion. Connected.

And that made him wonder, as he had more than once that day, if he might really be losing his mind somehow, slipping over the edge into some strange self-delusion.

On the mountain, in the snow cave, alone with his pain, he'd known he was going mad. He was crazy. And he was going to die.

On the mountain, he understood everything. He talked to Elias.

He was ready to go.

And there had been peace in that, a kind of completion.

When they dragged him back to the world, peace became the thing that eluded him.

Until tonight, for some unknown reason. Tonight, in the quiet of the dining room. Sharing a meal with Abilene.

It ended too soon. She got up, smiled again at him, said good-night.

"Good night," he answered, and watched her go.

The room seemed empty without her. Yet another sign of his current slide into total insanity.

Tomorrow, he promised himself, in the bright light of morning, the world would right itself. He would be the man he had become in the past year. Self-contained. Wanting no one. Needing no one.

Alone.

In her rooms, Abilene changed into the old pair of sweats and worn T-shirt she usually slept in. She brushed her teeth. And then she paced the floor for a while.

What had just happened, in the dining room?

She had questions for Donovan. And she'd fully intended to ask them. She had planned to be delicate about it. And respectful. But really, there was so much she wanted to know.

And she'd accepted that Luisa was right. If she wanted answers—about whether Donovan had been married, about his wife, if there had been one, about the child he had lost—well, it was only fair that she ask the man himself.

But then she'd turned from the doors to the courtyard to find him sitting there, so gorgeous, so self-contained, so guarded....

And she couldn't do it. She didn't even *want* to do it, to pry into his mind and his secret heart. To ferret out the answers he didn't want to share.

All she wanted was to be with him.

Simply. Gracefully. For an evening.

To share a meal with him, if not as a friend, at least as a temporary companion, a guest in his house. She was grateful to him, she realized, for teaching her so much, for guiding her at the same time as he prodded her forward. For demanding so much of her, for never letting her off easy.

For being such a fascinating man.

So she had done exactly what she wanted. She'd shared a quiet meal with him.

And now she paced her sitting room, feeling edgy and full of nervous energy, not understanding herself any better than she understood him.

Eventually, she gave up wearing a path into the hardwood floor. She got out her cell and called home, called her mom, and her sister, Zoe, who was just back from her honeymoon.

Yes, she was tempted to ask Zoe if she would speak with Dax, try to find out from him if he knew that Donovan had had a son. But she didn't. She reminded herself that Donovan was the one she should ask about the child.

If she ever asked anyone at all.

She called Javier to see how things were going with him—and then ended up going on and on about the design for the children's center, about the idea for the facade that still wasn't coming together, about how much she was learning from Donovan. As always, he encouraged her and he asked all the right questions.

By the time she hung up with Javier, it was after ten. She got into bed and turned off the light and told herself that she was glad she'd decided not to hound Donovan anymore about his past, about his secrets, about his private life.

From now on, she would do the job she had come here to do, period. She would be pleasant at dinner, in a thoroughly surface sort of way. And in three weeks, she would leave this house and the solitary man who lived here. She would build a special children's center and get a great job with a top firm.

And if she ever thought of Donovan McRae again, it would be with simple gratitude for the opportunity he had given her.

Donovan woke at ten after six Monday morning with the facade, vestibule and welcome area of the children's center clear in his mind.

He could see it. He understood it. He knew how to build it. He *had it,* damn it.

He knew how it should be.

He needed to draw it, fast. And then he needed for Abilene to see it. He couldn't wait to show it to her. This was the breakthrough they'd been waiting for.

After today, it was all going to fall into place. And fast. Even faster than it had up till now.

He sat bolt-upright in bed, threw back the covers and swung his legs to the side, unthinking. His feet hit the floor and he leaned forward to stand.

The arrows of shimmering pain brought him up short. He looked down at the deep grooves of scar tissue, scoring his thighs, the flesh over his knees, which were now made of metal and plastic, and lower, to his skinny, wasted calves.

He tossed back his head and laughed out loud.

It was the first time since the fall down the mountain that he'd actually forgotten there was a problem with his legs.

After that, he took it a little slower. But not a lot. He was a man with a mission, and the mission was to get the concept in his head down onto paper, to take what he'd discovered and to show it to Abilene.

What he'd discovered. Sometimes an inspired design element felt like that: like a discovery. Not as if he'd created it at all. But as if it had been waiting, whole and ready, for him to finally see it.

He rang Olga and asked her to bring him coffee in the studio. And then he threw on some clothes and wheeled at breakneck speed out of his rooms and down the hall.

In the studio, he turned on some lights to boost what

natural light there was from the skylights and the clerestory windows, so early on a gray winter morning. He got out large sheets of drawing paper and soft pencils and he went to work.

It came so fast, he could barely keep up with it, his hand moving, utterly sure, across the paper, every stroke exactly right, no hesitation. Just a direct channel to the idea that was waiting, so impatiently now, to reveal itself.

When he finished, he looked over and saw that Olga had come and gone, leaving the coffee he'd asked for, along with a couple of Anton's killer cinnamon rolls. He took time for a cup, ate half a cinnamon roll.

By then, it was after seven. And there was no way he could wait any longer. Even if Abilene came to the studio early, it could still be an hour before she put in an appearance. Before he could show her what he had.

He couldn't do it, wait that long.

So he gathered the drawings—the one of the facade, the one of the entry interior and the one from the floor of the welcome area, looking up. He rolled them, snapped a band around them, laid them across his thighs and went to find her.

Often she would grab breakfast in the kitchen, so he wheeled there first and stuck his head in. Anton stood at the stove stirring something that made his stomach growl.

"Abilene?" Donovan asked.

"Haven't seen her yet today."

"Thanks." And he was off down the interior hallway.

He reached the door to her sitting room and braked sideways to it, gave it a strong tap, called, "Abilene?"

She didn't answer.

He knocked again.

Nothing.

Was she still in bed? If so, she needed to get up. Now. She needed to see this and she needed to get herself together and get to work.

He tried the doorknob. It turned.

So he pushed the door inward. "Abilene?"

Still no answer. She must be a sound sleeper.

Too bad. It was imperative that he get her up, that he share with her what he'd found out. She was going to be so happy, so relieved. It was all coming together, and it would be a really fine piece of work, something they could both be proud of.

He wheeled over the threshold and into her private space. The bedroom door, in the far corner to the left as he entered, was wide open, so he went for it, rolling the length of the sitting room and then into her bedroom.

The blinds were drawn against the morning light, the bed unmade. And empty. The bathroom door, directly across from the door to the sitting room, stood open. The light was on in there. And he could hear the unmistakable sound of the shower running, feel the moisture in the air...

He backed and turned, approaching the bed. He saw the black dress she'd worn the night before, laid across the bedside chair. Saw her cell phone on the nightstand, beside a half-full glass of water, and a framed snapshot of a bunch of good-looking, smiling people. He picked it up, that picture, for a closer look.

Her family. They stood out in the country somewhere, in front of a weathered cabin. Father and

mother. Seven broad-shouldered brothers. Abilene—
but younger, her face a little rounder than now. And
another girl who resembled her.

Carefully, he set the picture back exactly where he'd
found it.

He knew where she had to be, of course. Had known
when he saw the light from the bathroom, heard the
sound of the water running in there. He knew he should
wheel around, roll into the sitting room, and on out the
way he had come.

But he didn't wheel away. All he could think was
that she had to see what he had to show her.

He backed up, turned his wheels toward the sound
of running water, and rolled on through that open bathroom door.

Chapter 7

She was in there, as he had known she would be.

In the shower. The doorless, open shower.

Wearing nothing but the slim, smooth perfection of her own skin, facing away from him, her head tipped up to the shower spray, eyes closed, soap and water sheeting down over her pink-tipped breasts, her concave belly, her gently curving hips, her perfect bottom, her long, lean thighs.

He stopped the chair without a sound.

And he watched as she turned her body in a gentle, side to side swaying motion, rinsing herself, letting the spray carry the bubbles away. He saw her from the back, and then in profile, and then full front.

At first, it was the same as when he watched her in the pool. A pure appreciation of something so beautiful, so smooth—her skin flushed, steamy; the secret shadow beneath her arm as she slicked her wet hair back. The soft, round curve of the side of her breast.

But in seconds, everything changed. It became more than just about the perfect picture she made, more than the slim, womanly shape of her, more than the frothy dribble of bubbles sliding down sleek, youthful skin.

He saw her as a woman.

Desirable to him.

More than desirable.

Wanted. Yearned for. Craved.

The reality of the situation became all at once blindingly clear. He had been lying—to her, and more than to her, to himself. He'd treated her callously, cruelly.

Because she stirred him. She…excited him. From their initial meeting, in the studio, when Ben brought her to him on that first day, he had felt it—the brisk wind of change on the air.

Felt a sense of possibility, of promise. As if she had marched into a darkened, stuffy room on those long, strong legs of hers, run up the shut blinds, and thrown the windows wide.

He'd been blinking and whining and sniping against the light ever since. Like some cranky old man.

Yes. Like an old man. An old man awakened abruptly from a long, fitful sleep. He'd been digging at her, taunting her, trying to get her to give up and go, to leave him in peace—but at the same time he couldn't help but be drawn to her.

She was not only a joy to look at, she had an incisive intelligence. She questioned everything, wanted to see beneath the surface, to understand the deeper truth. And beyond looks and brains, she possessed a kind and generous heart.

She was pretty much perfect. His ideal woman.

And he had met her too late.

All this came to him in an instant—the instant before she turned beneath the spray and opened her eyes.

She let out a shriek, blinked fiercely against the water that still ran into her eyes, blinding her—and looked again. "Donovan? What in the…?" She turned, twisted the knob to cut off the water, at the same time as she groped for the towel on the rack outside the shower stall.

He spun the chair to face the door, giving her the chance to cover herself, at least. And then he just sat there, the rolled drawings he'd *had* to show her waiting in his lap, feeling not only reprehensible, but shamed beyond bearing.

Was she wrapped in a towel yet? She was absolutely silent behind him. All he heard were the final hollow drip-drip-drips of water on slate from the shut-off shower heads.

And he couldn't think of a damn thing to say. Sorry was not going to cut it. And as for trying to justify what he'd just done? There was no justification. None.

She spoke then, her voice low and tight. "Would you just leave, please?"

It was the permission he'd been waiting for. She had released him. He didn't look back at her. He kept his gaze straight ahead as he wheeled out of the bathroom, across the dim bedroom, down the empty sitting room and out through the open hallway door.

* * *

Abilene's first thought, once she heard him shut the outer door behind him, was that she needed to go. She needed to get her stuff packed, throw it in her car and get out, go home, back to San Antonio where she belonged.

Really, she couldn't stay here anymore. She just couldn't.

She traded the hastily grabbed towel for the robe that hung on the back of the bathroom door. Her hair hung in snaky coils, still dripping wet, and she left a trail of droplets across the bedroom floor as she pulled back the door to the walk-in closet, went in there and grabbed an empty suitcase, the largest one of the three she had brought with her.

She hauled it back into the bedroom, tossed it on the bed, got hold of the zipper tab and ripped it along the track until she had it undone. Then she flipped the top back, spreading it wide.

After that, she just stood there, staring into the empty space within, still dripping on the bedside rug, feeling overwhelmed and awful and foolish.

And also numb, somehow.

She shook herself. Then she turned on her bare heel and marched back into the closet, where she grabbed a bunch of stuff, hangers and all, and lugged it back to the open suitcase. When she got there, she flung the whole pile into the yawning interior.

Bracing her hands on her hips, she stared down at the tangle of shirts and light jackets, knit tops and cardigan sweaters.

"What a mess," she whispered, to no one in particular. "What a stupid, crazy mess."

She turned, sank to the edge of the bed and gazed blindly toward the open door to the closet and thought how, if she was going to go, she shouldn't be just sitting here, staring off into space. She needed to finish packing, to put on some clothes, to dry her hair.

But she didn't get up. She continued to sit there. By then, she was thinking that she didn't really want to go.

She wanted to finish the design for the children's center. She wanted her chance to see it built.

And still, the yearning remained within her, to understand what was going on with Donovan, to…talk to him, or *not* to talk. Just to be with him the way they had been at dinner the night before. To enjoy spending time with him. Without having to be constantly on guard against his sudden, inexplicable cruelty.

She wanted to be able to laugh with him, to speak openly. Honestly. Without fear of emotional ambush or petty retaliation.

With a heavy sigh, she got up, scooped the tangle of clothing and hangers into her arms, carried them back to the closet, and hung them up again. She returned to the bedroom, shut the suitcase, zipped it tight and put it away.

She was just emerging from the closet when she heard the polite tap on the sitting room door.

What now?

"It's open," she called, and then went over and sat on the long, rustic bench at the end of the bed.

She heard the outer door open. A moment later, Donovan appeared in the bedroom doorway.

He stopped the chair there, hands tight on the wheels, and waited, his fine mouth a grim line, his eyes bleak.

She was still naked under the robe and her hair hung on her shoulders in wet clumps. But so what? He'd already seen everything anyway.

Carefully, she smoothed the robe on her bare knees. Then she drew her shoulders back and aimed her chin high. "You have something you want to say?"

He nodded. And then, finally, with obvious difficulty, he said, "An apology seems ridiculous. It's not as though I have any excuse for my behavior."

She said nothing. If he had some kind of explanation to make, well, let him go for it.

He didn't waver, didn't look away. "Ridiculous," he repeated. "But nonetheless necessary." His eyes were dark right then, haunted. Gunmetal gray. He drew in a slow breath. "And so I do, I apologize. For what that's worth, which I know is not a lot."

She fiddled with the tie of the robe, nervously. And realized the action betrayed her. So she let it go and wrapped her arms tightly around her middle. "These rooms are the one thing I have here, for myself, in this house. The one place I don't have to be on guard, ever. The one place you are not allowed to be."

"You're right. I know." He let out another careful, pained breath and lowered his golden head. In shame, she hoped.

Because he *should* be ashamed.

She accused, "And now you've not only invaded my space, you've wheeled on into my bathroom and watched me in the shower." She waited until he lifted his head and met her eyes. And then she gave him a look meant to sear him where he sat. "I turned around and you were…just sitting there, watching me. Why?"

"There's no excuse," he muttered low.

"No argument there. I'll ask you again. Why?"

It took him a long count of five to answer. "Because you're beautiful—or at least, at first, that was why."

She scoffed, "What? I should be flattered now?"

"No. Of course not. I'm just trying to explain myself. Not that anything I say is going to make it okay. But you should know that at first, it was a totally objective appreciation."

"Objective?" She let out a harsh laugh. "As in detached?"

"I suppose so."

"And is that supposed to ease my mind somehow? That you broke into my rooms, rolled into my bathroom and looked at me—*stared* at me without my clothes on—and you felt nothing?"

"I didn't say I felt nothing—I said I saw you...I don't know, without heat, I guess."

What was he telling her? She had no idea. She should leave it alone, send him away.

But she didn't. "You looked at me coolly? Dispassionately. Is that it?"

"No. There was passion. But it wasn't personal. It was more the way I would admire good art."

"Good art." She shook her head. "I have to tell you, Donovan. This is one strange conversation."

He wheeled a fraction closer—caught himself, and wheeled back to where he'd been before. "There's more. You should know the rest of it. There should be honesty between us, at least."

Honesty. Well, okay. She agreed with him about the honesty. She *wanted* honesty.

She wanted that a lot.

"What else then?" She looked at him sideways, needing the truth, yes. But contrarily, not really sure she wanted to know whatever he might reveal next.

He revealed it anyway. "I watched you swimming, too."

Her cheeks were suddenly burning. She pressed her palms to them. "Oh, great. And I need to know that, why?"

"Because it's the truth. It's what I did. And I don't want to lie to you, by omission or otherwise, about what I did. I owe you that much, at least."

She had no idea how to answer that. So she simply sat there, waiting, for whatever he would say next.

He went on, "And it was the same, when I watched you swimming, as it was at first a little while ago, in there." He gestured toward the bathroom. "There was appreciation. Admiration. A vague, faraway sense of longing, I guess you could say."

She sat forward, curious in spite of herself. "Longing for...?"

"I don't know. For the man I was once. For the past. For the present and the future, too. But not as they are and will be. As they *might* have been."

She thought of his child then, of the little boy. His lost son, Elias. She longed to ask him about Elias.

But no. Bringing up Elias now would only send them spinning off in another direction entirely. They needed, right now, to stay with the subject at hand.

The painful, awkward, weird—and thoroughly embarrassing—subject at hand.

She raked her fingers back through her soggy hair. "So. You felt appreciation. Objective appreciation."

"Yes. When I watched you swimming. And today, too. At first. But then it changed."

Her throat clutched. She gulped hard, to make it relax. "Changed?"

"That's right. It became…something more. I found I was attracted. To you. As a man is attracted to a woman. It stopped being objective. I realized I want you. And I haven't wanted anything or anyone since before the accident on the mountain—a long time before."

I want you. Had he actually just said that out loud?

Okay, she truly was not ready to be having this conversation. Maybe she would never be ready. To speak of desire, of attraction, of *sex* with Donovan McRae.

That wasn't why she'd come here, worked her butt off, put up with his antagonism and his ruthless remarks. She was here for the work, and only the work. She had absolutely no interest in…

She caught herself up short.

Who was she kidding?

She did have an interest in Donovan, as a man. She had a serious interest.

He had captivated her from the beginning. From the first time she saw him, as a dewy-eyed undergraduate, one in hundreds in the audience on that long-ago evening when he came to speak at Rice.

And since she'd been here, in his house, it was pretty much a toss-up over which fascinated her more: the work she'd come out here to do, or the man in the wheelchair across the bedroom from her.

In the end, it was pretty simple. Much simpler than

either of them were allowing it to be. She wanted him. And he wanted her.

They should start with that. See where it led them…

But really, *how* to start? *That* was not simple. Not with a man like Donovan.

She rose and walked past him, crossing to the French doors. She opened the blinds. The winter sunlight spilled in, filling the room, gray and cool. Outside, the wind found its way into the courtyard, ruffled just slightly the glassy surface of the pool.

He said her name, "Abilene."

She turned to look at him again.

His gaze didn't waver. He sat absolutely still at the threshold of her bedroom, waiting.

She asked, "But why?"

"Why, what?"

"Why did you come in here in the first place? I mean, it's one thing to look out a window and see me in the pool. It's another to wheel right into my bathroom when you can hear the shower running and have to be reasonably certain you'll find me stark naked in there."

He lifted one shoulder in a halfhearted shrug. In the morning light, she could see he hadn't shaved yet. Golden stubble shone on his lean cheeks and sculpted jaw. He said, "I told you, there's no excuse."

"You're right. There isn't." But there had to be something. "But I think there *is* a reason, isn't there?"

He blew out a breath. "Fine. Yeah. There's a reason." He didn't say what—really, the man was beyond exasperating.

She was forced to prompt him again. "Okay. *What* reason?"

And he finally gave it up. "I figured out the answer to our main problem. You must know how it is, when the solution finally comes." He held out both hands to the side, palms up. "Magic time. I woke up this morning and I knew what we had to do...."

"Wait a minute..." She felt suddenly breathless. Buoyant. "You mean you figured out what we need for the entry and the facade?"

He nodded.

"Oh, Donovan. That's huge."

He lowered his head and spoke with real modesty. "It seemed that way at the time."

"I can't believe it. This is fabulous. So you, what? You dreamed it?"

"Well, I wouldn't say that, exactly. I just woke up and I knew. I went to the studio. I couldn't get it down fast enough. And when I had it, I came looking for you. I couldn't wait to show you. It seemed important at the time."

"Donovan. It *is* important. It's everything—I mean, *if* you've really got it...."

"Oh, I've got it." A slow smile burst across his wonderful face. He looked so charming, when he smiled.

She remembered then. When she had turned in the shower and opened her eyes, saw him sitting there, big as life in her bathroom: there had been rolled drawings in his lap. "You had them with you before, didn't you?"

"Yeah."

"But where are they now?"

"I went back to the studio. I left them in there."

"Why didn't you tell me that up front? I mean, it

would have made what you did a little easier to understand."

"I told you. That would have been an excuse. And there is no excuse." He glanced away, then back at her again. "Do you...want to see them?"

"Are you kidding? I can't wait to see them."

"You're not leaving, then?" He looked so hopeful, his face open and eager.

And she saw, at that moment, the man he had been, the man she had glimpsed from a distance once so long ago, before he lost a child. Before he fell down a mountain. Before all the things that can kill a man inside, make him hard and cold, cruel at heart.

"No," she said. "I'm not leaving."

Already, he was backing, clearing the doorway so he could turn. "Then get dressed. Meet me in the studio...."

"Donovan." She said his name softly. But it was, unmistakably, a command.

He froze, his strong body drawn taut, rigid in the chair.

She said, slowly and deliberately, "Stay. Please. Stay here with me. Just for a little while, all right?"

He stared, perhaps sensing the direction of her thoughts, yet not really believing. And then he whispered, "But I don't..." For once, he didn't have the words.

She asked, gently now, "Would you come out of the doorway, please? Would you...come here?"

He started to come to her—then stopped the chair with a firm grip on the wheels. "Abilene..."

"Hmm?"

"You really don't want to go there."

"Don't tell me what I want. You'll get it wrong every time."

His dark gold lashes swept down, then instantly lifted again to reveal watchful, stricken eyes. "I only mean, it's not a good idea. We've cleared the air between us. You've decided to stay, to finish what we started. Now we can forget about all this."

"Forget?" It hurt, a lot, that he had decided to make what had passed between them just now sound so unimportant, so trivial. "Would it be that easy for you, to pretend this morning never happened?"

"You know what I mean. We can go forward, do the work that has to be done, leave the rest of it alone."

"The rest of it?"

He glanced beyond her, toward the open bathroom door. The light was still on in there. She followed his gaze briefly, long enough to see what he saw—the gleaming trail of water across the floor. Her towel in a damp clump, right where she had dropped it when she grabbed for her robe.

"It would only lead to trouble," he said gruffly, at last, still looking past her. "I'm no good for that, not anymore."

She made herself ask, "No good for what?"

He shut his eyes again. And that time, when he opened them, he met her gaze with defiance. And such stark, determined loneliness. "No good for any of it. Sex. Love. A future with someone with you."

She tried for a teasing note. "Love and the future, huh? Well, Donovan, we really don't have to tackle everything at once."

He laughed, as she'd hoped he might. But it was a gruff laugh, a sound with more pain than humor in it.

"And as for sex…" She was looking down again, at her own bare feet on the hardwood floor. She drew her head up to find him watching her, his focus absolute. Unwavering. Waiting for her to finish what she'd so boldly begun. She blurted out, "Well, does it work? I mean, *can* you…? Is there some kind of damage, or is it all in your mind?"

A silence from him. Then, warily, "How many questions was that? Four?"

She was not backing off on this. "So pick one."

He did, after a moment. "There's no physical problem."

"So it's a psychological issue, then?"

"Abilene." He said her name in a weary voice. "Psychological. Emotional. Mental. I have no clue, okay? In the past year, I never so much as thought about it. It wasn't as if I cared."

"Oh." Disappointment had her shoulders drooping. She whispered, "I see…"

"At least, not until about twenty-five minutes ago." Was that an actual gleam she now saw in his eyes?

"Oh!" She snapped up straight again. Of course. How could she have forgotten? He'd already said it—that he wanted her, in a man/woman way. "So you *can,* then? You're…able?"

"Yeah. I'm able."

She found she was grinning. And then he was grinning, too.

And then they were both laughing, together.

It felt so good, to laugh with him. As good as she'd

dared to imagine it might. She wanted to go to him, to touch him, to lay her hand against his beard-stubbled cheek, maybe bend down and press her lips to his.

But he had stopped laughing. He was watching her again. And his eyes were wary.

So she didn't approach him. She went past him, to the side of the bed, and sat down. The silence stretched out. Finally, she couldn't bear it any longer. "Well, okay. I'm relieved—not that we couldn't have worked something out. I mean, there are a lot of different ways to make love."

He said nothing to that, only arched a gold-dusted brow.

What? Had she said something that offended him? She felt breathless all over again. And embarrassed, too. But still, she refused to give up on this.

She suggested what she hadn't quite had the nerve to do. "Maybe just a kiss. Would that be all right? We could start with a kiss. For now."

He stayed where he was, in the doorway. And he asked, so gently, "Is that wise?"

"Oh, come on." She threw up both hands. "What do you mean, wise? Is a kiss ever wise? What kind of question is that?"

"You just need to be aware that I meant what I said."

"About…?"

"Love. A future for you and me, together. It's not going to happen. You would have to understand that, going in."

She realized she could easily become irritated with him again—she *was* irritated with him again. "A minute ago, you said there couldn't be sex, either. But it seems to me that already, you've changed your mind about sex."

He only nodded. Slowly. "I'm a man. Men are weak. On two legs—or on wheels."

She wasn't buying that lame excuse. "You're not weak. We both know that. Blind and stubborn and needlessly cruel, maybe. But weak? Never."

He held his ground—in the doorway, as well as in his intractable, impossible attitude. "You should think it over. Better yet, you should forget the whole thing."

She pressed her palms to the tangled sheets, braced forward on them. And tried, one more time, to get through to him, to get them back to the way it had been between them such a short time before. "Is that what you want, seriously? To forget this morning? Forget what happened? Forget everything that we said?"

He frowned. And then he said her name, so softly, with tender feeling, "Abilene…"

And for a split second, she *believed*.

She believed in him, in the possible future. In the hope of love. She was certain he would at least admit that there was no way he could forget what had passed between them just now.

For that beautiful instant, she could see it, all of it, just as it would go. See him shaking his head as he confessed that no, he couldn't forget, didn't *want* to forget. And then she could see herself rising, going to him, bending close to him, claiming his mouth in their first lovely, tender, exploratory kiss.

But then he said, "Yes. It's what I want. I think that forgetting would be for the best."

Chapter 8

And that was it. It was over between them—over without ever really getting started.

He backed, turned, glanced over his shoulder. "The studio, then?"

She nodded, pressed her lips together, made them relax. "I'll be there soon."

He left her rooms for the second time that morning, again shutting the door to the main hall quietly behind him.

"Ho-kay," she said aloud to the silent bedroom, once he was gone. "So we forget."

She rose, went to the bathroom, hung up her towel, dried her hair, brushed on mascara, applied a little blusher and some lip gloss. She took off her robe, hung it on the door, rolled on deodorant, spritzed on scent

Back in the bedroom, she got dressed.

Her stomach was empty and she needed her morning shot of caffeine, so she stopped in at the kitchen to grab something to eat. Anton gave her a big mug of fragrant, fresh-brewed coffee and told her that Donovan had already ordered breakfast for her. It was waiting in the studio.

She wanted to snap at Anton, to inform him in no uncertain terms that Donovan didn't get to decide everything, that where she ate her breakfast damn well ought to be up to her.

But it wasn't Anton's fault that she felt like biting someone's head off. She thanked him and went on her way.

In the studio, Donovan was at his desk. He glanced up when she entered.

She gave him a nod—one minus eye contact—and followed her nose to the credenza where Olga had left the food. Under the warming lid were light-as-air scrambled eggs, and the raisin toast she adored. She grabbed the plate and a fork and carried them and her coffee back to her work area, where she ate. Slowly. Savoring every bite.

Donovan didn't say a word. Not until she'd carried the empty plate back to the credenza and helped herself to more coffee from the carafe waiting there. She had no idea what he was doing while she was eating. She was very careful not to glance his way.

Not even once.

But the moment she set the plate back on the credenza, he said, "Come here. Have a look."

A sharp retort rose to her lips. She bit it back. *Forget,* she reminded herself. *We are forgetting....*

She went to him, circling around the giant desk, until she stood at his elbow. The drawings were spread out in front of him.

For a moment, she refused to look down. She sipped her coffee. She gazed in the general direction of the door she had entered through, thinking how she almost wished she could go out that door and keep walking.

Never come back.

"Abilene." He had tipped his head back, was looking at her.

She went ahead and did it, let herself look at *him.*

Zap. Like a bolt of lightning in the desert, visible for miles. Heat flared across her skin.

How stupid and pointless, to feel this way.

It had been better when she had been in denial about it.

Forgetting, she reminded herself. Again. *We are forgetting.*

She tore her gaze from his and turned her focus to the sketches.

And instantly, she felt better. Her injured fury faded to nothing. Because she had something else to think about. Something important.

Something that mattered as much—no. *More,* she told herself silently. Insistently. *The work matters more than whatever is never going to happen between this impossible, exasperating man and me.*

She leaned closer.

How had he done it? It was perfect. It was exactly right—a series of wide, overlapping skylit arches high above the entrance, like the wings of transparent birds, spread in flight. From the front, it almost seemed that the building itself was about to take to the air.

And from inside, in the entry and welcome area, the arches were wings, too, but now, wings seen from below, wings three stories up, wings spread wide, wings already claiming the endless sky.

She said, "Oh, Donovan, exactly. It's exactly right. Astonishing. Perfect."

"You think?" He sounded young again. Hopeful. Proud.

"I *know*," she told him. "It's what we've been needing, what we've been waiting for."

And she really did feel better about everything then.

After all, hadn't he said at the beginning that he would never work again?

And yet he *was* working.

The proof of that was spread on the big desk before her. He was working. He was changing. No matter how hard he tried to deny his own awakening, he was beginning to care how the whole thing turned out.

What was it Luisa had said? *He will come back, to himself, to the world.*

Abilene could see that now. He was already coming back.

And even if there was never any hope for the two of them, as lovers. Even if there was no future for them, together.

Well, she could live with that. It would be something, at least, to know that she'd helped him a little, that she had contributed to his finding his life and his work again. It would be a fair trade. More than fair—

for the chance she was getting, this fellowship that had miraculously become her own project, only better. It had become a cocreation, both hers. And his.

She said, "These wings…"

"Yeah?"

"The image should be everywhere. In the bottom of the pool."

"I like that."

"In the play yards, embossed in the concrete. In the floor of the cafeteria and the multiuse room…." She was already reaching for more drawing paper.

He handed her a soft marker. She began to draw.

It was a good week.

They did fine work. Now that they had the heart of the design down, they found a thousand ways to use it to enrich the rest of the building, so that the center really started to work as a structure with a specific purpose, a place where children who had started out without a lot in life would be free to learn and to grow, to reach for the sky.

They also had another guest.

Tuesday afternoon, one of Donovan's former climbing partners came to the door. Donovan could have had Olga or Helen, his new assistant, send the visitor away. But he went to answer the doorbell himself.

He even let the guy in. His name was Alan Everson. Alan was long-faced, lean and weather-beaten, a very serious man. He'd driven all the way from Albuquerque to see Donovan.

After dinner, Abilene left the two men alone. They went to the game room, where there was a pool table and a bar and tables for card games, very much like the game room at her family's ranch, Bravo Ridge. It was the first time, as far as Abilene knew, that Donovan had entered the game room since she'd been staying in his house.

She hoped they played pool, or maybe chess. And that they talked about old times, about who was attempting which mountain and when.

Alan left after breakfast Wednesday morning. Abilene asked Donovan if he'd enjoyed the other man's visit.

"Yeah," he said gruffly. "It was good to see him." But he didn't elaborate. And she didn't push him for details. Really, if he was willing to let his friends come around again, that was enough.

At least for now.

Thursday, in the early morning, just as they started working in the studio, Donovan got a call. Instead of telling Helen to deal with it for him, he took the phone.

Abilene was at her own desk, on the computer there, using the CAD software to get going on the key technical drawings the engineers were going to need. Later, more architects would be hired to produce the endless number of necessary drawings. But she needed to get the basics down—as well as a simple schematic CAD rendering of the center, which had advantages over manual study and presentation models. With computer-assisted drawings, the views could be expanded, manipulated, made to show any aspect of the design from within, below or in aerial views.

Yes, when Donovan answered the buzzing phone on

his desk and said, "I'll talk to her, Helen," Abilene could have taken a break, given him a little privacy.

But hey. She was curious. Was it Luisa? And if not, who else, beyond Luisa and Alan, was he willing to speak with, at last?

Her name, as it turned out, was Mariah. And Donovan didn't sound especially happy to hear from her.

His side of the conversation was mostly in the negative. "No, Mariah. I'm fine, Mariah. I'm sorry.... I know. I should have gotten back with you long before now.... No, I can't. I've got a lot to deal with at this point and..." The woman must have really started in on him about then, because he fell silent. He made a few impatient noises. And then he finally said, "Look. I don't think so...." Another silence from him, then, "Take my word for it. Move on. I meant what I said, and I said no." He hung up.

Abilene tried to decide whether to remark on his curtness. Or get back to work.

He made the decision for her by accusing, "I know you were listening."

She peered around the side of her computer screen. "Uh. Well. Yeah. Guilty."

He rolled out from behind his own wall of computers so he could see her while he lectured her. "You're always accusing *me* of being rude. But somehow, the rules are different for you. You could have given me a moment or two alone, to take that call."

"I considered it. But then, well, I was curious, so I stayed."

"You were curious. And that makes it okay to listen in on my private conversations?"

"Donovan. Do you really want to lecture me about respecting *your* privacy?" She gave him her sweetest smile. He glared back at her. But he didn't argue. She said, more gently, "Come on. If it was so private, *you* could have left the room—and I'm guessing that Mariah will not be coming to dinner?"

He stared at her, narrowed-eyed, from across the room. And then he grunted. "No, she won't."

She couldn't resist asking, "An old girlfriend?"

He actually volunteered a little information. "Mariah lives in Dallas. She's a successful interior designer. I met her when I was working on a project there. We went out, last year, for a couple of months. It ended abruptly."

"After the accident?"

"It seemed as good an excuse as any to say good-bye to her."

"Not a happy relationship, huh?"

He was glaring again. "You ask too many questions."

She widened her smile. She was thinking of Luisa right then, of how Luisa had told her that *somebody* had to stick with Donovan, had to drag him out into the world again.

"Here's another question for you," she said. "Will you please come with me to Luisa's bar tomorrow night?"

He made a humphing sound. "Didn't I already say no—and more than once?"

"What can I tell you? I'm an eternal optimist."

"Lot of good that's doing you."

Still craned around the edge of her computer screen, she braced her elbow on the edge of the desk and rested her chin on the heel of her hand. "Actually, in spite of everything, I do believe I'm making progress with you."

"Oh. Now I'm a job you've taken on, is that it? Something that either goes well, or doesn't?"

"Hmm. It's an interesting way of putting it—but no. You're not a job, Donovan. You're just someone I like. Very much. No matter that you act like an ass a lot of the time."

He grunted. "I'm an ass—but you *like* me."

"That's right. And deep inside you, there's a good man. A good man trying very hard to get out."

"Don't bet any hard cash on that."

"Come with me. Tomorrow night. It will be fun."

"I doubt that."

"Come anyway."

He slanted her a sideways look and muttered, "I'll drive."

"Am I awake? Or is this a dream? I could swear you just said yes."

Friday night, Abilene wore jeans that clung to every curve. The jeans were tucked into calf-high boots. Her silk blouse was the exact golden green of her eyes. And her jacket was the same camel color as her boots. Metal-studded leather bangle bracelets, several of them, graced her slim arms.

Donovan thought she looked great. Sexy as hell and ready for anything.

They went together into his underground garage. He wheeled along beside her down the ramp toward the van, still not quite believing that he'd let her talk him into going with her tonight.

"Need any help?" she asked when he stopped several feet back from the rear of the van, took a remote from his pocket and pushed the button that unlocked the doors.

"No. Just get in." He pushed another button and the back doors swung wide. The lift extended out from the van floor and lowered itself to the concrete.

She was still at his side. "Wow. I guess you have it all under control, huh?"

He only wished. He sent her a quelling look. "Get in."

She did, striding away on those amazing legs of hers. He waited until she pulled open the passenger door and swung herself up into the seat. As she shut her door, he rolled onto the platform and let the lift take him up to the floor of the van. From there, he wheeled along the cleared space between the seats and in behind the wheel. He drove from his chair.

They rode in silence most of the way. That was fine with him. Conversation with her could be dangerous. The past few days, he never knew what she was going to talk him into next.

Plus, he kept thinking about sex now, whenever he was around her—okay, maybe he'd *always* thought about sex when he was around her. Subconsciously, anyway.

But since Monday—specifically, since he'd seen her in the shower—he could no longer pretend that sex wasn't on his mind when he looked at her.

And to be brutally frank about it, he didn't even need to be looking at her. She didn't need to be anywhere nearby.

Suddenly, he was thinking about sex all the time. About *having* sex. With her.

Twice in the past few days, in the studio, he'd gotten hard. He was lucky both times, since he was sitting at his desk. All he had to do was to keep on sitting there until the problem subsided.

Still, he found the situation humiliating. All those months and months without a twitch. And now, all of a sudden, he couldn't sit at his own damn desk without a raging woody.

She hadn't known what was happening, he was sure. And he was grateful for that, at least.

If she'd noticed what was going on with him, she probably would have insisted they discuss it. Frankly. At length. In excruciating detail.

Discussing his current state of continuous arousal with her was the last thing he needed.

"There it is." She pointed at the turnoff up ahead. Beyond it, he could see the red neon sign: Luisa's Cantina, complete with matching zigzagging arrow pointing down at the front doors. The dirt parking lot was packed with pickups and SUVs, and glaringly lit by sodium vapor lamps. "You need to turn."

"Abilene. I know. I've been there before."

She slanted him a frown. "You are edgy tonight, even more so than usual."

He didn't answer her. He concentrated on turning off the highway and then into the lot and then on looking for a decent parking space—easily found, since Luisa had a few handicapped spaces not far from the door.

Men and women in jeans and boots stood out on the wide wooden porch that jutted off the front of the barnlike structure. They lounged against the raw pine railing, wearing jackets against the night chill. Even in the van, with the windows up, he could hear the country-western music from inside, muffled, but clearly distinguishable.

He eased the van in between two extended cabs, each with a handicapped sign dangling from its rearview mirror. The space was a few feet from the wheelchair access ramp. The special parking spaces and the ramp had been there for as long as he'd known Luisa. Even back when he could walk unassisted, he'd always noticed such things. It was part of his job, to include handicapped access in any public building he designed. But this was the first time he would be making use of it himself.

He glanced at Abilene in the seat beside him. In a cheerful clatter of bangle bracelets, she flipped a swatch of chestnut hair back over her shoulder—and winked at him. It annoyed him no end that he found that silly wink of hers sexy.

"Ready?" she asked.

Strangely, he *was* ready.

The edginess she'd remarked on as they left the highway had gone. He might be the only guy in a wheelchair to show up here tonight. Six months ago, he would not have been able to imagine himself doing this. He'd told himself then that he simply never would.

Now, thanks in no small part to the maddening and relentless woman beside him, he *was* here. And he was going farther. He was wheeling up that ramp and through the front door.

Maybe he would even have a good time. At any rate, it would be something of an adventure. A first.

He gave Abilene a nod.

"Well, all right then." She leaned on her door and swung those long legs to the ground.

He unhooked the locks that held his chair in place and backed cleanly between the seats to the lift. Once he'd ridden it out and down, he used the remote to close everything up again and engage the locks. Abilene was right there, waiting for him.

They headed for the ramp. A few of the cowboys on the front porch were watching them. Maybe they'd never seen a fully equipped wheelchair-ready van before. Maybe they were wondering if the guy in the chair would get up and dance—or maybe just admiring the way Abilene filled out those skinny jeans of hers.

Donovan decided it didn't matter. Whatever they were thinking was their business. There were nods and tipped hats as he and Abilene reached the top of the ramp.

One of the cowboys ambled over and held open the door. Donovan didn't need anyone holding a door for him. He preferred others to ask if he wanted help. Or to wait until he requested it.

But still, he got that the cowboy was only being polite. He gave him an extra nod and a muttered, "Thanks," as he wheeled on through into the din of Luisa's place on a Friday night.

The cantina was just as he remembered: rough plank floors and a long mahogany bar on the far wall, with mirrors behind, a never-ending supply of booze on glass shelves, and ten spigots for various beers on tap. Round tables with bentwood chairs rimmed the dance floor.

Luisa spotted them right away. She'd always been like that. She knew who came into her cantina and she knew when. She hustled on over, wearing jeans as tight as Abilene's and a red off-the-shoulder T-shirt, with Luisa's in black glitter emblazoned across her breasts.

"You came! I'm so happy!" Her smile was wide and her arms were outstretched. She hugged Abilene first. And then she came at him. When she bent down, he allowed her to wrap her arms around him. "Donovan. Oh, it has been much too long since I've seen you here." Her black hair brushed his cheek and she smelled, as always, of jasmine. She stood tall and braced her fists on her hips. "I saved you a table. See? I knew you would come. This way…"

Rounded hips swaying, she led them to a table not far from the bar and swept the reserved sign away. He asked for scotch. Abilene said she would have the same.

Luisa signaled for the drinks and took the chair beside him. She asked them how their work was going and then listened with half an ear as Abilene told her. Luisa was like that, in the bar. Always ready with the hugs and the questions. But as a rule, she hardly heard the answers. Inevitably, she would have to jump up and go deal with another friend who'd just arrived, or handle some mini crisis or other.

The drinks came. And Luisa left them.

They sipped scotch and listened to the music, watched the locals two-stepping out on the floor. It was nice, easy. Relaxed. If someone had told him two weeks ago that he'd be sitting in Luisa's with Abilene tonight, thoroughly enjoying himself, he would have called them certifiable.

Abilene leaned close to him. "Don't you wish you'd done this sooner?" Her hair swung forward. He could smell her fresh, tart scent—like green apples, watermelon and roses, all somehow perfectly blended together. He wanted to touch her hair. He wanted it bad.

And he had a thousand reasons why he shouldn't have what he wanted.

Screw all those reasons.

He lifted his hand from the table and caught a thick lock between his fingers. Warm. Silky.

He lifted it to his face, took in the scent, the feel, the essence of her. She made no protest—in fact, she leaned marginally closer. He heard her breath catch on a soft hitch of sound.

She didn't ask what was going on, what he was up to—she didn't say a word. That surprised him. She was always so ready to dissect and discuss his every action. But for once, she just let it be. He appreciated that.

It gave him permission, gave him the freedom, to do what he did next.

Which was to touch her cheek, to run the back of his index finger down the perfect curve, to feel the velvet-soft flesh, the elegant shape of her cheekbone beneath.

She sighed.

He wanted to kiss her, to feel the give, the texture, the heat of her mouth. To taste her, to know the warmth of her breath.

She said his name, "Donovan," on a whisper of sound. And he thought that no one, ever, had said his name the way she did. With tenderness. And complete understanding.

With acceptance. And the sweet heat of honest desire.

She leaned in just that fraction closer, a movement that told him she would welcome his kiss.

There was nothing else, at that moment. No one else in the crowded, noisy roadhouse. Just Abilene. So close to him, leaning closer.

He took her mouth. Gently. Lightly.

It wasn't the time or the place for a deep kiss.

But a tender one, yes.

A gentle brush of his mouth to hers was enough— enough to tell him everything he needed to know right then. That her lips were as soft and giving as he'd always known they would be, that the scent of her only got better, sweeter, more tempting, when he was tasting her, too.

With aching reluctance, he pulled back—not far. A few inches. Enough that he could see her eyes again: rich gold, lush green.

He ran a finger down the side of her throat, felt her slight shiver that said she wanted more. She wanted everything. And he thought of the thousand and one ways he had refused her since that first day, that first moment, when she entered the studio. All the small and petty cruelties, which in the end had served no purpose beyond forestalling the inevitable: the two of them, now.

Tonight.

Luisa came back to them, laughing, happy, all busyness and bustle. She dropped into the chair she had vacated a few minutes before. "So sorry to desert you. There's always too much to do here, for me, on a Friday night."

"No problem." Abilene sent Luisa a smile. And then she turned to him again. She met his eyes, glanced down at his mouth. He felt that glance as a physical caress, as if she had kissed him a second time. "We're doing fine."

"Ah." Luisa was catching on. "Yes. I see that you are doing just great. And I'm very pleased." She sounded smug, as if she herself had engineered it all—the evening, the moment, that perfect, brushing kiss.

He probably should have said something cool and ironic. But right then, the last thing he felt was cool. And irony seemed only another defense, another sad little way to reject all the basic human connections he'd set himself on denying.

For tonight, at least, for the short time he and Abilene would have together, he was going to let down his defenses. He was going to let the inevitable find him.

At last.

So he only smiled at Luisa and she grinned back at him and the band started playing a slow, romantic song.

Under the table, Abilene's hand found his, lifted it over the wheel between them and rested it on her knee. They twined their fingers, held on tight. Like a couple of kids in love for the first time, with their whole lives ahead of them, with the world before them, theirs to claim.

"I'll be back," said Luisa, and she jumped up again and headed off toward the bar.

Abilene squeezed his hand. "Want to play some pool?"

He'd taken the armrests off the chair before he left the house. It was easier to work the wheels without them, easier to get around in confined spaces. And also, as luck would have it, to get up close to a pool table to make a shot. "Eight ball?"

"Whatever you say." She leaned in close. He couldn't resist—didn't want to resist. Again, he brushed her lips with his. Her eyes drifted shut—and so did his. She was the one who pulled back that time. She whispered, "I have to warn you, I'm pretty good."

"I'll do my best. I just hope I can hold my own."

Her gaze sharpened. "You're acting much too humble. I can see I might be in trouble here."

"Want to back out?"

"No way. We're playing."

And they did. It was the second time he'd played since the accident on the mountain. The first had been that past Tuesday night, when Alan stayed over.

He'd discovered right away that there were advantages to playing from a wheelchair. Players on two legs had to bend over to get the right angle to line up a shot. From the chair, he was in a good position to begin with.

He and Abilene played best of three. She *was* pretty good. She won the first game.

He took the other two.

After that, there were coins lined up to challenge him. Abilene claimed a stool a few feet from the table and cheered him on. He beat three comers and then a tall blonde in a straw cowboy hat and studded jeans, with colorful tattoos covering both arms, stepped up.

She took him down, two in a row.

He shook her hand.

She tipped her hat at him and chalked her cue for the next game.

By then, it was almost midnight. The table they'd had

when they arrived was taken, so they found another. Luisa brought them a second round, sat with them for a few minutes, then took off again.

On the dance floor, couples swayed, dancing close and slow. He felt a small stab of regret—that he couldn't rise to his feet, take Abilene's hand, lead her out there and pull her into his arms.

Someday, he might be able to dance again. A slow number anyway, like the one playing now, the kind of dancing where you pretty much just swayed in place. But not in the near future. Not for months, anyway.

Maybe never.

That hadn't bothered him, until tonight. He hadn't given dancing so much as a thought since the accident. It was like sex, something that held no interest for him, something he'd left behind.

Abilene took his hand again, calling him back.

Into the moment, into tonight.

He looked at her. Never would he grow tired of looking at her. "You about ready to go?"

She squeezed his fingers, nodded.

Luisa appeared from the crowd as they worked their way to the door. She bent down and hugged him, pressed a kiss on his cheek. "Come back soon."

He promised that he would.

The drive home was as silent as the ride out there had been. Now, though, it was a silence of anticipation. There was a certain promise between them now, a promise made in a kiss, in the simple act of holding hands.

In the weeks she'd lived in his house, they'd done a lot of talking

But tonight was like that night almost a week ago, when they'd shared dinner in quiet companionship. Tonight was a night they didn't need words.

When they reached the house, he followed the driveway around to the garage entrance. They were in and parked, the engine idling, when she leaned across the space between her seat and his chair.

"My rooms?" she asked him, her face tipped up to his, her skin pearly in the dim glow from the dashboard lights. Her mouth, her husky voice, her night-dark eyes, the scent of her—*all* of her—invited him.

She made a low sound as their lips met. And she opened for him.

He swept his tongue in, groaning at the taste of her, the wet, tempting slickness. She put her hand on his shoulder, clasping, holding on to him.

That did it.

He was aching for her, growing hard.

She pulled back. Her eyes seemed haunted, a trick of the dim light. "My rooms?" she asked again.

His throat clutched. He felt absurdly inexperienced, as though this were his first time—which, in a sense, it was. Somehow, he managed a nod.

She reached out again, bangle bracelets clattering, her hand sliding warm and smooth against his nape, to pull him close for one last, hard, swift kiss.

And then, as quick as she had kissed him, she released him. She leaned on her door and swung those long legs out. She jumped down, pushed the door shut between them.

For a moment, she stood out there, beside the van,

looking in at him, as if she had something important to say. But in the end, she only turned and left him.

He pivoted in his chair, tracking her, watching her walk away around the end of the van, her boot heels tapping out a hollow rhythm on the concrete floor.

She headed for the ramp. Too soon, she was out of sight.

Once he could no longer see her, he had the strangest sensation—that he had lost her already, without ever letting himself have her. That tonight hadn't really happened. That he was alone.

Again.

That, he couldn't bear. Not now. Not yet.

He was backed out and down in record time. He shut up the van and made for the exit ramp as fast as his wheels would carry him.

Chapter 9

In her rooms, Abilene worked fast.

She took off her bangles and dropped them on the table by the bed. She took off her jacket, her shirt, her bra. Perched on the stool at the end of the bed, she tore off her boots, her jeans—everything. Naked, she grabbed the clothes in her arms, carried them to the closet, tossed them inside and shut the door.

And then yanked it open again.

Maybe greeting him naked was a little too...much.

She dug around in the pile of clothes until she found her silk panties. Once she'd wiggled back into them, she went to the dresser in the middle of the closet, where she started opening drawers and riffling through them, looking for something that was attractive, but maybe not too overtly seductive.

Not that she'd brought anything overtly seductive.

After all, she'd come here to work, not to have sex with Donovan.

In the end, she settled on the one nightgown she'd brought. It was cotton, a warm bronze color, very thin and wispy. It left her arms bare, but covered the rest of her to her ankles.

Not sexy, really. But not exactly unsexy. And certainly not as bad as greeting him in her Rice T-shirt and tattered sweats.

The bed was already turned back. Olga did that, nightly. So she ran around the sitting room, the bedroom and the bathroom, getting the lighting right—low, but not *too* low.

By then, a good ten minutes had passed since she left him in the garage. He would be knocking on the sitting room door any second now.

Wouldn't he?

He'd better be.

She went out to the sitting room and perched on the couch, where she stared at the door to the hallway, willing that knock to come.

It didn't. Endless seconds ticked by.

Eventually, she jumped up and went back to the bedroom, to check the time on the bedside clock: fifteen full minutes had gone by since he agreed to meet her in her room.

She went back to the sitting room, stood in the middle of the floor and tried to figure out what to do next.

What was going on here? He *had* agreed he would come to her rooms. Hadn't he?

He'd agreed with a nod, which clearly meant yes. But maybe she should have insisted that he say it out loud.

Then again, if he'd changed his mind after the fact, what difference did it make?

She paced the floor, trying to decide what her next move should be. Should she go to his rooms? Call him?

Or just forget it? Just take off this not-quite-sexy nightgown, put on her sweats and go to bed.

The knock—three light taps—cut her off in mid-pace.

In a rush, she released the breath she hadn't even realized she was holding. She considered calling out that the door was open. But then she ended up racing over there and turning the knob.

At the last second, she decided she'd better be sure it was him before she swung the door wide. When it came to Donovan, well, a woman just never knew....

So she peeked around the edge of the door.

And there he was, staring back at her, still wearing the same sweater and jeans he'd worn to Luisa's. One side of that wonderful mouth of his kicked up. "Changed your mind?"

"I most certainly did not." She stepped back, pulling the door wide. "I was getting a little worried about *you,* though."

He wheeled in.

Once he'd cleared the threshold, she shut the door and leaned back against it, turning the lock by feel, her knees suddenly rubbery and her chest kind of tight. "Is everything all right?"

"Abilene."

"What?" She sounded snippy. Somehow, she couldn't help herself.

"I went to my room, that's all. To get condoms."

She realized she'd failed to mention that they didn't need them. "I'm on the pill." Then again, well, you couldn't be too safe these days. "But I guess it's wise, to use a condom in any case."

"Well, all right, then." He looked her up and down, a lazy kind of look, a look that took its sweet time. When his eyes rose to meet hers again, he started backing the chair toward the center of the room. "Come away from the door." He said it softly, with wonderful, delicious intent.

And she felt instantly better about everything. It was obvious that he wanted to be with her. She could stop feeling that maybe she had pushed him into something he just wasn't ready for.

She took a cautious step.

"Nice nightgown," he said. He sounded like he really meant it.

But she felt suddenly shy anyway. She gnawed on her lower lip, fiddled with the wide straps that held up the top. "It's not exactly seductive...."

"It's perfect."

She felt a flush flooding up her neck and over her cheeks, and she had to look away. "I, um, thank you."

"Come here."

She took another step. "I feel...kind of awkward, you know? As if it's my first time, or something, which it's not. I mean, it's not like there were a *lot* of guys, or anything. But still, it's not as if I'm a virgin or anything...." She shut her mouth, swallowed. Yikes. Talk about an excess of information.

"I know what you mean." He said it low, roughly tender. "When you kissed me in the van, I was thinking that I felt completely out of my depth, like it was my first time all over again."

"You did?"

"Yeah. And it *is* the first time. *Our* first time."

Now she almost wanted to cry. "Oh, Donovan..."

"Yeah?"

"That was the perfect thing to say."

"You think so?" He looked kind of pleased with himself.

"I do, yes. The perfect thing."

"So you think you might come all the way over here, then?"

She did just that, stopping inches from his front wheels. He put his palms to his thighs, patted gently. She hesitated. "Will I...hurt you?"

"I'll let you know if it gets too bad."

"So it *will* hurt you, hurt your legs, if I sit on your lap?"

"If it does, a little, it will be worth it." He engaged the brake, locking the wheels into place. "Trust me to tell you, if something isn't going to work for me."

"Yes, all right." Her throat felt constricted. And her heart was just jackhammering away inside her chest. She could almost laugh at herself. She'd been so confident, at Luisa's, and when she kissed him down in the garage. Where had all that boldness gone?

But then he held out his hand to her.

She took it. And she found reassurance, in the steadiness and strength of his grip. She let herself relax a little, let herself feel again the electric excitement that charged the air between them every time they touched.

He gave a tug. She took his signal, gathering her nightgown in her free hand, lifting it high enough to get it out of her way. It was so simple, to hitch one leg over him, to slide her hips forward, so she straddled his lap.

With slow care, she settled her weight onto him, the skirt of her gown riding high across the tops of her thighs.

"You feel good," he said. He let go of her hand and clasped her bare thigh. Heat shimmered through her as he stroked her skin with his open palm. "Smooth."

She framed his face in her hands. "Oh, Donovan…"

"Shh," he said. "It's all right." And he kissed her, a slow, deep kiss, wet and sweet and so arousing.

His tongue slid over hers, retreating, and then gliding forward again, beneath hers that time, in a slick caress that brought a soft moan into her throat. The kiss went on and on and he touched her as he kissed her, first with long, exploratory caresses of her bare thighs. And then, more deliberately.

He cupped her bent knees in his palms. And after that, he took the caress lower, down the sensitive, thin flesh of her shins, and around, to learn the curves of her calves, the secret coves behind her knees.

She touched him, too. She ran her eager hands along the hard, thick muscles of his shoulders, over his chest, so deep and powerful, heavy with muscle even through the soft wool of the sweater he wore. Encircling his neck, she let her touch stray up into his close-cut hair. The short strands were warm, alive, between her fingers.

And then he ended the kiss, pulling away just enough that their lips no longer met. He pressed his forehead to hers. With a long, slow sigh, she braced her forearms on his shoulders and linked her hands behind his head.

Below, she could feel him. Growing hard. She tried moving her hips on him in a gentle, rocking motion.

It felt so good, she sighed again, let her head fall back and groaned his name, "Donovan..."

He pressed his lips to her throat, grazed the sensitive skin there with his teeth. "Yes..."

And then those wonderful strong hands of his were sliding under the hem of her nightgown, around the sides of her thighs. He cupped her bottom, over her panties, and he urged her to move faster—and then slower. And then faster again.

And again, they were kissing, mouths fused and hungry, as she moved on him, creating the sweetest, hottest kind of friction, and she was burning, deliciously. She was on fire, a fire that only flared hotter, that built and spread, all through her.

He tasted so good. He *felt* so good.

She let her hands stray downward, along his sides, so lean and compact, to his tight waist. For a moment, she lingered there, her hips rocking, her hands on either side of him, holding on good and tight, as the pleasure within her built in fiery waves.

Beneath his sweater, she felt his warmth. But she wanted more. So she took the sweater by the hem and tugged it upward. For a moment, he resisted, unwilling to let go of her.

But she was insistent. And finally, he gave in. He eased his hands from the folds of her nightgown and lifted his arms high.

With a moan, she pulled her mouth from his and whipped the sweater up between them. He did the rest, yanking it all the way off, tossing it to the floor.

And then they were kissing again. And he had those hands of his back under her gown, holding her, urging her onward.

And she was rocking him, rocking herself, rocking both of them, as she wrapped her arms around him, ran her hungry fingers up and down the hard muscles of his back.

She could have gone on like that forever, moving against him as he kissed her in that so thorough, so lazy, slow, delicious way he had. He still had his jeans on. She still wore her panties. But even with the barrier of their clothing between them, it felt perfect to her.

It felt absolutely right.

But he took it further. He trailed a hand slowly, up under her nightgown, along the lower curve of her back...and around.

To the front of her again. He pressed his palm flat against her belly. And then those skilled fingers of his slid lower.

He cupped her.

She froze. And she gasped.

He took that soft sound into him as he eased his fingers under the elastic of her panties and slid them into the wetness between her thighs.

Oh, it felt so good. So thrilling, so free. So exactly right.

She was open to him and he stroked her, continuing to cup her at the same time, holding her in place with one hand as with the other he did the most amazing, lovely things. He dipped a finger in, then two. And with his thumb, he found her sweet spot.

Oh, she was losing it. She hovered in a haze of building pleasure, on the far edge. She teetered on the verge of completion.

And then, she was there. She was going over. The soft explosion claimed her.

She grabbed his wrist, widened her legs even farther, held on tight, moaned low and helplessly, deep in her throat as the sweet, shimmering contractions took her. The pleasure increased in waves, taking her higher, and yet higher still. Until she hit the second peak, surged over it...and down.

The slow fade-off began.

She sagged against him, murmuring wordless things, boneless now.

He gathered her close to him, wrapping his arms around her. She felt the brushing touch of his lips in her hair, the warmth of his breath at her temple. For a time they just sat there, in his chair, together. Entwined.

Some time passed. Minutes. Forever.

When she finally lifted her head from his shoulder, he touched her cheek and she met his shining eyes. He stroked her hair, guided a heavy, tangled lock of it behind her ear.

They shared another kiss—a tender one, a light brushing of his mouth to hers.

And then he was gathering her nightgown in his hands, easing it up. She raised her arms and he pulled it off and away, dropping it to the floor on top of his sweater.

"So fine," he whispered, bending his head to touch his tongue to the tip of one breast. He pressed his thumbs to either side of her navel, holding her waist in his hands. And then he caressed his way upward, until he cradled both breasts.

She sighed and arched her back, offering him total access. He took it, bending closer, taking one nipple into his mouth, swirling his hot tongue around it, and then sinking his teeth in—not too hard, just enough to add to her pleasure.

He kissed her other breast, too, taking his time about it, making her moan again, making her clutch his big shoulders and whisper his name.

And then his hands were around her waist again, lifting.

She took his cue and transferred her weight to her toes. A little unsteadily, with her legs spread so wide, she started to rise. He helped her, taking most of her weight in his two strong hands. She hitched one leg back and then the other, clearing the large rear wheels of the chair. And then the smaller front wheels, too. At last she was able to find her balance upright, to bring her legs together.

He gazed up at her, his eyes heavy-lidded. She smiled down at him, admiring the beautiful musculature of his arms and shoulders, the hard perfection of his chest and belly. Such a gorgeous man.

And still very much aroused, his hardness straining the fly of his jeans.

He canted forward then, touched the side of her hip,

tracing the curve of it, following the shape of her, up into the cove of her waist, and then back down again. Little flares of heat burst along her skin in the most wonderful way, wherever he touched her.

He took hold of the bits of elastic at her hips and eased her panties down, over her thighs, to her knees. Then he sat back again. She did the rest, bending to slide them down all the way, stepping out of them, using her toe to kick them aside.

She rose to her height again.

Naked, she thought. *I'm standing here naked in front of Donovan McRae.*

And then she grinned to herself, as she realized that his seeing her naked really wasn't anything new.

"I know what you're thinking," he said, low and rough.

"Maybe you do."

Or maybe he didn't.

It made no difference.

What mattered was that they were here, together, in this intimate way. What mattered was that it was good, between them. It was honest. Open. True.

He said, "You're so beautiful. I never thought this would happen."

"I didn't, either. But it did. It is. And Donovan, I'm so glad that you're here with me...."

He asked, "The bed?"

She shook her head. "I was thinking, the first time, we could try it in your chair...."

His eyes grew darker. Softer. "Sure." His hands were already at his fly. He unbuttoned, unzipped.

"Can I help?"

He lifted one sculpted shoulder in a half-shrug. "I guess it would make things quicker."

"Your shoes?"

"Thanks. Yeah."

So she bent on one knee and took off his shoes for him, and also his socks. When she stood again, he'd taken the condoms from a pocket. He held them out to her. She set two on the nightstand, and kept the other, ready, in her hand.

With some effort, he began easing down his jeans and underwear. She stepped back a little. Partly to admire the view. Partly because if he wanted help, he would say so.

He paused with the jeans and briefs still high on his thighs and he snared her glance, held it, his square jaw suddenly tight. "You should be warned. It's not a very pretty sight...."

She only looked at him, steadily, without wavering. It seemed to her that there were no words for this. Her complete acceptance of him was what mattered, her ability to communicate that she wanted him exactly as he was, that the man he was now, at this minute, was enough for her—more than enough.

He braced his feet on the footrest and with a groan he tried to stifle, lifted his hips enough to take the jeans down to his thighs. Since he didn't ask for more help from her, she didn't offer it.

Bending at the waist, he pushed the jeans and briefs over his knees, down his calves and, finally, all the way off. And then he wadded them tight and tossed them away from him.

Slowly, he sat up straight again. He remained hard,

fully aroused. She had absolutely no doubt that he wanted her.

But his eyes had turned wary. He was watching her, gauging her reaction to the sight of his damaged legs. "Pretty ugly, huh?"

"No," she said. "Not ugly at all."

"Liar." But at least he said it with a tender smile.

She wanted to argue, to promise she wasn't lying, that his legs weren't ugly. But why go there? They were what they were. And in comparison to the buff perfection of his upper body, they did look sad and wasted—the right leg especially. It was much worse than the left, crisscrossed with ridges of scar tissue, some of it red and angry, the long rows of stitches still visible. His calves were too thin, his ankles slightly swollen.

He gave a low chuckle. "A lot of pins, rods and screws involved, putting them in, taking them out again. Believe it or not, this whole mess looks a hell of a lot better than it did just a month ago...."

"I believe it."

He searched her face, seeking the slightest hint that she might be having second thoughts—about tonight, about the two of them.

But she had none. And he must have seen that.

Because he held out his hand to her again.

She took it, and she came to him, easing a leg over him, straddling him as she had before—only now, there was nothing, not the slightest scrap of fabric, between them. They were flesh to flesh.

She kissed him, sliding her fingers free of his, peeling the wrapper off the condom and then slipping her hand between them and down, so she could encircle him. He moaned into her mouth when her grip closed around him.

He was silky. So hard. So warm. She moved her hips in rhythm with her stroking hand.

As she stroked him, he clasped her thighs, his fingers gliding underneath, so he could caress her from below. She felt her own wetness, her readiness for him.

And then he was lifting her, taking some of her weight on his arms. She helped him, rising to her toes, moving in closer against him, so her breasts brushed his chest and her toes, behind the rear wheels, could touch the floor.

She still had her hand down between them, around him, and she moved it lower, to the base of him, so she could hold him in place. She rolled the condom over him.

There. It was on.

She tipped her hips forward, lifting them. He helped her, raising her higher, into position to take him inside.

Yes. Just…there.

She felt him, so sleek and hot, nudging her, parting her.

With a long, hungry moan, she lowered herself onto him. He came into her in a sweet, hot glide. Her body put up no resistance. She welcomed him.

There was only pleasure. Only heat.

Only the delicious, complete, thrilling way he filled her.

She let her head fall back and a deep cry escaped her; it felt so very good. And he leaned into her, kissed her throat, her chin, opening his mouth on her, licking her, scraping her burning skin lightly with his teeth

Until she lowered her head and offered her lips. He took them. She parted to him eagerly, gave herself over to his deep, wet kiss.

With his powerful arms supporting her thighs, giving her something to brace against, she could take control. And she did. She moved on him in deep, hard strokes and he helped her, lifting when her body signaled him, lowering when she pushed down.

He felt so good, so exactly right.

And behind her eyes there was darkness, beautiful darkness. Darkness turning slowly to blinding, glorious light.

Chapter 10

Donovan woke in Abilene's bed.

For a moment, he lay there, eyes closed, unmoving. Remembering.

Every kiss. Every whispered endearment. Every hot, sweet caress.

It had been good. Damn good. Better, even, than in all his frustrated fantasies of how it might be.

He opened his eyes. He lay on his side, facing her. His legs hurt. But then, they always did.

She was still sleeping—on her back, one slim pale arm thrown across her eyes, her hair wild on the pillow, her lips slightly parted. Her breathing was shallow. Quiet. Slow.

He ached to touch her, to take hold of the blankets, pull them away slowly. To reveal every inch of her, every hollow, every soft, inviting curve.

It made him hard all over again, just thinking about something so simple as easing the blankets down so he could see her bare breasts. But the clock on the nightstand said it was nine-fifteen. Long past time that they should be up and at work.

Yes, it was Saturday. And yes, she deserved a day off.

But they couldn't afford that. They had two weeks and two days left until the agreed-upon presentation to the Foundation people. They were making fine progress.

But still, the timeline was an impossibly short one. There would be no days off.

She rolled her head his way, lowered her arm and opened one eye. "Oh, God. I know that look. It's the *get to work* look."

"We should have been up hours ago."

She groaned. "Can't I have just one kiss, please? Before you start cracking the whip again."

He eased a strand of hair out of the corner of her soft mouth. "It's after nine."

"Ugh."

"Work."

"Have I told you lately that I hate you?"

He grinned. "You don't have to tell me. I can see it in your eyes." And then he sat up, pushed the covers off his scarred legs and eased them, with great care, over the edge of the bed.

"You're such a romantic the morning after," she grumbled behind him.

He sent her a glance over his shoulder. "Don't tempt me."

"I wouldn't dream of it." She looked right in his eyes

and she eased down the blankets. Her full breasts with their pretty, puckered nipples came into view.

He was the one groaning then. "Unfair."

She laughed, a low, husky sound that stirred him even more than her nudity. And then she sighed and pulled the covers up again. "You're right. We need to work."

He continued to stare at her. He really liked staring at her. It felt good—freeing—to be able to do it openly now.

Finally, he shook himself and reached for his chair, which waited where he'd left it, next to the bed. It was easy, after all the months of practice, to lift himself into the seat using only his arms.

She was shaking her head as he dropped neatly into place. "It's amazing, watching you do that."

"It's all about upper-body strength and conditioning. Nothing any gymnast can't do and do well."

"Still, it doesn't seem humanly possible."

"I'm a fortunate man. I have my own personal gym and I can afford to hire good trainers. All I had to do was put in the time."

Her expression had turned chiding. "Don't minimize what you've accomplished, Donovan."

"All right, I won't. I'm amazing."

Her eyes went soft. "Yeah. You are. You definitely are."

He wanted to swing himself back into that bed with her. But no. Not an option. There was work that needed doing, work that wouldn't wait. "So, mind if I use your bathroom—just for a few minutes?"

"Be my guest. Take your time."

He backed and turned and aimed himself at the bathroom.

When he came out again, she was wearing sweats and a Rice T-shirt. His briefs, jeans and sweater were laid out neatly across the bench at the foot of the bed, his shoes and socks lined up beside them. He wheeled over there. "Thanks."

She nodded. "Need any help?"

"No, I can manage."

"I'm going to take a shower, then." She headed for the bathroom, pausing in the doorway. "Breakfast in the studio?"

"Yeah. We can eat while we work."

The day was a good one, Abilene thought. A very productive one.

Their routine was the same as it had been. She worked steadily, and he worked with her for a couple of hours that morning. Then, as always, he left her to continue on her own and he went to spend time in the gym. He returned briefly before lunch to check on her progress and make suggestions. Then he was gone again. Lunch, like breakfast, she had in the studio while she worked.

Donovan appeared again around three.

Anyone observing them that day might have thought everything was the same between them. As before, he demanded much of her. He could be very tough, and if he didn't like something she'd come up with, he told her what he wanted changed in no uncertain terms.

And she talked right back to him, same as she always had. He might be a genius and she might be really grateful to have this chance to work with him. But no way was she letting him get all up in her face. She demanded respect, too. And she could give as good as she got.

So everything between them was the same.

Except that it wasn't.

Now they were lovers.

Just the thought of that, of the simple words, *He is my lover,* brought a thrilling, heated shiver running beneath her skin. And every time she looked at him, she felt that little lurch in her belly, that click of recognition, that deeper knowledge a woman has of the man who shares her bed.

She worked hard and she kept her focus.

But still, through the whole day, she felt a rising sensation, a sweet anticipation. She wanted him.

And she would have him when the workday was through.

At five, when she was ready to stop for the day, he was in the studio with her, over behind that volcanic slab of a desk of his, puzzling through an issue with storage room access.

She straightened her work area and got up to leave. "I'm going for a swim. I'll see you at dinner."

He glanced up. Their gazes met. The shimmery, heated feeling within her grew brighter, hotter.

She wanted to run to him, to bend close to him, fuse her mouth to his. The answering flare of heat in his eyes told her he was thinking along similar lines.

But no. It was better, wiser, to wait.

The studio was their workplace. And she'd been tempted all day to give in to her desire for him and blatantly try to seduce him in that very room. Maybe on that enormous desk of his.

It should be possible. If he could manage to swing himself up there, she could do the rest....

Uh-uh. No. Better if she disciplined herself in here, during work, from the first.

"Dinner," she said again.

He gave a low, knowing laugh that sent little flares of bright heat exploding along her nerve endings. "Dinner. Got it."

She turned and headed for the door before she ended up behaving in a manner that was totally undisciplined.

"Your brother-in-law called me," Donovan said during dinner.

By then, they'd had their salad and Olga had just served the lamb chops and the lemon tarragon asparagus. Everything was delicious, as always, but all Abilene could think about was getting the man across from her alone.

For a moment she wondered which brother-in-law. Pretty pitiful, considering she only had one—a brand-new one, Dax Girard—who had married her baby sister Zoe at New Year's. "Uh. Dax, you mean?"

Donovan nodded. "He gave me a hard time for not taking his calls."

"I'm glad," she said gently, "that you finally did talk with him. Did you tell him what you've been through in the past year?"

"That I'm using a wheelchair now—is that what you mean?" He phrased the sentence as a question. But it wasn't, not really. It was a put-down, a warning that he didn't want to be quizzed on what he might have said to Dax about his physical condition.

She ignored the warning. She never would have gotten this far with him if she'd heeded his warnings. "Yes, Donovan. That you use a wheelchair is part of it, of course."

He made a low snorting sound. "Yes, I told him that my legs were badly damaged in the accident on the mountain—worse than I let it be known at first. Badly enough that I'm using a wheelchair now."

She smiled at him, a wide, approving smile. "Good."

He glanced away—to show her he was still annoyed with her? Or maybe to keep from returning her smile? Who knew?

And that he was defensive about what he'd said to Dax really didn't bother her, anyway. She was simply grateful, that he was willing, at last, to talk to his friends, to tell them what was going on with him.

Also, his frankness with her new brother-in-law freed her up to be more honest with her family. She'd yet to explain to them the challenges Donovan faced. It hadn't seemed right, as long as he was so guarded about it. But now, at last, he was letting people know his situation.

She prompted in an offhand tone, "So, what else did you and Dax talk about?"

Now, he turned to look at her again. It was a cool look—or at least, it tried to be. But Abilene knew him better than she once had. His dismissive remarks and icy glances were only defenses, ways to keep the world at bay after whatever had damaged his spirit so badly. Slowly, he was giving those defenses up.

And that was what mattered.

He said, "Dax tried to talk me into visiting him and your sister in San Antonio."

Dax was über-rich. His house, in one of SA's most exclusive areas, was more like a palace. And then there was the giant garage, where he kept his collection of classic and one-of-a-kind vehicles, there was the gorgeous pool, the tennis court....

Abilene sipped her wine and then suggested casually, "We should go."

He dismissed that idea with a lazy shrug. "Not going to happen. You know that."

"Things change. So do people. *You've* changed, Donovan, just in the few weeks I've known you. You've changed a lot, and for the better."

"I'm not going to San Antonio."

She brushed his objections away. "It's time, and you know it. And not only for you, personally. We're getting to the point where we need to be on-site. We need to bring in the other architects, start working with the builder."

His forbidding expression had only grown more so as she spoke. "What's this 'we'? You know I'm not going to San Antonio with you. You knew it from the start."

She set down her wineglass. "That's another thing I've been meaning to discuss with you."

He was openly sneering now. "You look way too damn determined. I hate it when you get that look."

"I only want you to consider that things are changing—*you* are changing. And for the better."

"You're repeating yourself."

"Some things bear repeating."

"I have not changed."

"You sound like a sulky kid, you know that?"

"Did I mention I don't like where this is going?"

"Too bad. You told me when I got here that you would never work again. Well, Donovan. You *are* working. You're doing amazing work. It's not going to kill you to admit that you are."

He made another snorting sound. "You're doing the work. I'm merely guiding you, giving you a nudge now and then, and only when you need one—which is rarely."

"Oh, please. You're the one who made it all come together. We both know it. You found the heart of this project. And you've been with me, creating it, every step of the way. As a result of what you created, we're actually ahead of our own impossibly tight schedule."

"You're overstating my contribution."

"No, I'm not."

He went on as though she hadn't spoken. "We're almost to the point now where you won't need me. And I took your inexperience into consideration when I chose the firm you'll be working with. The Johnson Wallace Group is the best."

She'd heard of the Johnson Wallace Group, of course. They were based in Dallas and their reputation was worldwide. "Donovan, you're not listening to me."

"I heard every word you said."

"But you weren't *listening*."

He sipped from his water glass. "Of course I was listening. Now, about Johnson Wallace. The two partners in the San Antonio office, Doug Lito and Ruth Gilman, are excellent architects—and they work well with oth-

ers. You'll be able to count on their support and considerable experience."

"I know Johnson Wallace is the best around. And
I've actually met Ruth Gilman and liked her. But that's
not the issue."

"There is no issue." He cut off a tender bite of lamb.
"It's a brilliant design and you're going to be ready to
take over."

She dropped her fork. Hard. It clattered against her
china plate. "Donovan. You're not hearing me. My taking over was never the plan, and you know it."

"It's been the plan, and *you* know it. I made that more
than clear the first day you got here." He ate the bite of
lamb, started cutting another.

She reached out, stilled his hand. "You know what
plan I mean. The *original* plan. The plan you proposed
to the Help the Children Foundation, the one you offered as a fellowship to me and a bunch of other hopeful beginners. You started this fully intending to be in
on it all the way. That was the contract you made with
everyone involved and that's why it matters, that you
see it through, that you come, too, when it's time to go
to San Antonio."

He shrugged off her touch. Then he set down his
fork and knife and sat back in his wheelchair. She, on
the other hand, sat forward, urgently, *willing* him to see
what he needed to do—and to finally agree to do it.

"What are you telling me, really?" His tone was as
cutting and cruel as it had ever been. "You're afraid you
can't handle it? You're just not up for supervising the
construction phase?"

"Oh, I can handle it. Not nearly as well as *we* can, as

a team. But well enough to get the job done, especially if Ruth Gilman has my back."

"Then there's no problem."

"Yes. There *is* a problem, the one you keep refusing to talk about. Whether or not I can handle it isn't the question. It was never the question. The question is what's holding you back, what's keeping you from carrying through on the commitment you made?"

He refused to answer her. Instead, he insisted, "There is no point in going on about this. I explained the situation to you the day you got here. You stayed, and by staying you accepted those terms."

"But I only—"

"We're done here."

"But—"

"I said, we're done." He took his napkin from his lap and dropped it on the table next to his half-finished meal. And then he backed and turned and wheeled away from her. She watched as he disappeared through the arch into the front room.

With a discouraged little sigh, Abilene sagged in her chair. She gazed glumly down at her barely touched meal.

So much for how far she and Donovan had come together.

Donovan wheeled fast down the hallway until he reached his own rooms. Once he rolled over the threshold, he spun the chair around, grabbed the door and gave it a shove.

The door was solid core, very heavy. When it

slammed, it slammed hard. The sound it made was supremely satisfying to him.

But the satisfaction didn't last.

He pulled a second wheelie, spun the chair again and ended up facing the sitting room fireplace. As well as the portrait hanging above it.

Elias. At two. Before Donovan even really knew him. Wearing some ridiculous little sailor-boy suit Julie had put him in, sitting on a kid-size chair, one plump leg tucked beneath him, clutching his favorite Elmo doll, his chubby face tipped back, laughing at something the photographer—or maybe Julie—must have said or done.

Sometimes, when Donovan looked at that picture, he could still hear the sound of his son's happy laughter. But not often, not anymore. As the years went by, the sound, when he did hear it, seemed to get fainter. A bright, perfect memory fading by slow, painful degrees.

He turned from the portrait, and his defensive fury at Abilene drained away, leaving him feeling foolish and petty and weighed down by regrets. Wheeling on into the bedroom, he avoided letting his gaze fall on the framed snapshot by the bed, of Elias at the beach. Instead, he went on into the bathroom. He turned on the water in the deep, jetted tub and stripped.

The water welcomed him. He sank into it with a long sigh. He closed his eyes and tried not to think about what a jerk he was being, about the evening he might have been having, in Abilene's bed.

* * *

Abilene called her mom that night.

She told Aleta Bravo more about Donovan than she'd

ever felt comfortable revealing before, including that he used a wheelchair—and that she cared for him. A lot. More so, each day.

Her mom was great, as always, accepting and supportive. She said she hoped she'd be meeting Donovan soon.

After talking to her mom, Abilene called Zoe, who instantly confessed she'd made Dax tell her everything that Donovan had said to him earlier that day.

"Dax tried to get him to come and visit us," Zoe said. "Donovan never quite got around to giving him an answer on the invitation—and he didn't invite us out there to West Texas to see him, either."

"I know. Donovan told me, tonight, during dinner, that Dax had invited him for a visit. And then we had a big fight about it."

"A fight?"

"Long story. Too long—and way too complicated."

"Ab, why do I get the feeling that there's more going on with you two than this fellowship you waited so long for?"

Abilene busted herself. "There *is* more. A lot more."

Zoe said nothing for a moment. And then, when she did speak, she sounded nothing short of philosophical. "Well, I guess I knew this would happen."

"Excuse me?"

"Oh, come on. You've been talking about Donovan McRae for years. You idolize him."

"I idolize Mies van der Rohe, too." Van der Rohe was one of the great pioneers of Modern architecture. "But that doesn't mean I want to get intimate with him."

"Isn't Mies van der Rohe dead?"

"Oh, very funny. You know what I mean."

"So…how serious is it?"

"It feels serious to me. But it's all new, you know?"

"What about kids? Does he want them? *Can* he…?"

"Wait a minute. Didn't I just say it's all new? Do we need to jump right to whether or not he can father a child?"

"You just said it feels serious. And it *is* an issue you would have to deal with—I mean, if you want children."

Abilene sighed. Really, the question didn't strike her as all that rude and tactless, given that it was coming from Zoe. After all, Dax had once sworn that kids and married life were not for him. Zoe had taken him at his word.

And that had created no end of problems between them, as Zoe had come to discover she did want children. Very much.

They'd worked it out and ended up together. And they were expecting their first, a boy, in May. So the big question of having babies—or not having them—was front and center in Zoe's mind.

"Ab, you still with me?"

"I'm here."

"Well?"

Abilene gave in and told her what she wanted to know. "The accident only affected his legs. So yes, as far as I know, he *can*. And yes, I do want kids. And next you'll be asking me if I really think I can deal long-term with a guy who uses a wheelchair."

Zoe made a humphing sound. "No way. I know you. You can deal with anything you set that big brain of yours on accomplishing. If you were a wimp or a quitter or prone to being overwhelmed, yeah, I might ask. But you? Uh-uh—and will you get him to come to SA, please? I want to meet him."

"I'm working on that. So far, as I think I mentioned, it's not going all that well."

Zoe laughed. "You'll make him see the light. I have total faith in you."

"Tell that to Donovan."

"I will, you can count on it—I mean, after I get to know him a little, once you get him to come to SA."

"He says he won't."

"You'll talk him into it. And keep me posted?"

"Will do," Abilene promised. She asked how Zoe was feeling.

"I feel great. You should see me. I actually look pregnant now. It's about time, I guess, almost six months along. And he's started kicking. I think he plans to be a football star." She sounded so happy.

But why wouldn't she be? She had a husband she adored, a baby on the way. And she also worked with Dax, at his magazine, *Great Escapes*. She loved her job. Zoe, the one who could never settle down and stick with anything, had finally found the life that suited her perfectly.

The conversation wound down after that. Zoe said goodbye.

As Abilene got ready for bed, she found herself thinking of Donovan's son again—the son he had never so much as mentioned to her. She'd spent nearly a month working closely with him. She'd made tender, hot love with him last night—and still he hadn't said one word about the lost Elias

Plus, there was the argument earlier, at the dinner table. She hated that she couldn't get through to him, make him see what he really did need to do. But more than that, she hated that his ultimate solution to a heated disagreement had been to simply wheel away.

She'd told Zoe that this thing with Donovan felt serious to her. And it did. But maybe to Donovan, it just didn't.

It hurt, to consider that he really might not care all that much about what was going on between them. It hurt her heart—and her foolish pride.

In the bedroom, after she'd put on her comfy sweats and brushed her teeth, she considered getting under the covers. But no way would she sleep.

She got some paper and a pencil and did some sketching—just kind of doodling, fooling around with ideas for houses and various other structures she might someday actually get a chance to build. When that got old, she put on some sneakers and went to the kitchen, where she dished up a slice of Anton's blackberry cheesecake. She carried the dessert into the dark studio, turned on all the lights, sat down at her desk and powered up the computer.

For a while, between bites of the creamy treat, she worked on the text of her proposal for the Foundation people. It was descriptive writing, designed to promote the project, to impress the client—in this case, to convince the Foundation that she knew what she was doing, with or without a master architect to guide her.

It didn't go well. Her mind kept wandering, as it had back in her rooms, to thoughts of Donovan. It seemed she couldn't escape him.

So she switched to the drafting board and her pet project, the one she always turned to when she was troubled or in need of distraction. She had hundreds of drawings of this particular structure already, of varying exterior views, of every room seen from every angle. It was her Hill Country dream house, the one she fantasized about building someday, for the husband and children she didn't have yet.

Sometimes she drew it as a rambling craftsman-style structure; sometimes it had a log cabin exterior. The floorplan kept changing, too, over time. Currently, her dream house was forty-seven hundred square feet—two thousand nine hundred downstairs, and eighteen hundred up. It had a vaulted great room with a floor-to-ceiling natural stone fireplace at one end and a formal dining room at the other. The built-in media center and carved double doors separated the great room from the home office, which had the same wide-plank floors and extensive built-ins. The kitchen, with walk-in pantry, center island and snack-bar counter, opened to a sky-lit second kitchen—an outdoor kitchen—with its own cooktop and oven and corner fireplace.

She was rethinking the purpose of a small interior section between the four-car garage and the outdoor kitchen, when Donovan said, "You're working late."

Her hopeless heart lifted. She glanced up to see him sitting in the doorway at the far end of the room—the door nearest his own desk. "Not working, just…daydreaming, really. Daydreaming on paper."

He rolled the chair, first back a few inches, and then forward, stopping in the center of the doorway, pretty much right where he had started. As if he hesitated to enter his own studio. "I went to your rooms first." It was a confession. "And then I tried the kitchen. When you weren't in either place, I figured maybe here…"

"Ah," she said, a warm glow flowing all through her at the thought that he had come to find her, that he *did* care about her, at least a little. And yet still, she wasn't going to prompt him. If he had something to say to her, he was going to have to get the words out all by himself.

Finally, he did. "I'm sorry, Abilene. I didn't want to hear what you had to say at dinner. And when you wouldn't give up and quit talking about it, I wheeled out on you. That was a crappy thing for me to do."

It was a step. A rather large one, actually. "Your apology is accepted." She turned her attention to her dream house again.

"May I see?"

She didn't look up. "Sure."

He entered the studio and wheeled down the length of it, rolling around the outer edge of her drafting table and stopping at her side. "A house…"

"My dream house," she said. "Someday I'll build it. Ideally, in the Hill Country."

He took a few seconds to look over the drawings she'd done that night. "Not bad."

She stuck out an elbow and poked him in the ribs. "Kissing up much?"

"I never kiss up when we're discussing architecture—what's this?" He bent closer. "A dog shower and grooming station?"

"I just thought of that. It's off the garage. Very convenient."

"Do you have a dog?"

"I intend to. Big dogs. Several—well, at least two. And a couple of cats, as well."

"Where's the cat grooming station?" He leaned her way—just enough that she felt his arm brush hers. She caught a hint of his scent, clean and earthy at once, a scent that stirred her, made her think of the night before, of what they'd done in his chair—and later, on the tangled sheets of her bed.

She looked at him then and saw that he was watching her, his gaze intent. All at once, the air between them felt electric, charged with promise. She said, with a slight huskiness creeping in, "Cats don't need one. They groom themselves."

He leaned a little closer. "I do like your dream house."

She only nodded. And it came to her that from now on, whenever she imagined her dream house, it would be with him in it.

And that was just beyond depressing. If it didn't work out with him—and it most likely wouldn't—she would have to dream up some other house to build for the man who *could* love her, and the children they would have together.

Really, she was carrying this whole thing between them too far—and too fast.

His eyes had changed. They were suddenly sad. And a million miles away. "It looks like a great place to raise your children."

"Well, yes. That's the dream...."

He caught her hand, brushed his lips against her knuckles. She felt that light kiss so deeply, in the core of herself.

Oh, I am going down, she thought.

Going down and fading fast. Just the touch of his lips against her skin and she was done for, finished, gone.

How could she have let this happen?

He was so not the man she'd imagined herself falling for. She'd always known that the man for her would be openhearted. And trusting. Someone kind and not cruel. Someone who would tell her all his secrets, someone who could love her without holding his deepest heart away from her.

Someone as different from the man beside her as day was from night.

And then, in a torn voice, he said, "I had...a child, Abilene. A little boy who died. His name was Elias."

Chapter 11

Abilene sat very still in her chair, her hand held in his.

He was ready, at last—ready to tell her about Elias. It hardly seemed possible, that this precious moment had finally come.

She forgot all about that other man, her ideal man. The one who loved her unconditionally, the one who never spoke harshly, who was always understanding.

Right now, there was only Donovan. He filled up her heart, banished her doubts.

It meant so much, proved so much. About how far they had come, with each other, *toward* each other.

Donovan said, "Elias was four when his mother, Julie, died."

She let out a low cry. "Oh, Donovan. His mom died, too?"

He gazed at her steadily. "That's right."

She asked, softly, "You were married then, you and...Julie?"

He shook his head. "We were together, for a while. But it didn't last long."

It seemed important, then, to tell him what she already knew. "That day I went to lunch with Luisa...?"

He made a knowing sound. "She told you about Elias." At her nod, he added, "I was afraid she might."

"Don't get the wrong idea. It wasn't a gossip session, I promise you. Luisa respects your privacy and your feelings."

"I know she does."

"She mentioned Elias, but only because she assumed that I already knew about him. When she found out I didn't, she wouldn't say much more. She said I should ask you."

"But you didn't." Donovan spoke gently, a simple statement of fact.

Abilene admitted, "I've been waiting, for you to tell me yourself, when you were ready. It seemed somehow wrong, for me to be the one to bring it up."

He almost smiled. "You rarely hesitate to say what's on your mind."

"True. And I did want to ask you about him, about Elias. About what he was like, and yes, how you lost him. But somehow, it never felt like the right time. I didn't want to ambush you with something like that. And I knew it had to be a really rough subject for you."

"Yeah." His eyes were more gray than blue right then, a ghostly gray. And his face, too, seemed worn. Haggard. "It is a rough subject."

"Luisa did say there used to be pictures of Elias, in the music room and the front room."

"I had all his pictures moved to my own rooms, months ago, when I got back from the first series of surgeries after the fall. So no one would ask me about him—which was seriously faulty reasoning, if you think about it." His voice took on a derisive edge. He was mocking himself.

She understood. "Who was around to ask you?"

"Exactly. By then, I allowed no one inside this house but Ben and Anton and Olga. And I'd already told them in no uncertain terms that they were never again to mention Elias. And they didn't. It was part of their job description, not to push me, never to challenge me, not to mention my son. I had everything under control, I thought." The shadows in his eyes lightened a little as he gazed at her, and a hint of a smile came and went. "And then you came along...."

She squeezed his hand. "Tell me about Julie. Tell me...the rest."

"Julie..." His almost-smile appeared again, like the edge of the sun from behind a dark cloud. "She was a good woman. Straight ahead, you know? Honest. After it was over between us, when she found out she was pregnant, she told me right away. I asked her to marry me. She said no, that we didn't love each other that way and marriage between us wouldn't last. But she did want the baby. I had money by then. And Julie was an artist, a struggling one. She was barely getting by. So I agreed to pay enough child support that she wouldn't have to work and she could be a full-time mom."

"That was good of you."

He chuckled. "No. It was convenient for me. And it worked for Julie, too. She was devoted to Elias and happy to be able to be with him, to raise him without the constant pressure of having to make ends meet. Everybody won—Elias, Julie. And me. I had no interest in being a real dad. Not until Julie died out of nowhere, of a stroke, of all things. She had no family. What could I do?"

"You took your son to live with you."

"I didn't see a choice in the matter, and that's the hard truth."

"So it was a big change for you."

"I dreaded it, to be honest, having a kid around. I worked all over the world. And when I wasn't working, there were mountains I wanted to climb. If Julie's parents had still been alive, I would have turned Elias over to them in a heartbeat. Or to my mother. But as you know, she was gone, too."

Abilene searched his face. "You're being way too hard on yourself, you know that?"

"No. I'm just telling you the way it was. The way *I* was. That first year, after we lost Julie, that was rough. Elias suffered, missing his mom. But he was a sunny-natured guy at heart. A miracle of a kid, really. From the first, clutching that beat-up Elmo doll he carried everywhere with him, he was following me around. He was looking up at me with those trusting eyes, asking me questions." Donovan smiled, but his own eyes were suspiciously moist. He shook his head. "Elias never stopped with the questions. And as the months went by, I found I was only too happy to come up with the answers he needed, only too happy to be a real dad. He was so curious. And as he got over the loss of his mom, he didn't have to carry his stuffed Elmo around everywhere. He became…fearless. I loved that about him. I took him with me, when I was working. I hired a tutor. And a nanny, to go with us. We lived in San Francisco and Austin. And then in Lake Tahoe…." Donovan drew in a slow, shaky breath.

Abilene waited. She sensed the worst was coming.

And it was. "That was where it happened, in Lake Tahoe." Donovan let go of her fingers then. He sank back into his wheelchair and gripped the wheels in either hand. "I had rented a vacation cabin there. The driveway was impossibly steep—and remember how I mentioned that Elias was fearless?"

"I remember."

"Six years old, and he loved nothing so much as to ride his Big Wheel down the steepest hill he could find—the driveway. And then he graduated to his first two-wheeler. That really freaked the nanny out, but I watched him and he was a natural athlete, lightning reflexes, great balance. I told her to back off, that Elias knew what he was doing, that he had sense as well as good reflexes—plus, she always made him wear his helmet. He would be fine. At first, she thought I was crazy. But then, after she watched him go flying down that hill a few times, she agreed with me. He was having a ball and he was perfectly safe."

A chill ran along the surface of her skin. "But he wasn't?"

Donovan shut his eyes, tight, as if he saw the worst all over again, and only wanted to block out the memory, erase it from his sight. "Elias rode that new two-wheeler down the driveway countless times without a scratch. And then there was the last time. The bike hit a rock—or so the medical examiner determined later. It was one of those freak things, out of nowhere. Must have caught him off-guard. Elias fell. He never wanted to wear his helmet. That time, apparently, he had it on to appease the nanny, but left the clasp undone. The helmet flew off. He hit his head. I found him at the bottom of the driveway. Just lying there. His eyes were open. He was gone, I knew it. But he seemed to be staring up at the pines, at the blue sky overhead...."

"Oh, Donovan." The words were useless, but she couldn't help it. She said them anyway. "I'm so sorry...."

After a moment, he looked at her. His face was so pale, suddenly. Pale as a man lying in his own coffin. As if he was the one who had died.

And maybe, in essence, he had.

"I didn't protect him," Donovan said. "He died because I loved his fearlessness. I ate it up, that he was such a bold little guy, that nothing got him down. I... didn't watch out for him."

She ached to argue, to insist that you can't possibly watch a child every moment of every day, that terrible things can happen, with no one to blame. But she had no doubt he'd heard all that before. And if Elias had been her child, such consolations, however true, wouldn't help in the least.

A father needed to protect his children. And if he failed at that, for whatever reason, nothing anyone could say would make the guilt and pain go away.

"The children's center?" she asked in a whisper.

He swallowed. Hard. "Yeah. The idea for the center

was a lot about Elias. My son was gone, but I hoped that maybe, if I could help someone else's child to have a better start in life, it would mean something, somehow. It would make up, at least a little, for the life Elias was never going to have."

"Oh, Donovan, yes. It's a good thing, what you're doing, an important thing. The center *will* mean a lot to children who need it." The words were totally inadequate, but she offered them anyway, in a vain attempt to draw him back to her, to the world of the living.

"I thought I was over it." His voice was no more than a rough husk of sound. "I thought I had made my peace with Elias's death. For a year or so, I grieved. And then I told myself I needed to let it go—let *him* go—to get on with my life."

"But you weren't over it. Not really."

He shook his head. "It all came back, after the accident, like some dangerous animal I had locked in a room and told myself I was safe, protected from. That animal got out. During those three days alone in that ice cave, that animal came after me. At first, I fought it. I told myself I could make it, I was going to be okay. But that, the fighting, the holding on, it didn't last long. Then I was wondering if I was going to die, and then I was *certain* that I would. I was making a kind of peace with death, an agreement. Death and I came to an understanding. We both knew it was time for me to go." He stared off into the far corner of the long room, past the shadowed open door down at the other end. And he was lost to her at that moment, lost to the world, gone from his own life.

She reached for him, touched his face. His skin felt

cool, bloodless. "Donovan." She urged him to turn to her. "Look at me. Please…"

He did turn his face her way. But his eyes were empty. He said, "I thought about Elias a lot during those three days. I thought of the life he would never have, of the complete wrongness of that. By the end, before they found me, I was talking to him, to Elias. It seemed I could see his face. I could hear his voice, calling me, asking questions, asking where I was, why I had left him alone. And I started thinking it was good, right, that I should die and be with him. I knew I was *ready* to die. I wanted it. To die."

He seemed a million miles away from her then, back on that mountain, in unbearable pain, with only his lost son for company.

She feared for him, truly. And she hated herself a little. For pushing him so hard, for challenging him, constantly, to open up to her, to face his demons.

What did she know, really, about all he had suffered, about how he might have managed to deal with the worst kind of loss a parent can ever know?

What right did she have, to rip away his protections, to drag him back to the world again? She could see a deeper truth now, one her own youth and optimism had blinded her to. She could see at last, that in his isolation and silence, he had found a kind of peace.

But then she had come and stolen his peace away, all the while telling herself it was for his own good.

His own good.

What did she know about what was good for him?

Desperation seized her. She found herself pleading

with him. "But Donovan—Donovan, please. You didn't die. You made it back."

He only went on staring at her through those blank eyes. "Not really. My body was rescued, I went on breathing. But for all intents and purposes, I was dead...."

It was too much. He seemed so far away now, gone somewhere inside his own mind, into a cold and lifeless place where she would never be able to reach him. She couldn't bear it.

She clambered up out of her seat and reached for him, wrapping both arms around his broad shoulders, from the side, bending across his wheelchair. It was awkward, trying to hold him like that. And it wasn't enough, either. She couldn't hold him tight enough.

So she eased one foot up and over him, sliding it between his white-knuckled grip on the wheel and the crook of his elbow. He only sat there, still as a living statue, as she squirmed to get her other leg into the space between his arm and his torso.

Finally, she managed it. She straddled him as she had the night before—only then, it had been for their mutual pleasure.

Now, it was for comfort. Comfort for him.

And for herself, too.

It was the only way she had left to try and reach him, to make him come back to her from whatever dark place he had gone.

She wrapped her arms around him and she buried her head against his neck. She held on tight, so very tight....

At first, it was no good. She was holding on all by herself. And that was unbearable, that he just sat there, unmoving, like the dead man he'd claimed he already was.

She held on tighter, she pressed her lips to the cool flesh of his neck, she whispered his name, over and over again.

And slowly, so slowly, his arms relaxed their steely grip on the wheels. He lowered his head a little, enough that she felt the soft kiss of his breath, stirring her hair.

He said, so softly she almost didn't hear the word, "Abilene…" And then those powerful arms came around her. He was holding her as tightly as she held on to him.

And she was whispering, frantically, "It's not true— you know it's not. You're here, with me. You're okay and you have to go on now. You have to learn to go on…."

He pressed his lips to her temple, a fervent caress. And then he was cradling her face between his two hands, urging her to lift her head, to look at him.

And she did look—and it *was* okay. He was all right. The color was back in his cheeks, and his eyes were focused, alive. He was there, in the studio, in the *world,* with her again.

She took his mouth—a hard, quick kiss. A claiming kiss. Once, and then a second time. "Oh, you scared me. You did. You really did…."

He eased her away from him enough that he could capture her gaze and hold it. "Okay," he said, firmly. Decisively.

She didn't get it, had no idea what he was telling her. "Okay, what?"

"Okay, you were right."

"Um. I was?"

"Sometimes I hate it, you know? How right you are?"

"I have to tell you, Donovan. Sometimes I don't feel very right. Sometimes I feel like I haven't got a clue."

"Coulda fooled me."

"Yeah. Well, I put on a pretty good act, I guess, huh?"

He searched her face. And then he gave a low chuckle. "You have no idea what I'm talking about, do you?"

"Well..."

"Do you?"

She was busted. "I hate to admit it, but no. I don't."

"I'm saying you were right, tonight, at the dinner table. And after I wheeled out on you, after I went to my rooms to sulk, I stared at the portrait of Elias over the fireplace, and I thought about how I let him down the day he died, by not watching out for him closely enough, by being too damn proud of him to do what was good for him, to tell him it wasn't safe, tell him no. And stick by it."

It was futile to argue that point, she got that. But she couldn't just keep letting it go, either. "Oh, Donovan..." She put up a hand between them, touched her fingers to his lips.

His gold brows drew together. "What?"

"Sometimes terrible things happen, no matter what you do to make sure that they don't."

He caught her fingers, eased them away. "I'm very well aware of that." The bitterness was there, in his tone, again—and in his eyes. "And it doesn't help to know that, doesn't help when people say it. It doesn't help in the least."

She lowered her head in surrender. "No," she said

quietly. "I can see that it doesn't." She reminded herself—again—that nothing she could say was going to make him stop blaming himself. He had to come to forgiving himself in his own way, in his own time.

He touched her chin, so gently. When she looked up, the anger was gone from his face. He spoke tenderly. "What I'm trying to tell you is that I get it. I understand. I made a commitment when I offered the fellowship for the children's center, and that commitment was not only to the children who need the center, not only to the Foundation, not only to you. It was also to Elias. For his sake most of all, I have to follow through. If I don't, I'll be letting him down all over again."

Her breath got all tangled up in her throat and her heart beat faster, with pure joy. It was happening. He'd seen what he needed to do at last.

And he'd decided to go for it.

He said, "You were right, Abilene, as you are way too much of the time. I'll be going to San Antonio with you, after all."

Chapter 12

He took her to his rooms. She saw the pictures of Elias, at last.

"Oh, I wish I could have known him," she said.

"He would have liked you." Donovan's voice was rough with feeling. He held out his hand to her.

She went to him. She kissed him. They undressed each other slowly and went to bed.

They didn't get to sleep until very late. But they were up at dawn, nonetheless.

Now that he'd made the decision to go, Donovan was wasting no time about it. He wanted to be in San Antonio, ready to work, within the week.

Sunday morning, he started surfing the internet, looking for a place he might stay for an indefinite period, somewhere with good wheelchair access. A few hotels offered what he needed. But he was hoping he could find a house to rent. After a couple of hours of looking, he'd come up with zip.

Abilene suggested, "You should call Dax. He and Zoe have plenty of room."

Donovan hesitated. He didn't want to put them out. It seemed presumptuous. They'd invited him to visit, not to move in on them while he worked.

Abilene marched down the length of the studio to his desk, grabbed the phone and shoved it at him. "They would love to have you. They have plenty of room. Their house is so big, you could move in there permanently. Unless they wanted to see you, they would never even realize you were there."

He slanted her a put-upon look. "Have I told you that you are one extremely annoying and pushy woman?"

"You have. Frequently. Make the call."

He took the phone she held under his nose and dialed Dax's number.

Dax said Donovan was welcome to live at his place, for as long as he wanted to stay. He and Zoe would be gone next week, when Donovan arrived. They traveled a lot, gathering material for his magazine. But he had live-in staff who would have Donovan's rooms ready and waiting for him.

Donovan thanked him, and explained what he needed in terms of access for his wheelchair. And Dax promised it was all workable. There was a suite on the main floor that should be ideal. Meals would be available at Donovan's convenience, since the cook lived in.

So it was settled. Donovan would stay with the Girards. Abilene had her condo waiting for her—though she wouldn't mind at all if she ended up spending her nights at her sister's, in Donovan's rooms.

Monday, when Helen came to work, Donovan asked her to accompany them to San Antonio. But she didn't want to leave her husband alone in Chula Mesa. So he had her call a San Antonio temp agency. They would send someone to Dax's as soon as Donovan got settled in. Also, Helen found trainers and a massage therapist in San Antonio who would work with Donovan while he was there.

Anton and Olga would remain in West Texas to take care of the house. And Helen would come in three times a week to deal with correspondence and anything else that might need her attention while Donovan was away.

As the week went by, Donovan spent a lot of time on the phone with the Foundation people. They were thrilled to learn that he and his protégé would be showing up very soon now. There were conference calls with Ruth Gilman and Doug Lito at the Johnson Wallace Group and with the builder, Sam Duncan of SA Custom Contracting. The site, chosen over a year before, was ready and waiting. The formal groundbreaking ceremony would be going forward on March first, as planned.

Abilene spent her days working feverishly to be ready to go—and her nights in Donovan's bed. She loved the picture of Elias in his sailor suit and talked Donovan into moving it back out to the main living area.

Wednesday night, at dinner, he told Olga to take the portrait out of his sitting room and put it back where it belonged, over the front room fireplace.

Tears welled in Olga's eyes. "Yes. Of course. An excellent decision. He was the sweetest boy. And we miss him, so much."

Thursday night, Luisa came to dinner. She told Donovan how happy it made her, to see that he'd put Elias's picture back in the front room.

"Blame Abilene," he said. "She made me do it." And he sent Abilene a look that melted her midsection and made her toes curl inside her high-heeled shoes.

Luisa wanted them to come to the cantina one more time before they left for San Antonio.

So Friday night, they drove out to the roadhouse. They had margaritas and played pool—and Donovan got his butt kicked again by that tall, tattooed blonde. They were back at the house before midnight and went together to Donovan's rooms, where they made slow, tender love and fell asleep in each other's arms.

Abilene woke Saturday morning in Donovan's bed. She watched him sleeping and found herself wishing she could wake up beside him every morning, for the rest of her life.

She loved him—was *in* love with him. And for the past few busy days, she'd been trying to figure out how to tell him. It seemed such a simple thing. She ought to just say it. *I love you, Donovan.*

But she didn't. Somehow, the moment never quite seemed right.

Strange, really. She'd always been the kind who said exactly what was on her mind.

But on this whole I-love-you thing, well, she kept

hesitating, kept putting it off. She didn't want to push him. Not about something so important as love.

Not about something as far-reaching as the possibility of forever.

On the pillow beside her, he opened his eyes.

She thought, *I love you.* But all she said was, "Good morning."

Donovan met her shining eyes and knew what he had to do. But somehow, he just couldn't bring himself to do it.

What he had with her, he'd never had with any woman—that sense that she knew him, knew who he really was. That she accepted him, completely, and yet still expected him to be the best he could possibly be.

He felt the same way about her. He *knew* her in the deepest way. He accepted her as the brilliant, pushy, tenderhearted woman she was. And he wanted the best for her. He wanted her to have the chance to make all her dreams come true.

She couldn't do that with him. He didn't share her dreams. He couldn't. Not anymore. He kept thinking about that fantasy house of hers—her dream house—about the husband and children she wanted to build it for. He was never going to be the husband in that house, or the father of those children.

He reached out and brushed the back of his hand along the velvety curve of her cheek, thinking that he somehow had to find a way to make her understand why he had to leave her.

Not now, though.

Not yet…

So he thought, *I have to leave you.* But all he said was, "Good morning."

Later that day, Abilene packed up her car. She would leave, on her own, early Sunday morning.

Donovan would fly to San Antonio on Monday. He'd offered to ride with Abilene, to keep her company. But they both knew an eight-hour car ride would be uncomfortable for him. In the end, he'd admitted it was probably wiser for him to fly. Helen had made arrangements for a van with a wheelchair lift to be available at the San Antonio airport, so he would have the use of a car when he got there.

That night, late, it rained. A real gulley-washer. Abilene heard the soft, insistent roar of it outside and woke. Beside her, Donovan slept on.

Slowly, with care, so as not to wake him, she rose from the bed, grabbed her robe from a nearby chair and slipped it on. Barefoot, she padded into his sitting room, where she gazed out at the torrent. It was coming down so hard it made the water in the pool churn and ran in little rivers along the courtyard pathways. Lightning brightened the sky and thunder boomed somewhere in the distance.

She stood there at the glass door for several minutes, watching the rain come down and the lightning flash, listening to the rumbles of thunder.

"Looks pretty wild out there," Donovan said from behind her.

She turned to him. "I didn't mean to wake you."

"You didn't. The thunder did." His white teeth flashed with his smile. In the darkness, his eyes were almost black. He'd pulled on sweats before he wheeled in to join her.

She went to him, bent to kiss him. He reached for her and pulled her down across his lap. She curved against him, her legs over one wheel, an arm around his neck, her head tucked beneath his chin.

He kissed the top of her head. "Ready for the big drive tomorrow?"

"All packed." She nuzzled his throat, breathed in the clean scent of his skin, thought how she hated to be apart from him, even just for a day.

Lightning flashed again. The room brightened.

She lifted her head and met his eyes as the room darkened once more and the thunder rolled off across the desert floor. "It almost feels unreal, that we're leaving. Five weeks out here, and it's as if I've been here, with you, forever."

"Five weeks," he echoed. "And I spent most of it making your life as miserable as possible."

"The past week is the one that counts."

He held her gaze. "They all count. You know that." And then he guided her head down to his shoulder again. "It will be good, though, won't it? To see your family, to go home…?"

"Um-hm." *I love you.* She thought the words. But she didn't say them.

Five weeks, she had known him. Five weeks was nothing. Even if it did kind of feel like forever.

And as he'd just said, only in the past week had they truly found each other.

They both needed more time.

At least a little more.

And a chance to be together out in the real world. His house was beautiful and so comfortable and lately, it had started to feel like her home, somehow. But it was a place apart, where the world outside could not intrude.

San Antonio would be the proof of what they had together. He would meet her family. And the work on the children's center would proceed beyond just the two of them.

Yes. It was good, that they were going.

And this strange feeling she had, the one she kept denying. The feeling that his going with her to San Antonio was an end instead of the beginning...

That would pass, like the lightning and the thunder, like a sudden midnight storm across the wide-open desert.

He smoothed her hair. "Back to bed?"

She lifted her head again, touched her lips to his. "Please." And then she shifted on his lap, turning to face front, bringing her legs down over his, out of the way of the wheels.

He rolled them both in a circle and back to the other room.

The next morning, she said goodbye to Anton and Olga and thanked them for everything.

Olga hugged her and whispered to her to come back soon.

"I will," she promised.

Donovan went with her down to the garage. She kissed him and told him she would see him tomorrow.

He said, "Call me when you get there?"

She promised that she would.

And then she got into her Prius and headed for home.

The drive was every bit as long and tedious as she remembered. But she finally arrived. At a little after five that afternoon, she lugged her suitcases into her condo.

Her place was pretty much as she'd left it—including the Christmas tree in the window and the fat red candles in festive holders on the mantel. When the summons had come from Donovan the day after New Year's, she'd had no time to put away her holiday decorations.

She called Donovan's cell.

He answered on the first ring. "You made it." The sound of his voice warmed her, banished all her strange, persistent doubts. "I've been waiting for you to call...."

She said, "It's crazy. We've been apart for eight hours and fifteen minutes. And I miss you so much."

He said nothing.

Her doubts came flooding back, drowning her. "Donovan?"

And then he confessed gruffly, "Yeah. I miss you, too."

She told herself she was being so silly—and definitely paranoid. And she asked, "Tomorrow?"

He confirmed it. "Tomorrow."

"I could come to the airport and meet you...."

"No. I'll have the van waiting. There's no point."

She wanted to argue that of course there was a point. To see him. To be with him as soon as she possibly could.

But she didn't argue. She told herself to get over this burning need to be near him constantly. Just because she loved him didn't mean she had to turn into some wimpy clinging vine.

She answered with determined cheerfulness. "Then I'll be waiting at Zoe and Dax's."

He said he would see her then. They said goodbye.

She felt let down and lonely—which was totally self-indulgent. So she ordered a pizza and called her mom. Aleta didn't answer the phone at home, so she tried the family ranch, Bravo Ridge, where her mom and dad usually went for Sunday dinner.

Mercy, her sister-in-law, answered. "Everyone's here," she said. "Why don't you come on out?"

"I'd love to, but I've been driving all day and my place is still decorated for Christmas. I need to take down all this holiday stuff."

"Next Sunday then. Family dinner here, as always. Think about it."

"I will. Thanks. Is Mom there?"

"Right here…"

Her mother came on the line. "You're home?"

"Yep. Safe and well."

"How about lunch, tomorrow?"

"Oh, I'd love to. But I can't. Donovan is coming in around noon and I—"

"Honey." Her mother's voice was full of love and patience. "I understand. Of course, you'll want to see that he's all settled at Zoe's."

"Yes. Especially, you know, since Zoe and Dax are out of town."

"Sweetheart, I agree. You should be there to greet him."

"Thanks. For understanding."

"I do want to meet him soon."

"Yes. Absolutely. Tomorrow will be impossible,

though, and probably the rest of the week. We have meetings and more meetings."

"How about next Sunday? You can both come out here, to the ranch, for dinner."

She pictured the wide white steps up to the deep front verandah of the Greek Revival-style ranch house. Wheelchair accessible, it wasn't. "Can I get back to you?"

"That will be fine. And call me any time you think you might be able to slip away for a bit, just the two of us."

"I will. I love you."

"Love you, too…"

They said goodbye.

The pizza came. After she'd devoured three big slices, Abilene got busy. She unpacked and went through the pile of junk mail that her neighbor had picked up for her. The houseplants didn't need watering. The same neighbor had kept an eye on them.

But the Christmas stuff really did have to go. She took it all down and packed everything away.

By the time she was done, it was after ten. She filled the tub and soaked for half an hour, easing away the kinks from those long hours on the road. And then, finally, she crawled into bed, where she lay wide awake half the night.

She missed the warmth of Donovan beside her, missed the soft, even sound of his breathing as he slept.

And she kept feeling that something was not right.

Which was silly, she reminded herself over and over. Everything was fine. Donovan would join her tomorrow. And on Tuesday, the next phase of work on the children's center would begin.

In the morning, she packed a suitcase and went to Zoe and Dax's house, which was just outside of San Antonio, in an exclusive gated community.

She gave her name at the front gate and then again at the gate to the Girard estate. In the cavern of a garage, she parked her little car between a Bentley and an Aston Martin, and left her suitcase in the trunk to bring in later.

Dax and Zoe's house was three stories and sixteen thousand square feet of pure luxury, the furnishings mostly modern, but with a lot of the interesting accent pieces that Dax had picked up on his travels all over the world.

The housekeeper welcomed her and showed her to Donovan's rooms, which were spacious and comfortable. Both the bedroom and the sitting area had views of the back grounds and the pool.

Abilene had been to the house twice before, during the holidays, after her sister and Dax had decided to get married. On the first visit, Zoe had given her a full tour, so she knew her way around inside and out.

Donovan had had his luggage sent ahead. The housekeeper, Pauline, led the way to the walk-in closet, where his shoes were arrayed on handsome wooden racks and everything else was either waiting on hangers or neatly folded and put away in drawers.

Abilene thanked Pauline and said that yes, she would ring if she needed anything. The housekeeper left her.

By then, it was ten-thirty. Donovan's plane wasn't

due to land for half an hour. It could be a couple of hours before he arrived at the house.

She went outside and strolled around the grounds for a while. Back inside, she stopped at the restaurant-size kitchen, where the cook gave her coffee and a warm chocolate croissant.

Her phone chimed as she was wandering back to Donovan's rooms. A text.

It was from Donovan. Just landed. No probs. C U soon.

She grinned like an idiot and texted back, Here. W8ing. She longed to add Luv U, but she stopped her eager thumbs just in time. She hit Send, fast, before she could change her mind again and do it anyway.

It was too early, she reminded herself for the ten-thousandth time. And besides, it would be just too tacky, to declare her love via text message. Too tacky. Too soon.

He answered with a simple, Gr8.

And that was that.

Danger averted. Love not so much as mentioned or in any way alluded to.

In Donovan's bedroom, she stood at the window and looked out at the pool and tried to figure out why she kept feeling so disconnected, so…wrong.

When no answer came to her, she went to the bed and kicked off her shoes and stretched out on her back. The room was quiet and she was pretty tired, since she'd barely slept the night before.

She closed her eyes, let out a slow sigh. Really, a half-hour nap might be just what she needed.…

* * *

Dax's housekeeper was waiting in the garage when Donovan pulled the van in.

She indicated the empty space a few slots away from Abilene's dusty Prius, and then waited some more as he unhooked his chair and wheeled to the lift and down.

"I'm Pauline. Welcome," she said, once he'd rolled off the lift and locked up the van.

Pauline led him out of the garage, down a wide hallway and up a short ramp, into another hallway somewhere in the back half of Dax's enormous house. She showed him the kitchen before she took him to his rooms. "Help yourself to anything you might like," she said.

"Thanks." The door in there, like every door he'd seen so far, was more than wide enough to wheel through. The doorways matched the house; everything on a grand scale.

"Abilene is in your rooms," Pauline said as they started down another wide hallway with a twelve-foot ceiling and a silver-flecked ivory granite floor.

Abilene. He'd been kind of wondering why she hadn't come out to meet him. He was anxious to see her. Ridiculously so.

"I checked on her a few minutes ago," said the housekeeper. "She's napping. I hated to wake her...."

Napping. He should have known. She worked so hard. And she'd spent all day yesterday on the road.

"Here we are," said the housekeeper, stopping at a half-open door. "Your suitcases arrived safely and I've had everything put away."

"Thank you."

"Is there anything in the vehicle that you'd like me to have brought in to you?"

"There's a briefcase and a small overnight bag. I'll get them later."

"If you need anything, just pick up the phone. House line is blue, to reach me. The green button is the kitchen."

He thanked her again.

She nodded and left him alone at last.

He went in, stopping to shut the door and engage the privacy lock behind him. The sitting room was big and inviting, furnished with simple, expensive pieces, mostly in reds and tans.

But he didn't hang around in there. He went through the wide doorway to the bedroom.

And found what he was looking for.

She was sound asleep, her silky hair spread across the pillow and a peaceful expression on her fine-boned face. She wore canvas trousers and a slouchy sweater and she'd kicked off her flat-soled shoes. Her slender feet were bare, her pretty toenails painted the color of plums.

His sleeping princess from his own private fairy tale.

He went to her, drawn as if by a magnet. When he got to the side of the bed, he shucked off his shoes, locked his wheels and, with great care, pressed his palms to the mattress beside her and levered himself out of the chair.

She opened her eyes as he lowered himself to a sitting position next to her. "Donovan. You're here." Her face lit up as if from within.

And he couldn't help himself. His heart melted.

He saw in her eyes what it could be, with them. He

was in it, he lived it—a whole, rich, wonderful life, at her side.

The fine work they would do. The bright, bold, unbounded happiness they would share.

The love they would make.

The troubles they would overcome, the dark times that would always, inevitably, give way to light....

No, it wasn't going to happen. But at that moment, in that large, well-appointed room, with the bright winter-afternoon sunlight streaming in across the tan cover of the bed, picking up gold highlights in her dark-toffee hair, he pretended that it would.

She reached for him, sighing welcome.

And he went down to her, ignoring the twinges in his messed-up legs as he hauled them up onto the mattress and then out as straight as they would go. With effort, he rolled to his side, facing her, and he gathered her into him, covering her soft mouth with his own.

They both groaned at the contact. Instantly, she opened for him. He speared his tongue inside, where it was wet and hot and oh, so sweet. She sucked on it, ran her own tongue around it, teasing him, laughing a little, deep in her throat, a rough purr of sound that vibrated into the core of him.

Already, he was hard, aching to be inside her.

And she was slipping her hand down between them, cupping him with another eager moan, pressing the length of him, caressing him as her body rocked against him, making him harder still.

"The door?" she whispered against his lips.

"Locked it."

"Ah." She went on kissing him—deep, wet, sucking kisses. Endless kisses.

Her nimble fingers worked at his fly. She had his zipper down in an instant, and she was slipping that slim, clever hand of hers under the waistband of his boxer briefs.

She encircled him. He groaned into her mouth as she pushed at him, urging him over to lie on his back.

He went, not even aware by then of his legs, of the twinges and twitches, the pain that was there, whenever he moved them. Right now, he felt a different ache. A good ache, dark and sweet, rolling through him in hungry waves.

Whatever she wanted from him, she could have. He was hers to command.

She left him—just long enough to get out of her trousers and little silk panties. And then she was back, pushing at his clothes enough to clear the way, easing his cell and his keys from his pockets, setting them on the nightstand, out of her way.

He shut his eyes, swept away by the sheer pleasure her touch always brought. And when he looked again, she was above him, straddling him, up on her knees, gazing down at him, her eyes soft and shining, her mouth curving in a sensual smile.

Slowly, by aching degrees, she lowered her body onto his, taking him within her, so deep.

All the way.

He made some absurd, lost groaning sound. And she laughed, low. Huskily. She knew her power over him. It was absolute. She bent down to him, kissed him.

But only briefly, a brushing touch of her lips to his, her hair falling forward around them like a veil of silk. When he tried to follow, lifting his head off the pillows to keep from losing the tenuous connection of that kiss, she laughed again.

And she rose up once more, pushing her hips down on him, locking her body to his. And she took that big sweater she wore and ripped it off, tossing it away, her beautiful hair crackling with static, lifting as she pulled the sweater over her head, then falling in a wild tumble to her shoulders again.

Her bra was nothing more than a bit of pink lace.

He reached up, curved his fingers around one lacy cup, feeling the warmth and fullness of the sweet flesh beneath. "Take it off." He moaned the words.

She reached behind her, undid the clasp and let it drop down her arms. He took it from her, rumpled the lace in his hand, brought it to his face, breathed in the tempting apple and watermelon scent that clung to it—and then he dropped it over the side of the bed.

He reached for her. She came down to him, fusing her mouth to his, kissing him so deeply now. He cradled her breasts, stroked her back and ran his hands up over her shoulders, into the lush silk of her hair.

She moved on him, deep strokes, slow and hot and overwhelming. He was lost—lost in her—never, ever wanting to be found.

When the finish came, she stilled above him. He wrapped her tighter in his arms, knew a breath-held wonder as they rose together.

And then the long, sweet pulse of slow release.

* * *

Not much later, his cell rang.

"Don't answer that," she commanded.

But then she allowed him to look at the display, at least.

"It's Jessica Nevis, with the Foundation."

She sighed. "Go ahead."

He spoke to Jessica, confirmed that they would meet tomorrow morning, at nine.

And he no sooner hung up, than Ruth Gilman's assistant called, from Johnson Wallace, just confirming, for tomorrow. Ruth would be there and Doug, as well, when they met with the Foundation people at nine.

And after Ruth's assistant, the builder called, too.

When he finally put the cell back on the nightstand and pulled Abilene close again, she asked, "Where is that temporary assistant when you need her?"

"That reminds me—I need to call the temp agency. There's not going to be any time to deal with the temp until Wednesday, at the earliest." He tried to reach for the phone again.

She caught his hand and kissed it. "Wait. Just for a few minutes."

He gave in and settled back on the pillow again, with her cradled close to his side.

"I have a confession." She pressed her lips to the side of his neck, whispered, "I brought a suitcase."

"What?" He pretended to grumble. "You're moving in on me?"

"Yes, I am." She snuggled in closer. "Don't try to escape."

"On these legs? I don't think so." He caught her

mouth. They shared a kiss, and then she curled against his shoulder with a sigh.

Idly, he ran his hand down the silky skin of her arm. She felt good in his arms. As if she belonged there.

And really, she did. At least for the next month.

He'd thought long and hard about when to end it, about whether or not he should get it out there now, have a long talk with her, remind her of what he'd told her that day he wheeled in on her in the shower, that love and forever were not an option.

But then again, when they had that talk, knowing her, there was going to be trouble. She was going to be really angry with him. He got that. He accepted that.

And right now, he didn't want her distracted from the job they needed to do together, didn't want her so furious with him that it got in the way for her. When he left her, he wanted her all set up as the supervising architect on the project—with the Foundation, with Johnson Wallace, with the builder, with all of them.

She had given him so much and he wanted her future assured. It was the least he could leave her with.

Or so he told himself.

At the same time, somewhere in his guilty heart, he knew he was a liar. The worst kind of liar, the kind who lied to himself.

The real problem was that he wanted more time with her. They'd only just found each other. And he simply couldn't bear to let her go.

Not so soon. Not quite yet.

Chapter 13

The Foundation people were thrilled with the design. They gave their full approval to proceed.

During the presentation, Donovan deferred to Abilene. He made sure they all knew that it was her dedication and talent that had made the design come together. He explained that she would be taking the position of lead architect as they moved toward construction, though of course, he would be available whenever he was needed.

Ruth Gilman, who was in her early fifties, slim and impeccably dressed, with short strawberry-blond hair, remembered meeting Abilene at some charity function or other. The two of them really seemed to hit it off. Donovan had been sure they would. Ruth had always liked to encourage up-and-coming architects, especially female ones.

They all went to lunch to celebrate—Donovan and Abilene, Ruth Gilman, Doug Lito and Jessica Nevis. Jessica left them after the meal. They moved on to the Johnson Wallace offices, where they met with the builder.

Around four, Jessica and a couple of others from the Foundation joined them. They went over everything, fine-tuning the basic design, working into the evening, and calling it quits around seven.

Donovan was tired when they got back to Dax's; his legs ached and twitched. But it hadn't been as difficult as he'd expected, to spend a whole day working from his wheelchair, dealing with a lot of people, never getting a break to go work out the kinks in the gym.

Still, he told Abilene he was exhausted. And that his legs bothered him more than they actually did.

And when she got on him for giving her all the credit with the Foundation people, he was able to convince her that she needed to accept the credit—and shoulder most of the work. He said he wasn't at the point where he could consistently spend whole days at Johnson Wallace, or at the construction site, for that matter.

She kissed him and said she would do her best.

And then she asked him to go with her to her family's ranch for Sunday dinner. She added, "That is, if you can bear the indignity of having one of my brothers carry you up the front steps." She looked adorably anxious, afraid he would be too proud to agree.

Meeting the parents. He shouldn't do that. It would be only another lie, another indication to her that he was thinking in terms of a future for them.

And it would have been so simple, just to mutter

gruffly that he wasn't comfortable with having one of her brothers carrying him anywhere, just to let her think his pride was the problem.

But he looked in her beautiful, shining, hopeful face—and he couldn't do it, couldn't tell that particular lie.

"Life is full of indignities," he said, and gathered her close. "What's one more?"

They were hard at work again by 9:00 a.m. the next day, spending the morning at Johnson Wallace and the afternoon at the cleared construction site. For Donovan, that day was actually easier than the day before. He saw possibilities for himself now, in terms of his future and his work, possibilities that he hadn't seen before.

But again that night, he lied to Abilene. He made a big deal of his exhaustion and pain.

Thursday morning, he finally got to meet with his temporary assistant. The first task he set her was to find him another place to stay, one with wheelchair access. A house to rent, if possible.

It bothered him to be taking advantage of Dax's hospitality, mostly because Dax was married to Abilene's sister. It was bad enough that he was lying by omission to Abilene about their possible future. He shouldn't be mooching off her family at the same time.

The temp didn't disappoint him. That day, she found him a nice house in Olmos Park, one that had just become available as a sublet for two months while the owners—one of whom was a paraplegic—were out of the country.

He left Abilene happily working with Ruth at Johnson Wallace and went to see the place. It was one story, with ramps leading up to all the entrances. It had space he could use for an office, a small exercise room and a kitchen specially designed with lowered counters. He could cook his own meals there, from his wheelchair.

So he took it, paid for both months, though if everything went according to his plan, he would only need it until the first week of March. Then he had his assistant find him a part-time housekeeper.

That night, during dinner, just the two of them, at Dax's, he told Abilene about the house he'd rented and that he'd be moving there the next day.

She set down her fork. "I'm…surprised. I thought it was working out well for you, staying here."

"It is. It's great. But I don't feel right, taking advantage of Dax like this."

She sighed and fiddled with her water glass. His gut knotted and he was sure that she would argue. That she would ask too many questions and he would end up saying too much.

But in the end, she only picked up her fork again. "I get it. You like your own…space."

"That's it, exactly." Well, okay. It wasn't all of it. But she didn't need to know that. Not now. Right now, she needed to put her boundless energy where it mattered—on the work she was doing, on the center she would be helping to build. And on the future she was creating for herself.

She looked at him sideways. "Do I get to see this house you'll be staying at?"

"Absolutely."

"When?"

"I'm thinking tomorrow, for dinner."

"Do I get to...sleep over?"

"I hope you will."

She laughed then. "I'll bring my suitcase."

She did bring her suitcase.

She stayed with him Friday night, and Saturday, too.

Sunday, they went out to Bravo Ridge, her family's ranch, where her brother Luke carried him up the wide front steps and he met her mom and dad and Luke's wife, Mercy, along with six other brothers, their wives and a few very cute children.

Over dinner, one of the wives, Irina, announced that she and Caleb, the fifth-born Bravo brother, were expecting a baby in August. Everyone jumped up, the men to clap a beaming Caleb on the back and the women to pull the serenely smiling Irina from her chair and pass her from one laughing, congratulatory hug to the next.

For Donovan, the moment was bittersweet. He envied Caleb. He envied all the Bravo men—whole and strong, married to women they obviously loved. Unafraid to be fathers, secure in the firm belief that they could protect their children and their women from harm.

Overall, though, Donovan enjoyed himself that day. They were good people, he thought. Abilene's mom, Aleta, was especially charming. He saw Abilene in her—in the way she tipped her head when she was listening, in the curve of her mouth when she smiled. And her father, Davis, was something of an architecture buff. He knew of the five-star hotel Donovan had designed in Dallas, and the headquarters for that office supplies conglomerate he'd built in Manhattan.

They all stayed well into the evening, playing pool in the game room and then returning to the dining room for a late dessert. At a little after eight, Luke carried him back down the front steps. Gabe, the second-born brother, brought his wheelchair down and set it up for him at the back of the van. Before he rolled onto the lift and in behind the wheel, he thanked them all.

Aleta bent close and hugged him and told him to come back any time.

"I liked them," he reassured Abilene, later, in bed.

She kissed him and whispered, "They liked you, too."

Monday was Valentine's Day. Donovan took Abilene to her favorite restaurant. They went home to his rented house and made slow, beautiful love. She fell asleep in his arms. He cradled her close and tried not to think about how fast each day was going by.

He wished he could hold back time, make it stand still. Just for a little while.

But time failed to cooperate. It flew by.

That Wednesday, Zoe and Dax returned, and the four of them had dinner together. Dax had always been a player, dating one gorgeous woman after another. But it was obvious that he'd found all the woman he needed in the six-months-pregnant Zoe, who had long red hair, a great sense of humor and a mind as sharp as Abilene's.

Later, the men retreated to Dax's study, where they drank very old Cognac and Dax tried to get him to talk about Abilene. But Donovan had a feeling that whatever he said would go right back to Zoe—and from Zoe, to Abilene.

So he was evasive. And Dax didn't push.

And that night, when they were alone, Abilene talked about how happy her sister seemed, how great it was that Zoe and Dax had found each other. He agreed.

She gazed at him expectantly. "A little like us, huh?"

Again, he lied by omission. He pulled her down into his lap, tipped her chin up and kissed her, ending a dangerous conversation before it could really get started.

Every evening, it seemed, there was someone new Abilene wanted him to meet. Friday night, he met Javier Cabrera, the builder Abilene admired so much. Javier was also the man whose estranged wife had once had an affair with Abilene's father—a brief liaison, which had resulted in Abilene's half sister, Elena.

Javier came to dinner at the rental house in Olmos Park. He was a compact, powerfully built man, with silver-shot black hair. He treated Abilene with honest affection and respect. Donovan felt drawn to him. There was loneliness in the older man's dark eyes, and wisdom, too. Javier said he was considering selling his business. That he didn't have the heart for his work anymore. That he was ready to retire.

As soon as the older man was out the door, Abilene turned to Donovan, tears in her eyes. "He seems even sadder than ever. I just want to grab him, you know? Grab him and shake him and tell him to go to his wife, go right away. To tell her he loves her and he forgives her for what she did all those years ago, to swear that all he wants is to get back together with her."

Donovan only shook his head. "Some things, a man has to figure out for himself."

Two fat tears overflowed the dam of her lower lids

and trailed a gleaming path down her soft cheeks. "And some things, I guess, just can't be forgiven."

He reached for her hand then, and pulled her down to him. She curled into him as if she belonged there, in his arms. He wished for the impossible, that he would never have to let her go.

The weekend passed, a weekend they spent together, he and Abilene.

She had essentially moved in with him. He shouldn't have allowed that, shouldn't have indulged himself so completely with her. But he did it anyway.

Every night with her was a night to remember, a night to treasure. He was hoarding those nights, storing them up in his heart. When he no longer had her with him, at least he would have the memories of her.

And during the day, he'd established a schedule much like the one he'd kept when she came to his house in the desert. He checked in and out with Johnson Wallace and the builder, making himself available when necessary, but pushing Abilene to the fore.

It went well, though by the end of their second week in San Antonio, he did notice a certain watchfulness in Abilene. She asked him Tuesday evening if something was bothering him.

He lied and said there was nothing. After that, it seemed to him, she was quieter, less lively somehow.

Except when they went to bed.

In his arms, she came alive. She burned with a bright fire, taking the lead, driving him wild. He was only too happy to be consumed by the flames.

By the next week, the third week in February, the

Foundation people, the Johnson Wallace team and the builder all seemed to have accepted that they were working with Abilene. That Wednesday night, again, she asked him if there was something wrong.

He denied it.

And then, both Thursday and Friday, he stayed away from Johnson Wallace, didn't even look in to see how the project was going. He knew he would hear from them if there was an issue and that Abilene could handle things without him hanging around.

He got no calls. No one seemed to notice his absence.

Or so he thought, until Friday night, when Abilene got home.

She came into the kitchen, dropped her big leather bag on the chair by the door and said, "Okay. It's enough. We've got to talk about this."

Abilene waited, her pulse a roar in her ears, her stomach tied so tight, in painful knots, as Donovan lowered the heat under the sausage he was cooking and turned off the burner beneath the big pot he used for boiling pasta. He wheeled over to the sink to rinse and dry his hands.

Oh, she did not want to go here. She didn't want to confront him.

But really, they couldn't just keep on like this. Pretending everything was all right, playing house in this cute little place he'd rented.

Finally, he turned to her. His eyes were a cool, distant gray. "Talk about what?"

Talk about what? The words bounced around in her

brain, and she wanted to fling them right back at him, *Talk about what? As if you don't know...*

Resolutely, she marched to the small breakfast table by the bow window, pulled out a chair and lowered herself into it. "Please." She gestured at the empty space across from her.

He didn't move, only suggested so gently, "Abilene, you don't have to do this."

A torn sound escaped her. "If I don't, then what?"

"Abilene..." His voice trailed off. He shook his head.

At that moment, she almost hated him. She *would* have hated him, if only she didn't love him so damn much.

She asked in a voice barely above a whisper, "Is it the groundbreaking ceremony? Is that the end? Is that when you're leaving me?"

He glanced away, which only made her more certain that it had to be the groundbreaking ceremony.

She pointed at the place across the table again, asked for the second time, "Please?"

And at last, he moved. He wheeled around the central island and took the space she'd indicated. When he stopped, he kept his hands at his wheels. As if, at any second, he would back and turn and roll out the kitchen door and away—from her, from this moment, from the words that needed to be said.

She folded her hands on the table. "I don't want to fight, Donovan. I just want to talk. To talk honestly."

His Adam's apple lurched as he swallowed. And he nodded. But he didn't speak.

It was up to her.

Fair enough. "For weeks now, I've wanted to tell you

what I feel for you, in my heart. But I kept thinking I shouldn't rush things, shouldn't rush *you*. Or myself. I kept telling myself that it was too soon to start talking about the future, that now was the time to just be together, to let the future take care of itself. I reminded myself to enjoy being with you, to allow what we have to be…open-ended, I guess."

"Has it been so bad?" he asked, carefully. "Just being together, just taking every day as it comes?"

"Oh, no. Not bad." She felt the tears rise. And she gulped them back. "Far from it. It's been beautiful. Perfect…"

He was leaning toward her a little now. "So, then. Can we leave it at perfect? Why can't we do that?"

Because you are leaving me. And that is about as far from perfect as it gets….

She cleared her throat. "I just, well, I can sense that what we have together is not open-ended, not for you. You know what you're doing, *exactly* what you're doing. You're giving me everything. Everything but the chance of a future with you. And today—which is the second day you haven't even put in an appearance on the project—today, for me, it all just got to be too much."

He tipped his head to the side, asked, "Is there a problem on the project?"

"No. Everything's going well. That's not what we're talking about."

"It *is* what we're talking about." He parsed out each syllable. "I'm available, if you need me. But you don't. You're up to speed. You can run this thing on your own."

She braced her elbows on the table and covered

her face with her hands. "I'll ask you again. Is it the groundbreaking? Is that when you're going back to West Texas?"

There was only silence from his side of the table.

She lowered her hands and she stared straight at him. "Just tell me, Donovan. Is it the groundbreaking?"

And finally, slowly, he nodded. "Yeah. After the groundbreaking, I'm going back to West Texas."

"Without me," she said in a hollow whisper.

He gave her a slow, regal nod of his golden head. "Alone."

Her throat locked up. She looked away, coughed into her hand to try and clear it. The effort was pretty much a failure. When she spoke again, her voice was tight, ragged. "Why?" She faced him. "Oh, Donovan, what are you doing, just throwing it all away like this, throwing *us* away?"

His gaze was gentle. But he wasn't budging. "I told you. I told you that morning I wheeled in on you in the shower. I'm no good for this, no good for…love."

"And I told *you* that people can change."

"Not me. Not about this."

Her anger mounted. She tried to tamp it down. She spoke through tight lips, with measured care. "This is not about what you *can't* do, and you know it's not. It's simply that you *won't*. You won't move on from the horrible things that have happened to you, from the loss of Elias, from those days on the mountain, when death almost found you, but didn't. You're like Javier, you know that? Unforgiving. He can't forgive the woman he loves, even though that's the only way for him to find meaning in his life again. And you, Donovan—you can't forgive yourself."

His hands were on his wheels again, gripping tight. He continued in that so-patient, infuriating tone, "You're young and you're beautiful. And you're a fine architect. Exceptional. You're going to do great work. And someday you're going to find the right guy, a really good guy, a guy who's not all broken up inside and out. You'll settle down together, have children, build that special house of yours...."

It was too much. She wanted to jump up, start shouting, to try and get through to him by sheer volume, since nothing else seemed to work.

But she didn't jump up. She refused to raise her voice.

She stayed in that chair and she spoke with furious softness. "Don't you get it? I love *you,* Donovan. You *are* the right guy. I want my children to be *our* children. Don't you know that? I want to build that house for *us.*"

He flinched as if she'd struck him. "Stop."

"But—"

"No more." He did back his chair from the table, then. But instead of turning and wheeling away, he jerked to a stop and told her flatly, "Never. No. I will never have another child. I couldn't do that, couldn't go through that again—and yes, I've been selfish. And wrong, to be with you, to give in to wanting you. I see that. I know it. I guess I knew it all along."

"Wrong?" She couldn't believe he'd actually said that. She did jump to her feet then. "Of course, it wasn't wrong. *This* is what's wrong."

"This." He glared up at her. "This...what?"

"This. You. Making my choices for me. *That's* wrong."

"I made no choices for you."

"Oh, yes you did. You decided to set everything up for me, to give me everything I've ever wanted, to make my life perfect for me—only without *you* in it. You decided that I wanted kids and you didn't, and then you decided that therefore it's impossible for things to work out with us."

He demanded, "Did you or did you not just say you wanted your kids to be my kids?"

"I only—"

"Answer me! Did you say it or not?"

"I did, yes. But nothing is absolute. It doesn't all *have* to turn out a certain way."

"Oh, right, Abilene. You go ahead. You tell me that you don't want to be the go-to architect for the children's center."

"I didn't say that."

"Tell me that you don't want children. Tell me that right to my face."

"Of course, I want children. But if *you* don't, well, we could at least talk about that."

He made a scoffing sound. "We could talk."

"Yes. Talk. Please."

His lip curled in a sneer. "What is there to talk about?"

"Plenty. Maybe I could live without kids. Did that ever occur to you? And even if I couldn't, how would you know what I can or can't get along without, if you haven't even asked me?"

He rolled back to the table. "All this is just so much noise. You have to know that."

"Noise? After all these weeks, we're finally talking, finally saying the things that need to be said—and you call it noise?"

"It's a waste of breath, to hash it out like this. Because it's not up for discussion. None of it is up for discussion. I was wrong, to get personally involved with you. I see that now."

She stared at him. The distance across that table seemed to be miles—endless, unbridgeable miles. Her knees felt all quivery. She sank back into the chair and asked, her voice breaking, "Wrong? You keep saying it was wrong. You really think that? That what we've had is wrong?"

"I've only hurt you."

"No. No, that's not true. You know it's not. Oh, why can't you see? We've had more, so much more than just this, just the hurting. And we could make a life, a *good* life. You know that we could. If you would only—"

"No."

"You keep saying that."

"Because you're not listening."

She was running out of arguments, running out of ways to try and get through to him. "Just…like that? Just, no?"

"I will be at the groundbreaking." His voice was quiet, resigned. "I'll play my part. And if I'm needed on the project, I'm there for it. But as for the rest of it…" He winced, turned his head away and stared off toward the bow window. It was dark out by then. All he could possibly see was his own ghostly reflection. "It's over. And it's time we accepted that."

It's over....

All the breath seemed to leave her body. She was empty. A shell. Finished in the worst, most final way. What more could she do? She had told him she loved him, that she wanted a life with him, a life on *his* terms.

And it had meant nothing to him.

Less than nothing.

He had denied her. He was sending her away.

And still, somewhere deep in her obstinate, hopeful heart, she wanted to fight for him. She did. She wanted to believe that if she could only find the right words, it would make all the difference, would make him admit that he loved her, make him beg her to stay.

But words had deserted her. And she didn't believe. Not anymore. He turned his gaze to her again.

She looked into his eyes and all she saw was a weariness to equal her own. The only thing left for her to say was, "I'll just get my stuff together, then."

Carefully, feeling as though she might shatter if she moved too fast, she pushed herself to her feet again. She put one foot in front of the other. She went out of the kitchen and down the hallway to his bedroom.

She took her clothes from the closet, went to the bathroom, got her toothbrush and hair dryer, her shampoo and her makeup. She packed it all up. When she had everything, she rolled the full suitcase back to the kitchen.

He was still sitting at the table. She was careful not to look directly at him as she got her tote from the chair where she'd dropped it, took out the key he had given her, and laid it on the counter.

He said nothing as she left him.

The silence between them was absolute.

Chapter 14

For Abilene, the days that followed were a grueling exercise in concentration. She found that if she could manage to keep the focus on her work—and not on her battered heart—she got through the daylight hours well enough.

Nights were another story. She had trouble sleeping. And when she did drop off finally, Donovan's very absence seemed to weave through her dreams, where she wandered, lost and disoriented. And cold.

She would wake to find herself curled in a ball all the way over on the far side of the bed—*his* side of the bed. Seeking his body's warmth.

Seeking *him*.

Four days later, true to his word, Donovan attended the groundbreaking ceremony.

Abilene wished he hadn't. She was suffering enough, thank you very much. Seeing him, hearing his voice…it only made the hurt sharper, made her poor heart ache all the harder.

He made a brief speech about the project—and about the brilliant young architect he had found to create the perfect space where children could have the chance they needed to learn and grow. He spoke from his wheelchair, using a wireless microphone, and he was as charming and inspiring as he had been all those years ago, the first time she saw him, when he came to give that talk at Rice.

Abilene thought he looked killer handsome, if a little tired—and then reminded herself that it shouldn't matter to her if he was tired. His well-being was not her problem. She'd been a fool ever to have imagined it was.

After the ceremony, a local gallery hosted a party in honor of the big day. Donovan put in an appearance. Abilene kept her distance from him and he steered clear of her, as well.

Her mom and dad were there, to celebrate her success with her. And three of her brothers and their wives showed up. And Zoe and Dax, too. They all knew that Abilene and Donovan were through. Out of respect for one of their own, they avoided him.

Except for Dax.

As the party was winding down, Abilene spotted the two men in an isolated corner of the gallery, speaking quietly to each other, both of them looking way too intense. Donovan glanced over and saw her watching.

Their gazes locked. She felt the floor drop out from under her, felt her heart tear in two all over again.

And then came the quick, flaring heat of her fury—at herself, for caring so damn much. At him, for turning his broad back on the best thing that had every happened to him.

She tore her gaze from his and turned away.

He left soon after that. She didn't ask Dax what he and Donovan had said to each other. She told herself she didn't want to know.

A week after the groundbreaking, Ruth Gilman offered her a position at Johnson Wallace. She accepted the job and also the great starting salary and nice benefit package.

And a week after she got her dream job, out of the blue, Ben Yates called. He said he'd kept her number and had been thinking about her.

At first, she was wary, afraid that maybe Donovan was using Ben to check up on her, to make sure she was taking full advantage of the "perfect" life he had set up for her. But Ben said he was living in Fort Worth and had managed to land a good job with a top firm. He said he hadn't spoken to Donovan since the day he walked out of the house in the desert.

And he told her that he'd been regretting the way he'd left, without even saying goodbye her.

"It's okay, Ben," she reassured him. "I understood why you had to go. And I'm happy that things seem to be working out for you."

"So, then. Good. And the children's center…"

"Under construction. I'm the supervising architect. And I'm at Johnson Wallace now."

"Congratulations. They're the best."

"Thanks. I love the job. It's working out well."

"So…are you seeing anyone? I was just thinking, if you're free some evening, I would catch a flight down to San Antonio. We could have dinner."

She really wanted to say yes. She liked Ben, so much. He was the kind of guy she'd always thought she would finally fall for. Fun to be with. A good guy, honest. Forthright. Without a lot of emotional baggage—completely unlike the man she was trying so hard to get over.

But she just couldn't do it, couldn't use Ben to try to forget Donovan. She needed to do the forgetting first.

And then maybe, someday, she would be ready for a guy like Ben.

So she laid the hard truth right out there. "I would like to be your friend, Ben. But that's all."

"I see," he said, softly. And then he thanked her for being honest with him. And he said he thought that maybe it was better, if they just let it go at that.

She hung up feeling a little sad, but grateful to have achieved something like closure with Ben. And she was also longing for Donovan.

She tried to remind herself that her broken heart would mend, that even the deepest hurt someday heals.

But the platitudes weren't helping. She loved him.

She missed him. She wished she could fast-forward time past the hurting and the yearning. She longed to be all the way over on the other side of heartbreak. To be at that moment when she could think of Donovan fondly, without that empty aching feeling, without wanting to wring his obstinate neck.

The next day, Ruth shared some gossip. She'd learned

from a colleague at the Johnson Wallace Los Angeles office that Donovan had accepted a commission to design a theater complex in Century City. Abilene pasted on a smile at the news and said how fabulous that was for Century City.

And it *was* fabulous. Even if he couldn't accept love in his life, well, at least he was working again. That was something. That was important.

She would try to focus on that, on how he was living a productive life now. She would tell herself that maybe she'd had a little bit to do with that, with waking him up from his long, painful retreat into solitude and loneliness, with bringing him back to the world.

Did it help, to think that she might have helped *him*? Not really.

In the end, she just had to set her mind on acceptance, on getting through the days away from him, on letting time do its job much too slowly, on telling herself that she was getting there, getting over Donovan McRae.

On the first Monday in April, Javier came to see her at Johnson Wallace. He told her that he had a client who wanted a house.

A very special house.

Javier said the client was a dear friend of his, a woman, a single mother with three children, a family law attorney. His friend wanted to adopt a fourth child. She planned to build her dream house for her family— and her three large dogs. She owned the property already, in the Hill Country—the perfect piece of land, with beautiful views.

He described what his friend wanted, how big the house should be, and the general arrangement of the rooms. Was Abilene interested?

Abilene almost said no automatically. Which was insane. She had a living to make. And she wouldn't get far if she started turning away potential clients, sight unseen.

And she *wasn't* turning down any clients. Her no had been merely a protective reaction. Because as Javier had described what the woman wanted, a chill had snaked its way down her spine.

Abilene knew that house.

It was *her* dream house.

The house that would always now, to her, be Donovan's house, too.

The house she needed to relinquish, because there was no way she would ever have it built to share with another man.

Javier asked, "So? What do you say?"

And she got it then. She saw that this could be an answer for her. Creating her dream house for Javier's friend and her family could be a big step in getting free of the pain, in letting her love for Donovan go.

She said, "Well, as it turns out, I have a house in mind, just from what you've told me. Something I've been tinkering with over the years. It's really pretty amazing, how close my design is to the house you just described."

"Ah," said Javier, the crinkles at the corners of his dark eyes deepening with his smile. "So maybe this is meant to be, huh? It's fate that you should design this special house."

"Well, I don't know about fate. But I'm definitely interested in meeting with your friend—and I wonder, is it possible for me to see the property first? I just want to make certain that the design I would propose is right for the setting." Okay, that was stretching the truth. What she really wanted was to reassure herself in advance that the property was right for the house.

And why shouldn't she want that? If she was going to give this single mom *her* dream house, well, it would have to be built on the ideal piece of land.

If the property didn't cut it, fine. She'd come up with something different for Javier's friend.

"I don't see why not," Javier said. "Let me call her, see if it's okay with her. And then I'll call you back."

Javier did call, the next morning.

He said his friend was excited at the idea that the architect needed to see the land first. In fact, his friend was hoping that maybe Abilene could meet her on the property. His friend would love to have the chance to show Abilene the spot where she wanted to put the house—a spot not far from the creek that ran through the property, with a view from the kitchen of a certain craggy peak, and from the master bedroom of a wide, open field, a field that was thick with Texas bluebonnets this time of year.

It seemed to Abilene a good omen for the project, that she and the prospective client viewed the process in a similar light. Abilene wanted to like Javier's friend, to be able to believe in the happiness that the woman and her family might find in the house.

So Abilene agreed to meet the client on the property. She gave Javier a couple of prospective meeting dates and times. He called back again later that day to say his friend would meet her the following morning at 11:00 a.m.

She laughed. "Don't you think it's about time you told me this woman's name?"

"Donna," he said. "Donna Rae."

Donna Rae.

Abilene felt that chill down her back again. Donna Rae?

It was just a little too close to Donovan, a little too much like McRae.

But really, she was being silly. The similarity between the two names was a coincidence, no more. She refused to get all freaked out because the woman's name reminded her of the man she couldn't seem to forget.

Javier said, "So then. I'll email you a map with directions to the property."

"Fair enough—and Javier, thank you for thinking of me. I'm excited about this, I really am."

"I'm glad," he said, his voice strangely somber. But then, Javier was too somber, too much of the time. "Call me tomorrow, after the meeting. Let me know…how it went."

She promised him that she would. And the next morning at nine-thirty, she was on her way.

It was a lovely ride. The Hill Country was beautiful any time, but never more so than now, in the spring, with wildflowers in bloom in every rolling, green field. She cranked the radio up loud and rolled her windows down.

At five to eleven, she turned onto the freshly paved road that would take her to the property. Live oaks lined the way, casting leafy shadows on the hood of her car as she sailed along. And beyond the screen of the trees, she could see open country, green and rolling and draped in a blanket of bluebonnets.

Yes, she thought. *This is exactly right. This is the place where my house should be.*

She slowed to make the turn onto the dirt driveway, stirring up dust as she rolled onto the unpaved surface. Limestone outcroppings flanked the way to either side and she was aware of the rising feeling of her own anticipation. She was almost there.

She rounded a gentle curve, saw the cleared space, the van parked and waiting.

And Donovan standing beside it.

Chapter 15

Fury. Longing. Hope. Joy.

The burning desire to make him pay...

A hot, knotted tangle of emotions warred within her, sending her heart rocketing beneath her breastbone, making her palms sweat, causing her knees to quiver at the very idea she might have to use them to stand upright.

Upright. Like he was.

It was the first time she'd ever seen him up on his own two feet—well, okay, he was kind of leaning against the side of the van, and his wheelchair was right there, behind him. Ready in case he needed it.

But still. He *was* standing. How wonderful.

If only she didn't want to kill him, she would be so proud of him.

He continued to lean there, against the side of the van, as if he had all the time in the world to stand there and stare at her through the windshield of her car.

She couldn't read his expression. He only *looked* at her. What was going through that frustrating mind of his? She shouldn't even want to know.

But there was no point in lying to herself. She did want to know. She *needed* to know. As much as she needed to draw her next breath.

And speaking of her breath...

It had clogged in her throat. Slowly, with care, she let it out. And then breathed in again, a conscious action. And out. And in.

Great. She was making real progress here. She could breathe again.

And her heart was still beating much too fast, but at least it had slowed down a little bit. It had stopped galloping along like a spooked horse. She felt almost certain her legs would hold her up now if she tried to stand on them.

So she pushed open her door, swung her feet to the ground and got out of the car. "Donna Rae," she said flatly. "A single mom, huh? A single mom with three kids—and a plan to adopt a fourth. A family lawyer, with three big dogs? Don't try and tell me Javier dreamed all that up."

He straightened, so his legs took his full weight. "Don't blame Javier. It was me. All me."

Down a slope of land, she could hear water rushing over rocks—a creek. She could see it, gleaming there, beneath the trees. And that craggy peak Javier had mentioned—yes, she saw it, too. Right where it should be, off in the middle distance, perfect for framing in a kitchen window.

She made herself look at Donovan. And she ached to go to him.

No way.

She broadened her stance a fraction, settling herself in place, and folded her hands protectively over her middle. "Oh, I'm killing Javier, too. Just as soon as I finish with you."

He put up both hands, palms out. Surrender. "I only…I didn't know if you would speak to me."

"How about a phone call? That's always a viable way to start."

"I was afraid you would hang up."

"I probably would have. Then you could have called again. And again. That would have been satisfying."

He took one step. And another. She watched in wonder. And in fierce, injured fury, as well. "I knew I had really screwed up with you. Screwed up so bad."

"No argument there."

"I knew that just telling you I love you, confessing that I was wrong, that all I wanted was another chance…" He took that last step. He was two feet away from her. The clean scent of him taunted her. And he was tanner than before. His hair gleamed, pure gold, in the spring sunlight. And her arms ached to reach for him. Her throat ached to speak her love.

And her heart ached most of all.

She only wanted to grab him, to pull him to her, to hold him fast and never, ever let him go.

She kept her arms around herself instead. And she

taunted him, "So you cooked up some big lie and got Javier to help you with it."

His strong jaw twitched. And he shifted, wincing. Evidently it still wasn't that easy for him to get around on his damaged legs. "Okay, it was a stupid idea. I should have just called you, I see that now. But I wanted...I *needed* for you to know that I'm not here just to talk. That I want you so much. I love you...so much."

"Love?" She could choke on that word. "You have no right. No right at all, to talk to me about love."

"I know. I get it. I do. I was a complete fool to have let you go. And so I thought that maybe, if you saw that I wanted to hire Javier to build your house, you would listen to me. You would believe that I've actually come to my senses. You would listen to me when I say that what I really want, more than anything, is to be the man who lives in that house with you..."

The tears rose, clogging her throat all over again. She willed them away. But they wouldn't go. They spilled over and slid down her face.

She swiped them away, furious that they wouldn't stop.

"Abilene." His voice was rough with emotion. "Come on. Don't cry." He started to reach for her.

She jerked back. "Don't you dare. You just keep those hands of yours to yourself."

He obeyed, even moved back a step and let his arms fall to his sides. "It's been...really bad. Without you."

Triumph surged within her. She knew it was petty, to feel glad that he had been suffering, too. But she did feel glad.

God help her. She did.

A sob escaped her. She swallowed it down, swiped at the tears again. "I thought it was what you wanted, to be without me. You said it was what you wanted. You said love was not an option, that you were no good when it came to forever."

"I was an idiot."

She almost laughed. But somehow, it came out as another sob. "Yeah. Yeah, you were. You definitely were." She put her hands to her cheeks, rubbed more of the wetness away.

His eyes were so tender, so full of regret. "I hate that I hurt you. I…didn't realize…" The sentence trailed off. He looked away, off toward the sloping of the land and the gleam of the creek.

She sniffed. "What, Donovan? You didn't realize, what?"

And he turned to her again. "I didn't realize that after you, after what we had together, there was no way I could go back to hiding in the desert. Back to the silence and the pain and the guilt over Elias. I don't think I'm ever going to be capable of forgiving myself for not protecting him, for not taking better care of him. But I am learning that I need to move on."

She felt her fury leaving her. She couldn't hold on to it. Her anger was nothing when measured against the love that still lived in her heart. And the tenderness in his eyes.

He said, "I finally get it. I do. It's what you tried so hard to get me to see. That I didn't die, after all. That I owe it to Elias's memory, to pick up the pieces, to do whatever I can to make the world a better place for *all* the children."

Her mouth trembled. She caught her lower lip between her teeth to still it. "I heard…that you were working again. I was glad for that. Truly."

He nodded. "My old literary agent called, offered me a new book contract. She wanted me to write the story of how I came back from near-death on Dhaulagiri One."

"And?"

His broad shoulders lifted in a shrug. "I passed on that. Maybe someday. But not now. Not so soon."

"Ruth told me, about the theater complex in Century City."

"Yeah. It's a complex that will include a children's theater and a place for kids to come to practice stagecraft, to get their first chance onstage. And after that, I'll be designing a preschool in Portland, Oregon."

"That's good," she said. "I'm really happy for you."

And then he said it again. "I love you, Abilene."

She only looked at him. Stricken. Yearning. Wanting to say she loved him, too. Wanting that with all her heart. And yet… "You hurt me. You hurt me so bad…."

His gaze didn't waver. "I know it. That I hurt you. That I don't deserve you. I know that I've given you a lot more grief than happiness in the time we had together. But please. Just consider coming back to me. Just think about it. If you give me one more chance, I swear to you, I won't blow it this time. I'll spend the rest of my life proving that I can be the man you always hoped I could be."

She turned away from him, unable, somehow, to look in his eyes at that moment. She made herself ask him, "And the children, Donovan? What about the children?

What about *our* children? Because I've had time to think about it, too, about what I want, about what I *don't* want to live without. And you were right about that, if nothing else. I do want children. I want them a lot."

He did touch her then. He took that one step closer and he put his warm hands on her shoulders. She felt his breath stir her hair and she trembled.

"I know that," he said. "I always knew."

She stared off toward the craggy peak. It shone silvery in the sunlight. "And?"

He dared to move in closer still, to clasp her shoulders more firmly. She felt his touch to the core of her and she sighed. He bent close. His lips brushed her temple, burning.

And he whispered, "I'm willing."

She gasped, whirled to face him once more, searched his eyes, wanting, needing, to know the truth. "You mean that? You're willing to be a father...again?"

He gave one slow nod of that golden head. "I know I'll be overprotective. And the whole idea of having more kids scares the hell out of me. It's not as if I'll ever be that fast on my feet, you know? And children, they need a dad who's fast on his feet."

Her tears spilled over again. She gave up fighting them. Unashamed, she let them trail down her face. "Children need a dad who loves them. That's what they really need."

He touched her cheek, smeared her tear tracks with his thumb. "Say yes," he whispered prayerfully.

She couldn't. Not yet. But she did say, "If we had children, I would be there, right beside you, whenever you needed me. And it doesn't hurt a child to learn to be a little self-sufficient. If you love them enough, if you teach them well, I don't even know that you have to be that fast on your feet."

He studied her upturned face, hungrily. Tenderly. "I love you, Abilene. You gave me back my work. You gave me everything. You made me hope again. You made me *live* again. And these last rotten weeks, without you…well, I see it now. I get it. You're what makes it all complete. And I swear I would get down on my knees to you, right now, here, in the dirt. If I only thought I had a prayer of getting back up again."

A torn laugh escaped her. "Oh, Donovan."

"Please. Say it. Tell me it's not too late."

She lifted on tiptoe, put her hands against his chest, felt his strength and his warmth and the beating of his heart. "You have to be sure. Absolutely sure."

"I am. Say yes."

She hesitated on the brink. "I didn't want to keep loving you…."

"Say yes."

She smiled through her tears. "But I did. I do. It's you, Donovan. Only you."

"Abilene. Thank God." He gathered her close, lowered his mouth to hers.

The kiss they shared held everything: their love, their sworn commitment, each to the other—and more. That kiss held the promise of the future they would share, including the house they would build on that very spot, with the craggy peak out the kitchen window, the field of bluebonnets and the clear, cool creek down the slope in back.

Their children would grow strong and tall there. And

it seemed to her that the bold, brave spirit of the lost Elias would be with them always, too.

When he lifted his head, he said, "Marry me."

She gave him the answer her heart had been holding, just for him. "Yes."

He took her hand. "Come on. Let me show you how I picture it—your house."

"*Our* house," she reminded him.

"Yeah. That sounds good. That sounds right. *Our* house. Let me show you...."

"I can see it already." She beamed up at him. "But show me, anyway."

* * * * *

We hope you enjoyed reading

SHELTER IN A SOLDIER'S ARMS

by *New York Times* bestselling author

SUSAN MALLERY

and

DONOVAN'S CHILD

by *New York Times* bestselling author

CHRISTINE RIMMER

Both were originally
Harlequin® Special Edition series stories!

Discover more heartfelt tales of family, friendship
and love from the **Harlequin Special Edition**
series. Romance is for life, and these stories
show that every chapter in a relationship has
its challenges and delights and that love can be
renewed with each turn of the page!

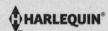

SPECIAL EDITION
Life, Love and Family

When you're with family, you're home!

Look for six *new* romances every month
from **Harlequin Special Edition**!

Available wherever books are sold.

www.Harlequin.com

NYTHSE0115

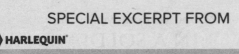
***

Allison sipped her wine. Dammit—her pulse was racing and her knees were weak, and there was no way she could sit here beside Nate Garrett, sharing a drink and conversation, and not think about the fact that her tongue had tangled with his.

"I think I'm going to call it a night."

"You haven't finished your wine," he pointed out.

"I'm not much of a drinker."

"Stay," he said.

She lifted her brows. "I don't take orders from you outside the office, Mr. Garrett."

"Sorry—your insistence on calling me 'Mr. Garrett' made me forget that we weren't at the office," he told her. "Please, will you keep me company for a little while?"

"I'm sure there are any number of other women here who will happily keep you company when I'm gone."

"I don't want anyone else's company," he told her.

"Mr. Garrett—"

"Nate."

She sighed. "Why?"

"Because it's my name."

"I meant, why do you want my company?"

"Because I like you," he said simply.

"You don't even know me."

His gaze skimmed down to her mouth, lingered, and she knew he was thinking about the kiss they'd shared. The kiss she hadn't been able to stop thinking about.

"So give me a chance to get to know you," he suggested.

"You'll have that chance when you're in the VP of Finance's office."

She frowned as the bartender, her friend Chelsea, slid a plate of pita bread and spinach dip onto the bar in front of her. "I didn't order this."

"But you want it," Chelsea said, and the wink that followed suggested she was referring to more than the appetizer.

"Actually, I want my bill. It's getting late and…" But her friend had already turned away.

Allison was tempted to walk out and leave Chelsea to pick up the tab, but the small salad she'd made for her own dinner was a distant memory, and she had no willpower when it came to three-cheese spinach dip.

She blew out a breath and picked up a grilled pita triangle. "The service here sucks."

"I've always found that the company of a beautiful woman makes up for many deficiencies."

***

Don't miss THE DADDY WISH by award-winning author Brenda Harlen, the next book in her new miniseries,
THOSE ENGAGING GARRETTS!
Available February 2015, wherever Harlequin® Special Edition books and ebooks are sold.
www.Harlequin.com

HSEEXPO115R

H HARLEQUIN®
™

SPECIAL EDITION

Life, Love and Family

Use this coupon to save

$1.00

on the purchase of any
Harlequin® Special Edition book.

Available wherever books are sold, including most bookstores,
supermarkets, drugstores and discount stores.

Save $1.00

on the purchase of any Harlequin® Special Edition book.

Coupon valid until April 7, 2015. Redeemable at participating retail outlets
in the U.S. and Canada only. Limit one coupon per customer.

52612187

Canadian Retailers: Harlequin Enterprises Limited will pay the face value of this coupon plus 10.25¢ if submitted by customer for this product only. Any other use constitutes fraud. Coupon is nonassignable. Void if taxed, prohibited or restricted by law. Consumer must pay any government taxes. Void if copied. Millennium1 Promotional Services ("M1P") customers submit coupons and proof of sales to Harlequin Enterprises Limited, P.O. Box 3000, Saint John, NB E2L 4L3, Canada. Non-M1P retailer—for reimbursement submit coupons and proof of sales directly to Harlequin Enterprises Limited, Retail Marketing Department, 225 Duncan Mill Rd., Don Mills, Ontario M3B 3K9, Canada.

5 65373 00076 2 (8100)0 12003

U.S. Retailers: Harlequin Enterprises Limited will pay the face value of this coupon plus 8¢ if submitted by customer for this product only. Any other use constitutes fraud. Coupon is nonassignable. Void if taxed, prohibited or restricted by law. Consumer must pay any government taxes. Void if copied. For reimbursement submit coupons and proof of sales directly to Harlequin Enterprises Limited, P.O. Box 880478, El Paso, TX 88588-0478, U.S.A. Cash value 1/100 cents

® and TM are trademarks owned and used by the trademark owner and/or its licensee.
© 2015 Harlequin Enterprises Limited

NYTCOUP0115

Discover four incredible stories from the biggest names in romance...

Pick up your copy today!